Lucy Vine is the bestselling author of novels *Hot Mess*, *What Fresh Hell*, *Are We Nearly There Yet?*, *Bad Choices*, *Seven Exes*, *Date with Destiny* and *Book Boyfriend*. Her novels have been published in seventeen territories, with *Hot Mess* optioned for a TV series in America. In a previous life, Lucy was a journalist, writing for publications including *Grazia*, *Stylist*, *Heat*, *Fabulous*, *Marie Claire*, *Sugar* and *Cosmopolitan*. You can find her on Instagram @lucyvineauthor and TikTok @lucyvineauthor. Her website is www.lucyvine.co.uk.

Praise for Lucy Vine

'The best Lucy Vine book yet – I felt so, so happy
when I was reading it, it's a proper love letter to
love stories and the people who read them'
Daisy Buchanan

'Opening a Lucy Vine book is the literary equivalent to
cocktails with your girlfriends . . . From belly laughs to
heartfelt emotion, this book is absolute peak romcom'
Lindsey Kelk

'I snort-laughed, I cried, I texted my sister and told
all my friends to read it. *Book Boyfriend* is a gloriously
funny romp about sisterhood, family of all kinds
and falling for fictional men. Absolute magic!'
Lizzie Huxley-Jones

'Like everything Lucy Vine writes, this is a hoot. A comedy
masterclass, a swoonsome treat for bookish girls everywhere'
Lauren Bravo

'It's brilliantly smart and wickedly funny, a double-helping
of romance with twists and turns that'll keep you hooked'
Justin Myers

'Gorgeously romantic, funny, sweet and bursting
with fun. Lucy Vine is fast carving out her niche
as a one-woman cheer machine. Loved it'
Milly Johnson

'*Book Boyfriend* is fresh, funny and full of lovable characters.
I loved the humour. A real joy from start to finish'
Portia MacIntosh

'She's nailed it again! *Book Boyfriend* has it all in spades; awesome
friendships, bags of humour and a sassy sibling relationship to boot'
Hannah Doyle

Also by Lucy Vine

Hot Mess
What Fresh Hell
Are We Nearly There Yet?
Bad Choices
Seven Exes
Date with Destiny

BOOK BOYFRIEND

Lucy Vine

**SIMON &
SCHUSTER**

London · New York · Amsterdam/Antwerp · Sydney/Melbourne · Toronto · New Delhi

BOOK BOYFRIEND

Narrator:

Well gosh, hello there, lovely reader, don't you look wonderful! I'm—

    'Aren't you going to open it?'

    Ahem, sorry for the interruption, I just wanted to explain that this is a novel told in three parts and—

    'Seriously!' *the woman with a voice a whole octave higher than it should be shouts, her eyes bulging out of reddened sockets.*

    She's not talking to me, of course. She's on a flight, where she would usually spend the whole journey clinging to the seatbelt, visualizing a burning, fiery death, surrounded by screaming families, while hanging oxygen masks violently knock into one another. But today! Ohhh, today she's been too intrigued by the haunted young woman beside her – whose name is Jemma, if you're interested. Jemma has been fingering an unopened envelope for hours. It's provided her seat partner with a tantalizing distraction from that dream she had last night – the one about the plane crashing into a mountain, where she had to eat her fellow passengers.

    The woman leans in closer, all the way over Jemma's arm rest,

1

giving up all pretence of watching the Sandra Bullock film on her tiny screen. She's very much in Jemma's personal space but Jemma's too polite to mention it.

'I'm sorry, I know I'm being nosy and your generation is all about' – she pauses, preparing to roll those red eyes as she does air quotes – '"boundaries".' She's practically in Jemma's lap now, puffing stale breath in every direction. 'But oh my god, I can't take it anymore. What IS it? And why aren't you opening it?' Her voice rasps, dry from excitement and recycled plane air, as she jabs a finger towards the envelope.

A subtle pinkness spreads across Jemma's cheeks.

Jemma usually resists any form of attention seeking. That's her sister Clara's area of expertise. In fact, Jemma's spent a whole lifetime trying to hide. She prides herself on being able to blend into any number of backgrounds. Physically, Jemma would describe herself as not being much of anything. In the dim light of this aeroplane cabin, her hair looks blonde, but she would pull a face and wave a dismissive hand if you told her so. It's mousey! she would insist. The kind of middling hair colour that hairdressers desperately want to highlight one way or the other. She'd also say her shape is average – too up and down to be described as curvy and too chubby to be called slim; a distinctly average height and weight that nobody would mention in the grand scheme of body positivity debate. She would, wittily, refer to herself as a beige buffet in human form.

But I would disagree. I think Jemma is shiny and brilliant.

Either way, right now – sitting in the centre aisle of this mid-flight aeroplane, fiddling with the edges of that still unopened envelope – there's no denying she's vibrating intrigue. *Jemma Poyntz is the most interesting person around for miles.*

Granted, she IS 10,000 feet in the air, so the pool is limited.

'Um,' Jemma hedges, clearly unsure how to answer the woman and probably wondering if her own eyes are also that red. She turns the creamy-white envelope over in her hands again, taking in the letters of her own name on the front and admiring the sloping, scrawled handwriting. She's thinking about how much she dislikes her name. Yes, she appreciates its sturdiness; its safe ordinariness. But that stupid *J* ruins everything. She's spent her whole life correcting the spelling and still gets 'To Gemma Poyntz' on every email and letter from British Gas.

She takes a deep breath. 'I'm sorry' – she turns slightly, feeling the woman's hot breath fully in her face now – 'I do want to open it – I have to open it – but I'm . . .' she finishes lamely, ' . . . scared.'

Jemma swallows hard, staring down.

A younger woman the other side of Jemma removes her earbuds. 'Are you talking about the envelope?' she asks, leaning in as well. Jemma is now squished on either side and the social-panic is obvious on her face. 'You've been fiddling with it since we took off, it's driving me crazy.'

'Me too,' Jemma dry laughs, her pink cheeks getting redder still. 'Believe me.'

'Is it exam results or something?' the older women asks, shaking her head, already knowing that won't be it.

'No.'

The red-eyed lady sags back into her seat and an angry passenger behind her kicks it in response.

'Who's it from?' the younger woman asks as Jemma frowns.

She laughs shortly. 'It's from my book boyfriend.'

Either side, both women look puzzled. 'What on earth is a book boyfriend?'

Jemma smiles. 'Erm, well, it's meant to be the sexy hero in a romance novel. The perfect man you obsessively fall in love with.' She glances between them. 'Because, y'know, it feels like a lot of real life men are terrible. Fictional men make more sense. They're more romantic and they don't let you down.' She sighs. 'Except THIS guy is real.'

The older woman frowns at Sandra Bullock's frozen features on the chair-screen. 'I'm still confused.'

Jemma sighs. 'OK, so it started a few months ago ...' she pauses, staring down into her lap, '... when my twin sister moved in with me.'

'Ohhh,' the younger woman interjects joyfully, 'that's so cute! I've always wanted a twin sister!'

Jemma shoots her a dark look. 'Everyone says that, literally everyone. But you haven't a clue.'

Red Eyes raises her eyebrows at this while Jemma breathes deeply through flared nostrils. 'The truth is, we've never got on. Clara's a selfish nightmare and the last few months have been awful. She basically ruined my life. And this' – she waves the letter – 'has been another complication I didn't want.' She sighs again. 'My life used to be so straightforward and predictable.' She looks between the women, both listening intently. 'And I LIKED it straightforward and predict-able. I don't need a rollercoaster of emotions, never knowing what's coming one day to the next. I was content in my stable little rut.' She narrows her eyes, glaring at the envelope. 'Until Clara and THIS came along.' She straightens her back and shoulders, determination lighting her eyes. 'Right, sod it, I'm opening it.'

She inserts an angry finger into the envelope edge, ripping open the top. Her hands are shaking as the two women either side watch on, agog.

At last, she's going to find out who he is, and – believe me, reader – it's going to change everything . . .

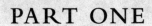

PART ONE

Chapter One

CLARA

'I'M HERE, EVERYONE!' I announce with a flourish to a hallway-full of surprised faces. 'CLARA! THE ONE YOU'VE ALL BEEN WAITING FOR!' I laugh dramatically, slamming the front door behind me as loudly as possible, and yanking on Harry's arm. 'C'mon,' I hiss at him before turning back to the room. 'And – drum roll, everyone – this is my gorgeous fiancé, Harry! Can you believe it?! We're engaged!'

Great-Aunts I barely know gasp, gathering and clustering around me as they cluck excitedly. I take in the array of quivering handbags, all in different ancient colours and textures.

'Oooh, isn't he handsome?' one squawks, as another fusses, 'Another family wedding! I can't wait!' A third at the back wails, 'Please have the big day soon, before I die!' A tall Great-Aunt I don't recognize at all seizes me and Harry by the wrists, her steely eyes burning into mine. 'Show us the ring,' she demands with something closer to fury than excitement.

I flick long hair off my shoulder, slightly regretting my grand entrance. 'It's being resized in Hatton Garden,' I tell her excitably. 'But it's *gorge*. Three huge mega diamonds, right, Haz?' I shoot him an encouraging look and he nods dumbly, eyes wide as he takes in the older relations swarming around us. He's probably wondering if this is how I'll look when I'm eighty-odd. But no fear, Haz, I plan to have literally all the available surgery the very *second* someone calls me madam.

'Right, uh-huh,' he swallows and I squeeze his hand reassuringly. Poor Harry. I mostly love attention, but I understand it's a lot for him.

'Let's go get a drink,' I say, pulling him through the throng of handbags to many shrieks of protest from the Great-Aunts.

The kitchen hasn't changed a single tile, I note, as we head for an array of bottles lined up along the counter. I help myself to a too-yellow wine, sloshing it into familiar wine glasses.

Huh, I thought I'd broken all of these as a teenager, but it seems at least a couple survived.

I hand Harry a beer and he takes it silently as I regard the room. Yet more weirdos – otherwise known as my extended family – mill about, sipping drinks and picking at bowls of orange crisps.

No Jemma, though.

I suppress a frustrated sigh. I've been gone for five years

with barely a postcard or a WhatsApp exchanged in all that time and my own twin sister doesn't care. She's abandoned me, hiding away in my hour of need.

I turn to Harry, who still looks overwhelmed. 'Hey, sorry about the relatives,' I tell him, laughing. 'Look—'

Another Great-Aunt throws herself at me from out of nowhere, ruffling my hair like I'm five, instead of twenty-eight.

'It's so good to have you home, Clara,' she says in a baby voice, bending down to speak to me, even though we are roughly the same height. She frowns disapprovingly now. 'You know your mummy has been *so* worried about you, running off like you did all those years ago. You've barely been home for a visit, it's *very* selfish.' She tuts. 'I'm glad you've at least returned to celebrate your mother's big day.'

'Um, yeah, that's totally why I'm home – Mum's engagement party.' I feel a thump of fear in my chest as I take in the banners and balloons around us. For half a second I consider blurting out the real reason I'm back; part of me would love to *really* shock this judgemental woman. Instead, I turn to wave in Harry's direction. 'And speaking of engagements . . .' I clear my throat, 'this is my fiancé.'

In milliseconds, her disapproval transforms into delight.

'*Fiancé?*' she howls at the moon, like I have achieved top life level. 'How *wonderful*! Your mother didn't tell me! So this is a *double* engagement party!' She beams. 'You and your mum *both* getting married!' She gasps. 'You should have a joint wedding!'

'I haven't told her yet,' I say quickly, waving my hand like this is unimportant, as I squeeze past. 'Come on, Harry, let's go find Mum and tell her the big news.' I grab his hand again, striding past the open-mouthed Great-Aunt and through into the living room.

Still no Jemma. Ugh, where the absolute fuckery fuck is she?

Actually, I know exactly where she is. She'll be hiding in the loo, like she always did at family parties when we were kids. She's always hated parties. But what's not to like? Booze, food, loads of people having fun? She's such a killjoy sometimes. I picture her now, sitting up there in the upstairs bathroom, trousers around her ankles, reading her latest novel and pretending she can't hear the noises of rowdy relatives hitting the sherry too hard downstairs.

I spot my mum across the living room, nestled in among the hallway aunts and arm-in-arm with her new fiancée, Angela.

I haven't met Angela in person yet. We've done some awkward waving through FaceTime and she seems . . . OK? She's a bit weird, but so's my mum. They've only been dating a few months, so this engagement is almost as much of a surprise as mine and Harry's.

I sigh internally, thinking Angela probably already hates me. After all, I'm the terrible black sheep daughter who ran away to the States five years ago and barely even rang home, never mind visited.

I watch Mum for a second across the room, and catch her squeezing Angela's hand. They exchange a look that makes my heart happy. I glance at Harry and then impulsively kiss his cheek. He looks surprised as I grin up at him and say, 'Let's go introduce you to my mum!'

As we approach, I spy a spotty teenage girl hovering moodily behind the couple. She must be Angela's daughter, I realize, studying her closer. She's pouting around the room, looking furious at the world. I feel you, sister.

I feel you, *step-sister*.

I brighten, thinking about winning this teenager over. I'm the cool, new, big sister, fresh from New York with a bag full of makeup and a fiancé on her arm. She's totally going to think I'm *awesome*. I'll finally have a sister I have stuff in common with. A sister who *likes* me.

'THERE SHE IS!' That tall Great-Aunt from the hallway is yelling across the room at us now, gesturing excitedly for me and Harry to approach. I meet Mum's eyes and her eyebrows shoot up. She cocks her head, giving me a perplexed look and I grin. Time for Harry to meet his brand new mother-in-law. The Great-Aunts giggle and trill about veils and venues as I make my way over.

'Clara, sweetheart, you're home!' Mum murmurs tearily through the din, opening her arms to pull me close. 'I'm so glad you're here, I've missed you so much,' she whispers into my ear. She releases me at last, regarding me with concern. 'They're saying you're getting married . . . is this . . . is this true?' She looks helplessly at Harry and then back at me.

I smile widely. 'Yes, Mum! I wanted to surprise you!' I

laugh shortly. 'And steal your engagement thunder. This is Harry! Harry, this is my mum, Sara Poyntz.'

She timidly offers her hand and he shakes it awkwardly. 'Great to meet you, Mrs Poyntz,' Harry says, and I can hear the tremor in his voice. 'And congratulations on your happy news, uhh, *too*.'

She blinks at him before answering slowly. 'Thank you ... *Harry*, it's lovely to meet you. You must call me Sara.' Her tone is kindly, but she still looks worried. She cocks her head at me again. 'You never said anything, Clara?' The question mark is loud and full of accusations.

'I'm telling you now!' I laugh a little defensively, feeling bad. 'You know what I'm like!' I catch Angela's eye and she smiles brightly, swallowing hard. I'm making her uncomfortable. I'm making *everyone* uncomfortable. This is so me.

'But ... but,' Mum splutters, trying to maintain her composure and quiet, 'how long have you been together and when did you ... how did this happen—'

Her concerned questions are interrupted by an angry voice behind me.

'What are you doing?' I visualize her face in my head before I see it, turning in slow motion to find my twin sister Jemma standing there. It's been a few years and she looks a little older, somehow, but not in any definable way. Not in the way that shows up in pictures I've seen on Instagram.

I probably look older, too. How awful.

'Hey,' I say, hating the pleading, neediness in my voice,

'you look great, Jim-Jems, how's it going? How was the bathroom? Anything new going on in there?'

She screws up her familiar face, looking between Harry and me. The confusion and fury is clear.

'I *said*' – she looks embarrassed, glancing anxiously at Harry – 'what are you *doing*?'

'Erm' – I roll my eyes – 'same as you, celebrating Mum and Angela's engagement and trying to keep the Great-Aunts at bay.' I realize they can hear me as Great-Aunt tuts echo around the room. A stab of guilt pierces through the bravado and I internally wince.

Jemma shakes her head. 'I *mean*, Clara, what are you doing with my housemate' – she gestures at Harry beside me – 'and why are you telling everyone you're engaged when you've literally never met him before today?'

I sigh, glancing around at the stricken faces. Great-Aunts mutter in asides, probably whispering about 'attention seeking behaviour' and 'American influences'.

Typical Jemma. Always ruining my fun.

Chapter Two

JEMMA

I *knew* I shouldn't have come out of the loo. I was perfectly fine, immersed in my library book, reading the latest note from my pen pal, and safely hidden away from all my Great-Aunts.

I mean, look what happens when you face real life. You have to deal with the Claras of the world, and their latest bout of attention seeking.

Standing in front of me, my sister shrugs. 'God, it's not a big deal, Jim-Jems. I just wanted to avoid a bunch of questions about my love life.' She says this like it's nothing. Like dragging my flatmate into her stupid lies and grandstanding isn't a big deal. She waves a hand now, dismissively. 'I thought it would be funny.'

Next to her, Harry is turning beetroot. 'I'm really sorry, Jemma' – he babbles when he's nervous – 'it all happened so fast. I was outside, about to knock on the front door, when your sister appeared out of nowhere and ...' He trails off, looking between us with fear. He's acting like his loyalties are divided. But he's *my* friend, not hers. We live together! And he and Clara have never even met before. Yet here she is, hanging off his arm, telling everyone they're a couple. She's only been here five minutes and I'm already exhausted by her behaviour.

Mum gasps, turning to Angela beside her. 'That's right!' she murmurs. 'I thought I recognized him. He's Jemma's housemate – we met him in passing when I helped her move in!'

Clara sighs. 'Yes, yes, it was all my idea. Mia cuppa!'

I squint at her. 'Do you mean mea culpa?'

Clara giggles. 'Or maybe I have a friend called Mia who wants a cup of tea?'

Mum frowns. 'Who's Mia? I don't remember a Mia.' She turns to Angela again. 'Do we know a Mia?'

Angela considers this, turning to her daughter for assistance. 'Buffy, haven't you got a friend called Mia? Didn't she come for a sleepover once?'

I only met Buffy for the first time earlier today, but I already know she won't put up with this kind of nonsense. She gives her mother a withering look. 'Don't talk to me. I couldn't give a shit about any of this.'

'Mea culpa!' I say again, my voice high. 'Clara meant mea culpa. As in 'my fault'. There is no Mia!'

A Great-Aunt throws herself forward. 'My middle name is Mia!'

I glare at Clara as Great-Aunts in every direction erupt

17

into debate about the Mias they know. One of them asks if Marias count and then announces that all the Marias she knows are dead anyway. This kicks off a loud, confusing chat among the Great-Aunts about how everyone they know is now dead.

Observing the mayhem, Clara grins slyly and throws her hands up with exaggerated innocence. 'OK, fine! Whatever. I was having a vape outside and saw this handsome thing approach up the driveway.' She winks at Harry and he reddens even more. 'So I asked if he'd mind pretending to be my date for the evening.' He turns slightly reproachfully to Clara.

'Yes, your date,' he says pointedly, some of his redness receding. 'I didn't realize you'd tell everyone I was your fiancé.'

Clara shrugs disinterestedly again.

'Haz, you should be thrilled to be my fake fiancé,' she smirks, then rolls her eyes at my expression. 'God, Jim-Jems, do you want to chill out?! It was just a laugh! I did it because I'm sick of everyone interrogating me constantly about my dating life, then looking at me all sad-face-emoji and telling me it'll be my turn next. As if I want the hassle of a bloke around, leaving pubes all over my stuff.'

This is a lot. This is Clara being her most … Clara. I glance automatically at Angela and her daughter for their reaction. The former looks frightened, the latter amused. It's the first time I've seen Buffy almost smile.

Clara sneers sideways at a slightly startled Harry. 'I mean, come on! As if I'd date this guy.' She catches my annoyed expression. 'Sorry! I mean, he's obviously good-looking and stuff! But he's not Mia cup of tea on any level, y'know? He's not ... I dunno? He hasn't got that' – she snaps her fingers in his face – 'je ne sais bad boy? I need a bit of whisky in my coffee, if you catch my drift. Sorry, Haz.'

He looks perplexed. 'Whisky in your – is that an actual expression?'

She shrugs, no trace of remorse. She's always mean to guys and I hate it. I also hate that they usually love her for it. I can feel my cheeks getting red. Stress always makes my rosacea flare up; just another reason to resent Clara being here.

Ughhh. Why did I come downstairs?

I hug the library book I'm holding close to my side, thinking about the note tucked away inside the front cover.

A month ago, some random woman left me a short, handwritten note in there, scrawled on fancy stationery. The mysterious note writer – who I'm affectionately calling Karen for now – scolded me for bending the front cover. Utter nonsense, for the record – and I told her so in my reply. We've been exchanging funny, silly notes ever since, swapping favourite book recommendations, best fictional characters, and – today's note – our top five romance tropes.

I consider making a run back upstairs to hide with Karen.

I'm suddenly aware of Mum at my elbow. 'So,' she says hesitantly, eyes searching my sister's, 'Clara, sweetheart, are you saying you're not engaged? This isn't your fiancé? Or even your boyfriend?'

'No, Mum, GOD!' Clara rolls her eyes at her, like she's the dumbest person ever.

'Oh,' Mum says, looking embarrassed. 'Well, it's all very confusing.'

Clara meets my gaze and tries to give me a complicit look, like, *Isn't Mum silly?* I narrow my eyes, glaring back, my face hot. We're not on the same side.

'Oh come on, Jemma!' She throws up her hands. 'I haven't seen you in years and the first thing you want to do is have a go at me? Over, like, nothing?'

I sigh, trying to calm down. Maybe she's right. Maybe I'm overreacting.

After all, the fake fiancé trope in romance novels was number one on that list I gave pen pal Karen, so surely this is ... funny? I glance over at Harry, who's watching me anxiously for a reaction. I push down any remaining anger, swallowing the hard lump in my throat. I put a cool hand to my boiling cheeks, trying to calm the redness there.

I don't really want this to be mine and Clara's reintroduction. Sure, I'm not exactly buzzing to see my sister again, but I should make an effort. She won't be here very long. It'll be a few days, maybe a week, then off she'll flounce, back to the US where she mostly wants nothing to do with us.

When she first moved over there, she messaged quite a lot, updating Mum and me about all her comings and goings. Revealing various temp jobs, detailing people she'd met or celebrities she'd spotted outside designer stores. But as her life picked up pace over there, she forgot about us so fast. For the majority of the last five years, we've mostly kept track of Clara's life via the regular Instagram posts: weekend hikes with friends; glamorous-looking nights out in fancy clubs; expensive meals I can't comprehend or pronounce. But emails and texts mostly went unanswered. And mostly unsent, if I'm being honest.

'Sorry,' I say begrudgingly, and I see Harry's shoulders relax an inch. I meet Clara's eyes and smile brightly. 'It's great you're home. How long are you staying anyway?'

Her eyes narrow and slide away from mine. I watch as she switches her weight from one leg to the other. She clears her throat.

'Hmm?' she says, examining her fingernails.

'Clara?' I prompt, trying to keep the panic out of my voice. I can feel the heat returning to my face because I recognize Clara's confessional body language.

She looks directly at me at last. 'Well, actually, I have good news!' She smiles widely – her fakest smile. 'I'm done with America. I'm moving home. Not moving, actually – moved! This is me, moved back to the UK. Aren't you pleased? I'm back for good!'

Chapter Three

CLARA

The Great-Aunts have gone at last, all agog with my oh-so-outrageous Harry lie – not to mention my announcement about moving home. I push down the twinge of embarrassment and remind myself that I don't care what they think. In fact, I've probably done them a favour! They'll be buzzing their tits off, gossiping about this for weeks. It'll probably give them a whole new lease of life.

I collapse on the sofa in the living room, shutting my eyes and hoping Mum will notice how exhausted I am and bring me a cup of tea.

A Mia cuppa. I snigger to myself, thinking how much that riled Jemma up. She's always been so easy to annoy. I've missed that.

The thing I've missed most of all, though, after five years in New York, was proper tea. As well as being waited on by my mum.

'You OK, Clara?' It's not Mum's voice, so I open just one

eye – warily. Angela is hovering over my face, eyebrows knitted with ... I dunno, fear? I wonder briefly what she must think of me – what Mum and Jemma must've told her – and fight an impulse to make a run for it.

'Hiya, Angela!' I give her my best approximation of enthusiasm. I want her to like me. I want her to be charmed by me. I want her to go out into the world boasting about the loveliness of her new step-daughter. And if Mum and Jemma have been bitching about me, I want her to think less of them after bathing in my sunshine.

'How's it going?' I say, opening the other eye, sitting upright and adopting my best interested face.

Angela and Mum met at a ballroom dancing class earlier this year, if you can imagine such a thing. It beats Tinder, I guess, but I wonder if they'll actually make it down the aisle. There was definitely something in the way they were looking at one another earlier at the party. A tenderness in the way they held hands in that sort of understated way. Like they were the only two people in the room, and not, in fact, surrounded by mean, watchful Great-Aunts looking for a spot of familial gossip.

But Mum's been engaged a couple of times before this – including to my dad a hundred years ago – and it's never worked out. So I don't necessarily hold out much hope for this latest romance. Though she's prettier than many of Mum's previous conquests; all legs and big red hair.

Angela smiles with relief, flashing small white teeth. 'Oh yes, yes,' she replies confusingly. 'Sorry to disturb you, I know you must be exhausted after your long journey. Did you sleep on the plane?' I shake my head and she tilts hers sympathetically. 'Did you know, in 1964, a student once went eleven days and twenty-five minutes without sleeping?'

I raise my eyebrows, like this is the most fascinating thing I've ever heard. 'I didn't know that, Angela, thank you for telling me!' I give her my most charming laugh. 'Sounds like me and that student were on the same GCSE revision schedule!'

She doesn't join in with my laugh and I wonder if Mum's already told her how badly I did in my exams. It was just after Dad buggered off, so never mind a revision schedule, I didn't turn up for half my lessons that year. Unlike Ms Smart Arse upstairs, Jemma, who never missed a second of school.

Angela is nodding again. 'I'll leave you to rest up. I just wondered if you needed anything?' Shaking my head, I smile widely, giving her the full-wattage beam.

'No, but thank you *so much* for offering, Angela!' I dial the smile down, aware I'm being too much. I shouldn't have used her name again; I sound like a Tory politician on *Good Morning Britain,* trying desperately to be relatable enough to justify re-election.

Angela turns to go, picking up stray plates and cups as she heads for the kitchen.

'Actually, Ange,' I call after her, 'I'd kill for a cup of tea if you wouldn't mind? No sugar, loads of milk?' She turns back and for a moment I think she will tell me not to call her Ange. Instead she nods happily, backing away again.

Jemma replaces her in the doorway. 'Already got them running around after you, I see,' she says dryly, and I turn to face her, sitting up straighter.

'Give me a break,' I tell her, feeling drained. 'I asked for tea! And I didn't even make the Mia cuppa joke! I only did it because Angela's clearly desperate to please. She *wants* to do stuff for me. It's like a bonding ritual; adults doing stuff for their kids.'

Jemma looks at me askance. 'We're not kids,' she says darkly. 'And you should be nice to Angela, she's really lovely.'

'Oh my god, I *am* being nice to her!' I cry out, feeling hard done by. Why does Jemma always assume the worst about me? 'You should've seen me, I was *so* nice. She will totally love me when she gets to know me.' I nod authoritatively. 'You'll see, I'll be like the daughter she's always wanted in no time.'

Jemma snorts. 'She does have a daughter.'

'Oh.' That's right, the teenager from earlier. I'd forgotten. 'Oh yeah. Well, what's her deal? Where is she anyway? Has she gone home?'

Jemma's eyes slide away and she looks shifty. 'Um, she's . . . she's upstairs.' We fall silent, something awkward between us. Jemma swallows before continuing quickly. 'She's kind of intimidating actually. She's just seventeen but she's basically terrifying.' She glances at me. 'Buffy, I mean.'

I sit up straighter as Jemma moves across the room, wiping surfaces littered with crumbs. '*Buffy?!* Jesus Christ, tell me the kid's name isn't really Buffy?!' I am delighted, but she shakes her head.

'No, I don't think so. Not really. I think it's a nickname. I asked her about it when we got introduced, and she gave me this aggressively withering look and said it's her username on Snapchat because she slays.' We regard each other with amusement and I shake my head.

'Surely she's too young for that reference?' I pause. 'Even *we're* too young for that reference.'

Jemma looks tickled again. 'I think the noughties are back. Haven't you seen all the thin eyebrows and huge coin belts?'

'God, *don't*.' I flop back onto the cushions again. 'New York was full of people wearing chokers and slip dresses.'

Jemma pauses, looking sombre, before joining me on the sofa. 'So you're really done with New York? I thought you loved it over there. You always looked like you were having a blast.' I stare down at my lap as she adds, 'What's made you decide to come back?'

I clear my throat then speak hurriedly. 'It's just the right time, y'know? I miss home, and I miss all of you.' She looks sceptical at this but I keep going. 'I was always going to come back at some point! I couldn't spend the rest of my life hearing people saying herb and aluminium wrong. It's time to move home and get my old life back together.' I perk up, thinking about my bedroom upstairs, still adorned with the old posters and teddy bears. 'Y'know, I'm actually really excited to stay with Mum for a bit.' I pause, feeling misty-eyed. 'I've lived away for so long, it's just the thing we need to rebond. A bit of one-on-one time together, y'know? Plus, I can get to know Angela better, when she's staying over – and even get friendly with her vampire slayer kid. It's going to be great!'

Beside me on the sofa, there is a chilly vibe emanating from Jemma. I try to read the atmosphere, without looking directly at her. She doesn't like people looking directly at her, it's too confrontational.

We haven't always got on that well – I always say or do the wrong thing around Jim-Jems – but we're adults now. I'm hoping things could be different with me being back in England. We'll take it slow, but maybe we could finally be . . . well, probably not like *normal* twins; the kind of twins you see on telly who do everything together and are like mirror versions of each other – but at least, I dunno, *friends*?

'Look, Clara, there's something you should know,' Jemma begins earnestly, just as Mum walks in, holding my too-full cup of tea in one hand and a bowl of orange crisps in the other. Angela is right behind her, looking fearful again. I must remember not to overuse her name.

'Did you eat anything, Clara?' Mum asks anxiously. 'I wasn't sure in all the excitement if you got any of the sandwiches? I can make you something if not?'

I catch Jemma rolling her eyes indiscreetly next to me. Ugh, she's such hard work. Is it my fault if Mum likes to fuss around me all the time? Whatever she thinks, it's going to be *so* nice being looked after for a while. I'm looking forward to fully reverting to child status while I'm staying here. After everything that's happened over there – everything that happened *with him* – don't I deserve it?

'I grabbed something at the airport on the way through,' I tell her, taking the tea from her. It's hot in my hands. 'But I'll totally take those crisps anyway! Cheers, Mum.' She places them beside me on a small table that's always sat next to this sofa. When I was a teenager, me and my friends used it for drinking games every Friday night. I grab a fistful of crisps and empty them into my mouth, enjoying the loud, satisfying crunch.

'Where's Harry gone?' Mum asks anxiously, glancing around her.

'He went back to ours,' Jemma says absentmindedly. 'Why?'

'Oh, I was hoping to get to know him better.' She looks wistful.

'You do understand we're not actually engaged?' I sit up again, crisp crumbs sprinkling in all directions.

'Well, yes, but—'

'Mum, they're not together *at all*,' Jemma interjects sternly. 'Like, not at all. Not even a little bit. They just met outside the house earlier. He's *my* friend. *My* housemate. Remember? You met him at mine last year? They don't know each other. *At all.*'

Wow, territorial much? Maybe she fancies him. Massive nerds were always her type. But, of course, now I feel bad. That would actually be a bit out of order if I've spent all afternoon clinging to a guy she's into. No wonder she's been so red in the face about it.

My wrist beeps, making Mum jump.

'What's that?' Jemma glances around anxiously and I tut.

'Don't worry about it,' I say, raising my arm straight over my head, waving it about towards the ceiling. 'So, gang, let's talk about me moving home!'

'Why is your arm in the air?' Mum looks flummoxed.

I keep waving the arm. 'It's just my watch,' I say by way of explanation, but she and Jemma still look just as baffled. I sigh, continuing, 'I'm supposed to stand up every hour for a minute or so. It's a fitness tracker, it thinks I sit down too much.' Jemma rolls her eyes as Mum slow-blinks at me with bafflement. I continue, 'Who can be bothered with that? If I wave my arm in the air like this, it tricks it into thinking I'm standing up.'

Jemma scrunches up her face. 'Why do you even wear it then?'

Of course she doesn't get it. I shrug. 'I dance sometimes?' I offer. 'Y'know, around the furniture at home and in bars on a Friday and Saturday. It likes me more when I do that.'

Jemma laughs. 'You're trying to *please* your fitness tracker?'

I nod. 'Oh yeah! It's very judgy. And it is not pleased with me very often. Honestly, I don't know what's more insulting – when it asks me if I've *finished working out* while I'm still exercising, or when it asks me *are you exercising?* when I'm just casually strolling between my bed and the fridge.'

'Goodness!' Across the room Angela looks just as baffled as Mum, then perks up. 'Did you know a man in Toronto once stood on one leg for seventy-six hours and forty minutes?'

I squint at her. Did someone buy this woman a Guinness World Records book for Christmas or something? 'Anyway,'

I say breezily, 'now that I'm back, I might take up jogging or something.' I glance at Mum excitedly. 'Ooh, do you think a Peloton would fit in my bedroom?' Mum gulps and stares at me, not answering. I roll my eyes at her continued confusion. 'It's an indoor bike? It killed Big?' She shakes her head, clearly out of her depth, and I try not to laugh. 'Actually, the internet would argue that technically Carrie Bradshaw killed Big, since she didn't call an ambulance and then left him to die slowly on the floor.'

'What is *happening*?' Mum murmurs as Jemma stands up decisively.

'Mum, you need to tell her.'

I feel a shot of fear. Tell me what? What does everyone know except me? Mum, Angela and Jemma all regard each other, communicating silently.

And, once again, I'm on the outside. 'Fine,' I laugh nervously. 'We don't *have* to get a Peloton. It's not like I can keep my room tidy enough anyway. I need the floor space for my clothes. You know what I'm like! No wardrobe can contain me!' No one reacts so I keep speaking. 'And I can always do a bit of aerobics here in the living room if the watch bullying gets too much, can't I, Mum?'

She stares at me, huge-eyed and silent. OK, this is freaking me out. What's going on? I glance at Jemma, who is still glaring at Mum. 'Tell her!' she says again, sounding upset and gesturing at me.

Oh god, Mum's ill. That's what this is, isn't it? She does look paler than I remember.

I swallow. 'Look, let me get my suitcases upstairs, and then we can talk. Whatever's going on, I'm here now. I'm here for you and I can totally help look after you.' I feel myself welling up, and get to my feet. 'I'll be back in a minute.'

'Wait!' Mum says suddenly and I freeze at the urgency in her voice.

'I'm just going to put my bags away in my bedroom, Mum.' I try to laugh. 'I'll be, like, ninety seconds.'

'You can't,' she says, sounding panicked.

I shake my head. 'What? Why not?'

From across the room, Angela's daughter Buffy appears from the kitchen. She's smiling wickedly, eyes twinkling. She speaks and her voice is high and young. 'Because it's not your bedroom anymore. It's mine.'

I feel my brow furrow as I turn to Mum. She looks at me pleadingly. 'I'm sorry, sweetheart, Angela and Buffy moved in a week ago. You haven't been home in years, I had no clue you were thinking of coming back, you didn't . . . I didn't . . . I'm so sorry, darling, there's no bedroom for you here.'

Across the room, Buffy smirks, then frowns at me.

'Er, why is your hand waving about in the air?'

Chapter Four

JEMMA

I'm actually living inside my own nightmare.

Or I will be, once she finally gets here. Because of *course* Clara is late. She's always late. She's a *late person*.

Late people are the worst. The worst! They think it's hilarious, this thing they've decided is a personality trait. News flash, it's *not* a personality trait, it's just plain rude and inconsiderate. You're leaving everyone waiting for you, as if their time isn't as valuable as yours. Just because you couldn't get up when your alarm went off. Or you wanted to stop for a coffee. Or you got distracted by some shiny thing on the way.

Clara always gets distracted by shiny things.

'Should we be throwing some sort of housewarming, d'you reckon?' Salma is looking at me quizzically, as she stirs her tea. It's my mug she's using, but I'm fine with that. Or at least I'm *almost* fine with it. Salma and I are working on me not letting small stuff like that get to me.

But it's my favourite mug!

'God, no.' I shudder, trying to focus on the question, instead of the mug she's now sipping out of. Ugh, now I want a cup of tea and I would've liked to drink it from *that* mug.

Never mind, it's not important.

'You only throw housewarmings for people you like. Y'know, for someone who is actually welcome in your home,' I say moodily and Salma spits a bit of tea back into my cup.

'You're such a fecking bitch!' she cackles, even though she is definitely the mean one in this friendship. 'She's your sister – your *twin* sister!'

'Fraternal twin,' I mutter, but Salma is undeterred.

'This is her hour of need, Jem. You have to be there for your sister – your *twin* sister!'

Everyone does this. Everyone acts like being a twin is something momentous and holy. Some huge sacred duty bestowed from on high by the heavens and I should be blessed and honoured to sacrifice my whole life to ensure Clara's happiness.

The trouble is, my twin sister is a selfish dick.

'The only reason she's moving in with us is because Mum didn't give me an option,' I warn. 'She knew we've been looking for a fourth housemate and insisted on Clara having the room. She said it was the perfect solution to both our problems, and Clara would be somewhere safe, where she wouldn't have to worry about her.' I sigh. 'I've never known Mum to be so pushy about something. She *never* puts her foot down. But of course she did it for her darling, precious, little Clara.'

Salma raises her eyebrows at my bitter tone and slurps from the mug that means nothing to me, I'm fine with it. She grins. 'Your generous mum has also – let's not forget – given us three months' rent *up front* to cover the room. It's not like we could've said no to that anyway!'

'Blood money,' I mutter furiously.

After Mum finally came clean last week, admitting to Clara that her old bedroom had been turned into Buffy's shrine to Olivia Rodrigo, there were a lot of tears. Mostly from Clara, who acted like it was the biggest betrayal to ever befall a human being. How dare our mother get on with her life, five years after her adult daughter willingly moved abroad, hardly to be seen again.

Mum told her she could stay on the sofa for a few days, but there literally wasn't anywhere else for her. My old bedroom has long since been a home office and is now full, floor to ceiling, with Angela and Buffy's belongings. Clara wailed for an hour and Mum promised she'd make things right – offering to cover her rent while she got back on her feet.

And then Mum looked over at me and got this happy expression on her face. Which is when I should've fled the room, house, country.

Of course Salma and Harry loved the idea of Clara moving in. We got left in the lurch by the last guy, who moved out practically overnight. And you wouldn't believe the number of weirdos who've so far called about the spare room. One bloke specifically needed to know if we 'walked around in bare feet' and another asked what our policy was on in-house nudism. The other day, I got quite close to offering the room to my bookish pen pal Karen while writing my latest note – I got that desperate! So, objectively, I can understand them being excited by the idea of Clara as a housemate. Who'd turn down a known entity that comes with a lump sum of rent?

Well, *I* would. Obviously.

Sadly, I didn't get a choice.

And – to be fair – Salma and Harry don't even know about the notes yet.

I don't know why I haven't told them; I guess I just like having a secret.

I march over to the kettle, refilling it and flicking the switch as Salma regards me with an amused look.

'I thought you couldn't drink caffeine after midday,' she comments, slurping from my mug, and adding grudgingly, 'I would've made you one.'

'Clara brings out my need for stimulants,' I comment dryly over the hissing kettle. 'It's so typical of her to fall on her feet like this. Mum's never offered to pay *my* rent. Or forced others to help me. But of course, there's always someone to catch Clara when she messes everything up.'

'You've never needed it, though, have you?' Salma points out unhelpfully.

'You're *my* best friend,' I remind her. 'You're not allowed to tell me when I'm being unreasonable, just tell me I'm right.'

'You're absolutely right, completely reasonable, and

definitely not being a bitter old hag,' she confirms in a loud voice.

'Thank you,' I say sombrely, choosing not to hear any sarcasm. I turn to face her, staring at her fearfully over my steaming tea. In a mug I don't like. 'I know I'm being irrational, Salma, but can you ... can you please promise me you won't end up liking Clara more than you like me?'

She looks shocked. 'What?'

I swallow, feeling vulnerable. 'I know it sounds silly, but our whole lives, everyone always fussed over adorable, fun Clara. She was the pretty twin, the one who got invited to parties, the popular one with a constant string of boyfriends.' I swallow again. 'Meanwhile I was just the loser nerd, obsessed with her books, hiding away in fantasy worlds, with fictional friends and imaginary boyfriends. At school I barely had my own name, I was always just *Clara's sister*. That's how people knew me – if they knew I existed at all. My name honestly felt like it was actually *Clara's sister* for years. I didn't have an identity of my own.' I pause and she waits patiently for me to continue. 'You don't know what it's like growing up, always being compared to someone.'

'I have sisters,' she protests and I shake my head.

'Not *twin* sisters. Literally everyone you meet wants to compare you. They want to know who's taller, who's fatter, who's prettier, whose nose is the straightest.' I sigh. 'Clara's nose is *so* straight.' Salma puts down her tea. I eye the mug moodily as she pulls me in for a cuddle.

'You are a beautiful, brilliant, kind person, Jemma. You're

no longer in your sister's shadow. You have a life, friends, a cool job working with the thing you love best – books – and who even wants a smelly boyfriend anyway? They only sweat and fart and leave semen stains everywhere.' She pauses. 'Actually, that's only if you're lucky. Mostly it's food stains.' I snort into her shoulder as she continues. 'Just because Clara's going to be living here for a few months doesn't mean you're going to end up being that lonely, rejected kid again.' She squeezes me tighter and I try to listen; to let her words sink in.

But she didn't know me at school. Salma and I only met a few years ago at a work party. I complimented her hair, and instead of saying the usual woman-stuff – 'Oh it's disgusting! I haven't washed it in a month! Look at the split ends! I'm an ugly monsterrrrrr!' – she replied, 'I know, it's amazing, isn't it?' Which was when I knew I had to make her my friend. Although obviously I don't tell people *that* origin story; I say it's because we both work in media. I'm a research assistant for an author and Salma's a radio presenter. Just a local station, but still, she was instantly the coolest person I'd ever met and remains so.

But I knew even back then – just like I know now – that we wouldn't have been mates if she'd met me as a loser teenager.

'I love you,' she says into my hair. 'You're my favourite person in the world, and if you need me to be mean to Clara I will, OK?'

I pull halfway out of the hug, a small smile on my face.

'Thanks,' I say quietly; sincerely. 'But that's OK, you don't have to do that. I know I'm being a dick.' I sigh. 'There's just something about Clara that turns me into a resentful kid again, I can't help it.' I sigh again, deeper this time.

'Are you having a moment?' Harry hovers awkwardly at the door. 'Or can I join in for a hug, too?'

'Get in here!' Salma yells at him and we all laugh as we fall into each other's arms.

'Is Jemma drinking *coffee*?' Harry squints at me. 'At this hour?' When he is shocked, Harry gets so much posher. He's already the poshest person I know, but the vowels get even more exaggerated when he's surprised by something.

'She said she needed stimulants to cope with today,' Salma shares solemnly. 'She's also just done a few lines of cocaine.'

'Have you really?' Harry blinks at me with concern and I laugh.

'Harry, you're always so gullible.' I give him a playful shove. 'You really should have worked out by now that Salma is a massive pathological liar.'

'Oi!' she protests, then adopts a thoughtful expression. 'Actually there was a guy on my show this week who's campaigning to get micro-dosing legalized and it sounded great. I might give it a go.'

'Micro-dosing?' Harry screws up his nose.

Salma snorts. She loves to shock the private school boy in him. 'Small daily doses of psychedelic mushrooms,' she explains, and he blinks hard.

'I've never done drugs,' I comment, a little embarrassed, and Salma looks amused.

'I only did them a few times at uni. The last time, I thought I was Mufasa from *The Lion King*. I climbed up on the table and started giving wise speeches from the sky. It was fun.'

I snigger as Harry nods agreeably. He's always very agreeable; I assume it's a posh thing.

See? See how good my life is now? I don't want things to change. I don't want anything – or *anyone* – to disrupt my perfectly calibrated existence.

But not much can get in the way of Hurricane Clara.

The front door bangs and my sister's familiar trill fills the house. 'I'm here!' she calls out breezily. 'I know, I know! I'm late. I got an email from 23andMe who said I have new DNA relatives. Jim-Jems, did you know we have a fourth cousin called Marjorie who lives in Utah?' She appears in the doorway, pink-cheeked, hair in a messy bun. 'Oh! And a relative called Denton somewhere over here! Isn't that a cool name? Imagine being called Denton. Think of all the doors that would open up for you. Everyone would just automatically assume you were awesome. You'd probably never have to apply for a job – everyone would just give you opportunities off the back of your cool name. He's probably, like, an influencer, or a baker with his own owl café in East London.' She takes a breath. 'Anyway, I've messaged them both and asked if they want to come to a family reunion I'm organizing. I'm sure Marjorie would be delighted to make the trip from America.'

My head lolls backwards and I stare at the ceiling. She's been here forty-five seconds and I'm already exhausted by her. And I *hate* being called Jim–Jems.

Salma is laughing like a traitor, waving my mug around and asking follow-up questions about Denton. Harry looks perplexed, but he hasn't told Clara to shut up, so he's a traitor, too.

'Where's your stuff?' I blurt, and she looks surprised.

'Oh! It's outside. It's just a few suitcases. I don't have much.' She shrugs, then glances at Harry. 'Do you mind, Haz?'

He shakes his head, backing out of the room to obey immediately. 'Of course not.'

'Clara!' I gasp. 'He's not your butler. You're late – as always – and now you expect everyone to drop everything and do your bidding.'

'Ugh.' She rolls her eyes. 'Chill out, Jim–Jems! I will totally go and help him.' She bounces out of the room. 'I need to tell him where to put everything anyway.'

I clench my teeth at Salma, who raises her eyebrows, looking amused. 'Don't let the small stuff get to you, Jem,' she reminds me lightly, dumping my mug on the draining board.

I nod tightly, fighting the urge to pick it up and hurl it at the wall.

Chapter Five

CLARA

God, early people are exhausting. So smug! Ooh, look at me, I know exactly what to wear for every occasion! I never get distracted by anything, not my phone, not my hair, not an email from ClearScore about my credit rating! Nobody buys early people a passive-aggressive watch for every birthday and Christmas present! What a bunch of show-offs.

What Jemma doesn't seem to understand is that being late is *pathological*. I am literally incapable of being on time. I *know* it's annoying and I've *tried* my best to change, but I don't know where the time goes. I will check the clock in the morning with an hour to go before I have to leave. Then, when I look again literally seconds later, fifty-three minutes have gone by. I sometimes feel like I'm living in an episode of *Stranger Things*.

Either way, I really wish Jemma would give me a break. Or even – y'know! – a chance. I've been so excited to come home and get close again, like we were when we were kids.

And sure, OK, I know I can be a bit selfish, but I'm a nice person underneath it all. I let people out at junctions when I'm driving. I gave a homeless guy a sandwich once. I stopped buying stuff from certain cheap fashion retailers the minute I heard they were evil. Well, OK, like *ten* minutes after I heard, but to be fair I get a lot of use out of that bag.

Upending my suitcase's contents on the bed, I take a second to review the room. It's a decent size, plenty of cupboard space. There's a weird smell, but Harry said the guy who rented it before was kind of a creep, so there's probably some sacrificed sheep heart hidden somewhere under the carpet. Candles and some white sage will sort that out.

I sit on the bed beside the piles of clothes and think about Jemma.

We must be able to find some common ground, surely. She's probably just mad I've been gone for so long, but I'm back now, and I want us to be friends. I want her to like me. We got on OK as children, didn't we? Sort of?

It wasn't so bad before Dad left. He thought I was hilarious and didn't give me a hard time about tidying my room or skiving off school. But he buggered off back to America when Jem and I were fourteen. And suddenly it was Jemma and Mum in it together, with their biggest joint problem being me. I had no one on my side. I was always getting into trouble and hiding letters from school. I really hated feeling like I was letting Mum down all the time, but I just couldn't get my head around anything the teachers wanted from me. Meanwhile Jemma sailed through, getting top marks and never missing a day. She never talked too much in class, or forgot her homework, or got shamed for the length of her skirt by a male teacher who couldn't stop looking. She was the good girl, and that made me the bad girl.

Is it any wonder I ran off to the US?

But now I need another fresh start here.

I stand up again, trying not to dwell on it all. I spare a small look at the mess on the bed but decide the unpacking can wait, I'mma go bond with my sister!

I find her in the living room, curled up in an armchair under a blanket. She's reading a book that is bizarrely covered in plastic.

'Hey!' I greet her enthusiastically. 'I love my room, thanks so much.' She doesn't look up so I try again. 'What are you reading?'

I catch a sigh she tries to swallow before she looks up. 'It's called *Too Good to Be True.*'

'Ooh, that's a fun title!' I offer, even though I think it sounds a bit nineties. 'Is it any good?' I try again and she eyes me warily.

'It's my favourite. I got you a copy for Christmas when we were fifteen.'

I ignore this, knowing there's no chance I read it. 'What's so good about it?' I move closer and feel hostility vibrating from her.

'It's hard to explain,' she says simply. 'I just love the characters and the story.' She hesitates and I wait, hoping she'll let me in a little more. She clears her throat, removing a small, white envelope from the inside cover and using it as a bookmark. 'It's a romance. There's a guy called George who's really grumpy and a woman called Julianna who's really nice, and they hate each other at first . . .' She trails off. 'It's just great, OK?'

I nod enthusiastically. 'It's cool you still love reading. It's all you ever seemed to do when we were younger!' I laugh and she frowns like she's trying to work out if I'm insulting her. 'I mean, it's awesome!' I add quickly. 'Really impressive! I was always so rubbish at reading.' I pause, thinking back. 'Actually, I think books lost me around the time I read *Jack and the Beanstalk*.' I giggle. 'I mean, when the giant shouts, "Fe fi fo fum, I smell the blood of an Englishman!" I was like, duh, hello? That doesn't even rhyme? "Fum" and "man" do not rhyme. It's literally made-up noises and they still couldn't get it to rhyme with "man".'

Jemma barks a surprised laugh and I feel a triumphant swell in my chest. I *will* get her to like me.

'So why is it covered in plastic?' I ask nicely, trying to keep up the momentum. 'Is it so you can read it in the bath?'

'It's a library book?' she says with a hint of impatience. But why would I know that? Libraries cover things in plastic? Do they get a lot of men wanking over the books? I move closer to examine the cover and she lifts it up, showing me a brightly coloured but worn jacket.

I frown. 'Why don't you get your own copy if you love it so much?'

She looks away, but answers quickly, 'I *do* have my own version. Loads of them actually. Hardbacks, paperbacks, a first edition off eBay.' She pauses. 'But they are just for look-ing at and admiring on my bookshelf.' She nods at the copy in her hand. 'This one is for *reading*. I've been checking it out since I was young. They have plenty of newer copies of *Too Good to Be True* available at the library, but this version, this *particular* copy, is special . . .' She blushes. 'It's dumb, I guess, but it's like my comfort blanket. When I'm stressed out or having a bad day, I pick this up. It soothes me. I tend to read this, then something new, then this again.'

I smile. It feels like we're getting somewhere at last. 'I can understand that,' I tell her as warmly as I can. 'Do you still go to the same library you used to?' She nods. 'God, I remember that place!' I laugh. 'I mean, I remember how much *you* went in there. Every time Mum and me went food shopping, we'd drop you off there, right?'

She smiles a little mistily. 'And I would go sit in the corner, reading my way through the children's section. I went there most days after school, too.' She unfolds her legs, sitting up straighter. 'It hasn't changed a bit in all these years. It still feels like a home away from home.' She looks shy. 'Actually, I work from there sometimes, too. I do interviews and tran-scribing in the work space.' She shrugs. 'I can do most stuff from home, but it helps me to get out of my room and have a separate place, like a pretend office.'

'You still work for that writer, yeah?' I enquire, really hoping that's right. I haven't asked her about the ghostwriting thing in years.

She nods, then sighs like it was a dig. 'Yes, I'm still a

research assistant.' She swallows, then adopts a determinedly bright tone. 'But it's totally better than being an author with all that pressure to sell books and reviews and mean internet trolls ...' She trails off, unconvincing. 'Anyway, we're working on a ghostwriting project right now for a famous mountaineer. His memoir.' She wiggles her eyebrows mischievously, leaning forward. 'He's really sexy actually! I'm doing a lot of interviews with him and loads of research! But ... not much writing.'

I widen my eyes. 'But that's so cool, Jim-Jems! And it's a lot more impressive than me! I have no career at all, and no idea what I'm going to do now I'm back.'

She looks at me sympathetically for a moment. 'What were you really doing over in the US? Even Mum never seemed to have a solid idea.'

I glance out of the window, taking in the small overgrown garden out there.

I should've been more in touch with Mum and Jemma. I feel a pang of intense guilt over what a crappy daughter and sister I've been. I always meant to call and message, but life goes by so fast. And suddenly huge, momentous, humiliating, horrible life stuff is going down and you feel like you can't call your family about it.

'Um, bits and pieces really. Agency waitressing, hostessing, bar tending.' I perk up. 'Oh! I did some voiceover stuff for a while, that was fun!' I sneak a look at Jemma, wondering if she disapproves. I smile away my anxiety. 'But mostly I was just focused on enjoying a year-round hot girl brat summer.

Or, if not *hot*, at least a lukewarm summer. Maybe a chilly girl rascal autumn?' I laugh and Jemma joins in, almost reluctantly amused.

After a moment, she clears her throat. 'So what made you come back then, if it was so great over there?' Jemma is watching me, I can feel it, though I'm staring out at the garden again. She's pushing this question. Does she know something about what happened over there?

'Never mind that!' I spring up, excitedly. 'I want to hear about *your* hot girl experiences. Are you dating?' I wave my hand towards the rest of the house. 'What about Harry? He's totally your type and seems really . . . sweet! Way posh, obvs, but cute! Like a young and nerdier Prince Harry with more hair. Thank god about the hair, right!' I giggle. 'Do you fancy him?'

Jemma frowns and I feel any warmth from our conversation fall away. 'No! Please don't say that. Harry and I are just mates; housemates. I hate that people act like you can't live with a boy without it being . . . more.'

'Oh come on!' I rib her, though warning alarms are blaring in the back of my head. 'You would be sooo cute together! Don't tell me you've never got drunk and accidentally shagged him? He sleeps in the room right next to you!'

Jemma stands up. 'I'm not like you!' she says in a tight, angry way. 'I wouldn't do that to a friend. I wouldn't mess with someone's head like that.'

'OK, OK, I just meant—' I begin, feeling afraid, but she cuts me off with a waved hand.

'Forget it. I'm going to the library. I have some work to get done and I need to return this.' She holds up *Too Good to Be True* for a brief second, the white envelope peeking out from a point near the end, and I swallow down competing emotions in my chest.

'Look, Jim-Jems, I'm—' I want to make this better. I want to say sorry – though I don't understand what happened – but she's already out of the living room.

A minute later, I hear the front door slam and I slump back down onto the sofa. I'm starting to think moving in was a huge mistake – as if my life wasn't enough of a fucking disaster. Maybe I should've stayed on Mum's sofa, listening to her and Angela cooing at each other. I mean, step-sis Buffy might've warmed up eventually. She might've even stopped insulting me in ways I don't understand because I'm too old. It would surely be better than being stuck here, in my smelly new bedroom, with a sister who hates me and no clue what to do next with my life.

I go back to my room, where I crawl under the pile of clothes on my bed, and fall asleep flicking through TikToks.

Chapter Six

JEMMA

Clara is covered in paint splodges. Pink paint. And she's wearing *my* jumper.

'What have you been doing?!' My voice comes out much higher than I'd intended. 'You know we rent this place, Clara? We're not allowed to paint or touch anything. *Anything.* The estate agents are absolutely *gagging* for an excuse to have a go at us and steal our deposit. You need to—'

Clara raises a hand and I shut up. 'I'm not painting the walls!' she laughs, and I feel silly until she adds, 'I have been upcycling.'

I narrow my eyes. 'What do you mean?'

She bounces across the room, excitedly waving a paintbrush in my face. 'Upcycling is when you take some ugly old bit of furniture and make it modern and cool! I watched a whole bunch of videos about it and got inspired.'

I sigh. 'I know what upcycling is, Clara. I also exist in

49

this world. I meant what exactly have you done?' I don't add *instead of looking for a job.*

'You had a rank old mirror in your bedroom that I have rescued and painted a gorgeous hot pink.' She raises her eyebrows, grinning. 'I just *tripled* its value – at least. And you're welcome.'

I feel myself pale and then get hot. My lovely, antique, wooden mirror that I got at a charity shop a few years ago? It's now . . . pink? I swallow hard, staring at her. She smiles widely, waiting for a delighted reaction. It doesn't even occur to her that . . . oh my god she's so . . . how could she think . . . RAAHHHHHH I AM SO ANGRY I CAN'T COME UP WITH WHOLE SENTENCES.

'You've ruined my mirror?' My voice is loud but I'm not shouting. I am not a shouter. I will not be reduced to being a shouter. Clara will *not* turn me into an awful, shouting person. 'YOU'VE RUINED MY LOVELY, LOVELY MIRROR *AND* MY JUMPER?' I shout, gesturing wildly at my favourite Vinted find, smeared with pink paint.

Sure, I actually only bought it to wear around Salma because she disapproves of my Asos premium subscription and says I need to wear more second-hand – but that's not the point.

Clara frowns. 'Ruined your mirror? No, I've *upcycled* it. I've made it amazing! I promise, Jim-Jems. I shared a TikTok of the whole thing and my thirty-four followers said it totally rocked.' She pauses. 'Well, obviously not *all* thirty-four of them, because my engagement is currently quite low. But that's to be expected, and the two people who did comment both said it was awesome.' She looks excited. 'I'm thinking this could actually be my new career, Jem – making shit, old furniture totally cool and then selling it on for thousands.'

'WHAT ABOUT MY JUMPER?!' I yell, trying to bring her back to the issue at hand.

She glances down, looking surprised. 'Oh!' She picks at the stains. 'It's just a bit of paint, it'll come off in the wash, I'm sure.' She looks up sheepishly. 'Actually, are you putting a wash on at all because I am completely out of stuff.' She laughs. 'That's why I had to borrow this.'

I feel my rosacea flaring up, hot and uncomfortable, and she cocks her head, looking mildly confused. 'Why are you annoyed, Jim–Jems? We always used to share clothes.'

'Yes, because we *had* to!' I explode. 'Because we were broke! And I hated it! I just wanted my own stuff. I hated sharing clothes. I hated getting joint birthday cards and joint birthday presents. I mean, how do you *share* a Tamagotchi anyway? Especially when you hogged it ninety per cent of the time and killed it over and over!'

'How can you say that?' Clara trembles. 'I *loved* our little Hikotchi and I did the very best I could for him.'

I sigh, trying to bring my volume down. 'Just . . . just don't take my stuff, OK, Clara? It's bad enough that everyone else thinks we're basically one person just because we're twins, but *you* should know better.'

She puts both hands up in surrender. 'OK! Jeez! No

problem, I won't take your stuff. But trust me, you're going to love what I've done with the mirror.'

I turn back to the washing up, trying to steady my emotions. I have been trying really, really, *really* hard not to get wound up by Clara in the week since she's been living here.

I have not succeeded.

It's like she has been designed by the universe to annoy me. It's like someone genetically engineered her to have all the traits that would most get under my skin. And I know it's just me, because Salma and Harry seem to find her *delightful*. They think she's hilarious and cool. Which obviously makes it all ten times more infuriating.

I steady my breath, adopting a friendly tone. 'I can show you how to use the washing machine, if you like?' I offer as nicely as possible. 'You said you've run out of stuff?'

'Oh yes, totally!' Clara sounds relieved at the overture. 'I'll go get my washing.'

She runs out of the room and I check the time. I have a meeting at the library in half an hour. It's with the sexy mountaineer, Aarav, whose memoir my boss and I are currently ghostwriting. I do all the interviews with Aarav, make notes, write them up, come up with sample outlines and chapters, but my boss does the actual writing. The finessing. He's the one who has the agent and publishers who love him. They throw more jobs at him than he can handle, which is why he needs me. It's really fun and interesting, but I wish I could do more of the actual writing.

But maybe I'd be no good. I'd probably be no good.

Either way, I'm really enjoying this project. Aarav is so impressive and hot. He was born in Nepal but has lived in the UK most of his life. He's broken all kinds of records with his climbing, and is just back from K2, where he and his team lost four toes between them.

I've been resisting the urge to tell him I'd scale his peaks any day.

I also need to return my library book – complete with a new reply for my pen pal Karen.

I feel a small thrill at my silly little secret. How long will we keep this up, I wonder, this fun, long-hand conversation? I hope at least a little longer. Yesterday, I bought a beautiful new letter writing set specially for our correspondence. It includes this elaborate blue hardback notebook with a floral border around the pages. I want to impress my bookish friend – but I also just bloody love stationery.

'Here we go!' Clara's muffled voice is back, this time under a swaying pile of dirty clothing that reaches almost to the ceiling. Even Aarav would struggle to find the top.

'Bloody hell,' I mutter, before clearing my throat. 'Right, er, OK, let's do this.'

I lead her to the machine, pointing out dials and drawers, but I can already tell Clara's not really listening.

'Oh, Harry! In here!' she cries as our housemate slams the front door, shouting out a greeting. 'We're adulting!' She sounds thrilled with herself, even though – so far – her contribution has mostly been staring out the window.

'Goodness me, Jemma.' He enters the room, gawping

53

bug-eyed at the giant pile of clothes I'm kneeling beside. 'Got a bit behind with your washing, have you?'

'It's not m—' I begin to protest, but Clara is already talking over me, bouncing excitedly.

'Oh my god, Haz! Jem! I've just remembered! They've made a TV series of that book!' She sounds excited and I stop loading stinky washing into the drum to listen. 'The one you're always reading from the library? I saw an advert for it earlier,' she continues happily. '*Too Good to Be True*, right? They've renamed the TV series *Book Boyfriend*, which is a bit of a relief because that name ... ugh, right? So dated!' She laughs and I make a mental note to lose at least half of her dirty socks. 'They said the show is based on the cult classic book – they even flashed up the cover – and is going to be airing soon.' I stare at her blankly. 'We can watch it together?' she suggests, then turns to Harry. 'All of us! It can be a house activity, every week, watching it together.'

Harry nods enthusiastically. 'Sounds like fun!'

'Are you serious?' I breathe out, horror dawning on me. 'They haven't!'

She frowns. 'I thought you'd be excited?'

I swallow hard. *Too Good to Be True* means so much to me ... How dare they rename it?! What else are they going to change?

I hold my breath.

'They usually ruin books, don't they, when they turn it into a TV show? What if they've ruined it? I don't want to watch it.'

Clara scoffs. 'Don't be mad. TV is sooo much better than books! Books just go on forever and are really boring.'

I glare at her so hard, it feels like fire will shoot out and burn her all up. I want it to.

'What are we talking about?' Salma bounds into the kitchen, stopping short when she senses the energy. 'Uh-oh, are we arguing? I can't have negative energy around me, I took my first micro-dose of mushrooms this morning and my emotions are way too raw and surface level.' She pauses, wide-eyed as she looks between me and Clara. 'I think I took too much actually. Unless Angela Lansbury is really in here with the magic bed from *Bedknobs and Broomsticks*?'

Clara shrieks with delight. 'I wish!' she says happily. 'And we're not fighting actually; we were just talking about watching a TV series together. It's based on Jim-Jems' fave book and starts next week. You're in, right, Salma?'

'I haven't agreed to anything,' I say quickly as Salma starts fiddling with the buttons on the half-loaded washing machine.

'Don't do that,' I scold her and she regards me with confusion.

'I'm just fiddling with the magic knob to make the bed fly,' she tells me and I gently guide her away from the sports setting.

'I have to leave in a minute,' I hiss at the other two. 'So Clara, please keep an eye on Salma today until this *Bedknobs and Broomsticks* phase wears off?'

I catch Harry mutter, 'What even is a bedknob?' as Clara smirks.

'I'll look after her, but only if you agree to watch the *Book Boyfriend* show with me!' She says this with a flourish, knowing I'm cornered. 'The first episode airs next week, OK? It'll be our new house show. And it'll be way, way better than the book, I guarantee it!'

Harry clocks my fury and clears his throat, stepping between us and helping a giggly Salma into a chair. 'Sounds like a plan!' he says cheerfully, regarding the half-dealt-with piles of laundry. 'Um, I actually need to do some washing, too.' He smiles helpfully between us. 'I can get this on for you guys, if you like?'

'Oh my god.' Clara is breathless. 'You *lifesaver,* Haz!' She skips out of the room and I pick up my rucksack angrily, heading for the front door. I have to get to the library for this meeting. Clara, her stupidity, and this news about *Too Good to Be True* the TV show can wait.

I turn back at the last moment. 'Oh actually, Harry, I've got a bunch of washing, too, if you're doing it?'

Chapter Seven

CLARA

'Jemma! We're in the living room. Get in here!' I call out as the front door slams with my sister's arrival home.

'Ugh,' comes the unenthused response floating through from the hallway. I start to reply but get distracted by someone's daring leap on the telly.

'Well, that's totally dumb, for a start!' I yell and catch Harry – across the room in the armchair – putting his head in his hands. Beside me, Salma stifles a laugh.

'What are you guys up to?' Jemma calls out.

'We're watching *Die Hard*,' Salma pronounces, as someone on screen spasms under a hail of gunfire. I sit up straight as the on-screen hero throws himself across a lift shaft or something. 'See? That would never happen, Haz! I've watched enough *Floor Is Lava* to know he would slide straight off that bit and into the lava.' I pause. 'Or into the German trap or whatever.' A small groan comes from the Harry corner and I give him a quizzical look. I glance up as Jemma fills the doorway, still wearing her coat, backpack in hand. We need a convo about that coat actually; it is hid-eeeeeee-ous. After all, if you see something that doesn't look right, see it, say it, sorted.

'You OK?' Salma asks Jem, as I turn back to the stupid movie.

'Hey, Jim-Jems,' I greet her. 'I've never seen *Die Hard* before, so Harry insisted I watch it.'

'Um,' he says to Jemma from between his fingers, 'I wouldn't characterize it like that. I would say more, I was watching my favourite movie, and your sister insisted on joining me to ruin the whole thing.'

'Potato, tomato,' I say, waving my hand.

'You're all watching it without me?' Jemma asks in a small voice, and I glance up at her. She's not annoyed, is she? She can't mind me hanging out with our housemates without her? I'm the one with no friends and no life, she can't *actually* mind me spending time with these guys? I internally sigh.

Honestly, everything I do seems to upset her, I don't know what to do. I don't know what I can do to fix things.

'Come join us, babe,' Salma says encouragingly, patting the space beside her.

Jemma shakes her head sullenly. 'I'm going to go read,' she mumbles like a big old martyr, jabbing at her bag's zip and pulling out a book. It's that novel from the library again – *Too Good to Be True*. Oh! I jump up, the sofa squeaking under me.

'Hey, Jemma, don't go, wait!' She cocks her head at me expectantly, crossing her arms defensively.

'What's up?' Her voice sounds forced.

I hop from foot to foot excitedly. '*Book Boyfriend* starts tonight!' I check my watch, ignoring the notification telling me to do more exercise. 'In fact, it's on in, like, twenty-five minutes.' Jemma doesn't say anything and I inch closer. 'You remember, Jim-Jems? You said we could watch it together? Like a fun, group house thing.' She still doesn't say anything and I add desperately, 'C'mon, Jemma! Give it a chance. It's based on your favourite book! It'll be fun! You never know, you might love it!'

She takes a deep breath, glancing at the book in her hands. I can see she is trying to find some enthusiasm. 'Let me go take my coat off and grab some dinner,' she says at last. 'I'll pop in and out, see if it's worth watching.' She turns to go, pulling at her coat sleeve as she does and almost dropping her book in the process.

'Whoops,' she mutters, as she grabs at the shiny plastic cover and something slips from inside it. A piece of paper. No, not paper – the envelope I've noticed her using as a bookmark.

Salma jumps up from her chair to retrieve the bookmark as it flutters to the ground. She casually offers it up to Jemma, who does not immediately take it. Instead – bizarrely – my sister flushes a deep, dark colour and begins stuttering.

'Oh, er, um, oh—' She reaches to take the envelope as Salma frowns, whipping it away again. Jemma is making the least amount of eye contact possible. 'Er, thanks, that's just . . . it's not anything . . . it's my . . . er . . . it's just . . .um . . .'

59

Salma narrows her eyes at Jemma, then examines the item. 'What? Why are you being so fecking weird? What *is* this?'

'Oh god, *nothing*!' Jemma replies, her voice high and strangled, eyes wild. 'It's just this silly ... just a thing ...' She swipes for the envelope but finds only empty air. Salma is too quick for her.

I watch Jemma floundering with fascination. Whatever this envelope is, it's ... *something*! I glance over at Harry, who's sitting up straight in his chair, watching with keen interest.

'Just tell us what it is, Jim-Jems?' I say, faux-casually. 'You can totally tell us anything. And it's not good to keep secrets!' I pause, feeling like a hypocrite, then add more forcefully than I can help, *'Just tell us!'*

My mind races with the many dramatic options: it's a secret will from a long-lost relative. It's newly discovered adoption papers and we're not really related. It's a million-pound offer letter from a publisher who wants Jemma to be the next ... er, hum. I literally can't think of a single wealthy author. Or any authors full stop, for that matter. Lorraine Kelly writes novels, right? She must be rich.

Jemma sighs, looking a bit defeated as her colour returns halfway to normal. 'Fine, I'll tell you,' she says, 'but it's all a bit odd, OK? So don't judge me.'

I suppress an excited gasp as me, Harry and Salma all lean forward to listen.

Jemma pauses, and looks me dead in the eye. 'It's a letter.' She takes a breath. 'From a stranger. It's a woman at the library. We leave each other notes in this copy of *Too Good to*

Be True. We talk about books, mostly. She's a big fan of *The Very Hungry Caterpillar* and—'

Salma holds up a hand, stopping Jemma in her tracks. 'Wait, wait,' she says, shaking her head. 'Back up, babe. What the hell are you talking about? When did this start?'

I bounce on the spot, excited, even though this isn't as good as a long-lost will.

'Yeah, Jim-Jems, spill,' I say, 'we want details.'

Jemma laughs, then hesitates, glancing again at the novel in her hands. 'OK, so it started about a month ago now. Someone left me a note. Here, in the inside cover of *Too Good to Be True*—'

I gasp with the thrill of it, then frown. 'Wait, a nice one? Or like, *give me a million pounds or I'll kill your favourite book*?'

Salma sniggers at this and Harry looks horrified. 'Do we need to call the police?' he asks in a serious voice. Bless him, he's adorable. I think he must've lived in a palace growing up, without a TV or phones, and no one around that ever lied. Apart from fun little lies about the Nazi origins of their family money.

Jemma opens the book cover to the library slip, where dates are listed – for returns, I guess?! 'No police required,' she says. 'It's just Karen. She'd left it here for me. She told me off for bending the book cover.' She looks up fiercely. 'But I bloody didn't! That's the point of the plastic anyway, isn't it?'

'How would she even know it was you who bent it?' Salma looks intrigued.

Jemma shrugs. 'There's only me and one other person who

61

checks it out. We take it in turns. I've tried to ask Anita the librarian about this mysterious other *Too Good to Be True* fan but she gets all GDPR-y on me. There are other copies of the book available – especially now there's this TV version coming out – but only me and one other person, Karen, check out *this* copy.'

'That's so mysterious!' I breathe out, enthralled.

Salma waves the envelope in the air. 'And this is that very first note, is it? Can I have a read?' Jemma nods and Salma pulls out an A5-sized sheet of paper. She scans the contents. 'Hold on, why are you calling her Karen?' she asks, glancing up. 'There's no name here. Did you do intros later?'

Jemma smiles shyly. 'No, actually. We haven't shared anything about our identities at all. I've just been calling her Karen in my head because she was so scoldy in that first message.'

I move closer to read over Salma's shoulder.

Dear fellow reader of this brilliant book. Please don't bend the front cover, it's a cardinal sin. I could only be more outraged if you bent pages over or wrote notes in the margins.
Sincerely, your TGTBT co-fan

'So wait,' I say slowly, 'how come you're assuming it's a woman writing the notes?'

Salma nods at this. 'Yeah, because there is definitely a flirty vibe to this thing.' She wriggles her eyebrows at Jemma, who looks startled. 'This whole message is so wink-wink. Even the cutesy note-in-a-book thing – it's like the plot of a movie.'

'Or indeed, a book,' Harry points out dryly.

I loudly gasp for the fiftieth time. 'Oh my *god*, Jim-Jems, imagine if this is some sexy man-stranger.' I cover my mouth. 'This would be the best meet-cute! Sooo much better than Tinder.'

Jemma rolls her eyes. 'Let's not get carried away here. Of *course* it's a woman! Only women read romance books, don't they?' She glances reprovingly over at Harry. 'Don't pout, Harry!' she cries. 'When did you last read anything that wasn't a boring war memoir or some motivational speaker nonsense from an Elon Musk wannabe?' She sighs. 'It's like men can't admit they'd enjoy reading about romance or their masculinity would instantly shrivel up and die.'

'Some men read romance!' Harry protests, his face pink. 'You don't know! This note could very easily be from a man. We … I … men are—'

'Not All Men!' Salma cackles and Harry shuts up.

Jemma rolls her eyes. 'OK, well, if we're saying it's not necessarily a woman writing these, it might just as easily be a freaky teenage boy with anger issues.'

Salma scoffs dismissively, then leans forward. 'What did you reply? Do you remember what you wrote?'

Jemma looks bashful again, before retrieving a notebook from her bag. 'I actually made a copy – there's a photocopier in the library – and I wanted to make sure I remembered what I'd written. All our messages are there.'

I leap forward, grabbing for the pile of notes in her hand and reading the first one out loud.

Hey, TGTBT co-fan,

Thanks for your note, though I'm outraged by your outrage. How is it fair that I'm being accused of such heinous book crimes, without the chance to defend myself?? Do you have any evidence of this so-called cover bending? They say don't judge a book by its cover, but that's just what you're doing. Anyway, I'm an open book, so send in your lawyers, as long as they do things by the book.

Too many reading puns?

More importantly, get over yourself. Books are made to be enjoyed! This one more than most. If a cover or two gets sacrificed along the way, at least we know it was loved in the process. Take a page out of my book and relax.

Sincerely, the OG fan

I groan. 'God, Jim-Jems, did you have to do so many book puns? How embarrassing!'

She reddens again, her nostrils flaring. 'She – er, they – liked it, thank you!'

Before she can stop me, I read out the stranger's reply.

It's true, I'm judgemental. I always have been. Especially when it comes to books. But I do agree that they are made to be loved, so I will forgive you any future book offences. Especially since you're so brilliant at book puns. Have you always loved reading? What was your favourite book as a child? I would say The Very Hungry Caterpillar *was mine, but that was George W. Bush's favourite, wasn't it? Which must've ruined a very lucrative income stream for that poor author.*

'*The Very Hungry Caterpillar!*' I screech, and it is too much for Jemma. She yanks the batch of notes from mine and Salma's grasp, then turns on her heel, heading in the direction of her room.

Salma, Harry and I regard each other excitedly.

'Well, that was fun,' Salma grins. 'Shall we get back to *Die Hard* before *Book Boyfriend* starts?' She waves at the frozen image of Bruce Willis on the screen.

I giggle. 'Ugh, you mean *Definitely Would've Died Very Hard In Multiple Ways Ten Minutes In,*' I correct and then dive for the sofa. 'Press play!'

I glance over at Harry as the action begins. He looks like he might cry and I suppress the urge to laugh at him again.

Chapter Eight

JEMMA

It's got to be a woman, right?

Only women have imaginations like this. Only a woman would be so madly in love with a romance book that she'd write a note to a stranger about it. Surely. But she – *they* – haven't technically given me any specific reason to think they're female.

I'd formed a picture in my head of Karen over these last few weeks. My mysterious 'TGTBT co-fan' is a tall, elegant brunette; about the same age as me. She's got big hips and a wide, unthreatening smile. I try now to picture someone else – a man – and everything goes wibbly. Suddenly the notes don't feel as fun and silly. They seem – I don't know – *charged*.

Is there a chance I've been swapping notes for a month . . . with a man?

I dump wet cutlery onto the draining board, trying not to feel resentful as I reach for dirty plates in the sink. When

I left the house this morning, everything was clean and tidy. Clara hasn't even had the decency to wash up her crap, despite clearly doing nothing with her day. I can't believe how at home she's made herself in just a couple of weeks — in *my* home.

And now she and the others have made me doubt everything about my pen pal.

I mean, if Salma's right — if the notes are flirtatious — then, apart from anything else, it's just not an effective way of doing it. What if someone else had checked the book out? What if the note had fallen out without me noticing?

I scrub at a particularly stubborn bit of crud on the back of a plate. How does Clara even get food on the *back of a plate*? It's almost like a talent how messy she is.

Behind me I hear my sister saunter into the kitchen, casually opening the fridge to inspect its contents. I bet she's been in that furry onesie all day. It must be filthy by now.

I internally sigh, trying to swallow down the resentment. It's not her fault I'm a petty, tidy person.

'It starts in a few minutes!' Clara calls excitedly across the kitchen. '*Book Boyfriend*, I mean. You're coming in, right?' She pauses when I don't react. 'You will give it a chance, won't you?' She sounds almost nervous, like she's asking me on a date.

'Sure!' I try to match her brightness, because she's *trying*. But I'm dreading this. *Too Good to Be True* just won't translate well on TV. It's too multi-levelled and layered. It's a bloody onion of a book. An uncooked, inedible, undigestible onion

Lucy Vine

that sits in the fridge – in the salad drawer – waiting to be peeled by the right pair of adoring hands and added to some kind of vegetable medley.

I've lost track of my own analogy.

Back in the late noughties, they actually tried to do a straight-to-TV film of the book, not long after it was published. It was bad. I mean, it was good-bad. Camp and kitsch with model-gorgeous leads who spent their screen time eye-boning the camera. The movie was hard-trashed by critics – those who bothered to review it, that is – but it kind of has a special place in my heart. It's a bit pure and well meaning in its cheesiness. *And* they didn't feel the need to rename it.

'Have you had dinner?' I immediately regret asking Clara the question. What am I, going to offer to make her food now? After she's sat around in her onesie all day, watching TV and ignoring all the mess she was leaving in her wake? Up her fucking bollocks I am.

I turn to face her and my bravado slips. She looks a bit pale. She needs looking after, she always has.

She shrugs. 'Kinda.' She regards me with big sad, cow eyes. 'I mean, I've sort of been grazing all day. For lunch I had a Toblerone I found in the cupboard, followed by some leftover spaghetti that was in the fridge. Then I had eight Ferrero Rochers, three of those mini Malteser Reindeers' – she pauses – 'which I assume were Christmas leftovers, so I hope they weren't out of date.' She waves her hand, not really caring. 'And then I had a Marmite sandwich because I'd overdosed on sweet stuff, but after the salty sandwich I fancied sugar again, so I had some biscuits I found in Harry's room. He also had a packet of beef Hula Hoops, which were delicious but now I keep burping. And they're like beefy, starchy, almost *solid* burps, y'know what I mean?' She gently punches herself in the chest, releasing more beefy gas into the room as I stare at her, my disgust growing. She swallows hard. 'I was going to come find some kind of vegetable or fruit because I worry about scurvy, y'know? But I didn't want to take the piss by stealing food.' She brightens. 'But if you're making dinner, I wouldn't say no!'

There is a long silence between us before I find my words. '*You ate my Toblerone?!*'

She grimaces. 'Oh, god, that was yours? I thought maybe it was Salma or Harry's, and I'm totally going to replace it, I swear.' She checks her watch. 'Look!' She changes the subject quickly and smoothly. 'It's time for the show!'

She flees the room, heading for the living room where I hear her flicking through channels, adverts booming for suntan lotion and garden centres. 'Starting in two,' she yells through as I breathe, trying to steady myself.

OK, so far, living with my sister again has been hell, but we just need to find our rhythm. We survived eighteen years when we were kids; we can manage a few months while she gets back on her feet.

I head for the living room, fighting a craving for beef Hula Hoops that will never again be satisfied. Flopping onto the sofa, I fold my feet under myself as the opening credits begin to roll on the TV.

And that is all I can manage.

I know immediately that I will – that I *do* – hate the adaptation. The music they've used and the font on the credits immediately grate, and they open with a scene I recognize as halfway through the book where the heroine – Julianna – is waiting on a date. Yeugh, how dare they.

I leave the room and head for the kettle, furiously filling it too full of water.

I'm evolved enough to recognize this as 'resistance to change', but ughhhhhhh, they're clearly going to wreck the whole thing. I can't watch it.

From the living room, I can hear the action unfolding as the kettle wobbles into life. A couple are bickering; full of charged barbs that will – very obviously – turn quickly into blistering chemistry. Even without seeing the action, I recognize them as the main characters from the book, Julianna and George. I don't need to see them to know the actors will be all wrong.

I place the *real* Book Boyfriend – *Too Good to Be True* – on the counter. Its shiny plastic cover is warm from my armpit and I stroke it lovingly as the kettle finally boils. I throw a peppermint teabag into my favourite mug and pour in water, ignoring Salma as she shouts from the living room, asking where I've gone.

This is an early edition from the mid-noughties. They've reprinted it with a new cover since then, and I know there will be another cover released soon, one featuring the two actors yelling at one another on the screen through there. I can't stand TV tie-in covers. I get that it's meant to attract new readers but it only ever puts me off a book.

'Oh my god!' Clara is shrieking as she appears in the doorway. 'You need to come watch this, Jim-Jems, the main guy is so *fit*,' she breathes. 'Come look at him!' Her eyes are wide, her pupils blackened. 'I don't think I've ever seen someone so good-looking before, he's all, like' – she waves her hands enthusiastically – 'square jaw, black eyes and thick, sandy hair. And the *shoulders*! They have to be seen to be believed.'

Yuck yuck yuck. I always pictured George in the book as being dark haired and slim.

I sip my too-hot tea and pick up my book, reluctantly following her through to the living room.

On screen, the heroine, Julianna – who is all wrong as predicted – is telling her friends about her terrible date with George. In my lap, I cradle *Too Good to Be True*, thinking again about the note writer.

Of course it's a woman. It's bound to be a woman. She's Karen with the good hair.

I open the front cover, the plastic lightly squeaking in my hand. Anita used to write the date it was due back on the inside sheet. But that's considered an old-fashioned way of doing things now. They use an electronic notification system these days. You get a text reminding you when your three-week session with a book is almost up, and a notification when a book you've requested comes in. I have a standing request set up for *Too Good to Be True* whenever it's taken out by someone else.

By the only someone else.

I account for about half the dates listed there in Anita's handwriting. The other person started checking out *Too Good to Be True* about a year and a half ago. I wish I knew more of who they are; this other obsessive reader of my favourite book. Of *this* copy. It's strange, right? Why would anyone take the same library book out over and over again? What kind of weirdo would . . . I mean, other than *me*, obviously. But I've always thought of myself as quite a unique weirdo. And I've been checking this book out since I was a kid; why would this person suddenly be interested in it?

Sigh. I just wish I had a name. Karen doesn't feel right anymore, not now Salma and Clara have tossed everything I thought up in the air.

Are our notes really flirty, like Salma said? And why haven't we exchanged at least some basic information about ourselves? It's so frustrating that the answers are at my fingertips. I *know* Anita knows exactly who the mysterious note writer is, but she's obsessively strict about stuff like that. Sometimes she acts like the library is MI5. Hmm, I guess I could ask the other librarian, Mack. But there's a good chance he'll tell me to eff off. Ever since he started, he's been a surly, mean knobhead. I don't understand why they hired him. After all, shouldn't librarians be friendly and helpful? Mack just glowers around the room, looking furious whenever anyone asks him anything. I can't stand guys like him, who think just because they're good-looking, they can treat people however they want.

But he might tell me something about the other *Too Good to Be True* reader – if only to make me go away?

I pull out the small, lined piece of paper and re-read that very first note, wondering about the person behind it. It's definitely a woman; it's *got* to be a woman. Maybe the flirty vibe Salma picked up on is because this female note writer thinks *I'm* a man! Or else I'm just being embarrassingly heteronormative.

Just for fun, I picture a tall man with dark hair scribbling out this note.

And then I picture some cranky old lady who tells racist jokes and tuts about women drivers.

Maybe I don't want to know the real person behind it. Maybe I want to keep the mystery because – let's face it – reality never matches up to the fiction. Maybe not knowing is more fun.

I sit up straighter, still ignoring the ongoing nonsense on the screen.

And who cares if it's a man or a woman! This person is my friend. We talk about books. We share a sense of humour and a passion for romance novels. This is someone I enjoy speaking to and it doesn't matter what Salma, Harry and Clara all think.

So why do I suddenly feel so freaked out?

Chapter Nine

CLARA

'You look intense,' Jemma comments from my bedroom door. Her hand is half raised awkwardly, as if she'd last-second thought better of knocking. It makes me a little sad. She doesn't know how to approach me. She cocks her head. 'Job searching?'

'Nah,' I say with a shrug. 'I'm making a list of things I'd buy if – sorry, *when* – I win the lottery. I know I need to get a house and stuff, but I don't want it to be the first thing, y'know. I'm thinking I book a really mega luxury holiday first. To Bali. Then I'll fly to Dubai, then St Tropez. Or wherever else the celebrities are all going. Then I'm buying a boat off the coast of the South of France.' I glance up at her unamused expression.

'St Tropez *is* off the coast of the South of France,' she says, and I grin.

'That works out well then. I can make arrangements for the superyacht while I'm holidaying there.' I pause. 'Oh, and obviously, I'll give you some! I mean, depending on the amount I win. If it's £50 million or more, you and Mum can have £500,000 each.'

She steps into the room. 'What the hell? You have £50 million – *or more!* – and we only get half a mill from you? That's so stingy!'

'Ugh.' I roll my eyes. 'Fine, £1 million *each*. Greedy.' I sit up in bed a little straighter and start deleting a line in my lottery Word doc. 'But that means I'm not giving any of it to charity. I'll need a lot to run my mcmega mansion. I hear being rich is expensive.'

'*Nothing* to charity? Oh my god, you're—' Jemma stomps fully into the room now, looking outraged, then stops. She makes her face blank. 'What happened to job hunting?' Her voice is neutral but I can hear something in her tone. Something judgemental.

But it's OK, I have an explanation. 'I was totally going to get on with looking for a job first thing this morning, but, like, I had to have breakfast first, *obviously*! It's the most important meal of the day or whatever.' I pause, gauging her reaction. 'And then I was really cold from my smoothie – which I made from scratch by the way! Did you even know you guys had a Nutribullet? It was right at the back of the cupboard, covered in dust!' Jemma doesn't look impressed. 'So anyway, afterwards I had to get back into bed to warm up, and then I thought I'd just watch, like, ten minutes of telly while I got cosy, and then I remembered I've been wanting to watch *Buffy the Vampire Slayer* ever since I met Angela's daughter. So I started it from the pilot episode – which is *so good* by the way – and I *somehow* ended up watching, like, seven episodes.' I grimace comically, adding, '-teen. Seventeen. It's just too good.' Jemma is still unmoved. I clear my throat. 'So, yeah! Then it was way past lunchtime and I ate too much, so had to have a quick nap. And I had this amazing dream about winning the lottery, so when I woke up I started making this list and now it's half five . . .' I trail off. I guess, now that I've said all of that out loud, it doesn't sound like the best reason to have wasted the whole day.

Ugh, it's not my fault I have no self-control. It's not something I'd choose as a personality trait!

And the truth is, I don't have any idea where to start with the job hunt, even if I could find the motivation to look. I googled 'new career ideas' last night, and – after baulking at the billion-plus results – clicked on a job quiz. I answered a few confusingly worded questions about my temperament, but all it did was reinforce that I have no idea who I am or what I want. This feels like a huge hurdle – like I'm facing a massive brick wall – and starting the search is just too big.

Jemma sighs and looks away, out the window. It's a Mum guilt move. 'Did you at least get loo roll and milk like I asked?'

'Yes!' I say too loudly, gesturing to the corner where my bag for life sits. Jemma left me with a list of chores for the day, including getting a few things from the shop. But the thing is, I literally haven't got any money. Last time I tapped my credit card to pay for something, it didn't request my PIN, it just dry-coughed and told me to go fuck myself.

So I had to improvise.

Jemma is peering into the bag disapprovingly. 'What am I looking at?' she says, sounding way too much like our mum again.

'I popped to the local Wetherspoons,' I explain, and she cocks her head, waiting for more. I'm excited as I explain. 'Don't you even know?! You can get free bog roll from their loos! And tiny sachets of milk. I nicked enough to keep us going all week.' She picks up a mini-pot of UHT milk and I catch a *Jesus* muttered under her breath. 'You don't even have to put them in the fridge,' I offer hopefully, and she stands back up, sighing.

'OK, thanks, I guess,' she says, turning to go.

'Oh wait!' I pull the covers off me, wincing at the rush of cold that hits my bare legs. '*Book Boyfriend* is on again tonight.' Jemma turns back, disinterest plain on her face. 'The second episode, remember?' I search her face. 'The first episode was *so* brilliant, I wish you'd stayed and watched the rest, you only gave it five minutes. I *loved* it. It's almost made me want to read the book!' I laugh. 'You really need to see how gorgeous the lead guy who plays George is. I looked him up, his name is Milo Samuels – it's a sexy name, right? He's a Brit! I totally assumed he was American, putting on an English accent.' I cock my head. 'Or maybe Aussie – like a Hemsworth brother or whatever. Honestly, I didn't think we made men that hot over here. We can't grow them, we don't have the climate.' I'm barely pausing for breath. 'Either way, I'm legit obsessed! I can't wait for the next episode tonight.' Out in the hallway, I hear a noise. 'HAZ? SALMA?'

Harry's head pokes in, closely followed by Salma. 'What's up?' he asks, as Salma piles past and into bed with me.

'I'm cold!' she declares by way of explanation, burrowing under my duvet. I catch Jemma watching her with jealous eyes and hold in a sigh.

'I was just saying to Jim-Jems,' I begin, 'that *Book Boyfriend* episode two is on tonight. You guys in?'

'Yes!' they intone together, and I beam at their enthusiasm. 'See, Jem? You need to give it a proper go tonight.'

Jemma nods non-committally but I refuse to be deterred.

The trouble is, my sister has always painted this picture of me in her head. She thinks I'm a shitty person, she always has. But just because she cares about stuff that I don't, doesn't make her nicer than me. I'm nice! I totally had giving to charity on my lottery to-do list until she demanded more money for her and Mum. Who's really the bad guy here?

If I could just figure out what to do with my life now I'm home, I think everything would fall into place. Jemma has it all together; this steady career, great friends like Salma and Harry. She's sorted. So of course she thinks I'm a loser layabout. I wish I had her motivation, her willpower.

'Stop being a spoilsport, Jemma!' Salma shouts at her from beside me. 'I've had a crappy day at the radio station. We had a competition winner in who we had to take out for a fancy lunch. He stole all the nice bread from the bread basket – left me only that crappy rye grain shit – and then kept asking the waiter for purloin steak.'

Harry looks delighted. 'Instead of sirloin steak?'

She nods as I cackle next to her. 'And did they go steal him a steak?'

'It's a full service restaurant,' Salma nods, straight-faced.

Jemma looks dreamy. 'This is making me hungry. Can't we just watch old episodes of *MasterChef* instead of this *Book Boyfriend* thing?'

Harry grunts a protest from the doorway. 'No way! I'm the posh one here and even I'm sick of the judges saying *unctuous* all the time. No one has ever used that word outside of *MasterChef*.'

'OK,' Jemma says at last, laughing a little. 'Fine, fine. I will give the second episode a go. But if I'm not feeling it in the first few minutes, I'm not staying. I have work to do anyway. And Clara has to promise not to constantly go on about the actor.' She rolls her eyes, but nicely. 'I bet he's not even all that.'

I throw a pillow at her as she laughs again. 'How dare you talk about my soulmate that way!' I nod half to her, half to myself as she waves her way out of the room. Something flips over in my stomach as I call out after her, 'He's The One, Jim-Jems, he really is! You'll see!'

Chapter Ten

JEMMA

After two wonderful years of marriage, we have mutually decided to amicably split. Please respect our wish for privacy at this time.

Total horse-do-do.

'If those years of marriage were so *wonderful*, why are they divorcing, huh?' I jab at the phone screen over Clara's shoulder.

'Don't say that!' Clara whines at me, wriggling further into the sofa as she turns her phone away – and with it, the showbiz homepage of the *Daily Mail* – from my view. 'You don't know anything about Greta and Indiana, or their relationship. They were so perfect together and their break-up is a national tragedy. They were amazing in all the films they starred in together.'

I throw myself down on the sofa cushions beside my sister. I can hear Harry and Salma bickering over snacks in the kitchen. I catch her telling him to 'go fuck a tin of Heinz beans.' Classic Salma.

'You don't know anything about those people!' I tell Clara hotly as she picks up the TV remote and flicks through the channels. 'That's my problem with celebrities. They're always performing, always faking it. You have no clue at all whether they were happy together, or if it was all a set-up. They probably signed a contract to be together for two years. I bet they hated each other the whole time.'

Clara looks stricken. 'Of course they didn't!'

I open my laptop on the coffee table before me. I pull up a folder with my latest Aarav interview, untangling my headphones and tucking my feet up beside me. I have a lot of transcribing to get done. I might as well do it while pretending to watch *Book Boyfriend*.

Salma and Harry join us, still arguing light-heartedly. Harry offers me popcorn from a large bowl.

'You left this in the kitchen.' Salma hands me *Too Good to Be True*, and I stroke it longingly. Maybe I'll read instead of working. That sounds much more fun.

Across the room, Clara is still on one. 'Salma, did you know Greta and Indiana split up? Can you believe it?'

Salma looks mystified as Harry leaps in. 'No way!' he says with outrage. 'I thought they were in it for the long haul. They were so great together.' Clara beams at his interest and I feel a spike of irritation. I hate how well they get on.

'The best you can hope for with those stars is half a story,' I comment, extracting the envelope bookmark from my novel and checking the length of the chapter ahead. Eight pages. Perfect. Short chapters make me feel like I'm a fast reader. Like I'm achieving something.

'Better than that rubbish.' Clara nods dismissively at the book in my hand and I feel hot with hatred. I loathe people who barely read and still feel entitled to comment on my reading choices. 'And,' she continues airily, 'I'd kill to have something as sexy and exciting as Greta and Indiana had.'

I snort. 'They broke up after only two years.'

'Two years and four months if you count their dating era,' Harry tells me defensively as Clara cries, 'And it's only because of, like, press intrusion and the stress of being an A-lister!'

I grin, actually quite enjoying the boost of serotonin I'm getting from teasing my sister instead of being furious with her. I'm trying really hard to be nice because I know *she's* trying really hard. Objectively I can see that this is my sister doing her best to be helpful and nice. Despite the Wetherspoons bog roll and long-life milk. What are we, students? I bet she also doesn't floss and drinks blue WKD.

I mean, I also don't floss, but I definitely don't drink WKD.

'Do you drink WKD?' I ask her innocently, and she nods happily.

'Oh yeah,' she grins. 'I drink it with Baileys and rum. I call it WKumleys – it's delicious.'

There, see?

But I'm trying to channel Salma and Harry, who both seem endlessly amused by my sister's hopelessness, rather than irritated.

'Ooh, it's starting!' Harry points at the TV, looking way too eager as Clara excitably turns up the volume. Pre-game adverts blast and Salma snuggles into me.

'I know you hate this,' she says in a low voice. 'But I'm glad you're still watching it with us.'

'I can't promise to give it my full concentration,' I say, smiling grudgingly and gesturing lightly at the book version in my hands.

'We'll take whatever crumbs you can offer us shallow TV people,' she laughs, then sits up. 'Oh, by the way, how's it going with the mountain guy? You were with him again today, right?'

I nod, raising my eyebrows. 'Yep, really good. I should be transcribing actually.' I sigh. 'God, Salma, I have such a crush on him.' I pause. 'Or maybe just a professional crush on his achievements? I mean, Aarav's done so much with his life! I feel both hugely inadequate and intensely hot whenever he's telling me about his adventures. I don't really want this project to ever end, but it's another tight deadline. A couple of months to do all this research and interviews, while the boss starts putting the structural edit together.' I frown, 'Although that dickhead librarian Mack kept interrupting us today.' I give Salma a dark look. 'He obviously hates that I use the library to work from, but the other librarian, Anita, has always said it's fine! It's what the desks are there for! If people like me didn't use the library, it wouldn't exist.'

Salma rolls her eyes. 'He's an arsehole, don't let him get to you.' She's been in the library to meet me a few times, and been subjected to the shitty charms of Mack. Last time he told her she couldn't come in if she didn't sign up for a library card. They nearly had a fist fight before Anita intervened and overruled him. I squeeze my book into my chest, speaking dreamily. 'Anyway, I could listen to Aarav's stories for hours.'

'Nobody cares about the mountaineer!' Harry is red-faced as he shushes us. 'The show is starting!' Salma and I exchange an amused look. He is very into this series, who'd have thought.

'There he is!' Clara squeals as our leading man strides across the screen. She turns to the room. 'Isn't he the dream-iest? I honestly think we're meant to be together.'

I snort at this, barely giving the screen a glance. Salma smirks in my direction. 'Jemma only has book boyfriends,' she tells the room, 'but I think TV boyfriends are just as legitimate.' Salma nods authoritatively. 'Mine will always be Colin Firth as Mr Darcy.'

'Which one is that?' Harry frowns. 'Is that his character in *Kingsman*?'

Clara turns to the group, momentarily distracted from her new on-screen crush. 'I know that film! It's the one where he has a stutter, right?' she asks and Harry shakes his head.

'No, that's *The King's Speech*.'

'No, wait.' Clara looks inspired. 'He was stuttering in *Love Actually*, wasn't he?'

'No!' Salma sighs. 'He was just trying to speak Portuguese to get off with his cleaner. And I'm talking about *Pride and Prejudice*, the TV series – obviously.'

'Of course,' I add supportively, though I've lost track of the chat.

Clara squints at Salma. 'Didn't Matthew Macfadyen play Mr Darcy?'

Harry shakes his head again. 'You're thinking of Matthew McConaughey.'

'Nooo,' Salma yells over them, turning furiously on Clara. 'Do not mention the *Pride and Prejudice* remake in my presence ever again. I'm talking about the only version that matters – the 1995 BBC adaptation starring Jennifer Ehle as Elizabeth Bennet and Colin Firth as Mr Darcy.' She takes a deep breath, before continuing her diatribe. 'I'm sure there are some people in this world whose Mr Darcy is Matthew Macfadyen, but something has gone deeply wrong for those people. That is a deep-rooted trauma that must be worked through in therapy.' Her eyes are wild. 'I mean, I'm sure Matthew Macfadyen is a perfectly nice person but he's also not and I hate him and how dare he.'

Clara looks at her kindly as she finishes this speech. 'Babe, Colin Firth played Mr Darcy in *Bridget Jones's Diary.*' She pats Salma's hand gently. 'It's an easy mistake to make, don't worry about it.'

I regard Salma's dumbfounded expression with some satisfaction. See? Clara *is* infuriating. It's not just me.

I clear my throat. 'To be fair, she's not wrong. His character *was* Mark Darcy. Just to confuse things even more, did you know Colin Firth is actually *in* the second *Bridget Jones* book? As himself, the actor? Bridget interviews him in her capacity as a really bad journalist. It's so funny. Much funnier than the films. The books are wayyyyy better than the movies.'

'You always think the books are better,' Salma says, half smiling, her colour returning to normal.

'That's because they are,' I mutter, resentfully watching my beloved Julianna on screen, laughing with her friends in a way that is all wrong.

Salma leans in closer, looking a little more serious. 'I think books and book boyfriends are great, pal, but don't you think . . .' She pauses. 'I don't know, when did you last go on an actual date with a real life man?'

I shrug, feeling put on the spot. 'I don't want to!' I tell her decisively, then try to make a joke of her question. 'I'm far too busy fantasizing about fictional men to worry about the real thing! I've been ruined by book boyfriends and everyone telling me I should settle.' I grin. 'I mean, why settle when there's a dreamy hero in the next book I pick up?'

Salma regards me silently and I swallow hard. I know what she thinks. She thinks my obsession with fiction is holding me back. We've talked about it before. She thinks I hide from real life. Like with my work. She'd say I've chosen to stay a research assistant for a ghostwriter because I'm too chicken to try being a writer myself.

From across the room, Clara suddenly starts wailing. 'Ohhh god no!' She looks up at me from her phone. 'Mum's just messaged to say she's got me a job interview! Tomorrow!'

'What?' I lean forward. 'Where? How? For what?'

Her voice rises an octave. 'At Angela's office!' She throws her phone down into the sofa cushions. 'It's a PA job, working for one of the execs.' She puts a hand to her chest like there is a chance she will start hyperventilating. 'This is not what I need right now. I need some time to figure out what I want to do!' She blinks at the three of us. 'I've just got back here, I've had a really bad—' She stops and looks down.

'What?' Salma prods. 'A bad what?'

Clara looks up innocently. 'Huh? Oh nothing. I just mean I'm not ready for this. I need more time.' She sighs and I grimace.

'Maybe it won't be as awful as you think,' I offer supportively. 'You could get there and love the office and the team! It might be amazing working in the same building as Angela. You could help her and Mum with some wedding planning!' She makes a face and I add, 'I'm joking – I don't think they've even started thinking about that yet.' I pause. 'At the very least, it'll be some decent interview practice.'

She sighs again. 'I guess so.' She stares longingly at the TV screen. 'I was just really hoping to dedicate some time to stalking my new crush.'

'Fair enough,' Salma says agreeably. 'And speaking of new crushes . . .' She turns to me excitedly. 'Have you had any more notes from your mysterious book boyfriend?'

I turn red. 'No! And stop saying it's a man!'

'Are you not still writing to each other?' Clara leans in curiously as I shrug.

The truth is, I haven't replied to the latest note. I feel weird about the whole thing now. This is why I kept it secret for a while – I *knew* it would get ruined by everyone else knowing. Now, every time I pick up my writing set to reply, I get all nervous, picturing some too-handsome man reading my silly words and laughing at me.

Clara looks outraged by my lack of enthusiasm. 'Oh my god, Jim–Jems, you *have* to reply! When do things like this ever happen to people like us? This is such a crazy, magical thing, you have to see what happens. You *must* keep going!'

'I will,' I say casually, staring down in my lap, adding in a low voice, 'probably.' I pause. 'I have to return the book to the library on Wednesday so I would need to do it by then. But I don't know, I think our conversation may have run its course. I don't know what else to say.'

'I agree with Clara, you should keep writing,' Salma says firmly.

Harry looks horrified. 'I don't think you should!' he says hotly. 'I mean, this note person could be anyone. It could be some absolute freak.'

Salma smiles serenely. 'Then it would be a match made in heaven, wouldn't it?' I lightly slap her on the arm and Clara shrieks with laughter.

'You really have to,' my sister says when she stops cackling. 'Otherwise you'd always wonder, wouldn't you? You'd always wonder what might have happened if you had. Who you might've met.' She looks serious for a moment. 'I'm not saying this is your soulmate or whatever' – she gestures at the screen – 'not like me and Milo Samuels—'

'Or me and Colin Firth's Mr Darcy,' adds Salma.

'Right!' Clara nods. 'But this is someone who seems to love *Too Good to Be True* as much as you. This could be a friend for life. Or at least someone you can bore on about it with.' She gives me a cheeky smile and I reluctantly return it.

'Let me think about it some more, OK?' I tell the room and Clara whoops.

To be honest, it's not like I'll be able to think about anything else.

Chapter Eleven

CLARA

'OK, great,' says the man whose name I forgot the moment he said it as he regards me with dead eyes. 'And finally, what do you think is your biggest weakness?'

I clear my throat and then offer with confidence, 'Kryptonite?'

I watched a video last night about acing job interviews, and it suggested this answer. It seemed like a hilarious solution to a shit question and I was totally sure it would break the ice. But the dead-eyed nameless man does not appear amused.

'Riiiiight,' he intones with disinterest, checking his watch. 'Before we finish up, do you have any questions?'

I know I've got no chance of getting this job. I'm sure this bloke only added me to the interview list as a favour to Angela, which is extra embarrassing – my *mum's girlfriend* getting me a job interview. I'm sure Mum had to beg Angela to set it up and I've mostly just made a tit of myself.

Oh god, what happens if they actually offer me the job? Because there's no way I could do it. I'd screw it all up, I know I would. Despite my pep talk from Jemma last night, I know me. And me messes everything up.

'Questions?' I repeat a bit blankly.

'Yep.' Dead Eyes looks past me at the door. 'Anything you'd like to know about the team or the culture here?'

That job advice video I looked at said I really should have something ready for this section of the interview, but I forgot to come up with a question. I was hoping something would occur to me during the conversation, but I was mostly internally playing the theme tune to *Home and Away* because the receptionist outside was Australian.

'My question is . . .' I hedge, hunting for something and finally hitting on a question I am genuinely curious about. 'Do you like my hair?'

His face goes slack and I raise my eyebrows.

'I mean,' I continue hastily, 'do you think it's, like, office appropes? I was going to do a ponytail, because that *defo* means business professional, but I haven't had my roots done in aaages and it looked really shi— bad. But it looks OK down, right?' I pause anxiously and he says nothing. 'It's too long, isn't it?' I ask, worriedly pulling at some split ends. 'I had a haircut booked in the other day but when I got there, the hairdresser had awful hair! What do you do in that situation? You can't trust someone with shi— bad hair not to give you shit, um, bad hair, too, can you? So I made a run for it.'

He takes a deep breath and I can tell he is annoyed. Even

more annoyed than he was a few minutes ago when he asked me about my work in America and I started singing the British national anthem. Or, at least, I sang what I *thought* was the British national anthem but turned out to be Eurovision winners Bucks Fizz's 'Making Your Mind Up'. Which really *should* be the national anthem.

I just didn't want to get into what I was doing in the US. And it's not like the many rubbish temp jobs I had over the last five years would've impressed him much.

He stands up and offers a hand for me to shake. 'I think your hair is fine. Thanks for coming in, Ms Poyntz.'

'Oh, sure!' I bounce out of my seat, feeling pleased with myself. I pulled things around, I reckon. That hairdresser chat was very relatable. 'I look forward to hearing from you, Mr . . . Sir.'

I head out into the early summer air, feeling excited. Sure, being a PA isn't exactly my dream job, but it might be OK, right? Until I figure stuff out.

I check my phone where there is a message waiting from Jemma. I feel an unfurling of something at the sight of her name. A thawing is happening between us, I'm sure of it.

> Hope the interview went well! I've been thinking about what you said re my note writer. Maybe you could help me with what to reply next? X

I let out a little squeal of delight and a man walking past with a Costa cup nearly drops it. I beam at him as he glares.

This is *great*. Jemma and I will bond over this mysterious book dude and maybe she'll fall in love and have me to thank.

I stop short, staring sightlessly into an M&S window. I hope this isn't a mistake. I mean, you'd have to be a bit of a nutjob to leave someone a note in a book, right? Or an absolute nerd.

My soulmate would never be such a geek.

An image of that *Book Boyfriend* actor passes across my vision. Dashing, gorgeous, charismatic, with the most dazzling smile I've ever seen in my life.

Milo Samuels.

I glance into another shop window while walking and feel a jolt as I realize I'm looking into his eyes. It's a poster – a screengrab from the show – as part of a large bookshop display. They're shouting about the novel version and it's got a new cover. One with the actors on it. I head inside for a closer look, wondering if I should buy a copy. It would give me and Milo something to talk about when we finally meet.

A group of giggling girls crowds past me at the doorway, and one points towards Milo's handsome photo.

'Have you seen that show?' one asks, followed by much squealing about his 'lushness'. I feel a pang of jealousy pulse through me and resist an impulse to yell *he's mine* at the whole lot of them.

I know it's a bit irrational, but he *does* feel like he's mine. After all, I've spent all week googling him, watching clips and reading interviews. I feel like I know him. I know he's in his early thirties and has only really done theatre until now. I know he has a brother and that he recently stormed out of an interview when a journalist asked him about his love life. And there's no point denying my penchant for a bad boy.

At the display table, I pick up a copy of *Too Good to Be True*. The cover features a steamy shot of Milo with his co-star. They've put *BOOK BOYFRIEND* in massive letters at the top, burying its original title down near the bottom. I giggle to myself, thinking how much Jemma would hate this.

I wish she'd give the series a chance.

I spot an overhead sign for the tills across the shop, meander over and join a long queue. I'm actually buying a book – check me out! Jemma's obviously having an effect on me.

I stare down at Milo's photo on the cover. He is … unbelievable. I genuinely feel a bit in love. He's exactly my type! I keep having this daydream where I'm a hard-hitting journalist, interviewing him for some highbrow newspaper, and then he gets really angry with me. He storms off, then returns all brooding and moody, and he throws me onto a bed that is also in the room for some reason – where he ravishes me.

Genuinely, if I'd ever written out a list of traits I wanted in my dream man, he would tick every single one of those boxes. Actually, maybe that's how I'll kill the rest of my day – a dream man checklist. I'll *manifest* him into my life.

If only there was some way I could figure out of meeting him.

But today isn't supposed to be about my dream man; this is about Jemma's meet-cute. I'm really excited for her. Because even if this book note person doesn't turn out to be a dashing, sexy male stranger, I still think my sister should reply. She is too secure in her little rut. Doing the same things every day, visiting the same library, chatting to the same two house-mates, checking out the same book every other bloody week. She needs an adventure and a bit of excitement and mystery in her life. I think that's why the universe has sent me here to her. It's not me escaping what happened in America, it's me running *towards* my sister. She needs someone to mess up her neat little existence a bit. Between me and this book stranger, we'll give her a big fat kick up the butt. Plus, this could finally be what it takes to bring us together. Helping her with this could persuade Jemma to let me into her life.

I hug the book happily as I check my emails, feeling only mildly deflated to find a rejection email Dead Eyes must have sent before I'd even left the building. I duck out of the queue, dumping the novel on a table. Sorry, Milo. No new job means I can't afford to turn over a new reading leaf.

Ah fuck it, when I'm married to a TV star, I won't need some stupid office job anyway.

Chapter Twelve

JEMMA

'Hello again, *Too Good to Be True* reader,' I read out loud as I write. Clara makes a wailing noise.

'God, no!' she cries. 'That is all wrong.'

I blink. 'All? Even the *hello*?'

'Absolutely wrong.' She shakes her head vehemently. 'Terrible, in fact. Disgusting.'

'Bit harsh,' I mutter as she switches seats, flopping down beside me and ripping the pen from my hand.

We're in our living room, debating my next response to the book note and it seems that – so far – I am not doing well.

'Maybe *hi* would be better?' Harry offers from across the room.

Harry is also here.

'Or *hey*?' Salma suggests eagerly, sitting up straight in the armchair.

So is Salma.

'*Hey*,' Clara says firmly. '*Hi* is slightly better than *hello*, but still very bad.' Harry looks crestfallen.

'I like *hi*,' I tell Harry nicely, and he perks up.

Clara snorts in his direction. 'I'm surprised you didn't suggest, like, *good day*, or *how do you doooooo*.' Salma barks a laugh as Harry's ears go a bit red.

'I'm not that posh,' he insists. '*Hi* is a perfectly normal greeting.'

'It's lame!' Clara tells him furiously. 'If you'd grown up around normal people instead of, like, the royal family, you would know that. And you—'

I cut her off. 'Can we stop arguing over greetings? It doesn't feel that important. You guys do know this is like the fourth note I've sent this person? Do we really have to crowd-source every word?'

Clara squints at me. 'You don't think what you say to the future love of your life is important?'

I splutter. 'The *love of my life*? We don't even know if this is a man or a woman yet. Never mind if they'd be age appropriate or a decent human. I'm still ninety-five per cent sure it's a stroppy lady with boundary issues.'

'The note has the air of thirty-year-old man,' Salma says confidently. 'There is a lot of main character energy here. I mean, jeez, even having the confidence and audacity to write a message to a stranger in the first place could only come from a man. When you've been brought up with society telling you you're number one and everything you do is fantastic, you believe in yourself.' She looks around the group, adding archly, 'For example, men don't have to crowd-source greetings.'

'I'm a man,' Harry points out meekly.

'Shush,' Salma tells him. 'You're a man, but you also went to an all boys' school where uniformity and falling in line was drilled into you. You follow the crowd, basically, Harry. We are the majority here and we are all shouting a lot. So you're falling in line. I bet loads of your school mates ended up in the military. But not in the normal military; in the fancy bit of the army that, like, the princes all served in, where there's not as much danger.'

Harry looks like he will protest but then nods dumbly.

'So, anyway . . .' I clear my throat, trying not to sound annoyed. I really regret letting this lot get involved. 'Shall we get back to the note and what I should write?'

Salma nods importantly. 'Y'know, it would really help if we could see your last few messages to each other.'

It's a fair point, and I reach for my bag where I've stored all our notes so far. I hesitate as my hand closes around the wad of papers. There is no reason at all for my reluctance. This person is a stranger and these are my closest friends. And yet, I feel like this is a betrayal, somehow.

'Come on!' Clara cries impatiently and I hand them over, my stomach on the floor.

'It's mostly just silly chat,' I mutter defensively and Salma shushes me as they all crowd around. They pull out one of my replies; one where I shared my own favourite childhood book.

I loved The Very Hungry Caterpillar, *too! He represented a simpler time – an easier life! – didn't he? He was a bug after my own heart. Except I feel like all that fruit he ate would get a bit boring after a while, wouldn't it? Personally, I'm more of a biscuit fan, so I'd go for one shortbread on a Monday, two chocolate Hobnobs on a Tuesday. On a Wednesday I'd have three digestives. On Thursdays I'd get four jaffa cakes. On Fridays I'd get five Viennese whirls and then it's a free-for-all on Saturdays, so I'd have a whole box of chocolate fingers. And instead of a green leaf on Sunday, I'd have a Garibaldi because they're practically healthy, right? All those currants?*

This whole thing has made me very hungry. A very hungry caterpillar.

I also still love The Tiger Who Came to Tea, *which – I'm realizing now – was also about a greedy creature eating everyone's dinner. I think this may explain some of my attitudes to food . . .*

Salma giggles, delighted by the silliness, and turns to the note writer's reply – much to Clara's irritation.

'I hadn't finished reading!' she cries with fury, and Salma sighs impatiently.

'Hurry up,' she instructs, but I see her eyes sliding over my pen pal's next note without waiting for the slower readers.

Hello again. I'm so thrilled to hear you're a biscuit person. I am, too. Although, I would swap out your Friday Viennese whirls for custard creams. And surely a ginger snap has to get a look-in? Maybe on free-for-all Saturdays? I have to say The Tiger Who Came to Tea *was a gamechanger for me. I made my mum take me to the zoo so I could throw buns and biscuits at the tiger enclosure. Can you believe they didn't seem that interested? It was incredibly upsetting, but I don't want you to feel sorry for me. I've tried to live a full life since then.*

'He's funny!' Salma crows with delight and I smile, feeling somehow proud. After another minute, Clara finishes, looking up with amusement.

'Bit weird if you ask me!' she says cheerfully.

'It's just a bit of fun,' I snap and she grins.

'There aren't many clues about their identity,' Harry points out, ever analytical, as Clara rolls her eyes.

'All this kid book chat – I don't get it,' she shrugs, and I grab for the remaining notes. Of course Clara doesn't get it – she doesn't understand me or my book friend – so she doesn't get to read any more of them.

To be honest, it's a lot more of the same silliness anyway.

Salma starts to protest, but Clara interrupts, looking faraway and dreamy. 'When I meet Milo for the first time, I'm going to have the perfect conversation ready. None of this caterpillar weirdness.'

I hold back a frustrated scream.

'Milo?' Harry frowns. 'Who's Milo?'

'The actor!' Clara looks exasperated by our blank faces.

'From *Book Boyfriend*? Come on, guys, I've told you his name loads of times!' I glance at the coffee table where the plastic-covered book sits ready to be returned to the library. She nods her head quickly. 'Yes, from your book – I mean, from the TV show.' She shakes her head again. 'This is confusing. I mean the main guy.' She waves at me. 'The one who plays George.'

'I haven't really been watching it, don't ask me,' I say.

'Milo?' Salma narrows her eyes. 'That must be a stage name, it's far too cool to be British.'

'He's British, but his mum is American,' Clara breathes happily. 'Yet another thing we have in common.'

I frown. 'Our mum isn't American,' I point out and she tuts.

'No, duh! But Dad was! So we're both half English, half American – we've got that dual-nationality, never-truly-belonging thing in common.'

'I've never felt at all American,' I tell her firmly. 'We were born here and Mum raised us. Dad's a knob.'

Clara looks like she will argue. She was always much more defensive of our dickhead dad. Even after he disappeared, never to be heard of again, she still found a way to defend him. Her mouth opens, shuts, then opens again. 'Whatever,' she begins breezily. 'Anyway, I looked Milo up, he lives here in London.'

'Handy,' I say. 'And it's certainly a nice name,' I add, trying to be supportive. Clara whips round.

'It's a *perfect* name! He is absolutely perfect.' She pauses.

'Last night I made a list of what I want in my future husband – have you guys all heard of *The Secret*? I put out into the universe what I wanted and he's it. Milo has every single thing on my list.' She starts ticking items off on her fingers. 'He's exactly my type, looks wise, he lives in the area, he's funny, super cool, a bit wild, a bad boy *and* he likes cats.'

'How do you even know that?' Harry screws up his face.

'I googled the absolute *shit* out of him,' Clara says brazenly. 'He's only done a handful of interviews promoting the show so far, and mostly they didn't seem to go very well.' She raises her eyebrows. 'It sounds like he has a bit of a temper!' When I frown, she adds quickly, 'Which is sexy! I like a man who runs hot.' She waves a hand. 'Anyway, I know he lives in North West London, I know he has family he's really close to. He has two cats and he's single.' She pauses. 'That woman he's been seen out with a few times is definitely just a friend, I can feel it.' She grins around the room, adding quickly when Salma makes a face, 'And he's straight! Definitely straight.'

'That came up in the interview?' Salma looks cynical. She's done her fair share of celebrity interviews through her job on the radio. She's told me about the endless restrictions put on what she can ask.

'Yes,' Clara retorts defensively, then shrugs. 'Well, not exactly. But I *feel* it. He's too perfect for me to be gay. The universe wouldn't do that to me.'

'Because the whole world revolves around you,' I say more harshly than I meant before I can stop myself.

'Exactly,' Clara laughs and I feel my face get hot. She's

always been this way. She's the main event and we're all just in the background, dancing in her peripheral vision. And it's becoming increasingly clear that – along with alcohol, stress and anxiety – my sister is another of my rosacea triggers.

Things have been better between us in the last few days. I'm trying to laugh more at her uselessness, and remind myself that she's doing her best to be an adult. She even used the washing machine before her interview yesterday – all by herself! I mean, it was a sixty degree wash with one random red sock in with the whites, transforming everything into tiny pink doll clothes, but that's better than nothing. Isn't it? Maybe it's not. She also asked me if she should wash the plates after dinner the other night. I was initially enraged because I'm not in charge. I don't want to be the house mother who has people asking my permission or approval to do things. She should just get on with the chores without checking in with me! But then I realized it was progress for her even to realize plates didn't magically clean themselves.

We're talking more as well. I've been trying to open up; telling her about my days, mostly spent interviewing and researching Aarav's life; battling with dickhead Mack on the library front desk; and now, bonding over this weird note business.

But I wish she'd open up a bit more to me.

I get the feeling something happened in America. Something that caused her to come home. She shuts down whenever anyone mentions it. A few months ago I would've defiantly refused to care if she'd been through something over there, but I ... care? I really do. I want to care and I want her to be OK. She might be selfish and useless and a massive narcissist but I really think she mostly means well. She doesn't intend to be a child.

I think part of the problem is that Mum has always done everything for her, and it's obvious that kids who never learn to do anything for themselves turn into adults who are constantly looking to other adults to do everything for them. They look for people who will mother them or control them.

So who was doing everything for her in America?

I sigh deeply. 'Right. So far we have *hey*. Does anyone have any other dazzling words of wisdom to offer?' I wave at my notebook before me and glance around quizzically. Everyone looks a little blank. 'This isn't really getting us anywhere,' I point out after a moment, and stand up.

'Where are you going?' Clara sounds panicked. 'You're not chickening out of this, are you?'

I shake my head. 'No, I'm going to the loo. I need a few minutes of quiet.'

In the bathroom, I slam the door behind me and lean on the sink, breathing deeply and examining my face in the mirror for redness. I've tried all kinds of creams and remedies for the rosacea over the years but nothing's particularly effective. I went to the GP last year, but he shrugged me off with an antibiotic gel that did nothing. Now I just try to manage it as best I can by avoiding triggers. But I can't avoid life, and life seems to be full of endless stresses lately.

I pull the notebook back out of my bag. I can do this

without that lot. I wrote the first lot of messages without them, didn't I? I'm just going to follow my instincts and be myself.

But I might as well stick with the *hey*.

Hey, TGTBT co-fan,

How are things? So sorry for the delay replying to you this time. I actually got a little . . . well, scared! It suddenly hit me how strange this whole thing is, and how bizarre it is to be writing to a stranger. But I'm really enjoying our chat, and I hope you are, too. I've loved our bookish conversation — and our biscuit chat! — but I'd also love to know more about you. About what you think of the world and about books that aren't just aimed at pre-schoolers. What is your favourite season? Which supermarket do you shop at? Are you a person who leaves long-winded voice notes on WhatsApp? Are you an early bird or a night owl? Have you ever been in an ambulance? Do you cry at adverts? All the important stuff.

I'm looking forward to hearing from you . . .

Before I can chicken out again, I take the note, folding it twice and shoving it securely into its small white envelope. I tuck it into the plastic cover on the inside page, my heart beating too fast.

It's my most intimate message yet. I'm wearing my heart on my (book) sleeve and I hope it's not too much. I don't want to scare them off and I'm not asking who they are — I don't think I want to know that just yet – but I do want to know *more*.

I'll return it to the library in the morning – and then who knows.

Chapter Thirteen

CLARA

There are twenty-four Milo Samuels on Facebook.

So yeah, sure, the likelihood of a famous TV actor having a Facebook page is slim but I'm! Staying! Positive! After all, he's v v v new to being a famous TV actor, and he might've forgotten he even had this profile. He may, like the rest of us, have forgotten Facebook exists altogether. And it's not like Instagram or TikTok are any use. Sure, there are fan accounts for Milo – which yes, I spent an hour scrolling through in slow motion, analysing his every red carpet facial expression – but every other possibility is majorly locked down.

I wonder again about the woman he's often seen out and about with in photos. She's in quite a lot of fan shots, always at his side, always standing too close. There's a kind of intimacy there. But you'd have that with a good friend ... wouldn't you?

She's pretty, I can admit that without feeling threatened. She's all delicate dark features and expensive-looking black clothes. Is she his girlfriend? Surely he'd have mentioned her in an interview if she was. I'm assuming he's single because – I don't know – wouldn't you be gushing about it to everyone if you were in love? I would. But maybe she's the reason he keeps storming out of interviews. I can totally imagine him being really overprotective and jealous.

Or maybe they *are* together, but it's all a sham for the cameras. A publicity stunt! Like Jemma said about celebrities like my faves, Greta and Indiana.

I roll over on my bed, cracking my back and trying not to smell the duvet. It's been a nice twelve hours, let's not ruin it by remembering I need to grow the fuck up and change my sheets from time to time.

Last night was fun, reading Jemma's notes and helping her compose a new one. I feel like the house is starting to accept me living here – that *my sister* has started to accept me living here. It's been really great, having this mysterious note thingy to talk about. I think – I hope – it's bringing us together.

But now it's time to focus on *my* love life.

I stayed up late into the night narrowing the list of twenty-four Facebook Milos down to a handful of possibilities, and I'm pretty excited about one of the accounts in particular. This one has a cartoon avatar, which could vaguely be a caricature of him, yellow *Simpsons*-skin aside, and the *about* section says he lives in London. The rest of his profile is locked down but I can see his *likes*, which include the Imperial War Museum – I've never been but I *bet* I would love it. He also likes the Crystal Maze Experience, which is a thing I've heard of and would probably be open to trying. He also likes a few bands I don't know, a mid-price face cream and TV.

I like TV! It's a match made in streaming heaven.

I can't see much else but! But! But! He has recently posted on Facebook Marketplace, offering up a very cheap old chest of drawers – for collection in North West London. Which is where he lives! I'm convinced this is my way in. I just need Harry's help.

I check the time – he won't have left for work yet – and slip out of bed. Pulling on my dressing gown, I pad down the hallway and knock on his bedroom door, calling out his name in my best helpless girl voice. He's a posh lad from an all boys' school. He won't be able to cope with what's coming.

'Come in,' comes the muffled voice, and I do so, bracing myself for boy stink.

'Hiya!' I say happily, trying to sniff subtly. It's surprisingly fine and I relax, heading in and throwing myself onto his bed. How does his duvet smell so nice? I'd been led to believe all boys did in their bedroom was relentlessly wank everywhere. This duvet has no crusty patches and smells like fabric softener. What a shocker.

'Er, you OK?' he asks, eyeing me warily. He's obvs not used to women in his room, never mind ones that throw themselves onto his bed in their pyjamas. I bask for a moment in making him uncomfortable. Then remember I need his help.

I sit up, folding my hands on my lap primly. 'As you know, Haz, me and the actor from *Book Boyfriend* are very much soulmates. Very much *meant to be*.' I nod with authority at him and, after a second, he nods back slowly.

'Um, right,' he says.

'So, all I need to do to is find a way to cross paths with him. He lives in London. I figured, how hard can it be to track him down?'

This time Harry shakes his head co-operatively. 'An absolute doddle,' he says, and for a moment I think he might laugh.

I ignore it. 'Sure, a, er, *doddle*. Anyway, it just so happens that Milo Samuels is potentially selling an item of furniture on Facebook Marketplace.'

Harry regards me, his mouth twitching. 'You think actor Milo Samuels is selling furniture on Facebook in the midst of promoting his new TV show?'

I narrow my eyes at him. He's definitely taking the mick. 'I'm just saying it's a *possibility*, Harry. And you have to take chances when it comes to love, don't you? You have to risk it all—'

'With Facebook Marketplace?' he interrupts, and I scowl.

'No! With *love*, Harry.' I wave my hands. 'This is destiny, my friend. And I happen to believe in fate and the universe. They will find a way to bring Milo into my life, so he can realize that I am The One. I just have to open myself up to the chances and grab onto these opportunities with both hands. I'm going to buy this piece of furniture, and put it out into the universe that acting superstar Milo Samuels will open the door when I go collect it.' I shrug. 'And even if it's not him, it just so happens that I am in my upcycling life phase right now, so I can take this chest of drawers and turn it into something *stunning*. It's the start of my new business, if not the start of my new relationship with Milo Samuels.'

Harry smiles widely. 'Gotcha. So what do you need from me?'

I grin sheepishly. 'I need investors and help with collecting the drawers.' He frowns so I continue quickly. 'I haven't got the funds to, er, fund this endeavour and I can't borrow any more off my mum or Jemma right now.' I pout. 'Stingy fucks. So I was wondering if you would be able to buy this chest of drawers from Milo for me? And then drive me to get it?' I speak even faster. 'I'm going to triple its value within days and you'll get your *investment* back.' I pause. 'With three per cent interest.'

Harry nods seriously. 'Make it three and a half per cent and you've got yourself a deal.' I can see he's trying not to laugh, but I don't care – he said yes! He's such a sweetheart! I jump up to give him a hug and breathe him in. He smells like the fabric softener, too.

You know ... he really would be *so* perfect for Jemma, I don't know why she's so weird whenever I've hinted about them getting together. Maybe she's scared about it not working out – that she'd ruin the friendship and make things awkward in the house? But, like I was *just saying* to Haz, you have to take risks for love, right?

That's it, I decide, if things don't work out for Jemma with this mysterious book note person – or they do turn out to be a Karen after all – I'm going to make it my mission in life to get her and Harry together. It would be an adorable match and they'd totally thank me for helping them get over their nerdy shyness.

'Er, Clara?' He interrupts my matchmaker plans by pulling out of the hug.

'Yes?' I look up at him, wondering why the atmosphere in the room has shifted. His eyes are large and dark as he regards me solemnly.

'Um,' he hedges, looking embarrassed.

'What is it?' I say encouragingly, reaching out to squeeze his arm. 'You can say anything to me. I am a safe space. We're business partners now, we *should* share everything.'

He nods, then gestures at my dressing gown, which I realize now is making a very loud buzzing sound. 'I was just wondering what that noise was?'

I know immediately that it is my vibrator. I am in the wanking-constantly stage of job searching, and unfortunately – I'm remembering now – I'd casually slipped the bullet into my dressing gown pocket earlier after a particularly enjoyable session. The on button is sensitive and it seems our hug has engaged protocol.

'Oh!' I say in a sort of forced casual tone. 'Right, yeah, ummmmm, that is . . . that is . . .' I search for a solution and pounce on the obvious answer. 'That is my phone!' I tell him with relief. Harry wrinkles his nose and looks pointedly towards my left hand – where I am, in fact, holding my phone. And it's not vibrating loudly.

'This?' I ask, holding it up. 'Right, yeah, this is actually my . . . personal phone. The phone you can hear . . . *ringing* right now in my pocket is . . . my *business line*. For . . . the upcycling business that I'm launching.' I pause to flick my hair over my shoulder in what I imagine is a businesslike move. 'Yeah, I just think if you're going to start your own business and be an entrepreneur, you need to take it *seriously*, Haz. Y'know? Invest in yourself. Get your ducks in a row. Grab that low-hanging fruit. Get your boots on the ground. Throw it up and see what sticks . . .' I mentally search for more shit office jargon, ' . . . synergy,' I finish lamely.

Harry gives a half nod, then says, 'Well, as your brand new business partner, I feel like I should be privy to any new *phone* expenses incurred.' His voice is smooth. 'I should at least make a note of the number, shouldn't I? For contacting you about the three and a half per cent?' He gestures at my pocket, waiting expectantly, eyebrows raised.

'Um, no, there's really no need at this stage.' I shake my head carefully. 'No need at all. If our . . . business arrangement continues beyond this one . . . chest of drawers, then yes, sure, obviously I will pass along my new business number for you to use. But for now, I'm going to suggest we table this and, um, blue sky . . . the conversation.'

Harry has been getting pinker and pinker as I speak, from what I had assumed was embarrassment, until he fully bursts out laughing. Tears spill out of his eyes and pour down his cheeks as he howls with hysteria.

'It's not funny,' I tell him hotly, and he shakes his head.

'It fucking is,' he tells me, barely able to breathe through the peals of laughter. It's funny to hear him swear – and actually kinda sexy when it's in such a posh accent.

The vibrating in my pocket continues as I turn on my heel and stomp towards the door. Harry calls out behind me in a voice shaking with mirth, 'Don't you think you should answer your business line, Clara? Someone is really, really keen to get hold of you.' As I enter my bedroom and yank the offending bullet out of my pocket, I hear Harry yell down the hall, 'Don't you have voicemail? It's been ringing for ages!'

I flick off the device and feel my breath slow.

OK.

For my first ever business meeting, I actually think that went pretty well.

Chapter Fourteen

JEMMA

I take a deep breath and inhale my happy place.

'Morning, Jemma.' Anita greets me warmly from the front desk, though she's already in conversation with someone having computer issues. Beside her, Mack swings in his chair, doing nothing. I catch his eye and he snarls.

I wave pointedly just to Anita, glaring back at Mack before heading for the returns box. Things have changed a lot since I used to come here as a kid, and there's now not really much need for front desk staff when it comes to returns. They have machines where you can check out or log the return of books. The notification system sending out messages about returns is automated. In fact, you can even access the library with a key card without any staff around. There are times and days when there isn't anyone staffing this place at all, but it remains open to the public – even on Sundays! Obviously I disapprove of the kind of sad cutbacks that have made that necessary, but I also love being here when the staff aren't. It's like being at school after hours without any teachers around.

I check for the thousandth time that the note is secure, now placed firmly in the spine of Chapter Twenty-Two. My favourite chapter. It's where George and Julianna finally admit they love each other, after weeks of pretending to hate one another's guts.

I ended up showing what I'd written to Clara, Salma and Harry, who all agreed it was 'fine' – Salma's pronouncement – 'delightful!' – Harry's judgement – and 'oi, what's wrong with long-winded voice notes?' – Clara. Their only edit was to suggest adding an X at the end. We debated it. Ohhh how we debated it. It took us hours, with Salma fully pro, and Clara one hundred per cent against. Harry got the deciding vote in the end; shooting terrified glances at my sister, he mumbled that he thought it was sweet and flirty, without being over the top.

Clara isn't speaking to him and is slamming doors all over the house. All over the twenty-fourth letter of the alphabet.

I return *Too Good to Be True* in the box, feeling nervous as hell about the person who will find this note. When we were just joking about *The Very Hungry Caterpillar*, the stakes felt lower, but what happens if some randomer decides to check it out for the first time now? The stupid TV series will surely bring in some new fans. It would be so embarrassing if a confused kid found my attempt at intimacy.

What if my note writer is here right now? I scan the rows of books, and slowly circle the library. Passing the children's section, I feel warmth moving through me. I spent every Saturday afternoon as a kid sitting on the floor in that very corner. Mum and Clara would head into Sainsbury's nearby, leaving me to read in peace.

Nobody else would understand the magic this place holds for me. It's so beige and so plain and so without soul – and yet so full of life for me. The rough, worn carpet is the same one I sat on as a kid. It used to give me a rash through my school trousers but I never cared. The walls are the same greying white from my childhood, with one yellow feature wall behind the front desk. The noticeboard is exactly the same as it's always been – full of easily ignored scraps of paper. I wouldn't be surprised if the notices haven't changed in twenty years.

Sure, there have been some additions to this place in that time. The group of desks, cordoned off as a work area. The newfangled check in and out machines by the entrance. And of course, a lot of the books have changed.

But enough haven't that I still get a rush of nostalgia every time I pass the rows of pastel-coloured Marian Keyes. My pupils still dilate when I clock the Jackie Collins pile, remembering how I gasped at the sex scenes as a teen. My heart flutters with trepidation when I spot the Stephen King stacks. This place often feels more like home than my real home.

'Looking for a new favourite?' Anita's voice right behind me takes me by surprise. She grins, pushing a trolley of books. I spot the newest Lindsey Kelk novel I've been dying to read. Anita's wearing one of her signature Christmas jumpers; she wears them all year round. 'I saw you've just returned *Too Good to Be True* – again! Are you hunting for something else to fill the time until you check it out again?'

I beam. She knows my routine far too well. 'Something like that, Anita.' I can't tell her I'm actually on the lookout for a person who I'm eighty per cent sure is unlikely to be an eligible man.

I glance around the room again, suddenly feeling so stupid. Look at the people who come here. It's mostly elderly people. Mostly elderly *women*. There's no way my note writer is a man – how have I let my housemates talk me into the idea? How many *men* read romance novels by female authors? Very, very few. In fact, most men are horribly sneery about the whole genre. They think if it's something written by a woman, by its very nature it must be trivial and shallow. Because all women's interests are trivial and shallow, right? The thing is, *Too Good to Be True* might be about romance – and yes it might have a good dose of smut running through it – but it's also about something much bigger. It's about life and friendship and making the most of every moment of happiness that comes your way.

Anita regards the stacks before us. 'Did you know that the ampersand used to be a letter? Until 1835, it was the twenty-seventh letter of the alphabet, after Z.'

'That is amazing trivia.' I forget my mission for a moment, agog. 'Are you on any pub quiz teams? My step-mum Angela is always recruiting.'

She shrugs. 'Unfortunately, my breadth of knowledge is

very limited. Mostly to word and letter facts.' She perks up. 'Did you know J, U and W were only added in the sixteenth century?'

'Wow!' I say with genuine enthusiasm, and she laughs warmly.

'There are a few benefits to working in a library,' she confides, leaning in. 'One seems to be people constantly telling you fun stuff about words.' She laughs again. 'I love it!'

'Me too!' I tell her. I take a deep breath, trying to decide how brave I'm capable of being today. 'Hey, Anita,' I begin carefully. 'You know how there's only one other person who ever takes out *Too Good to Be True*?' I've tried asking her about this before, but this time it's more than just idle curiosity.

She nods distractedly, checking something on her work iPad.

'Is it . . .' I'm not sure how much to ask. 'Is it a . . . man or a woman?'

She glances up curiously. 'Huh?'

'I know you probably can't tell me a name or whatever.' I swallow nervously. I don't want to scare her or make her think I'm a stalker. 'I was just interested, I guess! Y'know! Because you know how obsessed I am with the novel and I wondered who it is that's equally obsessed!' I laugh, aiming for breezy and coming out as manic. 'I know they started taking it out about a year or two ago, but I just wondered . . .' I trail off and Anita looks alarmed.

'You know I can't tell you about other users of the library,

Jemma, it's a privacy issue.' She looks around fearfully, checking for other staff members floating around. There's only Mack nearby, still in his chair behind the counter. He's checking something on the computer, jabbing angrily at the keyboard and muttering to himself.

'Sorry,' I mumble, feeling guilty. 'I was just . . . wondering.'

'I'd better get on,' Anita says and I pulse with embarrassment. I hate making people uncomfortable. She moves off and then hesitates, turning back and adding in a low voice before hurrying off, 'Ask Mack.'

Mack? I frown as she bustles away. Why would he help me? He hates me.

But I guess it's worth asking. Maybe Anita was hinting that he doesn't give a crap about library members' privacy? I watch him for a moment, sitting behind the desk. He actually looks genuinely upset – more so than usual. Something on his computer is really getting to him. I approach with trepidation.

'Er, are you all right?' I ask carefully and he looks up, surprised and annoyed.

'No,' he says shortly and I consider walking away.

'Anything I can help with?' I offer as nicely as I can.

'Help?' His eyes snap up to mine. 'No, there's nothing you can do.' He pauses, looking irritated again. 'Is there something you actually want?' he asks impatiently. 'I'm having a really bad day and I have to get back to this, it's urgent.' He waves at the computer and I nod, resisting a strong urge to tell him to fuck off with his oh-so important business.

'Um, so, er, you know the book I always check out? The novel called *Too Good to Be True*?'

He looks shifty. 'You think I take any notice of your reading choices?'

I frown. 'Well, no, that's not what I meant. I just—'

'What about it? Have you lost it? You better not have!' He looks genuinely upset. 'We'll have to charge you if so.'

'No, no!' I protest quickly, appalled at the very idea. 'I haven't lost it, the book is fine. I've just returned it actually.'

'Right, and?' He is distracted by his screen, typing quickly, concern on his face.

'You're clearly in the middle of something,' I say, any hope draining away, as I turn to go.

'Just say it, whatever it is.' His voice is a little softer and I turn back to find his full attention on me, his black eyes penetrating and hyper-focused on mine. He adds, 'What is it you want to know?'

'There's only one other person who checks it out,' I say quickly before I can lose my nerve. '*Too Good to Be True*, I mean. Can you tell me anything about that person? Anything at all?'

His expression changes, his eyebrows drawing together. He opens his mouth to speak, then closes it. His eyes dart side to side and I can tell he's suddenly deeply uncomfortable.

Why?

After another second, Mack turns away, returning his intense gaze back to the computer. 'I'm not allowed to share details about other members,' he tells me curtly.

'Of course,' I sigh, swallowing my disappointment.

He harumphs. 'But of course *you* thought you were above the rules of the library, like you always do. Always bringing your mates in here and using this place like it's your home office or something.'

'Oh, get over yourself!' I snap, starting to walk away. 'I just wanted a fellow reader's name for god's sake! It's not the crime of the century.'

He snarls to my retreating back, 'If he wanted you to know his name, he'd tell you.'

I keep going, but I heard it, my whole body flooding with adrenaline.

He said *he* – *his*. It's a he. A him! Something surges through me as I stomp away to the desk area. So it *is* a man! A man who reads and enjoys romance novels. What if . . . no. It would be stupid to let myself think . . .

I pause by the stacks, watching across the room as a handsome guy enters through the automatic entrance doors, heading for the thriller section. Maybe he's . . .?

For a moment, I allow myself to drift off into a daydream. What if this *him* writes back? What if it *is* that man over there? I study him for a moment and decide against adding him to my fantasy. He's too good-looking, too muscled. He looks like he spends seven hours a day in the gym. He's probably only getting a book out to leave beside the weights, to help him pick up women.

No, *my* fantasy book boyfriend doesn't care about looks. He's kind and thoughtful. He laughs generously and is sweet and funny. He loves the same things I do and enjoys early nights with a book. And he would fancy the absolute *pants* off me. He'd look at me under dark eyelashes, watching me with intense longing.

I've never really been looked at with longing. Definitely not *intense* longing.

Horniness, yes, a few times. But I want what the men do in books! I want them to – I dunno – *drink* me in. I want them to desire me and hold me and kiss me from head to toe. I want to be desperately *wanted*.

Across the room, Gym Man catches me looking and eyes me critically. He frowns with apparent contempt as he takes me in head to toe and I scuttle away to my writing desk in the corner. I need to stop obsessing over this note writer. He probably won't even write back, not now I've been so full on with my latest message. I have to think about other things. Like work! I need to catch up on some transcribing ahead of another meeting with my mountaineer next week. I have to focus.

But how can I, when this feels strangely like the start of something huge?

PART TWO

Narrator:

Hi!

OK, I'm going to start by apologizing. I can't believe I began my first ever narrator job earlier by saying . . . 'gosh'.

I'm so embarrassed!

Honestly, I'm not even usually a gosh kind of person. It just came out. I don't want you to judge me or think any less of me. I want us to carry on our professional relationship as narrator and reader without even THINKING about that gosh. Please? Promise me?

Anyway, let's get down to business.

Gosh, wasn't all that exciting!

Who is the mystery man writing letters to Jemma? Who is the mystery man Clara ran away from in America? Why are there so many mystery men in their lives? Can't we have some mystery women? #ImWithHer #YknowHerBeingThatMysteryWoman. Personally, I'm super intrigued by that Anita woman at the library. Like, why does she wear Christmas jumpers all year round? Did something momentous happen in her life that made Christmas important to her in some way? Can she not face the rest of the year for some deep, dark reason? #MysteryWoman

For now, let's return to the aeroplane, where our Jemma is holding that unopened envelope in her hands, ready to finally reveal the identity of her book boyfriend.

I'm zooming in on her now, exactly where we left her earlier, one finger still in the jagged, now-opened edge of the envelope. The women either side of her – the MYSTERY WOMEN, I might add – are still watching on, completely entranced.

And, predictably, Jemma freezes.

'I can't,' she whispers, voice trembling. 'I'm too scared.' She stares down at the envelope forlornly.

'Oh for god's sake!' The older woman with red eyes swipes for it, grabbing the note from Jemma's clutches.

'What are you doing?!' Jemma cries with horror. 'You can't do that!' She turns to the woman on her other side. 'She can't do that!'

'You're right, that's really uncool,' the other woman nods, her nose ring twinkling in the low plane lights. 'Haven't you heard of boundaries, lady?' They exchange vexed looks and Red Eyes sighs, defeated.

'Fine! I'll give it back,' she says, sounding annoyed. 'But only if you promise you'll actually read it.' She frowns furiously at Jemma, who visibly gulps in the face of such pushiness.

'Er, OK, I promise.'

Nose Ring leans in. 'She's lying,' she tells Red Eyes conspiratorially. 'It's so obvious she won't read it, don't believe her.'

'You just told me I had to give it back!' the older woman cries and Nose Ring shrugs.

'I didn't really mean it, I just wanted to say the right thing in the moment. I want to know what the letter says just as much as you.'

At this, the older woman huffs, yanking at the envelope and pulling out a sheet of lined A4 with force. Jemma gasps, covering her face as the intrusive (MYSTERIOUS!) woman unfolds the note paper, scanning the words.

'Your name's Jemma, is it?' she says conversationally, and Jemma nods into her hands.

'Please don't tell me what it says,' she mumbles through her fingers. 'I can't, I don't want to know, not yet.'

The red-eyed woman tuts. 'I don't understand most of it anyway. He's going on about names and – aha!' She stops there, grinning widely at Nose Ring, who nods encouragingly.

'What?' she asks eagerly, her voice high and excited.

The older woman smiles, showing off uneven but very white teeth. 'I've just got to his name!' She quickly scans the rest of the letter. 'Otherwise it seems to be a bunch of gobbledegook. Although' – she elbows Jemma, who makes a gargled noise behind her hands – 'he does want to meet up! He wants to take you for a very bizarre-sounding dinner.'

'Dinner?' Jemma peeks out from behind her fingers and the woman nods.

'Here, read it for yourself.' She offers up the note and Jemma takes it gingerly, like it's contaminated. She gently places it into her lap and Nose Ring barges into her personal space again, reading over her shoulder.

Jemma's eyes widen as she takes in his name and it's clear she's *experiencing an array of emotions, fighting to win out just under the surface.*

At last she nods with determination, folding up the letter and placing it back into the ripped envelope. She slips it into her coat pocket, her face an inflamed red, but her expression neutral. Nose Ring looks at her closely.

'What are you going to do? Do you know what you'll say back?'

Jemma swallows, then nods firmly. 'Yes,' she says at last. 'But first I have a more important mission ahead of me when we land.'

The two women look at each other wide-eyed as Jemma stands up from her seat, awkwardly climbing over Red Eyes. 'Sorry, excuse me,' she says. 'I'm going to the loo. It's where I go to think.' She shrugs, rubbing her stomach. 'But also, y'know, plane food, ugh.'

Chapter Fifteen

CLARA

I take a deep breath, trying to steady the pounding in my chest.

'Are you going to knock or what?' Buffy's annoying voice booms over my shoulder.

'Yep,' I confirm, my voice high and scared. I raise a hand to the knocker – and then let it fall away.

'Shall I do it for you, sweetheart?' Mum offers nicely and I want to scream at her that I'm not a fucking child any more. But also, I would actually really like my mummy to do this for me because I'm scared.

'We've only got the van until five,' Harry points out un-helpfully from the back as Angela pipes up with one of her facts.

'Did you know our days are getting longer because of the moon? Every year we pull another inch and a half away from its gravitational pull, which is slowing down the earth's spin.

So each century our days get an extra 1.09 millisecond of length.' She pauses. 'Approximately.'

The others ooh and aah as I tut. It's so annoying that I've had to bring all of this lot with me. I wanted my first meeting with my soulmate to be romantic and intimate – not surrounded by idiotic family members shouting about the moon. The trouble is, I need them. I'm here ostensibly because I'm buying a chest of drawers from a stranger on Facebook. I've been discussing the ins and outs on Messenger with 'M' for two weeks, and he insisted I'd need a van, plus a few hands to help carry the furniture.

I brighten, considering this. Maybe it'll actually work out well. This lot can deal with loading up the chest of drawers while I focus on flirting with Milo.

'Just knock already!' snarls Buffy, and I do so immediately, genuinely a bit frightened.

I hear movement inside and prepare myself, tugging at my collar to allow for maximum cleavage.

The door opens and my breath catches . . .

It's not Milo.

It's a woman. 'Hi!' she says warmly, taking in the small, eclectic group. 'I'm Amanda! You're here to collect the drawers, right?'

I blink at her, fighting tears. Where's Milo?

She frowns at my silence. 'Er, Clara? No?' She laughs nervously. 'Sorry, I was expecting someone to pick up some furniture.'

Harry steps forward. 'Sorry, yes, we are here for the

drawers. That is Clara, she's just' – he side-eyes me – 'shy?' I nod dumbly, trying to swallow my disappointment. He could still be here.

I take in Amanda. She's pretty. But not the mysterious dark-haired woman I've seen Milo with in pictures. Girlfriend? Sister? Friend?

'I'm Clara,' I say at last, and she smiles at me.

'Oh great! Come in. It's through here.' She leads us down a wide hallway, glancing back. 'I'm so glad you brought help, I did mention its size, right?' She looks at me nervously and I wave her concern away, clearing my throat.

'So, it's your chest of drawers, is it?' I ask innocently, and Harry shoots me a look. 'Or is it . . . someone else's?' Maybe that wasn't the most subtle of openings but c'mon!

'Um, yeah, it's mine,' she replies, then laughs. 'Well, *yours* now, I guess.' She stops in a large open plan kitchen diner and points across the room. 'There.'

Oh fuck.

It's fucking massive. Like, the biggest chest of drawers I've ever seen in my bloody life. I didn't even know they made them this big.

I glance anxiously at Mum, Angela, Harry and Buffy, who are all staring with horror at this Range Rover of a chest of drawers. 'It's, um, lovely,' I offer. Shit, I really should've paid attention to the measurements. I exchanged a lot of messages with 'M' over the last couple of weeks, and they kept flagging centimetres, but measurements don't really mean much to me, so I didn't give it any thought.

'Great!' I swallow hard. 'Let's, um, get this in the van then.' I wave at it and the group moves with misery towards the 800-stone item.

'So . . .' I clear my throat, watching them begin the struggle. 'Amanda, um, who . . . er, where is the person I have been messaging with? Um, Milo Samuels, wasn't it? I think? Maybe that was their name?'

She frowns, looking confused, before her face clears. 'Oh! No, Milo's my brother. I was using his Facebook account to sell this. I don't have a profile anymore, and he said Marketplace was the way to go. But it was me you were messaging!'

'No!' I say too strongly. 'It was an *M*.'

She looks a little alarmed. 'Er, yeah, Mandy. Amanda – Mandy. Sorry for the confusion.'

Fuck. OK, so Milo is her brother. This could still work. I just need to befriend this woman and get in with her family. This is actually way better! What lad doesn't fancy his sister's hot friends, right?

Across the room, Buffy is snarling at everyone as they inch the furniture monstrosity at a snail's pace towards the exit.

'Oh I see!' I grin. 'Totally get it.' I pause, searching for a subject. Something we can bond over. Something that will instantly make her want to be my pal.

The group makes it to the door with the chest. They're all red-faced and sweating. 'PIVOT,' Harry shouts, looking around expectantly but no one reacts. His smile falters. 'From . . . *Friends*?' he adds but still no one laughs.

'Ha,' I offer him politely, turning back to my new best friend. 'So Amanda – um, *Mandy* – why are you getting rid of it anyway, when it's so . . . so, um, lovely?'

She sighs, looking unhappy. 'I've just broken up with someone and I'm selling all their stuff.'

There. There it is. I know we can be best friends now. Bitter women mid-break-up are my forte. I can't tell you how many best friends I've made in club loos.

'Oh babe, that sucks, you poor thing. Exes are the worst,' I say and she gives me a look. For a moment I think I've crossed a line, but then her face crumples and she bursts into tears.

'I hate him so much!' she wails, and I open my arms, folding her sobbing body into my chest.

'Shush, shush, it's OK, Mandy love,' I say kindly, rubbing her back as she weeps. 'I get it. They're the absolute worst.'

'He's ruined my liiiiiiiiiife,' she cries into my shoulder, and I nod.

'I know, I know,' I tell her as loud grunts echo from the doorway. I lead Amanda over to the sofa and sit her down as she wails about always attracting arseholes. I'm catching every other word or so between sobs, nodding and oohing at appropriate moments, wondering how quickly I can steer this in a useful direction.

From the hall, I hear Harry trying his PIVOT joke again and complaining when it falls flat. It sounds like they've nearly got it to the front door. Fair play, I thought it would take them hours. It's now or never so I take a punt.

'We should go for a drink and talk it all out,' I offer, and she stops crying momentarily, regarding me with bleary eyes.

'You–you'd be up for that?' she asks all shuddery, shoulders up around her ears. 'All my friends are sick of hearing about it and I just need to talk about it for a few hours, y'know? Just go over the relationship in detail several times to understand where it went wrong. Really examine the whole thing piece by piece. I just need to *talk*.'

'Mandy, babe' – I take her firmly by the shoulders – 'I'm totally up for that. I'm here for you. We'll get through this together. How about this weekend?' I pause, wondering how much I can push it. 'Maybe your brother can join us? Y'know, as an extra shoulder for you to cry on?'

She cocks her head, eyes red and sore-looking. 'That sounds really good, I'd like that. I guess I can ask Milo, too. He's pretty busy at the moment, though.'

'Oh yes?' I say so goddamn innocently. 'Why is that? Um, any particular reason why he's so busy?'

'Well,' Mandy swipes at her eyes, 'he's actually—'

The front door bangs and Harry appears, sweatier than I've ever seen him. His thick hair is all mussed up – it suits him actually.

'We're done,' he says breathlessly. 'All loaded up.' He pulls a face. 'It only just fitted. Buffy's going to have to sit on your lap.' He pauses. 'Did you know she wasn't even *born* until years after *Friends* finished? Isn't that horrifying?'

Oh god, she's going to make sure I suffer for all of this.

'I'd better go,' I say apologetically to my new friend. 'I'll see you this weekend, though, yeah? You've got my number. You can talk it all out for hours and hours and hours.' I grin. 'And don't forget about Milo, right? I'm sure he could do with a night off from all his ... busy stuff.'

She nods, sniffing loudly. 'Great, thanks, Clara, I can't wait. I really need this. I'll see you to the door.' We file out and I lean in for another hug on her doorstep. 'Oh!' she pulls out, looking over my shoulder. 'Here's Milo now, actually. We can ask him about this weekend.' I spin around, my chest heaving. He's here! He's here right now. It's finally happening, this is it. The moment I've been— Oh, wait.

A man in a company-branded polo neck T-shirt approaches up the driveway. He's close to fifty, sporting a goatee and holding a clipboard.

'Milo!' his sister greets him. 'How was your day? Anyone pass or fail?' She glances at me. 'Milo's a driving instructor! It's his busiest season with all the teens rocketing towards the summer holidays.' She doesn't wait for my underwhelmed reaction, turning back to the imposter. 'Guess what, Milo! We're going out this weekend for drinks with my new friend, Clara!' She gestures at me and he takes me in, stroking his pathetic attempt at a beard.

'Sounds good to me,' he says in a reedy, horrible voice, leering at my tits.

This is not my Milo Samuels. This man could not be less my Milo Samuels. Fucking Facebook! Fuck you, Zuckerberg!

'Er, great!' I say, walking backwards and making a run for the van. 'We'd better get going now with our gorge new furniture. Honestly, the drawers are so gorge! See you both . . . er, really soon!'

'See you at the weekend, Clara babe!' Amanda calls out as we drive off slowly, weighed down by our gigantic, useless chest of drawers.

Chapter Sixteen

JEMMA

'Butthole hair, ohhhhhh butttttttthole hair!'

On the other side of the bathroom door, my sister is singing a song about butthole hair. And has been doing so for the last forty minutes. While I stand out here in the hallway, internally screaming.

Also, externally screaming.

'HURRY THE FUCK UP!' I yell again, knowing she can't hear me – or is choosing not to.

Salma appears behind me in her pyjamas. 'Do you think she means hair that grows *on* your bumhole or that clump of hair that always ends up in your crack when you wash your hair?'

'Who knows,' I sigh, my frustration growing with every passing high note.

'The song is so fecking multi-layered,' Salma murmurs.

'She's multi something,' I mutter churlishly.

We've never had a bathroom clash in the morning before

because, well, Clara hasn't been out of bed before 10am since she moved in. But here we are today, at seven in the morning, and not only is she up but she hasn't actually yet been to bed. She was out drinking with some new friend called Amanda. A woman she is for some reason referring to as 'Chest of Drawers Amanda'. I heard her crashing home about an hour ago, raiding the kitchen, and then hogging our one bathroom ever since.

'What is she singing?' A rough-looking Harry emerges from his room, blinking hard. His eyes are bloodshot, his skin pallid and grey.

'Oof.' Salma winces at his appearance. 'You don't look too good, mate.'

'Yeah,' he mumbles. 'I had a few with Clara and Chest of Drawers Amanda last night.' He gestures at the bathroom door as jealousy stabs me in the chest. Harry is my friend, not hers. He swallows hard. 'I couldn't hack it, though – those two are hardcore. I came home at about one.' His breath is ragged. 'I feel awful. How is Clara *alive*, never mind singing?!'

Salma raises a finger. 'Hold on,' she says, listening. 'This is the chorus again, I like this bit.'

'Butthole hair, ohhhhhh where do you come from, but-tttttttthole hair!' Clara yells tunelessly.

'CLARA, GET OUT OF THERE!' I screech, pummelling the door with my fists, furious that it sounds like I'm adding both percussion and harmony.

'Got somewhere to be?' Salma asks, looking amused by my outburst, and I suddenly feel a bit shy.

'Er, just the library. I'm meeting Aarav.'

I wanted to get to the library early today. Yes, I've got a meeting with my mountain climber later, but I've also had a notification that *Too Good to Be True* is back in stock already. He's returned her. And I know there will be a note waiting.

It's been nearly three weeks now since I left that semi-group-sourced reply. Three weeks since I found out from librarian Mack that my pen pal is a man. And our correspondence has since picked up pace quite a lot. He replied quickly – just a couple of days later – with answers to my silly questions. His favourite season is spring, he told me. His usual supermarket is Sainsbury's – which spun him off into an enjoyable tangent about whether there is meant to be an apostrophe (there is). He admitted to being occasionally guilty of recording long-winded voice notes, but only for old friends where catch-ups are long overdue. My pen pal is apparently an early bird, like me. He has indeed been in an ambulance, and relayed a scary story about a family member recently breaking their leg. Oh! And he does indeed cry at adverts, a confession that made my heart swell with such affection for this faceless human; a man capable of real emotion and honesty.

He had his own questions and I replied swiftly, relaying my childhood pet's name (Bonnie – a surly cat), my favourite swear word (fuck, though I try to use it sparingly), my first job (a dishwasher in a local National Trust tearoom) and my favourite takeaway (fish and chips, natch). The next library notification came just a day later, and I laughed, remembering how much those dings used to annoy me. That feeling has been replaced each time with a shiver of excitement through my whole body, knowing *Too Good to Be True* would be back on the shelf – with a new note hopefully waiting for me. And there was:

> *Hello you,*
>   *I adored your latest note, you make me laugh so much. I'm with you on fish and chips, although I am also a huge fan of a regular Chinese. Y'know, just for a bit of variety. Got to keep things interesting, right? Enjoy a wide range of fruits and veg. My first job was also as a dishwasher, but it was at my uncle's restaurant, and I'd much rather have worked for the National Trust. I secretly love a wander around a pretty old conservation site. I understand that makes me ancient but I can't help that – I am, after all, in my thirties now. And I am DELIGHTED to hear about Bonnie! She sounds like exactly the kind of cat I like – temperamental and mean. Big cat fan over here.*
>   *E x*

Ohhh, that E. How I've obsessed over that E. I spent an entire evening doodling E name options, wondering if my note writer could be an Edward, Eric, Evan, Earl, Edwin, Eli, Ethan, Eddie or Elijah.

We've exchanged several more since – with me now signing a J at the end – with the notes getting progressively less silly and more intimate as time's gone on. E told me how his mum got him into reading; how they would read together when he was young; and how his favourite literary characters are all women.

'*Becky Sharp, Katniss Everdeen, Jo March, Matilda Wormwood, and number one is definitely Elizabeth Bennet,*' he wrote in one note, adding, '*I also have a special place in my heart for all of George Eliot's female characters, but that's my mum's fault.*'

I replied with my own top choices: Julianna from *Too Good to Be True*. Mary Poppins, Miss Marple, Elinor Dashwood, and I agreed with him wholeheartedly about Elizabeth Bennet. I've always admired the way she metaphorically bitch-slapped Mr Darcy into being a better human. It felt like very relatable female energy we still don't see enough of.

We've talked about growing up as awkward book kids and struggling to make friends. He admitted to feeling lonely even now, as an adult, though he's close to his family. He didn't say what he does for a job, but did reveal it can be isolating. We teased one another a lot more about our preference for cats (him) vs dogs (me) and discussed a mutual revulsion for smelly cheeses. It's been intriguing, entertaining and – thanks to our running in-joke about *The Very Hungry Caterpillar* – still quite silly a lot of the time.

It also feels absurdly – stupidly! – romantic. I'm walking around with a fizz in my stomach all the time. I'm checking my phone constantly, checking my watch, checking my bag. For nothing. It's like my body is waiting expectantly for something to happen. I think about E a lot, and regularly open WhatsApp to send him a funny picture or meme, before remembering I don't know his name, never mind his phone number.

After each note, I feel buzzy with excitement. He seems so smart and knowledgeable. And *fun*. The whole thing feels dangerous and naughty. Like I'm passing notes at school. But it also feels risky in a whole other way. Because what if I'm starting to feel something for this guy and he turns out to be a monster? What if he's married? What if he's got seventeen kids? He mentioned being in his thirties, but that could easily be a lie. What if he's eighty years old? What if he's an eighty-year-old married monster with seventeen kids and *also* a fan of Andrew Tate?! Or – most likely – what if we meet and he is completely underwhelmed by the IRL me? What if I am a disappointment?

Clara keeps telling me to stop worrying. She says it's no different from exchanging messages with someone on Tinder. When I pointed out that you get photos, a name and an age on dating apps, she pfftt'd me and said everyone lies with those things anyway. Then she showed me the heavily filtered photos she uses on her Tinder account, and I honestly couldn't have picked my twin sister out of a line-up.

So I've decided to try my best to go with the flow and enjoy the mad feelings that are creepy-crawling around my stomach. I'm embracing lying awake at night, imagining what he might look like; who he might be. I'm delighting in staring at anyone and everyone who comes into the library, wondering if it could be him. I'm even enjoying the terror I feel at the prospect of falling in love with this man. Falling in love for the first time. Because, sure, I've dated before, but I've never had a serious boyfriend. I've never been in love.

Unless, of course, you count the men I've fallen for in books. There have been a lot of them. And that's part of the problem, I think. I've always thought fictional men were better – or safer at least. Sure, they're not real, but at least they can't hurt you.

Clara emerges from the bathroom at last, steam billowing around her as she blinks at the huddled group of housemates in the hallway.

'What are you all doing out here?' she asks with surprise, pulling her towel tighter around her. 'Are we doing a fire drill?'

'Just enjoying your lovely singing,' Salma snorts as Harry mumbles something about being sick. He pushes past the lot of us, slamming the bathroom door in my face.

'NOOOOOOOO, HARRYYYYYYYYY!' I scream helplessly at the locked door as Clara saunters off to her room without a care in the world.

Chapter Seventeen

CLARA

I'm still singing as I dry myself off, admiring my now-hairless bum in the mirror.

I'm feeling really positive for the first time in months!

A big night out was just what I needed and I actually – surprisingly – had a great time with Amanda, who thankfully left her brother at home in the end. We drank like we were teens, snogged some random men, and my Apple watch says I closed all my exercise rings – thank you, dancing all night in a club!

And most importantly, I've come out of it feeling clear-headed and ready for my future. I have a plan. Goals.

Out in the hallway, I can hear Jemma shouting at Harry to get out of the bathroom. He's clearly hogging it – he can be quite selfish at times.

What time did he leave us last night? I know it was super early. That guy cannot hold his booze at all. Although, to be fair, Amanda and I were pouring shots down his throat for a lot of the evening. I think she quite fancies him actually, which is so weird! But maybe it could be good. He could distract her from her awful ex-boyfriend. Amanda is a laugh, but she needs to learn how to push down some of her feelings. They're all so surface level! I tried to ply her with drinks to get her to shut up about the ex, which worked for a while. Until she got a few more drinks in her, and then she was mostly just crying about him again.

But still, it'll be nice to have a friend outside of the house. Outside of Jemma's universe. I think it'll make things easier between me and my sister. Sometimes I think she's pissed off that I get on so well with Salma and Harry. Like, for example, she's mostly been refusing to watch *Book Boyfriend* with us, but still acts like she's being left out when we all gather together for it on a Sunday night. It makes no sense! It's the fifth episode tonight and I hope she'll at least sit with us for it, even if she pointedly reads throughout the whole thing. Maybe I could even invite Amanda over for our weekly *Book Boyfriend* viewing sessions.

Out in the hallway, Jemma is shouting again. But this morning's histrionics aside, she seems happier lately. Nothing to do with me of course, and all to do with that incessant flow of lurve letters she and this 'E' guy are exchanging. She showed me a couple of them and, I dunno, they're kinda ... boring? Like, I don't get this guy *at all*. Who wants to chat about a caterpillar that much?! And then he seemed to be listing famous women I've never heard of that he fancied?! Who the hell is Becky Sharp?! Was she on the latest series of *Love Is Blind*? But whatever, Jem seems super smiley and more relaxed, which is making me happy.

I really hope it doesn't end up being a disaster.

'Hey, Clara, are you in there?' Harry's croaky voice floats through the door and I call for him to come on in. He does so feebly, shuffling across the threshold with effort.

'I've been sick,' he declares with something like pride.

'Well done!' I tell him warmly, and he responds with a weak smile. 'Wasn't last night fun?' I continue happily. 'Amanda's great, isn't she?'

He nods and I gesture for him to take a seat.

'Do you have my wallet?' he asks, collapsing onto my duvet. 'I can't find it.'

'Er, yeah,' I admit sheepishly. 'You gave it to us as I put you in your Uber. You told us to have some drinks on you.'

I mean, technically he said *one* drink, but he probably doesn't remember either way. And he totally owed us after I tracked his car all the way home to make sure he was back safe. I fish around on the floor for last night's handbag and hand over the black wallet.

'Thank goodness,' he mutters, then looks up at me, puffy eyes narrowed. 'Honestly, though, Clara, how the hell are you so perky this morning?'

I shrug. 'A-plus liver, I guess!' I consider this for a second. 'Or I might still be drunk, who knows. Either way, I feel *amazing*.' I take a seat on the bed beside him and lean closer, catching a whiff of booze wafting from his pores. Dude really needs a shower. He'll have to wait, though, as

148

I used up all the hot water. 'Haz, I've got a plan,' I tell him conspiratorially.

He raises a withering eyebrow. 'Another one?'

I frown. 'Shut up.' I pick up my hairbrush and start combing through my wet hair. 'The plan is two-fold,' I begin. 'Firstly, I'm going to become a mega successful and well-known upcycler, starting with the chest of drawers downstairs. I've messaged a few more people on eBay about some tatty old furniture. And,' I grin happily, 'after my epically bad, failed job interview at my step-mum Angela's office, I think she's been feeling bad, because she and Mum have offered to buy me some paint and supplies. I gave them a long list and I can get creating as soon as it all turns up!'

Harry nods, then turns green with the effort. 'Sounds great,' he says. 'I'm looking forward to that huge return on my investment.'

'Of course!' I say, trying and failing to gather my still-tangled hair up into a bun. 'Do you think Jemma would care if I sold that mirror I transformed for her? She doesn't even seem to like it, so I don't think she'd be bothered, do you?'

'Hum, I don't think … I don't know …' he hedges, quickly changing the subject. 'Anyway, what's part two of the plan?'

'Oh!' I grin. 'Well, that one you already know.' I take a dramatic pause. 'Find and marry Milo Samuels.'

He rolls his eyes. 'This again. I thought you'd got it out of your system with that wild goose chase to collect Amanda's drawers.'

I make a face. '*Amanda's drawers* sounds really . . .'

He nods. ' . . . grim. Yeah, I heard it, sorry. But you know what I mean.' He sits up a little straighter, regarding me. 'What is this obsession with Milo really about?'

I glare hotly. 'What do you mean? Milo is perfect for me! He's The One!'

He cocks his head. 'But, like, you don't know anything about him. Not really.' I don't answer and he continues, 'And what about you? What do *you* actually want in a partner? Do you even know? Do you know what makes you happy?'

His questions make my heart race and I stand up, pulling my hair back out of its bun. 'Of course I do,' I tell him, picking the hairbrush back up again and yanking it through tangles, wincing as I pull too much out.

There is silence in the room before Harry eventually speaks again. 'I'll help you find him then. If it's really what you want.'

'It is, thanks!' I say insistently, the subject firmly closed. Outside my room I catch Jemma yelling about the hot water.

Whoops.

Chapter Eighteen

JEMMA

My house is filling up with furniture. Every day the front door goes with yet another delivery of some crappy old desk or coffee table. Yesterday, we got an industrial-sized pallet filled with furniture paint and dust sheets, courtesy of Mum and Angela, apparently. Instead of saving up for their wedding, they're wasting savings supporting Clara's latest dream project. Honestly, I don't know how my sister talks people into colluding with her on her mad schemes. I'm pretty sure Harry has 'invested' too – he gets all sheepish when I moan about Clara's mess.

Either way, with our house increasingly becoming a storage facility, I'm spending more time at the library than ever. It's the only place I can get any peace and quiet.

I take a seat in my usual spot now, at a desk in the corner. I'm meeting Aarav again today and I have to focus. I'm behind on some of the research and my boss is getting antsy about our deadline. I pull out my Dictaphone, ready for some transcribing, and try not to think about E. There have been a couple more notes this week. We're mostly long-hand sharing our favourite passages in the book at the moment.

On page 129, second para down, George tells his friend Melanie that he's too damaged to ever fall in love again. That speech always gives me a vulnerability hangover.

Page 400, last line, when Julianna admits she's been lying about her step-father. I cry buckets every time.

I only dropped my last message off yesterday. The computer system probably won't have had time to register it, never mind update me on whether it's been checked out and in again yet. There's no way E will have collected it and replied yet. I won't even look. I have self-control, I don't need to look. It'll only be disappointing if – when – the book isn't back yet – or worse, is empty.

But what if it is? What if twenty-four hours later, there's another note? That would mean E had been here. Like, here-*here*! He could've literally been sitting in this very spot, reading my note and thinking about me. Maybe I should change up my routine, start coming to the library in the evenings so I can bump into him.

But do I really want to know who this person is? Am I ready to meet E?

Leaving my stuff where it is, I scurry over to the general fiction section, eyeing the usual spot. *Too Good to Be True* is there, but it will only be my note in there. It will only be me teasing E about caterpillars and asking if he ever watched *Murder She Wrote.*

My heart beating fast, I open the plastic cover, flicking quickly through the pages, holding my breath – and there it is. A new envelope. This time, it's tucked into Chapter Nine, where Julianna's friends try to talk her out of meeting up with George.

I hesitate. I have my notebook and envelope set in my bag. I could write back right now. This could be a new stage to our communications. We don't even need to check the book out anymore to pass notes. I hastily return to my desk, opening his note, sighing over his now-familiar handwriting, and scanning the words.

Hi J,

I feel a little embarrassed by how quickly I'm replying to you. We seem to be picking up pace but I can't help it. I look forward to getting your notes more than anything else. Which probably makes me sound like a bit of a boring loser – which I'm not denying actually. I'm hoping boring losers are your bag. Boring losers who are universally despised by tigers, despite best efforts with buns and biscuits.

Anyway, since we seem to be on a daily exchange of notes now . . . how is your day going?! I've got a busy one ahead, despite striving for boring loser at all times. I so often feel that all I want from life is to be at home with a book and a blanket. There should also be a big pile of food at my side, and, ideally, one really good friend on the other. A friend I'll mostly ignore as I eat and read. On the other hand, when things are quiet in my life, all I keep thinking is, 'Why haven't I been invited out lately?! What is everyone else up to that I'm not being included on?!' It's sad really.

And, oh look, we've come back around to me being a boring loser. Oh dear.

Please don't be too put off.

E x

PS Pages 59–63 where they keep missing each other at the funfair genuinely makes me roar with laughter every time.

PPS I watched a bit of Murder She Wrote, *but I was actually more of a* Columbo *guy.*

I laugh, delighted with his words, craving more. Impatient for the next instalment. I read the note again, drinking it in and dissecting the meaning. I turn to page 59 to re-read the scene he referenced through his eyes, and laugh out loud.

This letter seems somehow more intimate than before. Yes, we're still joking around and teasing, but there is more here. There is more realness. My heart beats faster as I re-read those words:

I look forward to getting your notes more than anything else.

I feel the same. I feel a lot for him – for E – actually.

And maybe he feels the same way? Is there a chance he has feelings for me, too? And wouldn't that be insane? After only speaking through these notes? It makes no sense. I chide myself for reading too much into it and pick up a pen.

What to reply? I could ask something more personal. We've talked about our lives, our values, what we like and don't like, but no real personal details. No identifying information. What does he do? How big is the family he's so close to? Who is his best friend? Does he have an annoying sister who brings home enormous pieces of furniture?

But personal questions could lead to identifying details. To a name.

I don't know if I'm ready for all that yet.

Hi E,

Put me off! How could you put me off when you're so clearly describing how I feel most of the time? I think it comes down to this: I want to be invited and included in literally everything everyone is doing. But I don't want to then have to go do any of it. Does that make sense? Because I don't think I'm trying to make sense. Most of life makes no sense to me. This, here – writing notes to a stranger – makes no sense.

But I look forward to it as much as you, I promise.

It's so strange to think of you being here, in this library at different times from me. Or maybe even the same time? Maybe we've passed each other in the stacks and not known. Does that blow your mind like it does mine? It feels sometimes like I'm talking to you from a parallel universe.

Oh god, this isn't The Lake House, *is it?*

And since you mentioned it again (you should really go through this with a therapist), I think – if we ever meet – we should go to a tiger sanctuary to resolve your issues. We'll take a variety of food, à la The Very Hungry Caterpillar, *and see what takes their fancy. I'll help you win them over with one shortbread, two chocolate Hobnobs, three digestives, etc. I'm not going to write it all out again, my hand is killing me only three biscuits in. I don't think I've written this much by hand since I was a kid. But I like it. Looking forward to hearing from you again soon, even if Jessica Fletcher kicks Columbo's butt every time.*

J x

PS Read page 312, where they have the most cathartic argument I've ever read. I want us to fall out just so we can have a conversation like that.

I'm interrupted by a deep, familiar voice as I sign the final full stop.

'Aarav!' I stutter, standing up and flushing beetroot. He stands tall and broad before me, always taking me by surprise with his bigness. I'd forgotten why I was here. Work. Our interview. 'Um, take a seat.' I gesture wildly across from me, shoving my note to one side. He grins, flashing that too-charming smile. 'Can I get you a drink?' I ask, nodding at the water cooler in the corner, and he shakes his head, looking amused by my flustered greeting.

'I'm fine, thanks, Jemma. Are you OK?' His handsome face creases lightly with concern.

'Yes! Er, yes, totally fine!' I exclaim, my voice too high. Aarav makes me nervous at the best of times, never mind when I'm caught writing secret love letters to anonymous strangers.

'Can I get *you* a water?' he offers, smiling nicely again, and I cough lightly.

'Actually, yes, that would be fantastic, if you don't mind?' He grins at me and heads towards the cooler. I examine his bum – it hardly moves as he walks away. Those mountains must be such a good workout. Maybe I should take up climbing? I watch him filling the cup with water, enjoying his dark hair and stubble. He has this wide back and you can see the muscles move under his shirt. It's so—

Ugh! Stop it! God, what is wrong with me? These notes seem to have awoken some beast inside. I've been celibate for so long, I think I've forgotten what it's like to feel things. To feel like *this*. I forgot how mad it makes you feel.

But I have to admit, I quite like it.

I try to order my thoughts. No more on *Too Good to Be True* or my note writer for now. I can obsess again later. Now I have to work. Aarav is my focus.

Chapter Nineteen

CLARA

So this is the magical, mystical, legendary library.

I'm not sure I get the big deal. It's kinda ... blah? Grey carpet, beige walls. And just loooooads of books. Rows and rows of books. I mean, I do understand that it's a library, but ugh, get a better hobby.

I take in the flaking paintwork and smile. I could *totally* upcycle this place.

I feel a little pulse of guilt at that thought. Not just because this is Jemma's sanctuary, but also because my upcycling plans have sort of stalled. Stalled in the hallway, in fact. The chest of drawers we wrestled home a few weeks ago – Amanda's ex's chest of drawers – ended up being too big to fit up the stairs. So right now, it's sitting in the entrance hallway, just inside the front door, blocking everyone's way. Not that there's space for it in any of the bedrooms anyway, because that's where I've started storing my other WIP furniture. And the cupboards are all paint cans, floor to ceiling.

Salma and Harry say they don't mind but it's pretty obvious the whole thing is driving Jemma mad.

It had started to feel like we were getting somewhere, with us living together, but this has definitely been a step back for our sisterly relationship.

I approach a weird-looking woman behind the counter. She's wearing a Christmas jumper with a unicorn on the front that's dancing in the snow. Are unicorns festive? Seems like they get to shine the rest of the year, and it should be the reindeers' turn to get some attention. Who even invented the unicorn anyway? I've never understood the obsession. It's literally a horse with a massive, vicious-looking spike driven into its head. It's basically a glittery zombie horse. Except if it was a zombie horse, a spike through its head would kill it.

Anyway.

'Hiya!' I greet the strangely dressed woman, and she starts, like no one ever comes in here. 'Er, I'm looking for my sister – do you know her? Jemma Poyntz?'

She stares at me, wide-eyed. '*You're* Jemma's sister?' she asks and I wonder what she means by that. Am I so repulsive that she can't imagine how we could be blood related?

No, it can't be that. I'm hot.

The woman beams. 'I'm Anita! I've known your sister since she was quite young.'

A good-looking but moody bloke joins us, glaring at me. 'Your sister takes the piss a bit actually,' he growls. He's wearing a black T-shirt that is too tight for him and I clock some serious muscles under there. He continues crossly, 'She's always in here taking up space that others might need. This library is for everyone, y'know?'

I didn't know. I kinda thought libraries were a closed club, exclusively for members. Like a really, really lame Soho House.

'Oh shush, Mack!' Anita scolds, turning back to me. 'Sorry about him! He's a grumpy sod.'

He glowers at her and I suddenly get Zayn Malik vibes. Like, back when Zayn was leaving One Direction and was peak sulky all the time. 'I'm not grumpy,' he growls grumpily. 'I'm just . . . ugh. You don't get it.' He throws up his hands and stomps off.

Anita giggles. 'Not grumpy at all!' she trills. 'Maybe just a little cantankerous? Crabby? Petulant? Mopey? Testy? Downcast? Definitely a bit melancholy and huffy!'

'Riiiiiight,' I nod, like I know what any of those words mean. What is she, a thesaurus? Actually, I guess that's part of the job description in this place.

I clear my throat. 'Anyway, is Jemma about? I think she's working in here today?'

'Most days!' she pronounces, gesturing across the room to an area of desks, where Jemma sits with her laptop.

'So anyway, are you a member of—' Anita is saying, but she's lost me, because oh my GOD, is that . . .? Jemma is sitting across from a gorgeous, rugged man I don't know and they're chatting animatedly. It *must* be the guy leaving Jemma notes in her book! E! They've clearly outed themselves to one another at last! And now they're finally having a real life chat! If so, Jesus, well done, Jemma! He's a stunner; all huge, rugged shoulders and thick, long hair. I would hit that in a second.

I march over, throwing a 'cheers' over my shoulder at the desk lady with the Christmas zombie horse jumper.

'Jemma!' I call out as I approach her and the bloke. I'm beaming as I turn to him. 'Well, hellooo! And what's *your* name?'

'Er, Clara, we're in the middle of—' Jemma begins.

'Oh I bet you are, Jim-Jems!' I interrupt her gleefully, offering my hand to the hot stranger. He looks a bit flummoxed but takes it.

'I'm Aarav,' he says in a low voice. 'And you are?'

'I'm Clara,' I frown. 'I thought your name started with an E?' He looks even more perplexed so I turn to Jemma. 'This is a *very* exciting development in the note passing! I can't believe you've finally met in real life! It was about time – it was all starting to get a bit weird, to be honest. All that caterpillar crap!' I don't stop for breath as I place a hand on his arm. 'God, I'm *so* glad you turned out to be a hottie. I was imagining all kinds of maniacs with two heads. But you're *gorgeous*.'

'Er, no—' Jemma begins and I wave her off.

'Don't try and deny it, you minx! I'm so glad you two finally met! It's all been a bit silly, hasn't it? Exchanging secret notes like you're teenagers at school! And now you can go on a real date!' I am crowing with delight, until Jemma abruptly stands up.

'Clara!' she says sharply and her voice is ice. 'This is Aarav, whose book I'm working on. This is a professional meeting.'

'Oh!' My eyes flit between them, as the panic sets in. That's right, Aarav is the name of her mountaineer bloke. The one whose memoir she's helping write. Well, god, how was I supposed to remember that?!

Ah shit, I'm in trouble. Aarav looks faintly amused, but I've never seen Jemma angrier.

She swallows. 'Sorry about this, Aarav, just give me a second, won't you?'

She grabs me roughly by the arm and frogmarches me across the room to the audiobook aisle. I'm distracted for a moment, wondering who still owns a CD player.

'God, sorry, Jim–Jems,' I begin. 'I was out for lunch with Mum and Angela and we passed this way and the atmosphere was, like, totally odd. I think they were having an argument, and Angela seemed like she didn't even want me there, so I thought I'd come in here and hang out with you. And then I saw you with that hot guy and I thought—'

'STOP CALLING ME JIM-JEMS!' she yells, and several people glance over. For a second of stunned silence, she looks mortified, then the fury returns. 'I *hate* that nickname, Clara.'

She does? I thought it was cute. I've always called her Jim-Jems.

'You just made me look like a fucking *idiot* there!' she hisses, waving back towards Aarav. 'This is my *work*! He has to take me seriously, and you come in, ranting about bloody notes and dates, all the while feeling him up!' She pants, and I stare down at the ground, horrified. 'You're just so *thoughtless*!' she half-shouts. 'And so selfish! No wonder Angela was in a mood with you – why are you crashing their lunch dates anyway? You're probably ruining their engagement, getting in the way! You should be *working*, but oh no, an office job just isn't good enough for you, is it? The world owes you something big and exciting, doesn't it? Everyone and everything has to revolve around *you*.' Her eyes are wild. 'God, Clara, you just take over *everything*! You've taken over my house and my life. And my fucking hallway with that stupid chest of drawers. And now you're here! In *my* library! Trying to sabotage my work as well!' She is red with anger, and I am red with emotion. She takes a deep breath. 'It's just not working, us living together.' After a second she adds a resentful, 'I'm sorry, you'll have to move out.'

I swallow hard, trying not to cry. I knew this was coming. I knew she'd want to get rid of me as soon as possible. I'm a fuck-up, and she's right about all of it. We've tried to make this work. *I've* tried. I know she doesn't think I have tried, but I really have. We're just incompatible; we don't work.

My heart is pounding and I try to steady my breathing. I'm a mess and I've infected Jemma's orderly life with it. Maybe it'll be better when we can get a bit of distance from one another.

After a long, cold minute, I shrug carelessly. 'OK, that's fine. I can stay at Mum's. I'll have the sofa for a bit. I don't think it'll be for long. It's pretty clearly not going to work out between her and Angela. I think it's just been a bit of companionship for them both anyway. I'll have my old bed-room back in no time.'

We are interrupted by a mad woman appearing at the end of the aisle. I think for a moment we will be told off for being too loud, but I realize in that second that it's Mum. Oh fuck, did she hear what I said about her and Angela? The last thing I need is to fall out with her as well. She's standing there breathing hard in her big coat; the outside cold hangs around her. I fight an urge to launch into her arms and weep, begging for a cuddle, like I did when I was little.

'Girls!' she beams, throwing her arms out for us. 'You'll never guess – we've set a date! Angela and I are getting mar-ried in a month!' She gathers us into a tight embrace, pulling Jemma and me closer than either of us would like to be in this moment. I regard my sister over Mum's shoulder and her eyes are full of the same kind of fear as mine.

They're really getting married. In a *month*. Which means I have nowhere else to go.

We're stuck with each other.

Chapter Twenty

JEMMA

God, I hate myself. Look at how disgusting I am. How *hideous*.

I turn to examine myself in the long mirror of the changing room.

What a monster I am! I hate me. I hate my sister, I hate my whole family. I hate my house and my friends, I hate my bedroom and that chest of bloody drawers in my hallway. What a miserable existence. I really thought by this point in my life, I'd have a husband, kids, my own house, a retirement pot. I've got none of it. All I have is a thousand plastic bags in another plastic bag, and a favourite ring on the hob.

I hate, hate, hate—

Oh wait, what's the date? Yep, OK, never mind, it's just my period on its way.

I take a deep breath, trying to see myself through non-hormonal eyes. I try to be kind to myself. Maybe this dress isn't— no, it's still hideous.

'Are you ready, sweetheart?' Through the curtain, Mum's voice floats over. She sounds excited. I paste on a rictus smile and pull back the curtain.

'Here we go!' I say with enthusiasm.

'Oh Jemma!' Mum says quietly, tears filling her eyes. 'You look *stunning*.'

I internally groan. Seriously? This bridesmaid dress might be the rankest thing I've ever seen. It's a mouldy, off-green-yellow with unflattering ruffles around my middle. Clara and Buffy emerge from the two neighbouring changing rooms, wearing matching dresses but very different expressions.

'Oh my god, I look *hot*!' Clara does a twirl, giggling as Buffy scowls. For a second I make eye contact with my twin and her face falls. We both look away.

We still haven't spoken since our fight in the library a week ago. Barely a word since I told her I didn't want her living with me anymore. Obviously she hasn't moved out, but she is being much more considerate around the house. In fact, I've hardly seen her. She's taken on some agency waitressing work, so she's been out most evenings doing events. Which also means she's been sleeping in most mornings. The fucking chest of drawers is still in the hallway, along with the rest of the untouched upcycling crap littered all over the place.

'You all look so beautiful,' Mum gushes, blinking hard.

Beside her, Angela nods enthusiastically. 'Those dresses really suit you. *In 2013 there was a wedding in Sri Lanka with a hundred and twenty-six bridesmaids*.' She smiles at my mum. 'I'm glad we only have three.'

'This colour is disgusting,' Buffy comments dryly. 'I'm dressed like a swamp.'

Clara twirls again. 'Actually, this colour is all the rage on TikTok right now. It's everywhere!'

Buffy gives her a withering stare. 'You are clearly looking at old people's TikTok. Don't act like you know what's cool.'

'Fair enough,' Clara replies cheerfully.

'Hellooo?' Mum calls to the boutique owner. 'Everyone loves the dresses, they all look beautiful. We'll take them!'

We get changed and regroup by the till as Mum pays. Clara bounces excitedly. 'I can't believe you're getting married in just a few weeks!'

Angela and Mum swap a loving look. They're heading to the local registry office with a handful of friends, a few of the Great-Aunts, and – obvs – the three of us, for a small ceremony. Neither of them wanted a long engagement or anything big, and somehow the whole thing seems way more romantic than some huge, expensive wedding ever could.

Beside me Clara coughs lightly. Awkwardly.

'So, look,' she begins carefully, 'I'm going to this thing tonight. It's a food festival in East London. Milo Samuels – the actor from *Book Boyfriend* – is meant to be making a guest appearance!' She sounds excited as she turns to face me. It's our first proper eye contact in days. 'I'm totally going to meet him and we'll finally get to fall in love. Do you want to come?'

I shake my head in disbelief. 'Do you seriously think he's just going to see you and that'll be it? He'll magically fall for you?'

She frowns. 'Yes! I know he's The One, I *feel* it. I've watched and read so many interviews with him now, I feel like I really know him. I know the way he moves and I know his facial expressions. I know how he laughs and the way his eyes crinkle. I know his favourite kind of biscuit and that he loves cycling. I know he can be super moody and hates having his photograph taken. Even his scowling is perfect! He's my soulmate and I'm falling for him. I know he'll feel the same once we actually meet.'

'That is . . . ridiculous!' I can't help it. She's being insane! 'It's a parasocial relationship, Clara, totally one-sided. It's just a fantasy of this person you don't even know. It's nonsense!'

Clara looks upset. 'Hold on,' she says, her voice wobbly. 'Are you saying my TV boyfriend is somehow lesser than your note-writing boyfriend? You don't know anything about him either, do you? At least I know what my guy looks like. I know what his name is, his age and how he speaks. You don't even have that much!'

My mouth opens to snap back that at least my weird relationship is *reciprocated*!

And then I realize she's right. Mostly.

I'm being a pompous ass. What harm is she doing, fancying some random bloke off the TV? We've all been there, haven't we? Mine have mostly been fictional men in novels, but I've fallen for plenty of romantic heroes before. They quite often seemed somehow more real – more flesh and blood – than the men I encountered out here in the world.

I sigh, feeling bad. I don't want things to be like this between us. 'You're right,' I say and she regards me suspiciously. 'I'm sorry,' I add, then as nicely as I can, 'I like your jumper.'

Her eyes flick up to my face. 'It's not yours,' she says quickly.

I roll my eyes. 'I know! I'm just trying to . . . I don't know.' I sigh again, then frown as I catch sight of her sleeve, covered in white, powdery stuff. 'Jesus, Clara,' I hiss, pulling her aside and slightly away from the family. 'Is that what I think it is?' I shake my head. 'I thought you were working all these evenings, but you've been partying, haven't you? Is it this new friend, Amanda?'

She shakes her head, looking confused. 'What are you on about now?'

I grab her sleeve. 'What is this? Drugs? Ricin?'

She barks a laugh. 'Fucking hell, Ji— er, Jemma, it's *toothpaste*. Dried toothpaste.' She picks at it and flicks it in my direction. I catch a whiff of mint.

'Oh.' I feel silly.

'And *ricin*?' She snorts again. 'That's a poison for fuck's sake.'

'I heard about it on *Breaking Bad*.' She frowns.

'Drugs? At my mum's bridesmaid fitting? That's what you think of me?' she says quietly, shaking her head. 'You always jump to the maddest conclusions.'

I shrug. 'I don't think it was that mad. It's not like I know anything about your life before you moved back here, is it? You've been so secretive about what happened in the US, what am I supposed to think?'

She looks like she's been slapped. 'Er, excuse me, but you never showed any interest,' she retorts. 'Remind me, how many times did you visit in the five years I was over there? You barely ever even messaged.'

'I—' Before I can reply Mum joins us.

'You all right, girls?' She smiles encouragingly and we both nod, silently. She continues, looking between us fondly, 'I'm going to be such a mess at the wedding! It'll be so emotional having both my girls with me by my side on the happiest day of my life.' She wells up again as she takes each of our hands. 'Having you back here in England, Clara, and having you girls living together again has brought me so much joy, I can't tell you. I've wanted this for so long, to have you close by and close to each other. I know you didn't always get along as kids, but I'm so glad it's working out, with you two getting to know each other as grown-ups. I'm sure living together isn't always easy, but it's obviously working out so well. It's all I want for you – for my baby girls – to be happy.'

Beside me Clara swallows hard, pasting on a smile. After a second, I follow suit. Looks like we'll be faking this a little bit longer. At least until after Mum and Angela's wedding.

Chapter Twenty-One

CLARA

'If we stay near the entrance, surely he'll have to pass by this way.' I glance at Harry for approval and he shrugs.

'I guess so? Unless there's a secret celebrity entrance the special guests use.'

I narrow my eyes at him. 'Negative thinking like that doesn't help me, Haz.' I feel snarly today and my irritatingly nice housemate with his irritatingly sweet face isn't improving things. I'm not entirely sure why I invited him along to this event today.

A group of giggling women shoulder barge past me, all wearing the same sort of oversized trench coats. I sigh. That's why I invited Harry. Because Amanda wasn't free and I have no other friends in the UK – or anywhere else if we're being really horribly honest with ourselves – and you can't turn up to a thing like this alone. Not when you're hoping to casually bump into a famous TV star.

I glance up and around, taking in the huge space, housing

every kind of food and drink you can imagine. It's a massive annual festival and last week they started shouting about their special guest for the day: Milo Samuels, my future boyfriend slash husband. He's here along with a couple of his co-stars from *Book Boyfriend*, promoting the series, and I'm fully sure we're going to fall head over heels for one another. Never mind what Jemma says.

I swipe at a passing tray of shots, grabbing a freebie for me and Harry. We both down the oddly creamy blue liquid, wincing in sync at the taste.

'Well, at the very least, we're right by the free samples area,' I point out, feeling the warmth of alcohol passing through me. Whatever that blue stuff was, it was strong.

Harry checks his watch. 'When is Jemma meant to get here?' he asks, and his eyes narrow when he catches my expression. 'Clara!' he continues accusingly. 'You said Jemma was coming along!'

I give him a shrug. 'I invited her but she hates me.'

Harry sighs. 'She doesn't hate you. And you can't lie to me like that! I really thought Jemma was coming – I was excited for a house outing with you guys.'

I smile wryly. 'You like her!' I accuse, with a finger in his face. He blushes deeply.

'No, no,' he stutters, looking away with embarrassment. 'We're friends, housemates, that's it.'

'Sure, sure,' I grin, knowing better and amused by his bashfulness. 'I really think she likes you, too, though, for the record.'

'You do?' Is that hope I can hear in his voice?

'Definitely.' I grab for another tray of drinks. These are clear. 'Drink up,' I instruct Harry, who obliges.

'Hey, Clara, I really think you two need to try to make things better between you,' he says after a moment, and I notice his voice is a little slurred.

How many free samples have we had so far? A lot. We should maybe find some food. And Milo Samuels, of course. The reason we're here. Where is he? Maybe I should ask someone before I have too many more of these free shots.

Harry's still speaking. 'I just mean, you're sisters – twins! – you should be best friends, shouldn't you? Isn't that how it works? All the twins on TV are best friends.'

I side-eye him. 'Don't ever mention Elizabeth and Jessica Wakefield in front of Jemma, OK? She hates that everyone used to say she was the Elizabeth.'

Harry considers this. 'Better than being the Danny DeVito to your Arnold Schwarzenegger.' I snort at the imagery from *Twins*.

'That is defo true,' I admit, speaking too loudly. 'But, as Jemma would point out, we're not even proper twins! Proper twins are one egg that splits into two. Originally one person! We're fraternal twins, which means we were two eggs. We're just sisters that ended up in the womb at the same time. It's inconvenient, is what it is.'

'Still!' he cries. He's also speaking too loudly. 'You should be super close!'

'Says who?' I turn to him, almost spilling another drink

I don't remember getting. This one is a graded sunset of oranges and pink. 'Why do people act like it's some travesty that me and my twin aren't close? It's an accident of birth that we're even connected. Just because we spent nine months huddled together twenty-eight years ago doesn't mean we share anything! In fact, I'm pretty sure we spent a lot of those months mostly kicking one another in the head' I lean into Harry's face and my brain takes a second to catch up. 'See this wonky nose, Haz?' I jab at it, mostly missing. 'I'm pretty sure she elbowed me when I was growing it, and caused this shittiness. She is the reason I have a bad sense of smell.' He gives me an amused look and I sigh. 'Whatever. Anyway, she's the one who hates me. Believe me, I've tried to make things better.' The look comes again. 'I *have*!' My voice is exasperated. 'She thinks I'm an attention-seeking party girl, with no depth.' I pause. 'And so what if I am? What's so wrong with that? Who am I hurting? I don't have any kids or pets. Why can't I spend my twenties – and maybe my thirties – enjoying some shallow fun?'

He shrugs. 'I don't think she hates you, I think you just need to—'

I cut him off. 'Don't tell me what I *just* need to.' I'm a bit annoyed now. I've barely known this guy for a couple of months and he thinks he knows me? He thinks he knows what me and Jemma have been through? Like he can *solve* us just like that? 'You don't have a clue, so just stop, OK? Leave it alone, because you are the last person I would ever take advice from. Yes, you invested in my upcycling business when I needed help, and I appreciate that, but that doesn't mean you get a say in my life. You don't know anything, you're just a boy.'

There is a second of awkward silence and then Harry speaks.

'I'm getting kind of sick of the way you talk to me sometimes.' His tone is serious, more serious than I've heard from him, ever. I whip around to take in the new Harry. He is slightly fuzzy round the edges but the geeky pushover-ness I'm semi-fond of has been replaced by a glowering bad boy that I suddenly ... *want*.

For a moment we glare at one another. And then – out of nowhere – we're lunging at each other, kissing without warning. It is hazy and messy, our hands pawing at one another in the murky gloom of this corner. Somewhere in the recesses of my brain, I am shocked by how good it feels to have Harry's tongue in my mouth. He is a *great* kisser. But it only takes one more second to realize this is the stupidest thing I've ever done. I know Harry likes Jemma and I know she likes him. I'm being the selfish, thoughtless person she always says I am. Taking something I have no right to take.

But the booze.

How much can I blame on the booze?

'Stop, stop!' I pull away at last, panting. 'I'm sorry, that was so dumb. I'm really, really drunk and this was a massive mistake.'

He nods, breathless, eyes blurry and unfocused. 'We're both just pissed,' he murmurs. 'Let's pretend it didn't happen.'

'Right.' I nod, looking away, feeling the creeping horror in my stomach.

I mean, *god*, I've made some foolish drunken snoggy mistakes in the past – *believe me* – but this is next level. I've really fucked up.

'Um, I'm going to find Milo.' I stand up, slightly woozy on my feet. 'You, er, stay here and I'll ...' I don't bother finishing the sentence, staggering away in search of the man I actually want to snog.

Oh god, I kissed Harry. *Harry.* What was I thinking?

It was the worst, stupidest thing to do for so many reasons. Firstly, Harry has become my friend in these last few weeks. He's my nerdy, posh boy pal and I genuinely like him. But I don't fancy him. He's like a walking pair of cargo shorts and he clearly sees me as a vacuous directionless moron with good hair.

He's never said that thing about my hair, but it's undeniably good and he has eyes.

Secondly, I really, really think him and Jemma would make a great couple and that they would make each other happy. That dumb snog neither of us even wanted may have totally ruined that. And third – C – it has been pointed out to me that I have a bad habit of looking for validation from men when I am feeling insecure. I have been trying not to do this since I got back from America. I cannot fall back into bad habits. I can't let what happened over there happen here. Just when things are looking up.

Oh, and D! I have also betrayed my beloved Milo Samuels.

He's out there waiting for me; waiting for our epic, sweeping, telenovela romance to start, and I'm over here pre-cheating on him with a pal I don't even fancy.

Ugghhhh! Right, that's it. From here on out, I'm going to be strong. Strong like Jemma. I'm going to be level-headed and sensible. I'm not going to get off with inappropriate people, or look for comfort in the wrong places. I'm going to be Zen and nun-like, and definitely, definitely not keep fucking everything up.

I lean on an outside bar for a moment, helping myself to another free shot and giving the barman a thumbs up. Then I open Tinder on my phone and swipe yes to the next fifty profiles, watching the matches ding ding ding in my notifications.

Maybe just a couple more fuck-ups.

I send a message to the first vaguely hot guy to DM me, suggesting we meet up for a drink tonight, and then I turn to go. I need to get out of this place and away from Harry. I need to get off with someone who isn't Harry so I can pretend it never happened. I need to drink so much I don't even remember doing it, so then I can't be a bad person. I need to find something to distract me from what a shitty person I really am.

And that's when I crash right into my future husband, Milo Samuels.

Chapter Twenty-Two

JEMMA

'I think it's time to ask him who he is.' Salma is examining an old school photo of me from when I was fifteen. I'm all glasses and big fringe.

I glance up at her. 'Oh god, really? Do I have to? Can't I just live in this fantasy world a bit longer?'

We're at Mum's house, sorting through boxes of my old stuff. Apparently Mum has kept literally everything I ever owned, made or bought since the minute I was born. But now she needs us to clear it out, to make room for the new members of our family. So far, it's mostly been about throwing away old craft projects we made in Design Tech. Oh, and quite a lot of tea towels we all drew on as kids in class that our teachers then sold to parents at an inflated price.

We've been here hours, but haven't made a whole lot of progress. I've been too busy chewing Salma's ear off about my book note writer, reading her each and every letter and re-examining each word, every bit of punctuation and the specific meaning of his sloping Ss.

Salma looks at me sternly. 'No, Jem. No more fantasy world. I love you, but you're too into your make-believe. It's about time for some reality.'

'Whyyyy?' I whine, and she sighs.

'I don't want you to get hurt!' she says, slumping down onto a desk chair. This is now my mum's office, when she works from home. 'And the longer this goes on – the more notes you exchange with this stranger – the more likely it is that you're going to get hurt.' She pauses, looking worried. 'What if you fall for him, for real, and then he turns out to be a hideous fifty-something six-time divorcee with headless wives in his cellar? Or, y'know, something even darker like an estate agent? You need to meet this person for real.' She waves her hands. 'Or at least get a name!'

'I have the letter E!' I protest, and she tuts.

'Well, there you go! What if it turns out his name is Ebenezer or something? You could never love an Ebenezer, could you? You need answers!'

I sigh heavily. 'I guess you're right.'

We're quiet for a minute, putting items into binbags and examining old photos. I heave another pile of clothes into the donations box. This stuff hasn't fitted me since puberty hit. 'Ugh, where's Harry anyway?' I moan. 'Shouldn't he be forced to help us go through all this crap as well?'

'Hmm?' Salma avoids my eyes and I glare at her.

'Salma?' I say in a warning tone. 'Where's Harry?'

She relents. 'He went off somewhere with Clara. She wanted help stalking that actor guy. You wanted help with this, so I decided we'd divvy you up.'

I frown, suddenly angry. Harry's *mine*, not Clara's.

'You're jealous,' Salma observes neutrally, and I stand up straighter.

'Of course I'm not!' I protest crossly, even though I know I am.

'Clara's our friend, too,' Salma says gently. 'I'm sorry if that bothers you.' She makes a vaguely impatient noise. 'To be honest, Harry and I feel a bit caught in the middle. Do you think it's fair to us that you can't be in the same room at the moment? That we have to split up to spend time with you both?' She sighs heavily. 'It's annoying, but also genuinely sad. I thought you guys seemed to be getting on better recently?'

I shrug. 'We were. We're not anymore.' My chest feels tight. 'But that's fine, good to know where Harry's loyalties lie.'

Salma huffs. 'Harry didn't even know! He thought he was going with you and Clara. I had to trick him into going so Clara wasn't left on her own.'

'Harry's a grown man, he can do what he likes,' I say hotly. 'I couldn't care less.'

She eyes me warily. 'Have you . . .' Salma trails off and I look up, expectantly.

'What?'

'Have you considered . . .' She stops again and I frown at

her until she continues. 'Have you thought about whether this note writer might be someone you know?'

'Huh?' This takes me by surprise and she puts down the pile of pictures she was rifling through. 'I mean, it could be. It could be an ex or an acquaintance or . . . a friend.'

This hits me square in the chest. Someone I *know*. It couldn't be, I'd be able to tell. Surely.

'I don't really have any proper exes,' I say warily. 'Not really.'

'You've dated plenty of guys,' Salma insists. 'Maybe not long term, but there are definitely some broken hearts out there. A few who might be looking for another chance with the Jem-Meister.'

'Jem-Meister?' I enquire, adding, 'I suppose it's better than Jim-Jems.'

She laughs. 'Are you still in touch with any of them? Any of your exes?'

I consider this. 'I still wouldn't exactly call them exes, but there are three guys I've shagged more than once.' I glance at Salma for confirmation.

'Only three? Are you still not counting that bus driver you were going out with for a while, who moved to Scotland to become a full-time Loch Ness monster hunter?'

'Shush, you!' I cry. 'We agreed never to mention him again.'

She hides a smile behind her hand. 'Fine. I'm pretty sure it wouldn't be him writing the notes anyway. He had a very specific fetish for slimy, aquatic monsters with long necks.' She pauses. 'And you only have one of the things on that list.'

I take a second. 'The long neck, right?' She looks away and I swat her.

'Anyway, I still follow all three on Instagram,' I admit, pulling out my phone and opening the app. I type in a name and show Salma.

'Oh god, I remember him!' she giggles. 'But look, he's got a wife and three babies now – ew. Thank you, next.' We visit number two. 'Nope,' she pronounces. 'He's living in Australia, so unless he's *really* committed to this project, the flight times back and forth to return the library book wouldn't be realistic.' She looks at me expectantly and I type in the third and final name. Someone I was with for seven months when I was twenty-three.

'He's hot!' Salma says, removing the phone from my grip and flicking through shot after shot of him living his hashtag best life.

'I have noticed he still watches my Instagram Stories . . .' I say bashfully. 'And he usually likes my posts.'

'That is very damning,' Salma says, nodding as she clicks on his Stories. Her face suddenly changes and she shrieks, throwing the phone at me. 'Oh god oh god oh god, I just accidentally video-called him!'

I scream, too. 'Oh god, why? *HOW*, SALMA?'

'I was watching his Stories and went to hit the exit button, but the call button is also in the top right corner!' she wails, looking traumatized.

From the phone, a voice pipes up, 'Er, hello? Jemma?'

'*You didn't hang up?*' I hiss at Salma and she pales, shaking her head.

I creep towards the phone, face down on the desk. Without picking up the phone, I yell in a dodgy Scottish accent, 'WRONG NUMBER!' and quickly hit the hang up button. Salma and I stare at each other for a long second, and then burst out laughing.

'Were you channelling the Loch Ness monster man?' she asks through silly tears.

'Shit, maybe?!' I say, giggling. 'Oh god, hopefully it's not him that's been writing the book notes, because he'll think I'm an absolute idiot now.'

'I mean, bloody hell!' Salma says, panting. 'Why is there even a call function on Instagram? WHO IS CALLING EACH OTHER OVER INSTAGRAM?'

We collapse laughing again.

'How are you girls getting on?' Mum's singsong question carries through from the hallway, her face appearing in the doorway.

'Fine thanks, Mrs Poyntz,' Salma intones politely, trying to pull herself together.

'Would you like a drink?' Mum offers in a child-friendly voice, like I'm having a playdate. 'A Coca-Cola or something?'

'No thanks, Mrs Poyntz,' Salma answers, like a well-trained puppy.

'OK, well, make yourself at home, won't you!' She disappears and Salma shakes her head.

'That phrase is my worst pet peeve,' she says, rolling her eyes. 'If I was *actually* making myself at home I'd go get in your mum's bed and dribble Mars ice cream across her pillows.'

I'm not really listening; I'm staring at the door after my mum. 'It's nice she's found happiness with someone again, isn't it? Angela seems like a good person, doesn't she?'

'She's mad as a box of frogs,' Salma comments, 'but so is your mum. And they're adorable together.'

'Hmm,' I ponder. 'I think a lot of finding the right person is locating the right person or frog to share your mad frog box with.' I turn to Salma decisively. 'OK, you're right.' She regards me quizzically. 'I need a name, I need to face reality. I'm going to write E a note telling him my name and asking him who he is. I want to know the truth.' I sigh deeply. 'Even if the truth ruins everything.'

Chapter Twenty-Three

CLARA

I'm sitting on the ground, staring up at Milo Samuels for a full ten seconds as he gabbles an apology.

'I'm so sorry, *so* sorry, are you OK? I didn't see you,' he's saying in that oh-so familiar London accent. His brow creases with concern as he takes me in on the ground. 'Are you hurt, love? Can I help you?'

Love. He called me love!

He offers a hand and I stare at that now, too. It looks soft, but a little weathered. Just enough to prove he's a man. There's a sprinkling of hair on his knuckles, but that's fine. It just makes him all the more *real*.

'Should I call someone? Or an ambulance?' He's starting to sound really worried and I hastily grab for his waiting hand and stand up. It's warm and rough and I don't let go.

'I think I'm OK!' I squeak and he laughs a little.

'That's good, because I imagine the ambulance probably

185

wouldn't turn up until at least tomorrow afternoon and I'm afraid I do actually have an appointment later today.'

Damn, I should've let him call me an ambulance.

'Good one!' I laugh hard. Too hard.

This is *actually* Milo Samuels. Right here, in front of me. The man I've been falling for on the TV every week for seven gorgeous, long episodes. He's here, in the flesh. And I'm still holding onto his hand.

'Er . . .' He nods at the hand now, smiling that winning TV star smile again. I allow him to extricate himself from my grip. My hand feels all cold now and I fight an urge to take it back, entwining my fingers with his.

'Sorry again for knocking you over!' he says. 'You sure you're OK?' He's looking at me with concern.

I can't remember any of the things I was going to say. I've spent entire evenings planning for this very moment. I'd got it all planned out; the perfect opener. I was going to be witty and clever and fun. I was going to make him fall for me instantly.

'I've got anaemia!' The words fall out of my stupid mouth before I can stop them.

He frowns. 'You've got . . . anaemia?'

I nod a lot. 'Yeah, I think I bumped my head when I fell over and now I've got anaemia. I can't remember my name or anything about my life.'

I mean, it's *kinda* true. I can't remember much right now, looking at his beautiful face.

His expression clears a little. 'Oh, do you mean, er, amnesia?'

It's my turn to frown. 'What did I say?'

'Anaemia,' he explains. 'I thought you'd been trying to donate blood and they wouldn't let you.'

'I can't remember if I've tried to donate blood,' I tell him. 'Maybe I've got anaemia *and* amnesia.' I pause. 'Wait, what's Ambrosia then?'

The concerned look is back. 'Right, goodness, well, we'd better find you a place to sit down.' He looks around anxiously and spots a group of sofas set back from the hubbub. He encircles a supportive arm around me and we cross the room together.

A young woman approaches, looking worriedly between us. 'Milo? They're waiting for us in the office.' I start as I realize it's *her*. It's the brunette I've seen in pictures; the one constantly with Milo. Is she . . .? Is this his girlfriend?

Fuck, she's gorgeous. Though a bit stern-looking in all black.

Milo nods reassuringly at her. 'Just give me a few minutes, Katies, this woman can't remember her own name.'

'Ambrosia,' I tell her sombrely and she glares, then shuffles off, speaking into a phone.

'Sorry about Katies, she's my publicist,' he tells me as we sit down carefully.

Publicist!! OMG!! I internally high-five myself. No girlfriend, just a stunning and terrifying female co-worker. I knew he was single, I *knew*— Wait . . . I frown. 'Um, are you saying Katies, like, *Katiezzz*?'

He laughs. 'I am actually.'

I shake my head, starting to believe in my own fake head injury. 'Wait, is her name Kate Teas? Or Kay Tease? Or like multiple Katies?'

He laughs again, his whole head thrown back. I'm making Milo Samuels laugh. It's happening, we're falling in love. It's really happening.

'It's Katies, like multiple Katies,' he confirms, his lovely eyes looking deeply into mine.

'What do you do with your possessive apostrophes?' I ask anxiously, suddenly feeling a lot like Jemma.

He shrugs. 'Same as the Jameses, I guess?'

'Blimey.' I breathe out heavily. 'That must be hell. Her parents must have hated her. I bet she has to explain it constantly. I bet she has to have a conversation every day about it.'

'Almost certainly,' he nods. 'I've just started having them on her behalf.'

I laugh at this. God, he really is perfect! Jemma was totally wrong about this all being a fantasy. Milo Samuels is actually here in the flesh and he's genuinely perfect. He's funny, he's sexy, he's cool, he's ... going to be mine.

'So,' he begins. 'Is there someone I can call? Do you need to go to the hospital? Because I could get Katies to call a car ...'

'Er—' Crap. I really don't want to go sit in A&E for the next ten hours, even if Milo were to come with me. It's not exactly the most romantic of places and I really don't want it to be our first date. Plus, I'm thinking there's no chance Katiezzz would allow him to take off with me.

I glance over at her now, still on the phone but glowering across the room at us.

'I don't think I need to go to the hospital,' I tell him confidently. 'I think I just need to sit here for a few minutes.' I try to look noble. 'I just need to *recover* from my *fall*, but if you need to go, I guess I can do that here, all on my own.' I duck my head sadly, trying to subtly watch for his reaction. He looks outraged.

'I'm not leaving you while you can't remember anything!' he says loudly. He glances worriedly over at Katiezzz. 'It's just that I'm technically here for work. I'm contracted to, er, do a thing and they're expecting me.'

I want to shout at him that I know. Of course I know!! What mad people out there haven't been watching *Book Boyfriend*? Who *isn't* in love with this man?

I squint at him. 'You know, you *do* look familiar,' I say very convincingly. 'Do we already know each other?' I grab his hand dramatically. 'Are you my boyfriend?!' He laughs and bites his lip, carefully removing his hand from mine.

'Um, no. We're not – *I'm* not – your, er, boyfriend.' He pauses, and I can tell he's debating whether to tell me who he is.

'Clara?' Milo and I both jump at the sound, glancing up at a perplexed-looking Harry standing over the pair of us. He looks much more sober than the last time I saw him. When he was smeared with my lipstick.

I cringe at the thought.

'Um, do I know you?' I ask, feeling a surge of fury at

Harry for interrupting this moment. Things were going so well! Milo was totally about to ask me out.

'Huh?' Harry's brow creases and I can see he's still not *that* sober.

Beside me, Milo bounces up and out of the seat. 'Do you know this woman?' he sounds excited. 'She's lost her memory and doesn't know who she is.'

Harry glances between us, his gaze landing on Milo. 'Holy fuck, you're— you're *him*!' He looks at me, eyes enormous, and I make a face that I hope conveys *shut the fuck up right now*.

'Oh, er, yes.' Milo looks bashful and Harry steps closer, excitedly offering a hand.

'Mate, you're brilliant!' he's saying too loudly. 'We all love you in my house. We've been watching *Book Boyfriend* religiously every week! I never want it to end!' His eyes are adoring and it's clear Harry is *almost* as in love with Milo as me. He swallows, getting too close. 'Honestly, you're the coolest! That outfit you wore in the fourth episode was . . . I found the shirt on Asos but it wasn't the right colour and the sleeves were all wrong and I—' He swallows again, trying to regain some composure. 'Anyway, yeah mate, we love *Book Boyfriend*. My friend Jemma is the biggest fan of the novel version, *Too Good to Be True*, and Cla—' He starts to wave in my direction and then sees my murderous expression, immediately shutting up.

'That's really kind,' Milo says, still looking embarrassed. He glances down at me and then back at Harry. 'So this is your . . . friend? Did you say her name is Clara?'

'Er, yeah,' Harry confirms, amusement plain on his face.

'Yeah, this is Clara.' He turns to me, saying in a slow, baby voice, 'Have you had a little accident, Clara? Did you bump your head?'

I glare at him. 'Yes, actually. I'm anaemic and you should probably take me to the hospital immediately.'

I catch Milo muttering, 'Amnesia,' to Harry, who nods, understanding. 'Well,' Milo says after a moment, 'I'd better get back to my ... thing then. If you're being looked after?' He stops and smiles kindly at me. 'It was really nice to meet you, Clara. I hope you feel better soon.'

Fuck, he's going to leave. This is my last chance. I need something – *anything*. 'Um, Milo, you know, I was thinking, my friend Salma is a radio host – she works for the BBC – and she would *love* to interview you. It's just local but she has a huge following. Loads of *Book Boyfriend* fans!'

'Oh?' He smiles with genuine warmth. 'I thought you couldn't remember anything?'

'Hmm?' Shit. 'Oh right, well, things seem to be coming back a little bit actually.' I squint into the distance and nod slowly. His dark eyes crinkle with amusement.

'That's very good news. And well, that's a lovely offer. Here ...' He fishes around in his jeans pocket and my eyes linger on the bulge down there. I let out a strangled noise and he looks up sharply. 'Are you sure you're OK?' I nod and he hands me a business card. 'Here are my agent's details, she can talk to your friend Salma about an interview.' He glances across the room. 'Don't worry, I won't make you deal with Katies!'

I jump up and pull him in for a hug. He tenses with surprise and then gently pats me on the back. I know this is a signal to release, but I don't. I just want to hold him a bit longer.

'Come on, Clara,' Harry says impatiently. 'We'd better get you to the hospital for your anaemia.'

Milo extracts himself and waves a goodbye, hurrying across to his impatient PR. Harry and I watch him go, both entranced by his TV star dazzle. And his hot butt.

After a moment, Harry turns to me. 'Did he say Katies?' He frowns as I nod. 'Like plural Katie?'

Chapter Twenty-Four

JEMMA

Salma is in my bedroom doorway. 'I'm on a wild, no-holds-barred, bloodthirsty, vengeance-y quest for chocolate. Got any?'

I turn away from the envelope in my hands. 'Period?'

She gasps dramatically. 'How dare you be so misogynistic! Am I not allowed to crave chocolate at other times of the month?'

I shrug. 'I guess you are.'

'Fuck you, yes, it's my period.'

I laugh. 'I don't have any, sorry. If I keep any chocolate in here, I will eat the chocolate, and then we begin the cycle again of having no chocolate in here.'

'That's fair. Want to come to the shop with me then?'

I stand up, the envelope burning in my hands. 'I'll come with you part of the way. I'm actually heading to the library to drop this off in *Too Good to Be True*.'

'Ooh!' Salma comes further into the room, staring at the

envelope. 'So this is the one where you finally ask him who he is?'

I nod, feeling shivery. This could be the last note I write to him. It could all be over after this.

Or it could all be starting after this.

We leave the house together, almost colliding with Clara on our way out. Things are a bit better than they were between us, what with all the enforced hangouts at Mum and Angela's, talking wedding plans. But I'm still livid with jealousy when Salma grabs her and says warmly, 'Babe, we still on for tonight? You better dress *up*!'

Clara nods excitedly. 'Tonight is the night, I just know it.' She looks at me and then away quickly.

'What are you guys doing?' I ask, trying to sound laid-back. Of course it comes off needy as hell. I've never been good at hiding my feelings.

'There's a big PR launch thingy at a hotel in West London later. I got invited through work and Clara's coming as my plus one.'

My sister bounces on the spot a little. 'And *guess* who's on the guestlist? Milo Samuels! I cannot wait to see him. I've got the perfect *in* now. I can just go right up to him and be like, "Oh hello, Milo, remember when we met at that food and drink festival thingy last week and you gave me amnesia? I remember my name now!" And he'll be like, "Oh wow! Let's get married and have babies!"'

I shake my head. How is she not mortified about that first meeting? When she and Harry told us about it, Salma and I laughed our arses off, and assumed she would be too embarrassed to continue pursuing this silly crush.

'It's going to be great,' Salma agrees, as I stare down at my feet. My twin sister and my best friend hanging out without me. At some swanky party. Without me. It's outrageous, I can't believe they'd do this to me.

I glance up and Salma is staring at me hard. 'Oi!' she says sternly. 'Stop looking so left out, you *never* want to come to these things. In fact, you've told me over and over to stop asking you. You said there was never going to be a chance in hell you would ever come along to one of my showbiz work parties. You said they sounded exhausting.'

Clara's mouth falls open. 'You know *celebrities* go to these things, don't you?' She sounds agog and I roll my eyes.

'I couldn't give a crap about celebrities,' I tell her and she looks aghast.

'Better than made-up people on pieces of paper,' she mutters, and I shoot her a warning glare.

'Anyway,' Salma moves us on smoothly, 'it'll be fun, and I'm sure I could get another name on the list if you did decide having fun wasn't beneath you.'

Clara perks up. 'Yes, please come, Jemma, it'll be really great!' She pauses, then says innocently, 'You should invite Harry as your, like, date or whatever.'

I take a deep breath. Her subtlety could win awards. But maybe it would be nice to have Harry come along. To have the whole house together for a night out. I can't even remember the last time I went out for drinks. I decided a long time ago that drinking wasn't really very *me*, plus it's terrible for my rosacea. But I find I'm actually excited by the prospect.

'OK.' I smile at them both. 'If you're sure you can get extra names on the guestlist, Salma?' She beams a yes and I pull out my phone. 'I'll message Harry and insist he cancel any other plans he might have, so he can join us.'

'Perfect!' Clara almost shouts. 'It's a date.'

I give her a disapproving look. 'It's not a date.'

'Where are you guys going now, anyway?' Clara fiddles with the buttons on her shirt.

Salma points to herself: 'Chocolate run,' then at me: 'She's going to deliver her latest note.' She leans forward excitedly. 'She's finally asking the book guy who he is!'

Clara gasps. 'No way! This is so exciting!' She looks at me hopefully. 'Can I come?' I swallow hard and she continues quickly. 'I know I made a mess of things the last time I turned up at the library. But I promise to behave myself this time! I'll even, like, shush other people! I can distract that hot, moody bloke behind the desk for you. And it's not like your sexy hills guy will be there this time anyway, right?'

'Mountains,' I say sharply. 'He climbs mountains. It wouldn't be much of a memoir if he'd lost two toes climbing Primrose Hill.'

'Still be impressive to me,' mutters Salma. 'I hate all inclines.'

I sigh at Clara. 'OK, fine, you can come. But no gossiping about this note situation. You have to be aware that it could be literally anyone in there! When you're shouting about it, he could be listening! It could be the stranger in the corner, y'know? Just promise you'll be cool.'

'I still think it's someone you know,' Salma says softly behind us, as we all head for the door.

The library is quiet and I internally groan at the sight of Mack behind the counter. No Anita today, just that sour-faced dick.

Beside me, Clara is muttering about upcycling the walls and I resist an eye roll. We're still climbing around the chest of drawers to get in and out of the house every day and I can't get to the washing machine thanks to a random bedside table. I thought she'd finally moved on from that hobby.

'Hi, Mack,' I greet the dickhead warily and he grunts a response. I lean into Clara, telling her in a low voice, 'You keep him distracted while I go slip the note in the book.'

She nods and I watch her transform into Flirty Clara, leaning forward onto the counter and lowering her voice. 'It's Mack, isn't it? I'm Clara and I think the walls here are genuinely hideous.'

He snorts and I stop short, shocked by the sound. I've honestly never heard him laugh. Literally never. OK, sure, it was *barely* a laugh but it's close enough to one to feel like some kind of revelation. I stare at him; his whole face is different when he is amused. He's always been objectively handsome but now he looks ... *nice*?!

'I have to agree with you actually,' he says to Clara. 'I've been complaining about the paint job ever since I started a couple of years ago.'

It's more like eighteen months but whatever.

Clara rewards him with a tinkly laugh and a hair flick as he continues. 'This whole place could do with a refresh – a bit of livening up – but nobody listens to me. Nobody likes change and no one has time to do anything. There are always excuses!' He shrugs and then – unbelievably – lets out an actual, real, honest-to-god *laugh*.

Clara glances discreetly at me and I slow-blink back at her. Maybe I'll have to bring her to the library with me more often if she brings out a nicer side of Mack.

I move away, my heart pounding as I head for the general fiction aisle. I stand for a moment, looking at *Too Good to Be True*'s spine.

Am I really going to do this? Do I really want to know who this person it? Isn't it better to keep things as they are – full of fun and excitement and possibility? Reality is so often just dull, disappointing and underwhelming.

I take a deep breath and – before I can lose my nerve – slip the note into the book. The last page. And hopefully the first.

Hurrying back, I find Mack and Clara in surprisingly deep conversation. I've barely had more than two syllables from him the whole time he's been working here. But of course, everyone finds Clara utterly charming. Typical.

As we leave, I grab her by the arm. 'I cannot believe that's the same Mack who's growled at me every day for the last year and a half,' I breathe. 'What were you even talking about?' I'm genuinely curious.

'I was telling him how much better he could make the

library!' Clara says with enthusiasm. 'And I don't mean just the shit walls and ugly carpets. I mean, like, you could have author events and book clubs and writer workshops – fun things! He said they don't do anything like that at the moment, can you believe that? It's so short-sighted!'

I give her a sideways look. 'That's actually really smart,' I tell her slowly. 'And what did he say?'

'He said it was something they'd get around to eventually. And then he got distracted by something on his phone.' She grimaces, glancing over at me. 'It seemed like bad news. Do you think he's OK? Maybe there's a reason he's so angry all the time.'

I raise my eyebrows at her. 'Maybe the reason is that he's a dickhead?'

'Maybe,' she snorts agreeably as we wait at a crossing. 'He's fit, though.'

I roll my eyes hard as the green man begins to flash. Clara would think the green man was fit if he glared at her long enough.

Actually, the red man is probably more her type. Walking red flags are her bag.

Chapter Twenty-Five

CLARA

I climb into my glittery jumpsuit, immediately getting tangled up. I'm too excited for complicated clothing – I can't focus or keep still enough.

This afternoon was great, hanging out with Jemma – dropping off her latest note – and tonight's going to be even better. I yank at the jumpsuit's sleeve, which I realize now is a leg, sending a spray of glitter across the floor.

If I can somehow get into this outfit-contraption, me, Jemma, Salma and Harry are heading to a fancy hotel rooftop bar that I've always wanted to check out. It's going to be wall-to-wall glitz and glamour, not to mention there's a guestlist that features my beloved Milo Samuels.

I'm also hoping tonight will put paid to any remaining weirdness with Harry. I think he's been avoiding me since our stupid drunken snog almost a week ago. We are on the same page of pretending it never happened, but we have undeniably been a little bit awkward. There has been a lot of uncomfortable staring at the ceiling and nervous laughter when we're in the same room.

And oh god it was *mega* awkward last night, when we all watched episode eight of *Book Boyfriend*. The whole thirty minutes was basically just one long sex scene – which would usually be totally Mia cup of tea, but when you're watching your future husband having fake sex with someone else, while sitting next to a lad you snogged the week before, while *also* sitting near your sister who clearly fancies that snoggee . . . well, it was a tiny bit bananapants confusing. I couldn't concentrate on the action at all, I was so worried about pulling the right facial expression and putting out the right body language. I didn't want to seem like the show was bothering me, like I'm some kind of prude, but I also *really* didn't want to look like I was aroused in any way.

Thank god for Salma being there. Halfway through, she started telling us about the last person she'd had sex with, and how she snorted a snot bubble in their face halfway through having an orgasm. That definitely helped break the ice. And then Jemma said her anecdote was like something out of a Jane Austen novel, and so I said, 'Or its TV adaptation star-ring Keira Knightley,' and we all started laughing. It got a lot less weird and tense after that.

'Are you ready?' Jemma pokes her head around the door. She looks lovely, in a yellow dress and cardi combo I rec-ognize from some Great-Aunt wedding years ago. Before I went to America. How does she always make old stuff look good? All the clothes I own feel dated and ugly halfway through their first wear.

'Just about.' I grimace, throwing another sleeve in the wrong direction. Jemma laughs and comes in, adjusting my outfit around me and doing up the zip. 'Thanks,' I tell her with genuine relief. I was starting to panic there.

She looks stern. 'Just don't be dragging me into the loos every twenty minutes to help you go for a wee.'

I hold up a hand in the Brownie promise. 'I swear I won't. I haven't drunk any liquids all day in preparation for wearing this jumpsuit.' I pause. 'To be honest, the main reason I'm wearing it is because it feels like a safe segue from the onesie I've worn for two months straight.'

She laughs and I study her. She looks *relaxed*. I'm surprised – I thought she'd be all over the place after leaving that note for her pen pal earlier. I mean, I'd be freaking out if I were her. Three solid months of chatting to this mystery guy and it's all about to be revealed. I mean, maybe. I suppose he could tell her his name is none of her business or ghost her.

To be honest, I thought Jemma would also be having a meltdown about going to an actual party for basically the first time in her life. She *never* goes out to stuff like this. But, taking her energy in now, she seems . . . excited? Maybe my predictable, rut-loving bookworm sister is finally learning to embrace the unknown – embrace an *adventure* . . .

An hour later, and I'm slightly missing my predictable, rut-loving bookworm, adventure-averse sister. She's had three shots, two large gins and is now draining her second large glass of wine. She grins sloppily at me now, her face red, her teeth and lips already purple.

'This is a *fantastic* party,' she stage-whispers at me, turning several heads with her loudness. 'Where's your man from the TV? Is he here?' She looks around, almost losing her balance, and I reach out to steady her. I feel a bit jealous. I want to be that drunk.

'Not yet, I don't think,' I say, shaking my head and scanning the room's occupants. But then – ohhhh – there he is! He's here. He enters the room from a side entrance that barely looks like a door. His publicist and definitely-not-his-girlfriend Katiezzz is right behind him again, annoyingly. But this time he's *here* to schmooze. It's a party. She can't drag him away – or glare me away – not this time. We're going to chat, and by the end of this night, that man is going to ask me out on a date.

'He's there!' I whack Jemma on the arm and she stands up straighter. Or at least, she attempts to.

Harry and Salma are suddenly upon us, fresh from the bar, drinks in hand.

'Have you seen?' Salma squeals. 'He's over there!'

Harry shrugs. 'I saw him,' he says, playing it cool. 'I've met him before, we're, like, mates or whatever.'

I laugh and our eyes meet briefly, before we both look away. 'I saw! He looks so hot,' I say excitedly. 'So, do I just *go over*? Just casual-like? And say *hi, it's me, Clara, the Ambrosiac?*'

'Amnesiac.' Even a drunk Jemma still has to be a right Jemma.

'Ignore her,' Salma instructs. 'Go do your thang!' She grabs my arm. 'Wait, do you want us to come with you?'

I blink anxiously. Do I? Yes, maybe I do. I want it to look like I have friends, and am not just some creep, alone at this party following him around. I nod decisively. 'Yes, please come with me.'

The four of us walk in a huddle – Jemma lolling in and out of our group – across the room, until we're a mere few feet away from Milo. He's waiting at the bar to order a drink and I wonder for a moment whether he will sense I'm here.

Milo, I whisper silently at him. *Turn around, Milo Samuels, and see me standing here.*

He doesn't, but I try not to see it as a sign.

'Go buy us a round,' Harry urges, downing his gin, 'and then, y'know, *happen* to notice him there, too.' He pauses to finish the drink he just bought. 'But also do genuinely buy us a round. I want another G&T, please.'

'Me too,' Jemma says. She leans into Harry and he circles an arm around her, keeping her steady. I feel a catch in my chest. It's not jealousy or anything – it's excitement actually. I'm excited that she's touching him, that they're touching each other. Tonight is the night they're going to realize their feelings for each other and embark on something special, ending in a wedding where I will be maid of honour. The note writer be damned!

I make my way to the bar, as casually as I can. Propping myself up, I clear my throat forcefully. 'Er, HARRY?' I say loudly over my shoulder. 'WHAT DID YOU SAY YOU

WANTED AGAIN, MATE?' He looks at me perplexed, but it works. When I turn back to the bar, Milo is looking at me.

'Oh!' he says. 'It's you! Um . . .' He snaps his fingers, trying to remember, and I squint at him exaggeratedly, as if I haven't got a clue. His face clears. 'Clara! Right? Is it Clara? Or Clare? We met at the food festival thingy last week?' I shrug, shaking my head like I don't know and he laughs awkwardly. 'Remember? You fell over – I pretty much knocked you over.' He grimaces. 'Sorry again about that. And then you couldn't remember anything.' He pauses, examining my face. 'Are you all better now? No more . . . anaemia?'

I nod suddenly. 'Oh right! Yes, of course! I vaguely recall the incident now. I am indeed Clara. Clara Poyntz. And you're . . . Miles, was it? Miller? Milly? Milepost? Military? Mileage—'

Behind me, I hear Jemma mutter, 'Those aren't names,' but Milo looks amused.

'Milo Samuels,' he corrects, offering a hand. 'Pleased to meet you properly, Clara Poyntz.'

'You too,' I say, chilled as you like.

I am determined that this time he will see me as a grown-up. Last time I was a silly little girl with a bonked head. This time he has to see me as an equal. A cool, enigmatic, mature woman, capable of keeping it together should I suddenly have reason to enter his celebrity world. I want him to see sharp edges like Angelina Jolie, a razor wit like Emma Stone's, a dark streak like Megan Fox. He could date any one of those celebrities, I have to be cooler than any of them.

'So you're all better?' he asks nicely. 'No more memory issues?' It might be my imagination but there is a hint of teasing in his voice.

I shrug. 'Weeeeell, y'know how it is, Milo. I live a hard life and I've had long covid for two years.' I pause. 'That or I'm just tired a lot. I'm not sure.'

'Uh-huh,' he says agreeably. 'That is . . . difficult.'

'Can I get you a drink, Milo?' I say breezily. 'I'm having a, er, whisky sour' – this is the coolest drink I can think of – 'and I'm getting a round in for my mates here because I'm incredibly generous.'

Behind me, I hear Jemma spit out a laugh and Milo turns to the group. 'Oh, are these your friends?' He smiles widely. 'Hi, everyone, I'm Milo.' He clocks Harry and waves an acknowledgement that they've met. Harry giggles with girlish delight at being recognized, unable to speak. Milo fills in the silence. 'Hey, everyone, let me get this round, what are you all having?'

Salma and Harry excitedly bluster a thank you, throwing drink orders at Milo, who beams back at them. He turns to Jemma, who is glowering sullenly at him. 'And what would you like? Sorry, what's your name?'

'I'm Jemma,' she says, 'and I don't want a drink from *you*.'

'Jemma!' I gasp, horrified, and turning to Milo, I say, 'God, sorry about her. She's a bit drunk.'

'I'm not drunk!' She sounds outraged, trying and failing to defiantly put her hands on her hips. 'OK, I *am* drunk – extremely drunk actually – but that's not the point.'

'What is the point?' Milo looks genuinely interested.

'YOU!' Jemma half-yells to a startled Milo. 'You are the point! You've ruined my favourite book.'

He frowns. 'I've ... huh? How have I ruined it?'

Jemma shakes her head – actually, *slumps it around her shoulders* might be more accurate. 'Y'know, with your ... making it into a TV thing thingy. You took the most beautiful, most important thing to me and you've ...' she waves her hands trying to demonstrate her elusive point, ' ... *ruined* it!'

Harry makes an apologetic face at Milo. 'Don't be offended, mate. *Too Good to Be True* is her favourite novel, she's been reading it since she was little.'

At this, Milo looks a little sad and I feel a wave of anger at Jemma. She's being totally mad – the TV show is brilliant and Milo is the best actor in the universe. How can she be so mean to him? Doesn't she understand this is her future brother-in-law?

'Don't listen to her,' I say earnestly. 'We all love the show, honestly.'

Harry and Salma nod. 'We do actually,' Harry interjects as Salma adds, 'And for all her noise, Jemma here has watched some of it, too, so she can't hate it that much.'

'I bloody do, and for the record, I've barely watched two minutes of it,' Jemma mutters, then squints at Milo. 'What other shows have you starred in and ruined?' She pauses, her bluster calming. 'And can I have a vodka, orange and lemonade?'

Milo nods, looking a little cheered. He turns to the bar,

then back, regarding Jemma curiously. 'Are you' – his eyes flick between us – 'are you two related?'

This takes me a little by surprise. Nobody ever thinks Jemma and I are sisters – we're so different.

'No, we're not related, how dare you?!' Jemma cries, then shrugs. 'I mean, technically, yes, we're twins, but not really. Fraternal twins don't count. You get all the competition and comparisons without any of the magic of one egg split into two people. It's fake twin shit.'

Milo looks mystified. 'Right, yes,' he nods, 'that actually makes sense to me. I have a brother who's only eleven months older than me. I used to feel like I was living in his shadow a lot.'

'You understand *nothing*!' Jemma says dramatically, leaning back and almost falling over. Harry puts an arm out to catch her and I note them touching, with detached disinterest. It's good they're touching, I *like* that they're touching. I love that he's *still* got his arm around her. They'll realize they're into each other any minute now!

Jemma is ranting some more, and Milo seems surprisingly interested. 'You have no idea what it's like to be a girl – or a woman! – you couldn't understand what it's like to be scrutinized by society the way we are! To be told over and over that your looks are all that are worth anything and ignored or sneered at for not trying to live up to those standards—'

Salma leans into me. 'Is she going to do the whole speech from *Barbie*, do you think? Because I might go to the loo.'

Jemma continues, still swaying. 'You don't have any idea

208

what it was like to be constantly compared with *her*!' She waves in my direction. 'Always hearing people going, *"Ooh, twins! Who's the pretty one? Who's the fun one? Who's the popular one?"* Spoiler alert, it was always *her*. It's bad enough being a friendless loser as a kid, but imagine how it feels to have a shining, shiny example of teen perfection you're constantly held up against. Believe me, it's ten times worse!'

Milo hands Jemma her drink and she downs half of it in one go. I study her for a minute, agog. She's never really said any of this before. I just thought she hated me and thought I was an idiot. But she was actually – what is this – jealousy? She was *jealous*?

I shake my head, trying to process the thought. I feel silly because it honestly never occurred to me. She's always been so wise and sensible. She always knew what she was doing and why. She was always so much *better* than me! How baffling that she sees things this way. And why did she never say it?

'And now,' Jemma continues dramatically, getting in Milo's face, 'you take my one safe harbour – my safety blanket, my sanctuary – and you turn it into a mass consumer product with none of the depth and heart of my book!'

She finishes her speech and her drink, eyeballing Milo, who looks surprisingly calm. After a moment he nods and says, 'I agree.'

Jemma's mouth drops open. 'You … *agree*?' She shakes her head after a second. 'What, with Clara being the pretty, fun, popular twin?'

He laughs, side-stepping the question. 'I actually meant about the book and the TV series. I don't think there's any way to really capture the essence of *any* book in just a handful of episodes, or even in a ninety-minute film. To even start to get close, you'd have to do something like the 1995 *Pride and Prejudice* five-and-a-half-hour epic.' He pauses. 'Absolutely brilliant in my opinion, by the way. Though I still prefer the book.' I catch Salma and Jemma exchanging an awed glance. Milo sighs. 'You can't beat books, not really, and I don't want to. I don't even want to compare what we made to the novel version. But I think *Book Boyfriend* the TV show was worth making, too, for its own sake. I don't think it takes anything away from the novel.' He hesitates again, looking sad. 'But I'm really, genuinely sorry you feel it does. I would never want that.' He looks intently at Jemma and she stares back.

'Well, er, now that's all resolved,' I say quickly, 'um, Salma, weren't you going to ask Milo something?' Salma looks a bit panicked, shooting me a confused mini-shake of the head. I prompt, 'Um, about your radio show? Didn't you want to get Milo on there for an interview?' Salma remembers her lines at last, nodding emphatically.

'Oh! Right, yes, sure! I'd really love that,' she says. 'I did email your agent about it, and they said they'd put me on the schedule for the next press junket. You're doing some round tables soon?'

Harry shakes his head at me, murmuring, 'What the hell is a round table?'

I roll my eyes. 'Duh, Haz, didn't you ever hear of King

Arthur? It's *obviously* what Milo's filming next. He's probably playing Lancelot or something.'

Milo smiles a slightly tired but professional smile at Salma. 'Yes, and of course I'm really looking forward to doing more round tables again.' He shoots me and Harry an amused look. 'Also known as group media interviews. They must be happening quite soon actually. The whole cast is heading to Australia in a couple of months to launch the series over there. They've bought the franchise, and it's in our contract to help promote it.' He wiggles his eyebrows. 'We're staying in Byron Bay. I haven't been there since I went travelling at nineteen.'

'Isn't Byron Bay a singer?' I ask, and Harry shakes his head.

'No, it's a place. In Australia.'

'No way, he was a singer!' I insist. 'In Roxy Music? Didn't he have an eye patch?'

Harry squints at me, uncertain. 'Bryan Ferry?'

I sigh. '*No*, Bryan Bay!'

Jemma covers her ears with frustration. 'It's a *place*, Clara!'

Milo laughs. 'I'm pretty sure it is. It certainly was thirteen years ago when I was there.'

I put my hands up. 'All right, all right! I believe you all.' I turn to Harry and quietly ask, 'Can you at least get there by ferry?'

'We could try!' he says, looking at me fondly. I quickly look away, checking Jemma didn't see anything. Not that there's anything to see! We're just pals. I sidle over to Milo at the bar, thinking about what he said. He's going to Australia.

That's like . . . a certain number of miles away! Probably a lot! I'm going to need him to fall in love with me soon, otherwise he'll be gone. All the way to the other side of the world for god knows how long, surrounded by gloriously gorgeous Margot Robbie-esque *Home and Away* actors.

'So, bloody hell,' I begin, 'flying to Australia, promoting your TV show! Doing, er, rounded table and chairs. It must be an exciting life!'

He laughs shortly. 'Yeah, I guess it is!' He pauses, swallowing. 'I mean, don't get me wrong, I really love what I do. The acting is everything I ever wanted from my life, but the rest of it is . . . um, a lot.' His eyes travel the high-ceilinged room bedecked with glittery lights and round to the crowds of people surrounding us in their finery, all clinking glasses and schmoozing. 'All of this is nice occasionally, I guess, but a bit exhausting.'

A memory from my Milo-stalking days flashes: him storming out of an interview. 'I can totally imagine,' I say sympathetically. 'You must *hate* having to do all that media stuff!'

He glances over his shoulder nervously. I'd hazard he's checking where Katiezzz is. 'Um, it can be quite rough,' he says in a low voice. 'And so much gets twisted and misquoted.'

I lean closer. 'I understand, Milo. Personally, I'd upend a table and storm out with all that press intrusion.'

He laughs hard at this. 'It's funny you say that!' he grins. 'There was a story recently claiming I did that! The truth is, I'd had a call about a family emergency – my brother broke his leg! – and I had to go. I apologized profusely to

212

the journalist and offered to reschedule, but that got turned into me behaving like a diva who'd thrown a tantrum. My publicist Katies went ballistic over it but there's no point trying to get a retraction. The internet seems to have enjoyed portraying me as a wild child ever since, sharing pictures of me constantly scowling. But that's not who I am.' He sighs as I reassess the bad boy image I'd painted of Milo. 'To be honest, it's a lot. I'm more comfortable at home, cooking dinner and watching *Escape to the Country*.'

I nod like I agree, but I've literally never seen that show. It seems like loads of different presenters in quilted jackets talking about views. Who gives a shit about views? You know there's such a thing as telly, right? Look at that instead! I pride myself on never having looked out of a window except to spy on people. And cooking? Ew. I'd rather *clean*, and I'm definitely not doing that either.

I change the subject. 'Right, it's definitely my turn to get the drinks in now,' I tell him. 'Though I'm not getting Jemma another one.' I make a face at Milo. 'Sorry again about her. I've never really known her to get drunk, it clearly doesn't suit her.'

He shakes his head, eyes wide. 'Don't apologize! I think your sister is really great. I love people who are passionate about things—'

He does? Fuck, what am I passionate about? Anything? Anything at all?

He continues with enthusiasm, 'Especially books. I'm a big reader myself; my mum was a librarian.'

'I went to the library!' I tell him, thrilled to have found

213

something we have in common. I add importantly, 'I was totally there, literally today.' I don't mention that I was only there for ten minutes and didn't even glance over at the books. I add gravely, 'I think it's really important to use these resources, or we'll lose them, right?' I echo words I've heard Jemma say and it works, as Milo nods excitedly.

'I really agree!' he says, regarding me with new eyes.

It's happening, he's falling in love with me.

'Yeah, I was giving the librarians some tips about revamping the place. Making it a bit *cooler*, y'know? They really listen to me about stuff like that. I'm a really trusted member there so they take me way seriously.'

He gives me a small smile. 'That's great.' He pauses. 'But don't make it *too* cool, will you? I think libraries are meant to be a little dorky and dated. Makes us nerdy types feel more at home!' He laughs a little and I consider this.

Nerdy type? Milo Samuels thinks he's a *nerdy type*? What the fuck.

'Sure, I promise not to make it too edgy!' I say smoothly. 'Jemma would never forgive me either actually. She loves the library.'

Milo glances over at Jemma, who is stealing half-finished drinks from a nearby table. 'You guys are . . . close?'

'Hmm,' I sigh, 'sort of! Jemma's just quite no-nonsense, and – if I'm being honest – I am quite . . . enjoys-a-lot-of-nonsense. It's hard to find common ground, y'know?'

'I do know,' he says nicely, and there is a beat of silence before we're invaded by his publicist Katiezzz

'Milo, darling!' she squeals, looping her arm into the crook of his elbow. 'I need you to come and meet this chap immediately – this second! He's only here for a hot ten, so now now now!'

Milo frowns and I feel my heart leap. He doesn't want to go! He's having fun with us! Even with Jemma being an absolute knobber, he wants to stay. He *likes* me.

'What are you even doing here, Katies?' he asks her in a low voice. 'You were supposed to finish up on Friday.'

She waves her hand. 'The temp can't start for another week and you needed someone with you tonight.'

'I'm not a child,' he says gently, 'and the baby could come any day now. You need to be at home, resting up.'

My eyes travel down her black dress, landing on the neat bump I'd completely missed.

'You're pregnant!' I blurt out pointlessly. It's such a mi-nuscule bump. I have more of a bump even on days when I *haven't* eaten 500 grams of pasta. What's the point of being pregnant if you can't just really go for it and get gorgeously fat? I can't wait to get up the duff so I can eat everything in sight.

Katiezzz turns to me with a blank expression. 'Pregnant? I am?!' she says sarcastically. 'Someone better tell my husband.'

Milo gives me a small, apologetic smile. 'She is, and she's meant to be on maternity leave.' He turns to her again, dis-approval clear on his handsome face. 'You've already put the start date off twice.'

She waves her hand. 'I'll be fine, it's just a few more days.'

Milo sighs. 'I'm serious, Katies, *go home*. I don't need to be looked after.' He pauses, then grins. 'Plus, there's only that one opening thing I have to do tomorrow, right? Then I've got a week off anyway. I love you, mate, but I can manage one event without you.'

Her eyes burn with indignation. 'Absolutely not, you need someone with you.' She sighs. 'I'll call the agency again and see if there's anyone they could send along tomorrow.'

My mouth opens and I am speaking before I can think any of it through.

'I can do it,' I say suddenly, and they both turn to look at me. I shrug, like it's nothing. 'I'm a publicist. Or I was, over in America where I've been living. I did all the big premieres over there, looked after all the Hollywooders.' The lies come so easily. 'You know the Hollywood Walk of Fame?' I nod at them as they regard me blankly. 'All those celebrity hands in the cement? Mostly arranged by me. I, like, *placed* their hands into the mushy concrete, y'know? Some of these A-listers have quite weak hands and I was, like, an *expert* at really making sure that handprint was done properly.' I wink at Milo. 'Couple of days with me and I could probably get you a spot on that sidewalk. I think they have a spare bit of pavement over there.'

His eyes widen and I can tell he is impressed. Or possibly amused. It's hard to tell which.

'It wouldn't be a couple of days,' Katiezzz snaps. 'It's one day – *one event*.'

'I think Clara would be great,' Milo says slowly, and if I

had to pick one or the other, I'd say his tone is now *definitely* amused over impressed.

Katiezzz narrows her eyes at me. 'What PR companies have you worked at then?'

'Ermmm' – I wave my hand – 'all the US ones. You've probably not heard of them because they're in, um, America. But y'know, that really big, main one ...' She continues to stare at me. 'Yeah, like, Top Publicity, that was a good one. I also worked at Celebs R Us and, um, The Best PR. Oh, and obviously I had all those good years at ... Lord of the High-Fliers.'

Harry's voice at my shoulder takes me by surprise. I had no idea he was listening.

'She's the best publicist I've ever met,' he says solemnly, and I fight an urge to laugh.

Milo grins. 'She's obviously qualified, Katies. Qualified enough to help me out at just one event! It's not like it matters if I have someone with me anyway.'

Katiezzz sighs reluctantly, looking me up and down. 'OK, fine,' she says, resigned. '*One* event. We'll pay you a day rate. I'll give you my email address so you can send over any questions or concerns.' She hands me a business card, adding, 'Send me a message right now, and I'll forward you the details for tomorrow.'

I pull out my phone to shoot off a greeting as Milo rolls his eyes. 'It'll be fine, Katies, stop stressing! And go home!'

She nods, stroking her bump fondly. 'Fine, I will.' She looks up with determination. 'But first, come and meet this producer chap, he's been asking after you.'

Milo laughs. 'OK!' He regards me with sad eyes for a moment and then takes a deep breath. 'Sorry, I'd better go.' He sounds reluctant. 'But this has been really fun and I'll see you tomorrow. Thanks for shielding me from the showbiz crowds for a few minutes.' He winks, adding quietly, 'Sorry we didn't get to upend any tables.' He turns to Harry and Salma. 'Feel free to come along tomorrow by the way, if you fancy it. And either way, it was great to meet you both.' Harry looks crestfallen. His new best friend has already forgotten him. As he debates correcting the record I notice Milo's distracted. He's watching Jemma across the room, where she is draining the dregs of strangers' drinks. He looks like he's going to say something but Katiezzz seizes her moment and drags him away.

'Bye, Milo!' I call, my stomach fizzing with anticipation. 'See you tomorrow!'

Holy shit. This is amazing. I'm Milo Samuels' new publicist.

Chapter Twenty-Six

JEMMA

This is a beast I have not fought for many years.

'Ughhhhhhh, help!' I shout, and listen out in the house for sounds of life. A rumble begins down the hallway and Clara appears breathlessly in the doorway.

'You rang?' she asks, grinning way too happily. 'Oh Jem, dude, you look WAY rough.'

'Cheers,' I mutter, rubbing my eyes. 'Please please can you get me some water? I'm so hungover, I can taste my lungs.'

Clara laughs, moving further into the room. 'There's a glass of the good stuff right next to you.' She nods at my bedside table and I gasp with relief, grabbing its cool watery-ness with my hot hands and gulping it down. 'Harry put it there for you before he went to work this morning,' she says, raising an eyebrow. 'He's *very* thoughtful, isn't he? Very kind to always be thinking of you like that.'

'Uh huh,' I agree, unable to muster the energy to fight her matchmaking nonsense. Right now I'd let her marry me off to Harry if she brought me pasta, a block of cheese and a Lucozade.

'Oh god,' I groan, collapsing back into the pillow. 'I feel so awful, Clara. Like, so awful that I can't even feel embarrassed about the way I acted last night. And I know I was an absolute knobhead at the event, and you guys had to put me to bed. But that is not even touching the sides, because the head pounding and nausea is too intense.'

She shrugs. 'I don't really get hangovers.'

If I was physically able to stand, I would honestly go murder her in this moment. Look at her, all perky and dressed for the day. What a bitch. Instead, I turn slightly, retching a little, and wonder how I'm going to survive the day.

It suddenly hits me. I left the note yesterday. E might actually have replied. There might be a letter with a name waiting for me *right now*. And I'm too deathly ill to get there!

'I need to go to the library,' I moan, trying to roll over and failing. 'The note!'

Clara looks sympathetic. 'I think maybe you should try to cure this hangover a bit first? Have you considered having a tactical chunder?'

'I *feel* horribly sick,' I say feebly, 'but I don't think I can actually vomit.'

Clara moves closer, bouncing herself down on the end of the bed. My brain see-saws with the movement. 'I'll share my secret with you if you like,' she says conspiratorially, and I narrow my eyes at her.

'I'm not putting my fingers down my throat,' I tell her with disgust and she looks offended.

'I'm not saying do that!' She leans in, bouncing the bed again and making me want to die. 'When I feel rough, what I do is go put my face over the toilet – get as close as I can handle to the bowl – and the' – she waves her hand evocatively – '*odours* and weird stains you can suddenly see up close always push me over the edge. Instant puke, every time.'

'Nice,' I say. And suddenly the visual she described hits me and I'm running for the bathroom.

I emerge five minutes later, sweat and tears mingling with mascara on my face. I feel too rough to care what a mess I am, but at least being sick has taken the edge off it.

'Oh, mate.' Clara emerges from the kitchen, looking at me with sympathy. She's holding a milky coffee and offers it up. 'Mia coffee?'

'I don't think I can,' I say weakly, and try for a smile. 'But thank you, you're very kind.'

She beams at me, delighted by the warmth, and I feel a pang. Am I usually so cold? I really have to get over it. Clara's a sweet person, and I've been pretty horrible to her since she's been back. I stagger through to the living room, collapsing on the sofa and feeling the momentary relief of cold cushions on my cheek.

'I need to get to the library,' I say again in a sad, low voice.

Clara sits down beside me and – very gingerly like she's afraid I will snap – puts an arm around me. I let her pull me in, enjoying being cuddled. I honestly can't remember us *ever* hugging. Can that really be right? Surely we have? We must've at least done it occasionally when we were little.

'I think the library might have to wait,' Clara says into my hair. 'I'll hit up the Lidl down the road for some hardcore carbs – that'll sort you out.'

I want to weep at this. It's the most generous thing anyone has ever offered to do for me. Ever. Or it feels that way right now anyway.

'I'll come with you,' I say, with determination. 'Some fresh air will help, and I think I need to *see* the food, to know what my hangover needs. I need to show the monster its prey.'

Clara releases me, then offers a hand to help me stand up. I make my way upstairs to pull a jumper on over my pyjamas, adding a coat to complement the lewk.

The cold air does its job and I feel slightly more like myself by the time we reach the supermarket. As we pass through the automatic doors, Clara is talking animatedly about her new 'job' as that actor's publicist.

'I thought it was only for one day?' I squint, picking up a basket as she examines a courgette. 'Like, literally just this single, solitary event today?'

'Whatever,' she says smoothly, moving down the aisle and calling back to me. 'It'll only take that long for him to fall madly in love with me anyway.'

I hide a smile, wincing a little at the sudden rush of head pain it causes.

'Excuse me.' A woman pushing a trolley taps me on the shoulder. 'Can you tell me where the nappies are?'

I blink at her. 'I don't work here.'

She looks me up and down. 'Oh. Never mind then.'

'Jemma!' Clara calls from the end of the aisle. 'I found pizzas!'

I hurry over and the pair of us stare in at the array of beige foods. I want all of it: pizzas, garlic bread, onion rings, chips, breaded mushrooms, croquettes, potato wedges, chicken nuggets. ALL OF IT.

A man steps between me and the food. 'Have you run out of baked beans?' he asks impatiently and I glare at him.

'I don't work here!' I tell him, matching his impatient tone. He tuts and strops off.

I turn to Clara. 'What is it exactly about my pyjamas that says I work here?'

She looks me up and down. 'To be fair, those are the shop colours, dude.'

'And the mascara smears all over my face just scream professional?' I comment dryly, piling items into the basket.

'Excuse me—' a woman tries to interject.

'I DON'T WORK HERE AND I'M NEVER WEARING THIS IN PUBLIC AGAIN!' I yell. Clara giggles as the lady scarpers, looking frightened. I sigh, turning to my sister, who's shovelling food packets into her basket. 'So, did that Katie woman send you the details for the job?'

'Katiezzz, not Katie,' she corrects me, groaning under the weight of trash-food in her basket. 'And yes, we have indeed been exchanging many professional emails this morning about my new job and what is expected of me.'

She grins at me happily. 'Genuinely, I'm thinking this could be it – my new career path! What if all these weeks of obsessing over Milo was actually the universe leading me to this cool new job?' She breathes out. 'And I'd be *amazing* at celeb wrangling, don't you think? I love going to fancy celebrity parties, I love talking about celebrities and bigging up celebrities, I'd love running errands for celebrities.' She pauses. 'I love, y'know, *celebrities*. And sure, this is only one day – one event – as Milo's PR, but I'm bound to be so great at it, they'll probably offer me the gig full time.' She frowns. 'Obviously once Milo and I start dating, it won't be professional for me to stay working alongside my man, but by then I'd be able to move on to other celebrity PR jobs. Probably for, like, Timothee Chalamet or maybe Leo Woodall. This is going to open all kinds of doors! It's my calling!'

She could be right, actually. She has always been celebrity-obsessed, so who knows? This could end up being the job for her. 'Sounds like a plan,' I agree, in part to shut her up because the hangover fog is descending again.

We pay at the self-service checkout with minimal frustration and head back out into the cold. Only one person in the car park asks me to find her a trolley and we head for home, laughing our heads off.

As we reach the house, Clara's chattering away, telling me about a threesome she once had in Barcelona.

'I thought it would make me feel sexy,' she says. 'Threesomes are always super-hot in movies, right?' She grimaces. 'And women seem to love it in porn.'

Even in my fragile state, I manage a laugh. 'You're not serious? Women in porn are always so unconvincing with their wild oohs and aahs.'

'Either way,' Clara shrugs, 'I thought it would make me feel liberated and sexy, but it was shit. The other woman kept hitting me in the face with her hair extensions. And at one point the bloke poked me in the eye with his elbow. I left in the end – they didn't notice.'

'That's a sad story,' I tell her sombrely, feeling a rush of affection for my sister.

It's not just the hangover making me more loving, I genuinely am starting to enjoy having her around. She's fun and silly, and she's been working hard on being less of a pain around the house. She's not forcing her will on everyone quite so much. I think Harry's been coaching her on how to be a better human.

I insert the key in our front door, my hands only slightly shaking. 'Let's get the oven on,' I say desperately, my mouth already watering at the prospect of all this food. 'And then you can tell me what this thing is later with Milo.'

'It's actually the opening of a new sports centre,' she says casually, as I head for the kitchen and dump heaving carrier bags on the counter. 'Milo and one of his co-stars have agreed to take part in a kickboxing class for a social media campaign. It's to, like, encourage kids to be more active or some other important crap.' She titters. 'I have to join in apparently, so I'm not just standing there looking like a creepy spectator.'

I glance at my watch. 'Is 10.45am too early to eat sausage rolls and onion rings?'

'I've signed you up, too.'

I'm not listening as I read the cooking instructions on the back of a packet of crinkle cut chips. 'It says 190 degrees, but if I stick it on at 220, it'll be ready faster, right?'

'And Harry and Salma.'

'Sod the pre-heat time, it's going in now,' I sing, throwing the tray into a lukewarm oven. Even the prospect of carbs on their way is making me feel better.

'It starts at 4pm, so we're leaving here at three.'

I set a timer on my phone. 'It says twenty-five minutes but I don't think I can wait more than twelve. I'll just eat them cold and solid, who cares.'

'Amazing,' Clara says happily, fiddling on her phone. 'I'm so glad you're up for it. I've just sent the confirmation email.'

I look up at Clara, taking in some of what she's saying at last. 'We're leaving what at who?'

Her smile is a rictus. 'Weren't you listening? Oh well, too late now!' She laughs. 'Katiezzz said I should bring people to the kickboxing class to make up numbers, so I'm taking you, Harry and Salma along.'

'What?' I freeze halfway through emptying Doritos into a salad bowl. Delicious irony.

'It'll be fun!' she says breezily. 'Taxi is coming at three because I now have an expense account.'

'You have a . . . wait.' I shake my head, the hangover clouding her words.

'Well, not *technically* an expense account,' she acknowledges. 'But Katiezzz said I can send a receipt, which will be reimbursed. Harry said he'd cover the taxi for now.'

The waves of sickness that had started to recede are back. 'Hold on, Clara.' I try to steady my breathing, focusing on the oven door where food-redemption lies. 'Just stop talking for a second.' She waits for me to continue. 'Are you saying we're going somewhere – in a taxi – at three today? Did you say . . .' I fight the panicky nausea, ' . . . *kickboxing*?'

'Yep!' She nods excitedly like this is the best thing ever, and not, in fact, the worst thing ever. I mean, GOD! Going to a kickboxing exercise class on a good day would still be at the bottom of my to-do list. It wouldn't even be on my list. It would be on my anti list. My don't-do list. The list of things I would never, ever do, thank u next.

And with a hangover???

'Oh god, no,' I stutter, 'I can't do that! Are you kidding me, Clara? I *can't*.'

She fishes out a Creme Egg from the plastic bags and unwraps it. 'I've told them you're coming, you can't bail now. The list is locked in.' She bites off the top, fixing me with a hard stare, 'Plus, you do actually owe Milo an apology for being so mean to him last night.'

My hands fly to my eyes. 'Nooooo!' I cry. 'Please don't shame me! I feel awful enough with this hangover, I can't deal with an emotional, humiliation hangover, too.'

I peep through my fingers to find her lovingly tonguing

white fondant out of the egg hole. This is why I never drink. I'm an awful drunk, I hate Drunk Jemma.

She eyeballs me. 'Just say you'll come later and we'll never mention any of it again,' she promises. 'Including your massive argument with the loo attendant over a paper hand towel.'

The chip timer goes off as hazy memories from the party accost me. 'Oh god,' I murmur. 'Just let me eat seven tonnes of yellow food and then ...' I sigh, '... OK, I'll come.'

She squeals excitedly, yanking the chips out of the oven, then peering at them disapprovingly. 'Jem, these are not cooked at all. They're barely even warm.'

I grab the tray from her, throwing cold, hard chips into my mouth. 'I don't care. I have to go *kickboxing*.'

Chapter Twenty-Seven

CLARA

To: katies.lea@GrandPRbranding.com
From: ClaraPoytnzcoolgal69@gmail.com
Subject: Milo S

Hey Katies!!!!!!!!!!!!!!!

Got your email, thanks babe. So great to hear you finally got
hold of my reference and glad it was all good – of course,
I knew it would be!! My old boss Harry was always saying
how incredibly impressed he was with my publicity work at
Celebs R Us.

LOVING the sound of kickboxing, and yep, we'll be there
from 3.30pm as requested. I've rounded up three extra
people for the class like you asked, to top up numbers. I've
got the taxi booked – yay expense account!!!! It'll be a huge
success, you can definitely trust me. And also, I'm actually
AMAZING at kickboxing, I've been doing it for years – I did

three classes just last week. You don't have to worry about
ANYTHING. I've got Milo covered, you just focus on growing
some more, like, toenails and eyebrows inside your womb
or whatever – LOL!! Do babies even have eyebrows?!!!
Anyhoo, speak soon, lots of love.

Clara xxxxxx

To: katies.lea@GrandPRbranding.com
From: ClaraPoytnzcoolgal69@gmail.com
Subject: Re: Milo S

Hey Katies!!!!!!!!!!!

Totally get it, no more weird questions about your baby,
PROMISE!! And yes, I do understand it's not an expense
account. I'll keep the receipt.

Quick one – did Milo say anything about me? Like, is
he excited for us to be working together? Excited to be
collaborating on this venture? Can you tell him I'm SUPER
excited and can't wait? I know we're going to be a brilliant
team, our vibes are very similar, y'know? Don't you think I
should have his personal phone number? So I can text him
a few quick Qs???

Speak soon!!

C xxxxx

To: katies.lea@GrandPRbranding.com
From: ClaraPoytnzcoolgal69@gmail.com
Subject: Re: Re: Milo S

Hey Katies!!!!!!!!

No problem, agreed this isn't school and *vibes* aren't everyone's Mia cup of tea. Don't worry, I can totally be professional!!!

Are you sure I can't have Milo's number? I reckon he'd want me to have it! It would only be for, like, *really* important stuff. Emergencies only!!!! BTW, what's his fave colour??? I think it would be so cute if we wore matching colours at the event tonight!!!

C xxxx

To: katies.lea@GrandPRbranding.com
From: ClaraPoytnzcoolgal69@gmail.com
Subject: Re: Re: Re: Milo S

Hey Katies!!!!!

Sorry, Mia cup of tea is an in-joke, but you're right, I shouldn't make any more jokes.

Gotcha re the outfit, I will just wear the usual gym clothes. I think I probably have a sports bra somewhere???!!! Might have to buy one! OK to stick it on the expense account?

Oh, and you didn't answer about his fave colour . . . I bet it's like a dark swirling hazel, right? To match his eyes? Or a sandy beach textured yellow? Like his hair???

C xxx

To: katies.lea@GrandPRbranding.com
From: ClaraPoytnzcoolgal69@gmail.com
Subject: Re: Re: Re: Re: Milo S

Hey Katies!!!

Yes, you're right, I did say I've been doing kickboxing for years, so obviously I have a sports bra. Loads of them, of course. I just meant I should probably get one in Milo's fave colour, just to be safe (is it midnight blue?? Emerald green??). But no wozza!!! I know it's not an expense account, you don't need to use all caps!!!!

C xx

—

CLARA POYNTZ
|Brand consultant|

Personal publicity assistant to famous actor Milo Samuels, star of smash hit TV series *Book Boyfriend*, rated almost four stars on IMDb

To: katies.lea@GrandPRbranding.com
From: ClaraPoytnzcoolgal69@gmail.com
Subject: Re: Re: Re: Re: Re: Milo S

Hey Katies!

Totally no problem! Signature deleted!!!!

C x

Chapter Twenty-Eight

JEMMA

I'm going to vomit. I'm a thousand per cent going to vomit. And we haven't even started the exercise part yet.

I look out of the taxi window, taking in the busy roads whizzing past. We're a few minutes away from this sports centre and I just need to focus on something – anything – that isn't me being sick.

Today's hangover has not improved and I never made it to the library. It's possible eating a large pile of uncooked fried foods didn't help, but I've decided to wholly blame the prospect of this mad exercise. Who the hell would voluntarily attend a charity kickboxing class in front of the world's social media? I glance over at my sister.

Clara.

'Oh my god, I cannot *wait* for this!' Salma shouts from the front seat.

And Salma, it would seem.

Beside me in the cab, Clara and Harry bicker happily

about how he performed on the phone as her fake manager this morning, when he had to give a reference to Katies.

'I still don't think we needed to create an entire fake LinkedIn profile,' says Harry, bouncing lightly in his seat as we mount a speed bump too quickly.

'Of *course* we did.' Clara is exasperated. 'Katiezzz is very thorough. You think she wouldn't have checked your LinkedIn to see if you really were the managing director and CEO of Celebs R Us?'

Harry grumbles. 'But did we really have to make an entire website for Celebs R Us?'

'Yes!' Clara scolds.

'It was really very convincing,' Salma adds nicely. 'I particularly enjoyed the page listing all the fake celebs you represent. Who knew Beyoncé, Adele, Brad Pitt, Barack Obama and Leonardo DiCaprio were all clients of Celebs R Us?'

I nod, trying to gather my frayed thoughts. 'I also thought it was a brave choice to claim you represent Princess Diana when she's been dead for thirty years.'

In the front, Salma snorts, adding, 'My favourite part was the section of the website exclusively dedicated to rating the hotness of various famous men called Chris.'

'That was my idea,' Clara says proudly. 'I'm going to add in a poll so the public can vote with me.'

'Ooh, I missed that!' I say, pulling out my phone and finding the Chris page. 'Hmm,' I frown, 'personally, I'm not sure I would've had Christopher Walken ranked higher than

Chris Evans and Chris Hemsworth, but I guess we are a rich tapestry of different tastes.'

Harry laughs as Clara looks stricken. 'I don't think that was meant to happen,' he says as she quickly examines the website on her phone.

'Shit,' she says, 'I've put Christopher Plummer above Chris Martin, too. And Christopher Lee is higher than Chris Rock! Chris Rock is so much hotter since he got slapped at the Oscars.'

Harry opens his own phone, suddenly looking frantic as he scrolls. 'Where the hell is Chris Messina? If he isn't in the top ten, I don't know what hot is anymore.'

'Chris Pine is my Chris,' sighs the taxi driver out of nowhere.

We exchange a look. 'Er, cool,' Clara says, eyes darting back to her phone.

'Oooh, I forgot Chris Klein ever existed!' I cry, looking up from my own phone. 'He was my *American Pie* crush.'

'Whoops!' Harry makes a face. 'Looks like Chris Brown has ended up being pretty high on the list, too.'

Clara grimaces. 'OK, I know he's the worst, but I do actually fancy him a tiny bit.' She brings her hands up defensively. 'I know, I know! There's something wrong with me.'

We all regard her with horror as the taxi driver mutters something about tanking her rating with a one star.

Clara looks worried, knowing she's lost the room. 'Um, I think we're nearly here.' She leans forward. 'Anywhere here, please, mate,' she says robotically and the taxi driver sighs, pulling over.

'That is the twenty-fourth time someone has said those exact words to me today,' he whispers in a sad, quiet voice as we all pile out shouting our thanks.

There is a buzz around the sports centre reception, with people milling about excitedly, talking in animated whispers. It would seem the 'celebrities' have already arrived.

'Shit,' Clara mutters, checking her phone for the umpteenth time. It's almost four, but it's her own fault we're late.

After crawling into a ball in the shower, I successfully managed to throw on a pair of jogging bottoms and a hoodie, emerging – on time – in the hallway to find Clara sitting on the chest of drawers giggling with Harry. She practically hissed when she saw my outfit, immediately insisting on re-dressing me. I had no energy – mental or physical – to fight her, so now I'm here, wearing tight, high-waisted pink leggings and a stripy crop top. My boobs are so smooshed together and yanked up, I keep grazing them with my chin. It's obscene and I feel hideously self-conscious, but I'm also too ill to care.

Our arrival attracts a few head turns, followed by disgust at our civilian-ness. I catch a few interested eyes lingering around my chin-tits and pick up speed as we head through the entrance. I mean, I *would* hang my head in shame, but there are two sacks of fat in the way.

'Come on!' Clara shouts, sounding a bit panicked. 'I'm supposed to have met Milo half an hour ago.' She flags down security and we're directed down a corridor that smells like fresh paint.

Music is blasting from a room up ahead, and we exchange panicked looks as we realize they've started without us.

'Shit, what do we do?' Clara is crestfallen, then glances anxiously around our group. 'Shall we just leave? Make a run for it?'

I'm about to agree wholeheartedly when Harry jumps in, looking quite cross. 'No!' he tells her firmly. 'You can't do that. We've committed to this – you've committed to this, Clara.'

Salma nods firmly. 'We just have to go in, be brazen. Come on.' She gestures at the door and Clara looks to me anxiously. At last she mutters, 'Fuck it,' and leads us through the glass door, where the music is suddenly overwhelmingly loud. The large, already-sweaty group have paired off and are pounding each other, wearing big gloves.

A huge man at the front shoots us a disapproving look but Clara has spotted her client.

'Milo!' she squeals loudly, waving over and leading us to his corner spot. Phone cameras are pointed in his – and our – direction as he pauses, mid-punch.

I am mortified, staring at my feet as we cross the room to him, people tutting in all directions around us. The sickness recedes, replaced by the acceptance that I am among the worst of people who ever lived.

How am I here? How am I in a live-streamed exercise class – *kickboxing*, no less! – with the worst hangover of my life, my face on fire, surrounded by strangers and celebrities? And I was *late*.

This isn't me at all.

'Clara!' Milo looks genuinely happy to see her. He pulls her in for a quick hug and I see her breath catch momentarily.

To be honest, I can't blame her. I wouldn't admit it out loud, but the guy is *unbelievable*. Offensively hot. Even in his shitty gym clothes, you can see he's all angles and sexy bumps. His hair is a touch too long, as is the stubble on his face. It's just enough to make him seem real. I've barely taken any notice of *Book Boyfriend*, but I've definitely seen him in something else. A film, maybe? Something much better than stupid *Book Boyfriend* anyway.

We must only be a few minutes into the class, but perspiration already dots his forehead; he's been working hard.

He turns to the rest of us. 'Hey, you lot,' he greets us amiably, his eyes stopping at my chin. Or a few inches below. I feel my face burn redder.

'Hi,' I say shyly as Harry throws himself in Milo's direction.

'HEY, MATE!' he practically yells, startling his man crush, who takes another second to return the smile.

'All right, Harry?' Milo replies, dazzling with that TV star charisma. Salma, Clara and Harry all swoon under his gaze and I feel myself straighten up, determined not to follow suit. However embarrassing this whole thing is; however red my face is; no matter how much my nipples are currently stroking my ears ... I *will* not succumb to this idiot's good looks. I know I was horrible to him last night about the show – and he didn't deserve it – but also he kind of does. After all, he is still guilty of the crime: he has ruined my favourite novel with his stupid show.

'ERRRR,' the teacher at the front is glaring over, 'WE HAVE STARTED THE WARM-UP, CAN WE ALL GET BACK TO THE CLASS, PLEASE?'

Shame-faced, we pair off to pound on each other. Salma takes the pad and I don the gloves, trying to throw punches that cross my body. The teacher shouts at us to work harder, but I can't. The waves of sickness come with every beat of the music. Every pathetic, weak little punch I throw brings with it a painful thud in my head. Within a few minutes I'm smelling myself, and I smell like red wine. It's all so, so bad.

'Booze is seeping out of my pores,' I whisper to Salma, who nods sympathetically.

'I know, babe, I can smell it,' she admits, grimacing.

'Oh god,' I murmur, praying for a break. I just need the teacher to give us a thirty-second water break, so I can disappear to the loo and not come back. I stare over at him, willing him to call a halt to things. Please, I silently beg. *Pleeeeease.*

'OK, hold it there!' shouts the buff instructor and I pant with relief. 'We're swapping partners around.' What? No! Give us a break, for the love of GOD. He moves around the room, personally pairing people up as I anxiously seek out an exit route. Could I just make a run for it? No way, there are too many excitable boxers between me and the door. There's no escape.

Huge hands grab me by the shoulders and physically move me away from Salma.

'You,' the instructor shouts in my ear, 'are going to be kicking … *him*.' He dumps me in front of the worst possible partner and I stare at the ground, mortified.

It's Milo Samuels. Not only am I horrified by my drunken actions last night but I'm also well aware of all the camera phones now directed straight at me and him.

I glance over at Clara, who is eyeballing me. *'Apologize!'* she mouths and I sigh, trying to meet Milo's eyes.

There is a long silence. He's looking at me with trepidation. 'You OK?' he asks warily.

I must be an absolute state.

I lick my lips and swallow hard, tasting my own sweat, which is easily twenty per cent proof.

'Yep,' I say abruptly, then regret it. Sighing, I try again. 'I'm … Clara says I have to … I mean, I am very … um …' I take a deep breath as the instructor starts screaming at us to roundhouse kick the pads. 'Milo,' I try again and he waits patiently. 'I'm very sorry about my behaviour last night.' My chest gets tight. 'I was very drunk and I really don't drink very often because, well, I mean … you saw. Drunk Jemma is a twat.'

He laughs heartily, then looks embarrassed as people glance over.

I take a step back, attempting a kick and nearly falling over. I continue speaking quickly, in a low voice, 'But being drunk doesn't excuse my rudeness, so I am very sorry.'

He braces against a pad as I try again to kick it – and fail. 'You don't have to be sorry, Jemma,' he says, and something in my stomach flips at the way this handsome man says my name. I'm starting to see what Clara's been talking about. 'I thought you were funny,' he adds, half smiling. 'And I liked how much you care. It . . . matters, it really does, and I like that you said how you felt. Even if it took all the alcohol in the room to get you there. I liked . . . all of it.' He smiles slowly and my stomach goes again. I think I actually kind of—

Oh wait.

No, that's not fancying, none of this is fancying feelings – it's puke. I gag, my mouth filling with sick, and his face falls. We stare at each other, my chipmunk cheeks full of acidic liquid.

'Are you . . .?' he asks, and I nod slightly, trying so desperately to stop. It takes another half second but I manage to swallow it back down. I have never been more disgusting in my life.

'Wow,' he says, eyes wide as the instructor at last calls – after seventeen thousand hours – for a break. 'Maybe you should go to the loo?' Milo suggests nicely, understandably horrified, and I nod, too ashamed to say anything.

I turn to go, speed-walking through the throngs of people drinking from expensive-looking water bottles. The door is there, thank god, but before I can reach it, I come face to face with a familiar dickhead.

It's the last person in the whole world I'd expect to see in this weird gym class in the middle of London; it's fucking *Mack* from the library.

Chapter Twenty-Nine

CLARA

That whole thing went *amazingly*.

I mean, aside from being super late, interrupting the class, Jemma disappearing halfway through to be sick and us now getting *ever so slightly* lost in this oversized sports centre ... Aside from all that, it was great!

'Don't worry about a thing, Milo,' I say smoothly. 'I'm totally in control of this situation.' I hope I don't sound as panicked as I feel. Because we've been walking down actually quite dark corridors for a good ten minutes now, without seeing a single other soul, and I have no clue what to do.

Would Google maps work in here?

After the class finished, people started crowding around Milo, asking for pictures and autographs, so I whisked him off, like the professional publicist I am. I was taking my job seriously. I was *saving* him. But that meant leading him possibly the wrong way, deeper into this massive building that is apparently only half finished.

It feels disturbingly like the beginning of a horror film.

'I think there's a lift over that way?' Harry shouts from the back of the group.

Salma replies quickly, 'No way, the front of the building is definitely this way!'

'Why the hell am I even following you lot?' Mack growls from behind me. And honestly, I don't have an answer to that. It's so weird he's even here!

'Sorry, what was your name?' Milo asks him politely and he's rewarded with something like a snarl.

'Mack,' comes the short, sharp reply. 'And you're Milo Samuels, I know you.'

Hmmm, that's interesting. Mack knows who Milo is? 'Do you like *Book Boyfriend* then, Mack?'

'You mean *Too Good to Be Tr*—'

'There's a sign!' Jemma screams, finger pointed down a left corridor fork like she's seen a ghost. Bless her, I've never seen a person look *so* pale, while simultaneously having such pink cheeks. The smell of booze and sick around her is truly *potent*. Poor thing.

I'm so grateful she came.

'It says the exit is that way,' Jemma continues, her voice trembling. We cheer and bundle forward, almost running as we spot lifts.

Sure, they look like they might be service lifts that haven't ever been used. They're slightly rickety and wobbly, but we just need to get to the ground floor and find our way out of here.

We pile in, relief palpable in the air around us. It's crowded with the six of us, and I eye the max capacity sign warily. It says four persons only.

It'll be fine.

I reach across Milo, push the G button and the contraption rumbles into life, the doors shuffling closed.

'Thank fuck,' Harry murmurs from directly behind me as we start to move. 'This has been like the last thirty minutes of *Saw V.*'

I glance over my shoulder at him and he offers me some chewing gum, grinning sweetly. I pop a piece gratefully into my mouth, thinking what a good dude he is for coming. He didn't have to and I can imagine it was the last thing he wanted to do on a random Thursday evening. He's such a good friend.

The lift stops and we collectively look to the doors. Nothing happens. There is silence for a moment and then . . . everyone starts talking at once.

'Are we stuck?' Jemma's voice is high and frightened.

'What's going on?' Salma shouts from the back.

'Oh god, no!' Harry yells as Milo sighs loudly.

'I don't have time for this!' complains Mack as I let out a silly little scream. Everyone looks to me, their faces a mix of sheeny fear. Am I supposed to be in charge here? What do I do?

OK, I'm a professional. I'm here as the official publicist of Milo fucking Samuels and a little thing like a broken lift with six people crammed inside is not going to faze me.

'Shit,' Milo mutters, pulling a phone out of his back pocket and looking down at the caller ID. 'Katies is ringing me! It looks like she's tried a few times.'

Somewhere in the melee, I catch Mack asking, '*Katies? Like plural Katie?*' But I'm too struck with terror to respond.

Katiezzz! If she's calling, it means I'm in trouble. She's supposed to be resting at home. Does she know about me being late? Does she know I got Milo lost? Does she know we're trapped in a lift?

I suck in my breath, suddenly very afraid, and the gum lodges itself in my throat. I start to choke, looking up frantically at Harry. He frowns, then whacks me on the back, forcing the gum to fly out. I watch in slow motion as it soars through the air, landing smack bang in the middle of ... Milo's beautiful hair.

Oh fuck.

Oblivious, he's still staring at his phone, as Katiezzz' name flashes angrily. Harry and I exchange a wide-eyed look of pure horror as Jemma starts wailing loudly on the other side of the lift.

'I don't like small spaces!' she cries. 'Where's the call for help button? What are we going to do?' Milo slides his phone away, turning to Jemma and stroking a soothing hand across her back.

'It'll be OK,' he tells her so nicely as she looks up at him, fear obvious across her features.

Harry and I are still staring at each other with a different kind of terror. What are we going to do about the gum in

Milo's hair? Can we pretend we know nothing? Do we tell him and hope he doesn't go mad? Suddenly Harry's face lights up. Reaching into his backpack, he carefully pulls out a tiny pair of nail scissors.

What the fuck is . . .? Oh my god, he's surely not suggesting . . . he thinks we should *cut the gum out*! Can we . . .? Dare I? Is it actually possible? I examine Milo's beautiful hair. It's close to my face in this small space, as he continues to comfort my sister. It *is* quite long, he might not even notice if we remove a chunk? I subtly retrieve the tiny scissors from Harry and lean closer to Milo. He smells delicious.

Am I really going to try this? I glance again at Harry who gives me an encouraging nod. '*Do it!*' he mouths and I sigh quietly.

Feeling like a ninja, I reach up and snip at the gum . . . missing entirely. The small sound gets Milo's attention, though, and he turns to me, his eyebrows knitted together.

'What—' he begins, and then my incredible, brilliant, helpful sister throws up all over the floor at Milo's feet.

'Oh my god!' Jemma groans, as Milo turns back to her. 'I'm so sorry!' She's mortified, but Milo looks like he's trying not to laugh.

'It's OK!' he's saying, far more generously than I would be. And – while he's distracted by the pooling sick around his trainers and Salma's screaming with horror and Mack's moaning with disgust – I reach up and confidently snip off the offending blob of gum-tangled hair.

Harry gives me a mini-high five, just as – to a collective

sigh of relief from the lift's occupants – the doors open. The smell of vomit wafts out to an area where . . . oh shit . . . waits Katiezzz.

She's outside the doors, and her face is absolute thunder. Fuck.

She takes in the scene before her. Milo surrounded by the lot of us, his shoes covered in Jemma's sick. Jemma, soaked in sweat, pale, shivery, with tits on the verge of bursting from their restraints. Harry and I beside him, holding a clump of Milo's hair tangled with gum. I mean . . .? At least Salma is in one piece and behaving herself.

'What. The. Fuck,' Katiezzz says after a moment, and I clear my throat.

'Hey, um, Katies! What are you doing here?' I begin, as Harry kindly retrieves the hair clump from my hand.

'Are you fucking *serious*?' she asks, looking unbelievably so. 'They told me you'd turned up late, then disappeared off somewhere with Milo. His car has been waiting outside for thirty minutes. I thought you'd kidnapped him! I was going to call the police!'

I gape at her as Mack pushes through the group from the back. He looks clammy and miserable. 'I'm out of here,' he snaps, stomping off.

'Er, bye, Mack!' Salma calls after him.

Katiezzz continues, rage making her face purple. 'I had to use the Find My Phone app to track you, Milo. Are you OK? I was so freaked out when you weren't answering your phone, and then I find you trapped in here!' She turns to me, eyes blazing. 'Have you been fucking holding Milo hostage in a stinking, vomit-covered service lift? Cutting off pieces of him for some kind of fucking tribute or ritual sacrifice? Or – what? – to sell on eBay?'

'Huh? You did what?' Milo looks to me in confusion, and I gulp, eyes wider than ever before. Harry takes a step forward out of the lift.

'Um, look, we can explain all of this—' he begins, but Katiezzz is having none of it.

'And who the fuck are you?' she spits out as he offers a hand to shake – before realizing he's still holding the gum-hair.

'Hi, I'm Harry and I've—'

'*Harry?*' she narrows her eyes. 'As in, Harry the managing director and CEO of Celebs R Us?!'

'Oh! Um . . .' Harry shoots me a terrified look and I freeze.

Katiezzz snorts now, but it's not with any humour at all. It is a furious snort of furied fury. 'Clara, you are sooo fucking fired,' she says coldly, grabbing Milo by the arm and literally dragging him away from us.

He glances back as they reach the exit and I offer a sad goodbye wave.

He doesn't return it.

Chapter Thirty

JEMMA

We wait outside for the taxi in silence.

'I don't think I'll be able to expense this actually,' Clara says quietly after a few minutes. Harry throws an arm around her shoulders.

'Don't worry,' he says softly. 'I've got it.'

Salma and I move closer, wrapping our warm arms around a sad Clara too, so we're in a tight huddle, heads touching.

'It'll be OK,' I whisper to her, feeling protective. She tightens her grip on my arm, so I say it again: 'It'll be OK.'

A voice behind us interrupts the tender moment.

'Oh you've got to be fucking kidding me!' We turn to see Mack, throwing up his hands in irritation. 'I can't get away from you lot!'

'I thought you left,' Salma says with a frown and he shakes his head.

'I've been trying to. My tube line is down, so I came out here to grab a cab.'

'Do you want to come get a commiseration takeaway with us?' Harry offers amiably as I shoot him an annoyed look. We do *not* want this guy coming with us.

'God no!' Mack says, to my immense relief. Then he cocks his head. 'Wait, why is it a *commiseration* takeaway?'

I look at Clara glumly and Salma grabs her hand for another squeeze. 'Clara got sacked,' I explain quietly.

'And really – like *really* – told off by a scary pregnant lady with a silly plural name,' Harry adds helpfully. Clara snorts, looking a bit cheered up.

'Wait,' Mack says slowly. 'You're not Milo Samuels' publicist anymore?'

Clara sighs. 'Nope. Not that I ever really was. It was only a one-time gig. I couldn't even manage that.'

'Right,' he nods, 'so are you interested in a trial period at the library or what?'

The four of us gape at him. Harry is the first to recover. 'Huh?'

Mack sighs, irritated, but makes eye contact with Clara. 'All that stuff you were saying about the library needing a revamp and more fun events, it makes sense. It's something I've wanted to make happen since I started, but there were always other things going on; other stuff on my plate. Anyway, my colleague Anita is just about to go on sabbatical—'

'She is?' I ask anxiously. I can't believe she didn't tell me! I don't like change, she knows that.

He tuts at my interruption. 'Yes. She's spending some time

travelling around Finland apparently. Totally bizarre if you ask me.'

I smile to myself. That makes sense actually. Finland is where Lapland is. I bet she's heading over there to search for Santa Claus. Those Christmas jumpers she wears are just the tip of her obsessive festive iceberg.

Mack waves his hand. 'Either way, it means there's room in the budget to try out a new role. A sort of head of events, if you're up for it?'

Clara gasps. 'Are you serious?'

He rolls his eyes as Salma squeals. 'This is amazing!'

I step forward. 'She'll take it,' I say firmly. My sister may not be into books, but she is incredibly charming, creative and great at corralling people and organizing joyful things. This is what the library needs to inject a whole new energy and life into the space. '*Clara* is exactly what the library needs.'

My sister gives me a gooey look, then screams and throws herself at Mack for a hug. He recoils with genuine horror and blushes deeply. It's kind of endearing.

'I'm going,' he says shortly. 'You can start on Monday. Two-week trial period. I'll email you so we can talk terms.' He leans closer. 'The pension contribution is *amazing*.'

'Thanks so much!' she shouts after him as he run-walks away, towards the taxi rank. 'I can't believe that just happened,' she murmurs as our car finally arrives. We start to pile in, everyone immensely cheered up, when a figure runs up to the door.

'Guys, wait!' It's Milo Samuels and he's breathless as he leans on the open car door. 'I just wanted to say I'm sorry you got fired, Clara,' he tells her genuinely, as we all stare at him, open-mouthed. 'I think you were the best PR I've ever had.'

'Really?' she says, beaming at him.

'Really.' He smiles back, then frowns, fingering a bit of missing hair. 'I mean, the gum thing was weird . . .'

Harry leans in and says, 'It was my fault. Overly en-thusiastic Heimlich,' he explains, and Milo takes a second then nods.

'Er, OK.' He glances over at me, a strange look on his face. 'Are you feeling better, Jemma?'

I nod. 'I owe you another apology . . .' I say, '. . . er, about throwing up on your shoes. Um, sorry. You can send me the cleaning bill.'

He bites his lip to stop from laughing. 'You don't owe me anything.' He's looking at me intensely, his dark eyes boring into mine. 'I think it was probably better than swallowing it.' He raises his eyebrows and I feel my face flame. I cannot wait for this awful day to be over, and yet, I like this moment right now. 'I'd better go,' Milo says after another, brief, moment. 'I can't risk Katies calling the police on us; she's been quite close to it all evening.'

He grins as we all say our goodbyes. Clara is glowing with happiness as we finally take off in our taxi. She bab-bles excitedly the whole way home about her plans for the library.

'Everything's worked out *perfectly*!' she declares, bouncing in her seat and holding hands with Salma and Harry, either side of her. 'This job is so right for me, I can't tell you. I'm totally going straight home to start researching authors who are on tour and how to set up local book clubs! It's going to be brilliant!' she beams. '*And* things aren't completely ruined with Milo, right? I can't believe he came out to say bye! I think he actually likes me, don't you think?' Harry lets go of her hand, looking out the window. 'And you've got that radio interview booked in with him, right, Salma?'

Salma nods her confirmation. 'In a couple of weeks. To coincide with the final episode of the series. It's the same day as your mum's wedding actually, but it's late afternoon. I can still make the vows and wedding lunch.'

'I'll come with you,' Clara says eagerly. 'And then I'll finally actually just give Milo my number. No more messing about. Everything's going to come together exactly as it's meant to.'

I smile, listening to her, feeling all warm inside. Yes, I've had a disgusting twenty-four hours of being a drunken mess, followed by being a vomity mess. I've humiliated myself on so many different levels – in front of a handsome TV star no less! But I still feel happy. Because Clara is happy. I'm happy for her.

I've really misjudged her these last few months – these last twenty-eight years in fact. She's well meaning. All the immature selfish stuff that bothered me so much seems dumb now.

I've not been fair on her. Not for a long time.

We climb out of the cab back at home, with Harry

leaning across to pay, as we laugh about ordering yet another takeaway.

Oh. There's a man on our doorstep.

'Er, hello?' I call out, interrupting Clara debating the nearby Thai place versus the local Chinese.

'Hi,' he replies, lifting a hand in greeting. Even from that one syllable I can make out an American accent.

Beside me, Clara freezes, dropping her gym bag on the pavement. 'Careful!' I scold, then catch her expression. She's white as a ghost, staring at the man. Shit, is he a recent one night stand or something?

'Clara—' he begins, and at that one single word, she turns around, literally running away down the high street.

I stare after her, completely stunned.

What the hell just happened? I turn back to the American stranger, my face a question mark.

'Who are you?' I ask, and he takes a deep breath, shrugging.

'I'm Clara's husband,' he says.

Chapter Thirty-One

CLARA

I don't stop running until I get to the tube station, and from there, I head for Mum's house.

I just need to get away. That's all I can think. My brain is panting the words *run away* in time with my steps. I can't face him, I can't. And I definitely can't face Jemma's judgement, or Harry's disappointment, or even Salma's probable shocked amusement.

I let myself into Mum's, listening for noises in the house. I can hear her and Angela in the kitchen, laughing about wedding flowers for their big day in a couple of weeks. I hear Mum giggle about not knowing the difference between mauve and violet, while Angela explains how the human eye can see ten million different shades. It's scintillating stuff.

I turn away and towards the stairs, making a dash for my old bedroom. Of course Buffy is in there – it's her room now after all – and she's lying on my old bed looking at her phone. She growls when I burst in.

'Shit,' I exclaim, realizing this is not a safe space for me. 'Shit.'

Seeing my expression, she stops growling. 'Are you OK?' she asks warily. The words sound wrong coming out of her mouth and I can see she has startled even herself with the compassion.

'No,' I tell her, shaking my head. 'Just had a . . . shock, or whatever.' She regards me coolly, and then nods.

'You can sit down if you want.' I do want, and I do sit.

In my coat pocket, my phone buzzes multiple times. It's Jemma, of course.

What the fuck, Clara? Where are you?

Is this man really your . . . husband? How could you not have said anything?

Come home right now and deal with this. You cannot just run off like that.

I do the right thing and turn my phone off completely.

Jemma can't tell me what to do! When *she* has a husband turn up at her house one evening after months of silence, when he should be three and a half thousand miles away, THEN she can decide how to handle things.

I look down at my hands – they're shaking.

Buffy reaches under her bed and pulls out a half-empty bottle of vodka. She offers it up to me and I take it without comment. See, if Jemma were here, she'd probably be shocked or tell Buffy off, but I'm *cool*. I was getting drunk all the time when I was her age, why shouldn't she? Although I was under the impression Gen Z weren't big drinkers. It seems Buffy – much like her nickname – is a Millennial throwback. How nice.

I take a long swig, trying not to gag at the nasty, acrid taste. I don't really want it, but I also don't want Buffy judging me for being uncool. I'm SUPER cool.

'Thanks,' I say, and she shrugs, turning back to her phone. I sigh heavily, looking out the window. It's starting to get dark. 'It's just that my—'

She looks up. 'We don't have to talk about it,' she says quickly. 'I don't care.'

'Right!' I nod, thinking that she's right. We *don't* have to talk about this stuff! Why should we have to? Jemma's annoyed with me for not telling her about Brandon, but we don't have to tell each other everything! In fact, she's the one who's kept me at arm's length since I got back to the UK. If she wanted to know I'd got married, she should've asked that specific question!

'It's just that Jemma doesn't get it!' I blurt and Buffy huffs dramatically. I ignore her resistance, continuing apace. 'I mean, what's so bad about running away from your problems anyway? That's what running is for. It's why we have legs!' I wave towards mine. 'It's what our dad did and I bet he's super happy wherever he is, having a fun, no-strings-attached life without complications.' Noises start squawking from Buffy's phone as she embarks on a loud exchange on Snapchat.

'I bet me and Dad would have a lot in common if he'd stuck around,' I carry on anyway. 'When he disappeared on us, Jemma dealt with it by hiding away in her books, and I dealt with it by, y'know, *having fun*. We were teenagers! And she acted like it was some kind of cardinal sin that I was getting on with my life, seeing mates, snogging boys. But that's what you're meant to do as a teenager, isn't it? I bet it's what *you* do!' I don't wait for her to agree or disagree. 'It wasn't like I was *ignoring* what happened, I was just getting on with things.'

I try to think back to that weird time of my life. It all feels so long ago and faraway. Actually, I think Jemma and I got on OK before Dad left. Like, she'd always been really into reading and schoolwork – she was always a lot more . . . I dunno, *studious* than me – but after Dad went, that was when we really started to grow apart. We gradually just had less and less in common. She was at home, looking after Mum and doing her homework, while I was out *living my life*. Because what's the point of all this if you're not enjoying yourself? If you're not *choosing yourself*? That's what Dad did and I don't blame him. Why can't I?

And they didn't want me there anyway.

I was always the third wheel in the family; the reject. I was the younger twin Mum never planned for – never wanted. She'd tried for a baby, and they'd got Jemma, plus one. I was the mistake, the accident, the extra burden they never would've asked for.

I take another sip of the vodka, instantly regretting it. Yeugh.

'I've never fitted in with this family,' I say fiercely and Buffy turns up the volume on her phone, trying to drown me out. I continue regardless. 'They're all so *boring*.' I glance at her. She's not taking any notice but I add quickly, 'Not you, obviously.' She doesn't react so I keep going. 'They can all, like, hold down jobs and homes and friends. They don't annoy everyone around them just by *existing*. They have direction and purpose. They're not . . . *too much*. That's how I feel most of the time. Like I'm too much.'

My throat feels dry from the alcohol, so I take another gulp. It doesn't help.

I rearrange myself, finding a comfy spot on the floor, and we sit there for a while – Buffy on the bed taking filtered selfies, me cradling the warm bottle of booze, mind racing. The light outside dims and I consider asking Buffy how Mum and Angela are; how the wedding planning is going, just to get her to talk to me. But I find I haven't got any words left.

What is he doing here? Why is Brandon here, in the UK?

I close my eyes, picturing him now, standing there on my doorstep. What must Jemma think of me? Never mind Harry and Salma. They're probably all sitting around our living room talking about what a freak I am. I hate that image so much, it burns in my chest.

'Clara?' My vision of Jemma is so vivid, I can practically hear her in the room with me. Her voice comes again, more insistent this time. *'Clara!'*

I open my eyes and it is actually her, standing there shouting at me in the bedroom doorway. She still has her gym clothes on and the smell of sick is wafting around her, though all of that seems like days ago.

I scramble to my feet. 'How did you know where I was?' I demand, feeling caught out. She snorts.

'Where else would you be? Plus,' she shrugs, 'Buffy messaged me. She said you were here.'

I turn to my step-sister, shooting her furious daggers.

She glowers. 'You wouldn't stop talking at me.'

Jemma shakes her head. 'Don't pretend you weren't looking out for her, Buff.'

I swallow. 'She messaged . . . you?' Of all the people Buffy could've texted, it was Jemma she automatically reached out to. My mum and step-mum are both literally downstairs, but she contacted my sister.

Jemma nods. 'Yep, and I got in a cab straight here.' She gives me a hard look. 'Are you OK?'

I consider this. 'Um, kind of. I guess so.'

There is a momentary awkward silence and when Jemma starts speaking, her voice is cold and detached. 'I thought we were finally getting closer.' Her words hurt. 'I actually thought you were . . . growing up a bit for the first time in your life. But this . . . this is *so* awful and immature. I'm *stunned*. Shocked that you could . . .' She doesn't finish her sentence and I feel my hackles rising.

'You don't know anything!' My voice is raised, and she nods.

'That's right, I don't! Because you never told me. Who doesn't tell their family that they're *married* for god's sake? Who doesn't tell their *twin sister* they're married? Who the hell gets married after only knowing a guy for a few months, and then abandons him and flees the country without a word after only a few days?'

I feel my face go slack from shock and she nods again, almost gleefully. 'Yep, that's right, Brandon told me everything. How you'd only been dating a short time and then ran off to elope and never told anyone. Presumably because you were too embarrassed about rushing into something so stupidly fast.' She pauses, her breath sounding ragged. 'And how you left him out of the blue, without a word. You abandoned him out of nowhere and moved back here to start a new life. I'm guessing you couldn't face up to the reality of a real, adult conversation with real feelings, so you thought you'd just dump and run.' She delivers the killer blow. 'Just like Dad.' She glares at me and I glare back before she continues. 'You're so immature and selfish, Clara. Treating someone like this is just . . . it's just fucking reckless! You've been nothing but trouble since you got back here, like an emotional wrecking ball, destroying everything in your path; relying on everyone else to bail you out all the time; never taking anything seriously!'

I explode back at her, 'YOU take life *too* seriously! You're a total coward who's afraid of actually living your life. You hide away in your books – in your fictional world – watching everyone else have fun. You've never travelled, never experimented, never even *tried* anything outside of what you know. I might run away from things, but you've never let anything or anyone get close enough to ever risk needing an escape!'

Now I'm the breathless one as we glare at one another furiously.

After a moment, Jemma looks away. 'Brandon's at that Malmaison hotel down the road. He's in room 212,' she says at last. I feel bile rising up my throat and swallow hard. She repeats herself quietly, this time emphasizing the shocking part. 'Your *husband* is waiting to talk to you. I think you owe him a conversation, a proper conversation. But I don't want to talk to you anymore, you're impossible. I'm going. I hope it works out with your husband because I've had enough of The Clara Show.'

As Jemma storms out I turn to Buffy, whose eyes are huge and enthralled by all the revelations she's just heard. She stares across at me and I can see her mentally wondering, 'Who *are* you?'

Honestly? I'm asking myself the same thing.

Chapter Thirty-Two

JEMMA

I wake up the next morning with a belly full of rage.

I'm so done with my stupid bloody sister. SO DONE! Why did I think things could be better between us? That *she* could be better? Why did I think we could be friends after all these years?

I roll over in my bed, feeling hot and uncomfortable. It's been a stressful, sweaty night of tossing and turning, trying to escape anxious, furious nightmares. I remember only bits and pieces, but I know I was chasing Clara. I remember that much. Chasing my sister around rooms full of surplus furniture, all of it half painted hot pink. I kept trying to get her to stop and talk to me, and she kept laughing and slipping from my grasp.

I angry-yawn, wondering if she's here in the house. Would she have dared come back after our fight last night? Surely not. Hopefully she's gone to see her *husband*, Brandon. She owes him that much, at least.

I still can't get my head around it. A *husband*. All this time. WTF? *A secret husband!* A secret husband she apparently dumped out of nowhere, leaving him without even a goodbye text to move back to the UK? And she never said a word to any of us! She had this whole other life I knew nothing about.

And how long would it have been before she disappeared from our lives without a word?

My phone vibrates beside me on the side table, and I reach for it, feeling nervous. I can't handle any more confrontation. I feel emptied out and hollow.

It's Mum.

> Morning, darling! Just checking you're still on for cake tasting with me and Angela at 10am? Clara's not going to make it, sadly. She's here on our sofa and not feeling too well – poor thing! ☹ Hopefully see you soon. Lots of love xx

I groan, as the memory returns. Cake tasting. Today! Goddammit. I could not be less in the mood for pasting on a joyful smile and pretending I care about vanilla icing.

But this is important to Mum and I can't bail. Especially not if Clara already has. Yet another reason to hate her.

Mum and Angela pick me up in their car an hour later, and I try not to cry as Mum folds me into her chest for a full body hug. I let myself be crushed, immersing myself in her unconditional love. As we drive, the happy couple in the front chat animatedly about ganache vs buttercream, as I nod, trying to stay engaged.

I shouldn't be doing this. I should be moving forward with my life, I should be working, I should be heading to the library to see if E has replied. I think about E as the busy roads whizz by. I wonder whether there's a note waiting for me in the library *right now*, containing his real name. I'm the one who asked for it, but I suddenly, intensely don't want to know who he is. I don't want to ruin this magical, lovely thing between us by bringing it out into the light. It will only be a disappointment. He will be a disappointment and I will be a disappointment. Reality never lives up to the dream. Nothing is as good as it should be.

And I'm so angry with Clara for making me stop believing.

I wonder briefly if she will go and see Brandon. She flew halfway around the world to avoid a difficult break-up conversation, so avoiding him here should be just as easy for her.

Angela pulls up in front of an adorable little specialist bakery-cum-café. There are ornately handwritten signs in the window promising fresh, handmade produce.

'What exactly *is* red velvet?' Mum murmurs as we head inside. 'Does it involve any actual velvet?'

Angela looks baffled. 'We will ask,' she says confidently. 'I definitely don't want to eat velvet.' Mum agrees, then starts crooning, 'Red velveeeeet,' to the tune of 'Black Velvet' by Alannah Myles. They giggle intimately and my heart squeezes tightly for them.

See? Maybe it is possible.

'What are *YOU* doing here?' an unpleasantly familiar voice slices through the moment.

'You have to be kidding me,' I mutter under my breath, taking in Mack from the library standing before me. He's wearing a branded apron and a cross expression, his hands defiantly on his hips. His lips curl with fury. 'Are you following me?'

'What?' I bluster. 'Of course not! We're here for black velvet – I mean red velvet. I mean cakes. Cake tasting. Wedding cake tasting!'

Mum and Angela are suddenly standing way too close at my shoulder, panting excitably in my face. 'Who is THIS?' Mum squeals and I feel my cheeks reddening.

'Er, this is Mack,' I mumble, mortified for some reason. 'He's . . . he works at the library, and we did an exercise class together yesterday.' I immediately regret sharing this. It makes us sound close. Intimate. Like friends or something.

Mum moves closer, offering her hand. 'Hello, Mack!' she says with delight. 'I'm Sara Poyntz!' She pauses. 'The library? But surely you work *here*?' she asks, gesturing at the apron.

As Mack shakes Mum's hand, his whole expression – his entire demeanour – changes. He straightens up, his face transforming into a wide, dazzling smile.

'It's so lovely to meet you, Mrs Poyntz!' he says with warmth. 'You're absolutely right, I do work here! I work at the library five days a week, and then here one day.' He grins cheekily. 'Keeps me out of trouble.'

Mum giggles, absolutely charmed as I watch the exchange,

totally agog. Who the hell is *this* guy?! He greets Angela with the same charm, offering more little bons mots and cheeky asides. He ushers them through to the tasting room, where a variety of small cakes are laid out. My mouth waters as I take in the array of chocolate, vanilla, caramel, coffee, buttercream and – oh yes, there it is – red velvet.

'Please take a seat,' Mack says gallantly to Mum and Angela, pulling out chairs. 'Can I bring you champagne? Let's make this a truly special morning!' Fluttering around them, I try to marry this friendly, engaging man with the scowling dickhead I see almost daily at the library. How can this be the same person who stormed off into the dark after last night's escapade? I don't know *this* Mack at all. Not one bit.

And why does he have a second job? Six days a week is a lot.

He turns to me. 'Are you sitting down or not?' he asks curtly as Mum and Angela giggle excitedly, pointing out fondant fancies and icing sugar flowers.

'Er, yes, I guess so,' I say meekly, unsure how to respond to this Dr Jekyll and Mr Hyde nonsense.

Mack hands around glasses full of sparkling liquid, and our fingers accidentally touch as I take one. He jerks away, eyes flashing. 'Be careful,' he snaps.

'What is your problem?' I hiss at him, checking Angela and Mum aren't listening. They're deep into a conversation about textured, drip style decoration. I shuffle closer to Mack. 'What are you even *doing* here?'

He discreetly checks around. 'Look . . .' He turns to face me and, for a second, I am deeply horrified by my appearance. Yesterday I was covered in sick and sweat, and today I'm dressed in an old jumper and joggers. It's not exactly been my finest set of hours. And just because Mack's a dick, it doesn't make any of it less embarrassing. Especially with him looking . . . well, undeniably good. He clears his throat. '. . . I like baking, OK?' His nostrils flare and he looks down. 'And yes, I need the money.' He pauses, then snaps, 'It's none of your business why. So don't even ask.'

'Fine!' I hold my hands up in surrender, adding, 'I'm not interested anyway!'

He stomps off to get another bottle and I put my own still-full glass down on the table. There's no way I'm drinking that. I've never been a morning drinker – not even for special occasions – and I can still taste yesterday's hangover. No more alcohol for me for a while.

I take a piece of creamy chocolate ganache, letting it melt in my mouth, and watch as Mack moves across the room, fussing over the older women. He smiles happily, topping up glasses and asking excitable questions about flavour preferences. He's actually good at this. Maybe he's just miserable at the library? Maybe he hates books, and that's why he seems so pissed off all the time.

'Have a bigger bite!' he gleefully instructs Angela, like he's a whole other person. It's *fascinating*.

I said I wasn't interested in why he needs money, but obviously I *really* am. I am desperate to know what his story is. Who is this Mack? And is he – oh my god – could he be a real life *human being* underneath all the tight black clothes and scowling?

What a terrible thought.

I sigh. There is at least one thing I can say for Mack: he's taken my mind off Clara and her secret husband.

Except . . . what happens if she goes back to America with Brandon? After saying she wants that job at the library? I watch Mack as he delivers more cake to the table, smiling broadly the whole time.

He'll hate me even more. And why does that bother me?

Chapter Thirty-Three

CLARA

My heart is hammering as I slow-motion knock on the hotel room door.

Maybe he won't answer? Do I want him to answer?

On my wrist, my watch flashes angrily, asking if I'm exercising because my heart rate is 130.

Fuck you, I mentally tell it. *You have no idea how stressful this is.*

I sense movement from inside the room, before I hear anything. It takes another minute but suddenly Brandon is standing before me, huge and looming in the door frame.

Oh god. I was not prepared.

He looks even more handsome than I remember. So large and burly and – I dunno – *square*. His face is tanned and symmetrical, stubble too long. Eye bags underline those huge dark eyes; he looks exhausted – but even that suits him. He's wearing a rumpled version of a shirt I remember, with the buttons undone to his chest. I catch a glimpse of some hair and it makes my watch beep crossly again.

The same thought I had the first night I met him flashes across my consciousness now: these are genes I would want for my babies.

We stare at one another for a full ten seconds. I break the eye contact first, swallowing hard and staring down at my feet. This is going to be so fucking awkward, I shouldn't have come, this is—

Suddenly he grabs me around the waist, picking me up, circling me around in the air and pulling me to him in a bear hug.

'Clara!' he breathes into my ear, laughing. 'I've missed you so much, babe!'

'Put me down,' I say, trying to sound upset but laughing despite myself. He does so and then kisses me, hard and full of purpose. I let it happen, hating myself. This is why I didn't want to see him – it is impossible not to fall back into something so familiar.

A voice in my head tells me to stop.

'We should talk,' I say, gasping a little and stepping back. Away from the heat of his body. I've come here to end this properly. No more running away, it's time to be honest. Jemma thinks I'm incapable of being a grown-up, but I'll show her. 'Listen, Brandon, I—'

'Babe, please come back to me,' he cuts me off. 'I'm lost without you, I really am. Give us another chance. You know we're right for each other. I'm sorry for everything that happened, and I forgive you for disappearing like that.'

'You forgive me . . .' I trail off, feeling confused.

'Yeah!' he says, sounding sad. 'It was the worst thing any-one's ever done to me, I've been a wreck these last couple of months. You ignored my calls and messages, I thought you were dead!'

'Apart from my very-much-alive Instagram posts?' I ask dryly and he tuts.

'It's not funny, Clara, it was an awful thing to do to me.' He sighs. 'But I can get past it. I forgive you.' He places enor-mous hands on my shoulders, looking deep into my eyes. 'We're *married*, babe. Married! That's no small thing, it means something. You have to give us another try! You left over nothing really – nothing! It was a little fight. We have to try to make this work, Clara, we can make each other happy. I love you and you love me. I know you do! And think about how good it was at the beginning! We were amazing. We can get that back.'

My head swims with confusion. I don't know what to think. This is all so ... OK, yes, he's right, we were amaz-ing at the beginning. And maybe I have been the one in the wrong, but I thought ... I was so sure I needed a new start, a clean slate. I thought coming back here to my family was the right decision. I thought running away was the right thing. I thought it would be impossible to stay married to Brandon and I'd be better off here.

But what have I got keeping me here?

Jemma?

Fuck her! I've tried so hard with my sister, *so hard*. I've done everything I could to make her like me. To make her *understand* me. I've tried for months now! But she doesn't give a shit about me and she never will. That argument last night was the final straw. There's no going back after that. Not after the things she said. Not after the things we said to each other.

I'm done with this place – with this country. Why would I stay somewhere no one wants or cares about me?

'Come back to America with me, Clara,' Brandon says seriously, grabbing my hands. 'Give us one more chance. You owe us that – you owe *me* that after everything you've put me through.' He winks. 'And I've already bought you a plane ticket. Please?'

I take in his beseeching face. My husband. He's so handsome. And maybe things will be different this time! We'll both be better. We'll both try harder and give it everything we have. Every marriage takes work and this is my chance to be truly happy. No more running away. I need to give *this* my everything and forget about the disaster of the last few months, trying to be something I'm not.

I reach for him. 'OK,' I say simply as he grins and leans in to kiss me again.

I'm going back to America. I'm going home.

PART THREE

Narrator:

Noooooooooo! Clara, noooo! Jemma, noooo!

I won't lie to you, readers, I'm distraught. They finally seemed to be finding common ground. Even if that common ground was the Lidl superstore in the frozen aisle, debating breaded mushrooms.

Sigh. It's very disappointing.

But maybe these two are just not meant to be friends. Personally, I'm a big proponent of chosen family and these two don't have to choose each other.

Although it would be nice if they did.

I wish they could see the kindness in each other's hearts. It's better common ground than breaded mushrooms.

For now, let's return one final time to Jemma on that plane, and — oh look — she's just left the loo. I'll be honest with you, reader, I really think she would've stayed in there for the duration of the flight, trying to figure things out, but someone kept banging on the door.

Jemma negotiates a drinks trolley, as she heads back towards her seat, down the plane aisle. She knows her mysterious pen pal's name now, of course, but her face gives nothing away as she spots her nosy seat companions.

She sighs, and I don't blame her – do you? Those two are exhausting, though I will admit I'm rather glad they made her read the letter. I mean, gosh (sorry, I can't help saying it), how much longer could she have put it off?

She pauses, hovering in the aisle, frozen with indecision.

'Excuse me!' An impatient fellow passenger doesn't wait for her to move before pushing through and past her.

'Sorry,' Jemma mutters despite herself, feeling herself shrink. She turns around, her eyes roaming around the rows of passengers; some sleeping, most staring at the screens from under blankets. It's clear she's decided not to return to the red-eyed woman or Nose Ring – and is now looking for someone else instead.

She moves back in the direction of the loo. I half expect her to go in again, knowing her penchant for hiding, but she doesn't. She continues on, towards the rear of the plane, her eyes still searching. She gets all the way to the end before sighing sadly and turning back – where she almost bumps head first into a familiar figure.

At the sight of him, her face breaks out into a delighted smile and she lurches forward and into his arms.

He laughs lightly, pulling back after a moment.

'I found you,' she says softly, looking into his face and squeezing the letter in her hand. Into the face of her housemate and old friend, Harry.

Chapter Thirty-Four

JEMMA

'Whoops, Ange, look at the time!' Mum leaps out of her chair, gesturing for Angela to join her. 'We have to meet Gina in twenty minutes.'

'Who is Gina?' I ask through a forkful of mashed potato.

'She's our officiant!' Angela beams at me, as she stands up, pulling on her coat. 'She's delightful.'

Salma leans in. 'I love the name Gina. It's so close to being Vagina.'

I snort at her immaturity and Harry – on the other side of me – joins in. Across the table, Buffy glares at the three of us.

We invited Mum, Angela and Buffy over to ours for dinner. I think we're all feeling a little fragile and wanted to be together. It's been four days since Clara flew back to America with Brandon. Five since our fight in Clara's old bedroom – now Buffy's room.

I haven't heard anything.

'Do you think the name Vagina will ever come into fashion?' I ask, and Salma sits up straight.

'One day I hope!' she pronounces, and eyeballs Buffy. 'Can you make it trend on TikTok?' Buffy looks away, disgusted not so much by the question but by being spoken to at all. Salma continues, 'Our generation was taught to be repulsed by our vaginas! We all use stupid euphemisms like foof and lady bits because we can't possibly be proud of our sexual organs.' She pauses, muttering again, '*Foof!* We're adult women, imagine how stupid it is!' She stops to shudder. 'Wouldn't it be brilliant if women got brave enough to actually call a kid Vagina!' She nods defiantly. 'That's it, I'm totally going to call my daughter Vagina. Or Vulva.'

'Isn't that a make of car?' Buffy looks intrigued, despite herself.

'That's Volvo,' Harry explains helpfully, then looks wistful. 'Hey, Buffy, you and Clara should've got to know each other better. I feel like you guys would've had a lot in common.'

I stand up at this, taking my plate into the kitchen and dumping it loudly in the sink.

I don't want to talk about my selfish sister. Especially not in some sad, sappy, nostalgic way. She's let us all down! She's disappeared just when I – when *people* – were getting used to having her around. And even though Mum's maintaining a brave face about it all, I know for sure that this has broken her heart. I'm the one who had to tell her Clara was married. I'm the one who had to tell her she'd only come back to us to avoid having a difficult conversation with her husband. And I'm the one who had to tell Mum she'd gone back to him and was missing the wedding.

I'm the one who had to watch our mum's bottom lip wobble and her eyes well up as she insisted it was fine and she understood.

I listen to her out in the hallway now, fretting to Angela about where her glasses are.

She was so excited about having the three of us as bridesmaids this Friday. She was so thrilled about having her two daughters by her side for her big day. It meant a lot to her, despite all her protestations tonight. She keeps waving her hand and saying it's completely fine that Clara's gone and it's just a small ceremony anyway, but I know she's really devastated. I'm so mad at Clara for doing this to her.

And I'm so mad at this lot, who already seem to have pre-forgiven her! She's not even said sorry or begged for forgiveness. From what Salma's said, she's been ignoring all of their texts completely. And yet here they all are, being soppy and sad about her absence.

'We'd better get going!' Mum calls to Angela from the hallway, popping her head around the doorway. 'I bought pudding, it's in the kitchen. Enjoy. We'll be back in a couple of hours to get Buffy. Thanks for having us, it's been lovely.' She smiles, but I can see the sadness underneath.

'Have fun with Gina,' I call, matching her bravado.

'Give my best to Vagina!' Salma echoes innocently as Harry laughs. Even Buffy breaks out a small smile.

'I'll get dessert,' Buffy says, leaping up gracefully, and returning moments later with a Tupperware of brownies.

'Found them!' she says gleefully, yanking off the lid. We all dig in, shovelling in two each, before Salma breaks the brownie-induced silence.

'You know . . .' she sounds sad. 'It really sucks that she's gone. It's the season finale of *Book Boyfriend* this week – we'll finally see if George and Julianna get together. Clara would've wanted to see that. And I've got that interview with Milo Samuels on Friday afternoon – after your mum's ceremony – I was going to bring her along.'

'Not that she cares about Milo anymore,' Harry says quickly. 'She's back with her husband, remember. She's getting her happily ever after with him instead.'

'Ughhh!' I throw up my arms. 'Why do you two keep bringing Clara up? She left! I was right about her all along. She's selfish, secretive, narcissistic and just plain knobheady. She lied to all of us about her life. She abandoned me, you guys, the house.' Another wave of anger floods me. 'And do you know how embarrassing it is that she's skipped out on the job at the library? I haven't even been able to face going back to see if there's a note in *Too Good to Be True* waiting for me! I told Mack Clara was the right person for the job and she wouldn't let them down – but of course she did. That's all she does to people. She's let us down, she's let my mum down just before the wedding, and she'll probably let down this guy Brandon that she married on a whim. I can't believe he's willing to forgive her after what she did. She's disappeared on him – it's awful!' I shake my head, furious. 'I told you how sad he was about it all? He looked so broken. And yet of course he's forgiven her, like everyone always does! She's the most selfish person I ever met and I shouldn't have to be nice to her just because we're related. I never want to see or speak to her again.'

There is a quiet around the table, as Harry and Salma stare down at their laps.

My mouth flaps open, trying to find more words. The *right* words. I need them to understand that I'm right. I need them to comprehend that I'm the only one who truly knows Clara. Who knows what she's like. I grew up with her. I *know* her.

'Look—' I begin, but I'm interrupted by a loud knock at the front door. Salma jumps in her seat as Harry sighs under his breath, reluctantly getting up to go answer it.

I look down, feeling both Buffy and Salma's eyes burning into me. In the silence, we hear the low hum of Harry speaking to someone out in the hallway. The voices gradually get louder and we exchange curious looks, leaping up to see what's happening.

The woman at the door is wild-eyed and frantic, her hair loose and messy around her shoulders.

'Who the fuck is that?' Buffy asks in a loud voice.

Salma answers in a murmur, 'Clara's mate, Amanda.' She regards her with amusement. 'Buffy, didn't you go with them to get that furniture? You must've met her?'

Oh! This is the famous Chest of Drawers Amanda.

Buffy shrugs. 'I have face blindness for anyone over the age of twenty-five.' She shudders at the idea, then sneers at Salma. 'Honestly, I don't even know who you are.'

Across the hall, Amanda raises her voice. 'I'm not going until you tell me where she is!' Her voice is firm and Harry looks a little frightened.

'I already told you, Clara's not here!' he replies, but she shakes her head.

'Yes, but *where* is she?' She holds her hand against the door even though Harry isn't trying to close it, eyeing her old chest of drawers sitting in the hallway. 'And why isn't she replying to my messages? I'm worried about her! Has something happened?'

Harry glances helplessly over at me, Salma and Buffy. I don't know why he's trying to protect my sister; she doesn't deserve it. I step forward, folding my arms across my chest crossly. 'She went back to her *husband*.'

Amanda regards me blankly and I await the barrage of confused questions. Instead she frowns. 'Brandon? No, you're not serious?'

I gape at her, my chest tight. So Clara told this random woman she's known for two sodding minutes about her secret husband. But not us. Not her flatmates, not her family, not her *twin sister*. Unbelievable.

I turn to head back into the living room, shouting over my shoulder, 'Yep.' I collapse onto the sofa, reaching for another brownie. Sugar is the only thing I can think of that might help right now.

After a few seconds, the group follow me in. Amanda is with them.

'Sit down,' Salma is saying nicely as Harry fetches Amanda a glass of water. 'Would you like a brownie?' She looks at me. 'Jem, are there any left?'

I casually shove the Tupperware in their direction and Amanda takes a slab, that worried expression still plain on her face. 'Do you really mean it? Clara's back with Brandon? She got back with him? Why would she do that?'

'I told her to,' I say with a shrug, staring forward, eager for her to leave.

She squints at me. 'You *what*? Why the hell would you do that?'

I sit up straighter, feeling defensive under the heat of this stranger's judgemental gaze. 'Because it was the right thing to do,' I reply. 'They're *married* and she left him without an explanation over in New York. He was heartbroken and miserable. She's a coward.' I sniff. 'I can't even believe we're related. I could never walk away from someone I love like that. Letting them think I'm dead or injured. Letting them fear the worst like that, it's so low. She's – there's no other word for it! – she's *cruel*.'

Amanda looks alarmed. '*He's* the cruel one!' she cries. 'She *had* to leave him like that.' She sighs deeply. 'Brandon had her under some kind of horrible spell, and believe me, I know.' Her breath gets shuddery. 'She confided in me because my ex was the same as Brandon: awful, mean, cheating constantly.' She swallows and looks down in her lap. 'When I tried to end things, he'd suddenly become charm personified, showering me with love and promises. Brandon did the same to Clara. She couldn't resist his manipulative pull.'

There is silence in the room as horror dawns on me.

'No.' I start to shake my head. 'No, he can't be . . . that can't be . . . she would've said something . . . he didn't seem . . .'

Amanda laughs shortly. 'Yeah, they never *seem*. That's how they get you. It's how they keep you confused and controlled.' She stands up abruptly. 'I'm sorry to barge in like this, I'll go now. But you need to know this is a bad guy. You should call her, tell her to come home. He's not a good person.'

I look up at her. 'She didn't tell me,' I say quietly, pleadingly, and Amanda nods.

'I didn't tell my family and friends either. I think Clara was embarrassed to admit the truth.' She regards each of us in turn, taking in Harry, Salma, Buffy and me. 'She felt so stupid about it all. Believe me, it's humiliating. It feels like it's your fault. But she really loves you all. Really, really.'

There is a long silence before Harry stands up. 'We have to go get her,' he says with determination in his voice.

'No,' I say firmly, also standing.

'Jemma!' Salma shouts, furious. 'This is not a competition between you!' She sounds more exasperated than I've ever heard her. 'She's our friend, too. You can't stop us caring about her. Life was just better with her around. And yes, all the stuff you said earlier is true. She is a selfish, immature nightmare, but she's also a real person with a good heart. We have to help her. We have to get her away from this bloke.'

Harry nods, leaning closer. 'It's true, Jemma.' His eyes are wide and sincere. 'I know Clara teases me all the time, but she's all bluster. Underneath it, she's kind and sweet.' He smiles fondly at me. 'I see a lot of you in her actually.' I automatically bristle at this as he continues, 'The fact is, she's just as insecure and scared as the rest of us. She puts on this front because she's afraid people will see the real her – and maybe won't like what they find.' He eyeballs me. 'And you know it! You were starting to warm to her, too, towards the end there. Don't try and deny it!'

Salma laughs dryly. 'And you know what's funny, Jem? You chose me as a best friend, and I'm actually *really* like your sister! You claim that you've wanted to get away from her your whole life, but you picked someone just like her to be in your life every day!' She and Salma both look at Buffy for her turn and she shrugs.

'Don't look at me,' she says. 'I thought Clara seemed like a loser pick me girl.'

I sigh. 'I know all that. I didn't mean *no, we can't help her,*' I explain slowly, 'I meant, *no, this is not a we thing.* I have to go get her myself. I have to see my sister and I have to help her get away from this dickwad. And, if it's at all possible, I have to bring her home – where she belongs.'

It's all suddenly so obvious.

Chapter Thirty-Five

CLARA

Enya's sofa is a lot lumpier than Mum's.

I wiggle across the cushions, yanking with frustration on a sheet that's caught up under my right buttock. Pulling on it only frees my feet, which I reflexively pull up out of the cold and onto a scratchier area of upholstery. Of course, Enya has a sofa that is all show and no substance. That's her all over.

I've slept on this sofa a whole bunch of times over the years, but usually I'm too trashed to notice what a monstrous uncomfortable beast it is.

I sigh, turning over again and trying to shake off this feeling. It's a bad feeling.

Why am I here, on Enya's sofa, instead of over at Brandon's? He wanted us to immediately pick up where we left off, living together in his fancy penthouse in Greenwich Village, but I said I needed a bit more time. I said we should start off slow — try dating. We haven't even had sex yet, which has come as even more of a surprise to me than him.

I prod the bad feeling, trying to identify it. Should I be living back with him? Throwing myself fully into this relationship again? Giving him my all? It's what he wants, but no . . . I'm not ready.

Usually, when I give myself a fresh start – or, as Jemma would put it, *run away* – I feel better. I feel relieved and excited. I can't wait to start again. But not this time. This time I feel restless and hot and itchy. And not just because of the scratchy texture of this sofa. Being back in America, being back with Brandon again, it feels . . . *wrong*.

I give up on sleeping, reaching for my phone on the coffee table and squinting at the too-bright screen.

Mindlessly I open Safari and google *Milo Samuels*, tapping the Google Images tab. His handsome face fills the screen

OK, here we go. *This* is why I'm feeling sad. This is why I'm feeling unfulfilled and confused, like I have unfinished business. Because I've run away with Brandon just when things were going well with Milo. We'd bonded! We were definitely going to meet up again and it was going to work out.

Sigh. Who am I kidding?

Let's be realistic here. I was using Milo, wasn't I? He was a lovely, handsome fantasy I was using to distract myself from real life. I don't even really *know* Milo Samuels. Not really. And what I was starting to know about him didn't exactly gel with the image I'd created of him in my head. I thought he was this wild, sexy bad boy; the classic treat 'em mean type. He's not that person at all.

It's time to be a grown-up. And being a grown-up means trying to make your marriage work. That's what I'm doing here, with Brandon. I need to make this work. It's definitely the right decision. It is. I have to try.

So what is this weird pit in my stomach? This solid mass of *wrong*?

Maybe I just miss my friends back in the UK.

Not Jemma, obviously, but Salma, Harry, Amanda. And Mum of course. Oh, and Buffy and Angela.

That might be the bad feeling. Leaving just before the wedding like that.

But Brandon had already bought my plane ticket and he needed to be back over here for work. It was all a rush, I didn't have a lot of time to think about it.

Actually, I've hardly seen Brandon since we got back, he's been so busy. We're meeting up for a 'date' later. I hope it'll be OK. I have to try to make it OK.

Harry's sweet face suddenly fills my vision. I *do* really miss my friends. And it's not like any of my pals over here were particularly excited to hear from me when I announced my return. Enya was the only one who even replied to my messages and she was only ever really a peripheral mate; someone to go drinking and partying with. We never really *talked*. To be honest, I never really talked to any of the people I hung out with over here. It was all just surface level. And I didn't realize that until I started sharing a house with Harry, Salma and Jemma. Lovely, fun, kind, generous people who laughed with me when I made a joke and told me off when I was being selfish. They picked me up when I'd given up hope and helped me when I couldn't help myself. They *cared* about me.

I really, really miss them. Even Jemma.

And maybe Harry most of all. Just because he was so kind, y'know. And so fun to tease! He always took it with a smile and looked after me when I was making a mess of things as usual. I think Harry is my best friend actually.

But we can still be mates from afar! Once things have cooled down a bit. And now I'm out of the way, hopefully he and Jemma can make things work. Now I'm not cock-blocking them with my presence and that giant chest of drawers.

It's still sitting in the hallway.

But I'm sure, now I'm gone, they'll just get rid of it! They'll sell it on or dump it and life will go on. They were all fine before I barrelled into their lives and they'll be fine now I'm gone.

Especially Jemma.

I yank angrily at my duvet, wrestling with it. God, she's hard work! One minute she's annoyed I'm in her space, taking over her life, and the next she's mad at me for not telling her stuff and not sharing enough! I mean, make up your mind, sis!

'*You're making a mistake,*' a small voice in the back of my brain whispers.

I'm not making a mistake, I tell myself firmly. I made too much of a mess of things over there, I can't go back. And Mum will get over it. It's not like we had much notice for this wedding anyway! She will forgive me, she always forgives me.

'*You could've explained,*' the voice whispers. '*You could've been honest with all of them. They deserved that. Not everything has to be glossy and amazing, you can tell them the truth instead of sabotaging it all.*'

I shake my head. It's too late. I've ruined everything. Jemma hates me, Mum probably does, too. The library must think I'm an absolute tit, disappearing before I even got to day one of the new job. And Salma and Harry – oh god, what must they think of me? Some guy they've never heard of turning up out of the blue and announcing we're married after some crazy whirlwind romance? They must think I'm mad.

Maybe I *am* mad.

'*You're pushing everyone away again.*'

'Oh FUCK OFF,' I yell into the darkness, then hide under the cover when I remember Enya's in the bedroom next door. I hold my breath, waiting for the noise of an angry host, but there is nothing but city noise through the thin walls. I pull out my phone and find the album with our wedding pictures, flicking through glossy, shiny photos of me and Brandon. We were happy. We are happy. This is going to be fine – great! Wonderful!

The bad feeling in my stomach disagrees as I turn over, diving back into uncomfortable cushions.

Chapter Thirty-Six

JEMMA

I'm pretty sure I'm about to do the stupidest thing I've ever done.

'This is the best thing you've ever done,' Salma says sombrely, throwing a jumper at me from the wardrobe. 'And it can be rainy in New York, even in July. Don't just take T-shirts.'

I roll my eyes. 'I'm only going to be there a couple of days,' I say, unzipping my carry-on suitcase and shoving it in. Salma glares at me and I sigh. 'Fine, what else have I forgotten to take? I never leave the country – I barely even leave our postcode – so please explain to me what I need to know.'

Salma looks delighted and gently shoves me out of the way. She empties out my bag, frowning with horror at what she finds. 'Useless!' she declares, tutting, as she fetches things from my drawers, rolling them up carefully.

'Are you ready yet?' Harry is at the door, looking excited with a suitcase in his hand. I beam over at him, feeling so grateful he's coming with me.

After I insisted this had to be a solo mission to fetch Clara, there was a moment of sincere, respectful silence, then they all burst out laughing at me. Harry said there was 'no bloody chance' I was going without him. Which filled my insides with gooey warmth.

Salma pouts. 'I'm really jealous you two are going to America without me.'

I laugh. 'Dude, we're only going to find Clara and make her come home with us. I have to be back for Mum's wedding on Friday. This is not a fun jolly.' I sigh. 'We couldn't even get seats together on the plane. I've got a crappy middle seat up the front and Harry's – I don't even know where – miles away at the back.'

'I'm dying first if the plane rips in two!' Harry calls out cheerfully. 'So I'll be getting druuuuuunk in my back-of-the-plane seat!' He bounces out of the room.

'You know that's not true,' Salma muses. 'Back of the plane is much safer.'

'Oh, cheers!' I tell her, genuinely a little horrified.

She ignores me. 'He's so brilliant to come along,' Salma says warmly, when Harry's gone. 'I feel better knowing our Haz will be with you, holding your hand.' She laughs at my sideways look and throws my makeup bag in the case. 'I meant metaphorically! You don't have to hold hands . . .' she winks, '. . . unless you want to.'

I ignore this. 'Am I ready? We'd better head to the airport.'

She checks her watch. 'Good god, woman! You've got ages!'

I feel a wave of anxiety as I help her zip up the suitcase. 'I know, but I'd rather be really, really early. Then I've got plenty of time to, like, figure out, y'know, check-in queues or security thingys.'

Salma raises an eyebrow. 'Security thingys? What do you mean?' She eyes me carefully. 'Jemma, when did you last fly anywhere?'

I blink at her. 'Never,' I admit, and she looks shocked.

'*Never?* Blimey. Well, the least you can say for your sister is that she's forcing you out of your comfort zone. This is the most spontaneous, adventurous thing I've ever known you to do!'

'You said I should do it!' I exclaim. 'You said there was no other option!'

She brings her hands up in a defensive motion. 'I know! But, to be honest, I didn't think you'd actually do it! After everything you said about Clara, I thought . . .' She shrugs. 'I don't know. I'm just . . . really glad. I'm happy for Clara that you're going to show her you love her, but I'm also happy for you, that you feel you *can* show her. You have those' – she picks up the suitcase off the bed, lowering it to the ground – '*walls* up. It's hard to persuade you to lower them sometimes.'

I feel shy suddenly. She's right, of course, I know she is. I can be a closed book and I don't like that about me. I don't want to be rigid and cold and unfeeling! I want to be open and loving and fun and . . . a realization hits me. Those are all things Clara is. I want to be more like Clara! And I want my sister to be OK. I do want her to know I care. I need her to know that I love her. Whatever's happened with that Brandon guy, she's my sister and I need to tell her, to her face, that I love her and want her in my life. I need her to know she's too good for some dirtbag cheater, and that she's ... *enough*. That we want her home, with her family.

'Well, this better bloody work!' I laugh away the sincere moment. 'I'm using all my savings for this round trip.' I grab the handle of my case. If Salma won't let me turn up six hours early to my flight, I can at least go put my bags and coat by the front door and stand there anxiously.

'So, what about the note?'

I freeze. 'The note?' I turn and Salma is frowning.

'I've been meaning to ask what's going on with your book boyfriend,' she says, looking at me intently. 'We've been a bit distracted by everything that's been happening with Clara. Have you checked the library for a reply yet?'

I look away. 'No, not yet,' I say. 'I haven't had a chance. I'll get Clara sorted, then deal with that.'

'Boo!' she shouts after me as I head down the stairs, dragging my suitcase behind me.

'Fuck it, shall we go, Haz?' I shout to the house, and Harry answers with a whoop.

'We'll get there *so* early,' he replies happily. 'I love getting to airports early, there's so much Baileys!' He suddenly gets super posh. 'Oh Jem! We have to drink some champagne and eat oysters at the Fortnum and Mason bar!'

I hear Salma taking the piss out of him, imitating his

excitement in a plummy voice. I line up my suitcase, grabbing my coat from its hanger.

Before I put it on, I feel for the pocket, where the envelope sits.

I lied to Salma before. I *have* been to the library, I went there last night. There was a new envelope waiting for me, as I'd expected. But I haven't been able to make myself open it yet. I can't quite bring myself to do it. I want to know but I also don't. My brain feels a bit too fizzy and full. I'm not ready to know E's name yet. I don't want to know the identity of this man I don't know, but already like so much.

I pull on my coat. I've got an eight-hour flight ahead of me for my brain to calm down.

I'll open it on the plane.

Chapter Thirty-Seven

CLARA

'Morning, Enya!' I greet her cheerfully from across the kitchen, but she raises a finger, a signal for me to shush. She's writing something down, her phone talking in front of her.

Whoops, she's obviously working. I can't remember what she does for a job – or maybe we've never actually talked about it – but she looks deep into things right now. I head to the sink and find myself picking up Enya's dishes to wash up. Yuck, Jemma's had too much of an influence on me.

'Sorry, babe!' Behind me Enya stands up. 'I was just listening to my gal pal's voicemail! She goes on and on, and I forget everything I need to reply about, so I have to make notes. Like a voicemail agenda.'

'I totally do that!' I tell her enthusiastically, scrubbing at some kind of dried oaty mess. See, Enya and I have stuff in common after all! Maybe I could stay here a bit longer.

'So!' Enya's voice is breezy with an undertone of awkward. 'You're really back! I thought you were in the UK for good.'

At the sink, I nod. 'I sure am! I've really missed New York. It's the vibe, y'know? It can't be beaten by stinky old London. Who needs all those buildings over fifty years old and stiff upper lips? I can't wait to, like, catch up with everyone!' My voice is hollow. I *want* to mean all that but I just . . . don't. I haven't missed being here and I don't want to catch up with anyone.

'That's awesome!' she says with enthusiasm in her Texas drawl. 'We should hit up the clubs to celebrate. I'll get us on some guestlists.' She pauses, then adds a little coolly, 'And obvs bring Brandon since you guys are back together.' I turn to grin at her excitedly – though I suddenly feel tired by the idea of it. She continues as I balance a dripping plate on her draining board. 'And of course, if you need, you can totally stay here for another . . .' she pauses, ' . . . night.' My heart sinks.

Where am I going to go? I'll have to move in with Brandon after all. Why does the idea make me feel so miserable?

But at least I'd have somewhere to stay. At least I'd be safe. And isn't that why I married him in the first place? Because I thought it would make me safe.

Enya laughs. 'Maybe even an extra two nights if you're going to clean up after me! Thanks, girl! I don't remember you being so well house trained last time you crashed here!'

I think the last time I *crashed* at Enya's was last year. We had a wild night out for Independence Day – which I only found out that night *wasn't* named after the Will Smith and Bill Pullman movie. I just thought the Yanks really, really liked that film.

It was the same bar where I later met Brandon.

I consider again the way Jemma looked at me when he turned up in London like that and told her who he was.

I haven't replied to her messages. Or anyone's. They've all tried to get in touch – Jem, Salma, Harry, Mum, Angela. I even got a Snapchat from Buffy, but it was mostly just to ask me to bring her a job lot of Twinkies the next time I'm coming home.

My phone buzzes and I dry my soapy hands on a damp tea towel. It's Jemma again. I sigh, ready to throw the phone in the sink along with the dirty water, when the message preview catches my eye.

We're at JFK.

I gasp, flicking the whole message open as more texts come in.

Me and Harry have come to see you, and if you don't tell us where you are, or where we can meet you in the next hour, we will bill you for the flights.

Her next text comes in just seconds later.

I can see the double ticks, so I know you're reading this. Reply immediately or I'm going to ring 911 and report you as a missing person.

And another one:

> Harry says he's come to cash in on his investment in
> your upcycling business – he says you owe him and
> you can't just leave the country to avoid your debt.

I double gasp and Enya looks over curiously. 'Do you need my notepad?' she offers kindly and I shake my head.

Harry's here, too?

My heart races. Have they come to confront me? To tell me to my face what an absolute arse I've been and how much they hate me?

But they're *here*. How can they be here? They've come all this way, I have to go see them. Even if it is to let them tear shreds off me. They certainly deserve it.

'You wanna hang out today?' Enya offers. 'I'm going to a life drawing class.' She pauses. 'I'm the model.'

Well, that decides things.

'That sounds amaaaazing,' I say, 'but I'm actually going to meet my sister. Turns out she's in town.'

Enya looks unimpressed. 'Cool.' Does Enya have family? I really should know this stuff about a so-called friend. Especially the only friend I seem to have in New York. Back in England I could list the entire extended list of cousins Harry has dotted around Buckinghamshire – and the order in which he hates them most.

I message Jemma back, my heart hammering in my chest. I suggest a coffee place near the airport. It's quiet and inexpensive. Y'know, in case she makes me pay for the drinks in her fury. My hands shake a little as I add three kisses.

You never know, maybe the Xs will make her hate me a tiny bit less.

Chapter Thirty-Eight

JEMMA

Harry is the first to spot Clara. She's sitting in a booth in the darkest corner of the room. She's hunched over and in on herself, like she's hoping we won't spot her. But she waves when she sees us, almost like she's excited.

'Jemma! Harry!' she calls happily, but her face falls as we approach. 'I can't believe you're here, this is mad!' She pauses, then gushes emotionally, 'I'm so sorry, I'm *really* sorry. Please don't shout at me.' She looks between us. 'Well, obviously you *can* shout at me if you want to – I know I deserve it – but please don't. I've done so much crying these last few days, I am incredibly dehydrated.'

Harry laughs, pulling her in for a hug. She freezes for a second, looking thunder-struck, before relaxing into it. They hold onto one another and I can see Clara is close to crying – again. Harry pulls away at last. 'You silly goose,' he says with affection. 'Why did you run away? We were all really worried.'

Clara gapes at him and then looks to me.

I frown, then try not to. Everything in me wants to hug her – to check her over for lumps and bumps and emotional bruises – I've honestly been so worried. But I'm also not quite so ready to forgive and forget. I have stuff to say. Stuff to ask.

I feel for the envelope in my pocket. And stuff to *tell*.

I was forced to read the letter on the plane. Forced by two strange women, sitting either side of me. And now I just don't know what to think. I have answers, but I also have more questions.

But right now, my only questions are for Clara.

Harry looks between us and clears his throat. 'Listen, I'm going to leave you guys to chat for a while.' He glances at me. 'I'll go get us checked into the hotel, OK, Jem? Come find me whenever you're ready.'

I nod, unable to say thank you out loud. He's been so good. So kind. And only a tiny bit drunk and useless on our journey here.

Clara leads us back into the booth and I see her swallow hard. We sit in silence for a minute.

I take a deep breath. I guess I'm speaking first.

'Amanda told us the truth about Brandon,' I say quietly, and Clara's head shoots up. Her mouth opens and closes as her eyes fill with tears. I resist the urge to reach for her while I continue, 'I don't understand what happened, Clara. I thought we were starting to be in a good place – weren't we? Couldn't you have trusted me to listen to what you had to say? Couldn't you have told me he was a controlling arse? Instead of running off again?'

She looks up, a pained expression on her face. 'It's not about trust, Jem.' She frowns. 'At least I don't think it is. It's just . . . I don't know, an instinct? I had to get away. I couldn't face your disappointment. I know you don't like much about who I am. You think I'm selfish and immature, and I couldn't face you being right about me – again.'

A wave of emotion washes through me and I take a moment, letting them settle down. After a minute, I put a hand on top of hers. 'I'm so sorry I've always made you feel that way, you don't deserve it. You're a good person, Clara, and I . . . I do love you.' Her fingers find mine and we sit there, holding hands for the first time since we were kids. 'I guess a lot of it stems from when we were young. Everything seemed so easy for you. I was jealous, I suppose. I probably still am.'

She shakes her head. 'Everything seemed so easy *for you*! You had it all together, everything sorted. You weren't wasting your life chasing silly boys around and making friends with people whose names you couldn't remember a year later.' She gestures at me. 'Look at you! Jemma, you're *so* sorted. You have the loveliest friends in the universe, you have a cool job that means you get to spend your days in your favourite place, you have enough money to hop on a plane to New York with a few hours' notice!' She grimaces. 'Meanwhile I'm up to my arse in debt with no idea where I'm even going to stay tomorrow night.'

'You're not staying at Brandon's?' I ask with a frown.

She looks away. 'We're, um, taking it slow.'

I take a moment, then say, 'You can't get back with him, Clara.'

She swallows hard. 'It's complicated. Amanda doesn't know the full story. It's . . . there are . . . I'm *married*, Jem. And I can't keep flip-flopping, running back and forth between the UK and America.' She laughs shortly. 'I can't afford it, for one thing.'

'I'm sure Mum could lend you some more money,' I offer.

She nods, embarrassed. 'Probably. Even though she must hate me.'

I grin. 'I think I know how you could persuade her to forgive you.'

Clara gives me a toothy smile back. 'Come to her wedding?' She looks down. 'I'm sure she doesn't even want me there anymore, not after I ditched and ran like that.'

I give her an impatient sigh. 'Of *course* she wants you there!' I pause and then ask carefully, 'Why do you think you do run away from things? Do you think it's—' I don't finish because Clara is looking away. She knows what I'm going to say.

'Dad?' she offers quietly and I nod. 'I guess so, maybe.' She meets my eyes. 'But how come I got the stupid, cowardly escape genes and you got the reliable, see-things-through ones?'

I shrug and half-laugh. 'I think everyone is different – even twins. It's like how some children of alcoholics become alcoholics themselves, and others are disgusted by alcohol and never drink a day in their lives.' I swallow, adding, 'You know you started disappearing – running away – back when we were teenagers, just after Dad did.'

Clara regards me, smiling. 'Well, *you* started disapproving just after Dad left.'

'Fair enough,' I laugh, then pause. 'I actually had a feeling you'd left America because of a man. But I suspected it was Dad. I thought you'd tracked him down somehow, and he'd let you down again.'

Clara brightens. 'Ooh, maybe we *should* track him down!'

I look at her hard. 'Why?'

She shrugs. 'I dunno! It might be cool to get to know him. Don't you think? It's been nearly fifteen years. Maybe he regrets how he left things . . .'

I hesitate, uncertain how to confront this. We've just made up, I don't want to upset her again. I don't want to send Clara running for the hills. God knows how far she'd flee this time. But I can't understand how she can still see Dad as some goofball who, like, forgot to come home one night. 'Um, you do understand that our dad's an arsehole, don't you, Clara? You get that he abandoned his wife and two children and literally never got in touch?'

Her body language is immediately resistant. She crosses her arms and shakes her head. 'Yeah, but . . .' She struggles for the words, looking away. 'I can understand that impulse to run. Like I said, I have his coward genes. I can see how things might've got too scary. We must've been a lot to deal with − *I'm* a lot to deal with.' She swallows hard. 'Maybe that's why I've always defended him: I'm like him.'

I put a hand gently on her arm, and it's enough to stop her speaking. 'No,' I say carefully. 'Really no, Clara. I know you guys were close, but he *left*. Can you imagine doing that to Mum and two young kids who need you?' I swallow. 'I know that you have this instinct to escape things, but that doesn't make you anything like him.' Clara frowns, then looks down at the table between us. I carry on. 'I'm so sorry I said that in our fight. You're *not* like him, Clara, I was wrong or hurt or just − I don't know − lashing out. You're nothing like him. I know you think you are, but you're *not*.' I sigh, leaning back. 'I've never told you this, but I did get in touch with him a few years ago.'

She gasps at this. 'You did? What did he say?'

I nod slowly, feeling pulses of guilt for never telling her. But she was in America and we weren't close. And the truth is, I knew it would hurt her, and − despite the physical and emotional distance − I didn't want that.

'Yep, it was surprisingly easy. He was just there, on Facebook. I sent him a message explaining who I was and asking if he would be interested in talking after all these years.' Clara's eyes are huge and expectant, and I feel awful as I continue. 'He replied after a couple of weeks to say he had a new partner − a new life − and wasn't interested in revisiting long-forgotten history. He didn't even say sorry.'

Clara's bottom lip trembles, but her arm cross gets tighter. 'But maybe . . .' she tries weakly and I shake my head.

'No,' I say softly, and after a few seconds she nods back.

'OK,' she acknowledges and then releases her arms. Her shoulders slump with something like exhaustion. 'OK, he really is a piece of shit then.' She looks up at me anxiously. 'But you honestly don't think I'm like him? Or at least, you think that I can be better than him?'

I grab her hand and hold it tightly. 'You are a million miles better than him! You love people a lot and care about them. Can you imagine *ever* sending a message like that to your own child? Or even to a stranger?'

She shakes her head vehemently. 'God no!' She takes a deep breath, letting it out in a low whistle. 'I think I convinced myself Dad wasn't so bad because I really thought I was like him. But I think I can be more like you and Mum if I try.'

I laugh shortly. 'I've just decided to try being more like *you*! You're fun and chilled out. I want to try to be less . . . I don't know, *rigid* about stuff. Less judgemental. I'm going to go with the flow.'

Clara machine-gun-laughs at this. 'You're going to go with the flow? You!'

'Fuck off,' I say mildly. 'I can go with the flow!' I sit up straighter. 'And I'm going to live my life a bit bigger, I think.' Clara's eyes widen. 'I actually loved that plane ride! Nosy seat mates aside, it was awesome. I want to do more of it. I can travel and try things and have adventures – outside of my books.' I frown. 'Though I'm definitely not sacrificing them. They can come with me. Or maybe I'll finally give in and get a Kindle.'

Clara's face is alight with happiness. 'And I'm going to stop running away. I'm going to face reality, find a real life with real friends and a real job. I will do the washing up and I won't impulse buy stupid gigantic items of bedroom furniture or paint antiques without permission.'

I beam at her. 'For the record, I actually really love my hot pink mirror. I just didn't want to admit it.'

'You do?!' She looks thrilled. 'Maybe there *is* some mileage in upcycling then ...'

'Oh god,' I laugh, then I stop. Squeezing her hand, I ask the big question. 'What are you going to do about Brandon?'

Clara looks away. 'I don't know yet.' She inhales deeply. 'And I want to tell you everything – the whole story – but I just need a minute. Can we just ... can I just ...'

Her eyes are wild and fearful, so I cut her off. 'There's no rush. Let's go find Harry and start exploring. We're in New York for god's sake! And we're only here until tomorrow night, so you have to show us around. Harry says we have to get trashed and dry hump the Statue of Liberty.' I shake my head. 'I don't know what these fancy private schools are teaching our young men these days.'

Chapter Thirty-Nine

CLARA

'So where's the coffee shop?' Harry is turning on his heel in circles, searching for something.

I frown. 'There are loads of them.'

He looks exasperated. 'Central Perk!' He waves his hands like I'm stupid. 'We're right next to Central Park, there is surely a *Friends* coffee shop called Central Perk?'

I shrug. 'I think someone said there is a coffee place in that location, but god knows where that building was even filmed.' I pause. 'You know there's like 843 acres of this park?'

Jemma's eyes widen at my knowledge. 'How do you know that? Did Angela tell you that?'

I give her a smug look. 'The Sponsored Snog. A couple of years ago a group of us decided to try to snog someone in every acre of this place.' I grimace. 'It was gruelling but I knew I couldn't give up. I covered more than my fair share, but still only managed to snog fifty-six people that year.'

'Wow!' Jemma looks intrigued. 'How much did you raise for charity?'

I shoot her a confused look. 'Huh? Ohhh right, when I say *sponsored*, I just mean we were, like, in it together and, y'know, *supported* each other. I bought sooo many drinks for people.'

'That's not what sponsored means on any level,' Jemma points out, but Harry looks super impressed. And then a bit grossed out.

'So anyway, how much of this park do you actually want to see?' I ask, hoping they'll say this is enough. Central Park was on the list of touristy places Jemma and Harry wanted to visit, but a park is still just a park. And I've been sleeping on a really crappy sofa for a few nights, I'm not sure how much more walking I'm capable of.

'Shall we go see the Met now?' Jemma says eagerly and I squint at her.

'The . . . Met?' I enquire. 'What the hell is that? Like the Met Office? You want to know about the weather? Or do you mean the Met Police?'

Harry jumps in. 'No, she means the New York Mets! Baseball, right, Jem?'

Jemma looks horrified. 'No! God no! To all of those suggestions. Why are there so many things called the Met?' She looks at me penetratingly. 'Clara, are you telling me you lived here for five years and you've never even *heard* of the Metropolitan Museum of Art?'

'Erm,' I hedge, 'oh yeah, that's totally a thing I've heard

of.' I pause. 'And have been to, of course! It's full of, like . . . paintings?' Jemma snorts at my expression and I giggle. 'OK, fine, I don't know it.' I give her a hard look. 'And I'm pretty sure you don't care about art either. I know you love books, but I've literally never heard you mention art or artists in your life. And you don't even have any pictures on the walls in your house!'

'Only because the letting agents would have us boiled alive!' she protests.

'No way!' I smirk. 'You're just trying to sound clever.'

For a second I think she will get annoyed, but then she bursts out laughing. 'Fine, you got me. I don't really care about the Met. But at least I'd heard of it!'

'Yes, fine,' Harry interrupts us. 'We're all dumb-dumb philistines, and let's agree to strike any museums or galleries off the to-do list.' His eyes light up. 'I'm starving, let's go to a really traditional, renowned American restaurant.'

Twenty minutes later and we're sitting in a Five Guys eating burgers.

'How is this so much more delicious than the Five Guys we have around London?' Jemma asks, drooling sauce down her chin.

'It's the smoggy New York air!' I tell her happily, through half-chewed fries. 'It makes everything taste better.'

Jemma stops eating, looking serious for a moment. 'You really love it here, huh?' She swallows hard, though there is no food in her mouth. 'Are you going to stay?'

Harry stares down at the table before us as I wonder how

to answer this. I've been waiting for this conversation, but I still don't feel ready for it. There is a long, expectant silence around the table.

Harry leans in. 'What actually happened between you and Brandon?' he asks in a soft voice. 'Why did you leave him all those months ago to move back to the UK like that?'

'It's a long story,' I say shortly, but neither of them look away or resume eating.

After a minute, Jemma says gently, 'You said you were going to stop running away from things, Clara. I know it's scary talking about this stuff, but it's important. You can talk to us.'

I still don't answer and Harry looks uncomfortable. 'Shall I go? I understand if you want to talk about this, just the two of you.'

I shake my head quickly. He deserves to hear this, too. 'OK.' I pause. 'So, Brandon and I met on a night out.' I pause again, trying to steady my fast breathing. 'Right away, he seemed mad about me. There were expensive presents, fancy dates.' I shrug. 'He's rich. He said he'd fallen for me within a couple of weeks and that he'd never met anyone like me before. He wanted us to be together for ever.' I sigh. 'I thought it was that one big, sweeping, dramatic love we're meant to get in our life and that I was being swept off my feet like in the movies.' I inhale slowly. 'But it turns out love is hard work – *marriage* is hard work. I get that now.'

Jemma's eyebrows are knitted together as she reaches across the table for my hand.

314

I continue, hating the words coming out of my mouth. 'He proposed after only a few months, and we kept it secret because I thought everyone would think we were mad. I guess I was a bit embarrassed. And then, a few weeks later, I found out he was cheating on me.' Even all these months later, the humiliation burns through me. I'm fighting everything in me that says *run*. But Jemma and Harry deserve to hear the whole thing. I take a deep breath.

'Anyway, Brandon persuaded me it was a one off – a final fling before we committed ourselves to each other for ever. I broke things off with him, but he wouldn't leave it alone; sending more flowers, jewellery, other gifts.' I wave at my wrist. 'He got me this stupid high-tech fitness watch and I *hate* it. Anyway, we got back together and it was all perfect again for a few weeks. Then it happened again. He begged for forgiveness and we decided to try again.' I stare down at my hands. 'To be really honest, I felt like I was going a bit mad, like I was addicted to him. We ran off to Nevada and got a licence, then got married the next day.' I shrug, feeling silly. 'I thought it would make things secure between us, like *of course* he wouldn't cheat on me again once we'd said "I do". I was so sure . . .' I trail off.

'We were going to drive to San Francisco for our honeymoon, but I found messages on his phone that night from some other woman. On our wedding night! Can you believe that? He was literally sending messages on Tinder a few hours after we'd exchanged vows.' I add with fury in my voice, 'I left the next day, got on a plane, came home.'

I look at Jemma, whose eyes are full of sympathy. 'But he says he's really changed now. He seems really serious about making this work.' They both look at me with such pity, I feel a surge of humiliation as I continue, 'I'm not the same naïve idiot I was before. I'm in this with open eyes this time. And if it goes wrong again, then I'll know for sure.' I look at Jemma. 'But it's like you said, we're married! I have to give him another shot. And I hurt him, too, didn't I? He said he was broken by me leaving. So I'm ... it's me ... I don't ...'

'It's not your fault.' Harry has been quiet until now, but moves closer, circling his arm around me. His arm is bare and warm and I instantly feel better. My chest fills with new air. 'It's not your fault!' he says again, stronger this time.

'Clara, I'm so sorry,' Jemma whispers. 'I never would've ... I shouldn't have ... if I'd known he ... I don't know why I didn't ask ...' She trails off again and then grabs my hand, repeating, 'I'm so sorry.'

We sit quietly, holding each other, and then Jemma shakes her head.

'What are you *doing*, Clara? Do you actually want to give this guy another chance? Do you really love him? Do you honestly think he's changed?'

The dam inside me breaks and I lean forward, head on arms, and start crying. 'No,' I say through wails. 'No, I don't think he's changed at all! I don't know what I ever saw in him. He's *repulsive* to me! I didn't want to see him back in the UK because I was in thrall to that loser for so many months. I'm a stupid idiot who got sucked back in by his lies and charm. He's a snake.' I look up at them through watery eyes. 'But I'm scared that I'm not strong enough to get away again. He says all these things and it confuses me. I get so overwhelmed.'

'You are strong enough!' Jemma says fiercely. 'You are so strong. You got away from him once and headed for the best place you could – a safe place with your family! – and you worked on yourself. You did what you had to. But you don't have to do it alone this time. We're here with you. We're here for you.' She nods at Harry, who nods back firmly. 'Everyone back home is with you, too. Salma, Amanda and Mum. And Angela – even Buffy! She pretends not to care, but I think she does. She's been sending me loads of messages today, asking if we've found you.' She pauses, looking a bit abashed. 'And asking me to get her Twinkies. I don't even know what Twinkies are.'

Harry squints. 'I think they sell them at the Met?'

I nod, laughing a little. 'I'll get her some at the airport.' I look between them. 'When I come home with you tomorrow.'

They both grin from ear to ear. 'Seriously?' And I nod, relief flooding through me. I don't have to see that arsehole Brandon ever again. I don't love him – I don't think I ever really did. I think I was just running away to find something I already had. Or have now.

'Phew,' Jemma replies with genuine delight. 'I'm afraid of what Salma might've done if we came back without you.' She takes a second. 'When we get home, we'll help you – we'll *all* help you – figure out how to file for a divorce. If that's what you want.'

I start to cry again, using grease-stained napkins to dry my eyes. 'Thank you,' I say at last when I can speak. 'Thanks, both of you. And I'm sorry.' I swallow. 'I've already got a lawyer,' I admit quietly. 'I looked someone up when I first got back to England. I wanted to get the whole thing annulled since it's been less than six months and I totally feel like I got defrauded.' I sigh. 'But apparently an annulment is really hard to get and it's easier just to go through a divorce.' I sit up straighter. 'Either way, I don't ever want to see that twat again.' I brighten, smiling at the pair of them. The knot that's been tight in my stomach since I got here – the bad feeling – has gone at last. 'And I can't wait to get back home with you guys.'

The three of us hold hands across the table in a weird circle, smiling at one another. And for the first time in a week, that voice in the back of my head telling me what a fuck-up I've been finally shuts up.

Chapter Forty

JEMMA

Oh my god I LOVE FLYING! Look at these little care packages they give you! Blindfolds! Headphones! Some other confusing crap! I tap the screen ahead of me as we take off, enjoying the sensation of the plane lifting up into the air. My stomach flips; it's like being on a rollercoaster! And I never thought I even liked rollercoasters, they seemed unnecessarily dangerous. I flick through the array of movies available, marvelling at the choice. Oh my god, and there are *games*, too?! I'm totally going to get into travelling after this. Especially after such an epic couple of days seeing the sights of New York.

I choose a rom-com to watch and immediately ignore it, instead mentally making a list of places I want to see. More of America, for sure. Also Italy, definitely – it's always seemed so romantic. Germany, Denmark, Portugal, Poland, Finland, Slovakia, Sweden, Australia, Spain, Serbia ... there are so many places, so many choices. I feel really excited about what's to come. And maybe Clara will come along on a trip! I know she wants to visit Denmark. Then maybe Harry and Salma can come with me to Germany.

Maybe E can join me in Italy?

I smile, considering that letter in my pocket. I might know his real name now, but he'll always be E to me on some level.

'Hey, babe.' A familiar voice interrupts the movie in my headphones. It's Clara, towering over my row from the aisle. She and Harry are seated nowhere near me, scattered in different directions around the plane.

I sit up to reply, but realize she's not speaking to me. 'Babe, babe?' She waves in the face of the man sitting beside me. He frowns, but removes his headphones.

'Yes?'

'Babe,' Clara begins again to the man, using her best babygirl voice. 'See this gorge young woman sitting beside you?' She gestures at me and I feel myself reddening. What the hell is she doing? Clara beams at the man. 'This is Jemma, my twin sister. That's right, my *twin*! We're the closest two human beings can be, but we've been cruelly forced to sit apart. Any chance I can swap with you? So I can sit with my darling, beloved twin sister? I'm in 24C, up that way.' She pushes her hands together in a prayer position and the man looks between us.

Eventually he sighs and says, 'Fine.' He sounds exhausted as he removes his flight paraphernalia.

'Oh my god, Clara, you're *so* embarrassing!' I hiss at her as he vacates and she collapses into the seat beside me.

'What?!' She blinks innocently at me. 'Just because I'm trying to be a more grown-up, mature version of myself doesn't mean I'm going to stop trying my luck.' She winks. 'And he totally could've said no!'

'We'll get in trouble with the air stewards,' I add, glancing anxiously around me.

'Hey,' she warns, 'I'm trying to be less annoying, but you're meant to be taking more risks and not being such a goody-two-shoes.'

She elbows me and I give her a begrudging smile. 'OK, fine.' I lean back into my seat, and then remember. I nudge Clara. 'Do you fancy a trip to Denmark one day?'

She gives me a quizzical smile. 'Sure! I mean, it'll have to wait until I've paid back some of my debts and clawed together some savings. I'm going to be paying Mum back for a long time, I reckon.'

I nod. 'Very sensible, I'm impressed.'

She grins. 'But I'm so glad you've enjoyed your first big trip abroad.' She pulls a small, plane-issued water bottle out of her bag and cheers me. 'To many more of them!' I clink her plastic bottle with mine and she turns in my direction a little more. 'Hey, I've been meaning to ask – what's going on with the notes at the library? Do you have a name yet?' She doesn't give me a chance to consider whether to lie before she's off again. 'Because I totally have a theory!' She grins at me excitedly. 'Don't get annoyed when I say this, OK? Just hear me out . . .' She gives me half a second and I frown, waiting. 'I think the man writing the love notes to you might be ...' she leaves a dramatic beat of silence before adding, ' ... Harry.'

I burst out laughing so hard, the person in front turns around to shoot a disparaging look, while the kid behind kicks my seat.

'Harry?' I repeat through giggles, disbelief in my voice.

Clara looks a bit offended by my reaction. 'Yes! It could be. You know I think you guys would be perfect for each other and I *totally* think he has a thing for you.' She ticks items off her fingers. 'He knew *Too Good to Be True* was your favourite book and that you check it out of the library constantly. He knew your schedule so he could make sure he never returned it or left a note when you were there to spot him. He's been encouraging you to reply the whole time, hasn't he? He even knew exactly what to say in those notes to win you over. Because he *knows* you.'

I try not to laugh again, but I can't help it. 'It's not Harry,' I say with amused certainty. 'It's one hundred million per cent *not* Harry.' She looks perturbed as I shake my head, continuing, 'I know it's not him. And also – you absolute bloody idiot – Harry's not into me, which I know for a fact, because he's clearly, *obviously*' – I pause to triple check she's definitely listening – 'without any question ... madly in love with *you*.' I let this sink in for a second before I hit her with the second big revelation. 'And, Clara, you moron, you're also in love with him.'

Clara shakes her head, snorting. 'With *Harry*? Fuck off!' She forces a laugh. 'Harry's not ... I'm not ... He's, like, such a boring ... He likes, y'know, *Star Wars* and action movies, and he's, like ... *nice*. Jem, he couldn't be *less* my type. I like bad boys! I go for shitheads who ... I ... I swear to god, I would never ever, ever ... I mean, yes obviously he's totally the best. He's too good for me, really. He's lovely and fun and sweet and so ... But I ...' She trails off, her eyes suddenly widening in abject horror. 'Oh my god I do! Jemma, oh god, I love him. I love Harry. I'm, like, *desperately* in love with him.' She turns to me in disgust. 'Ew! Jesus! How did this happen?! How could I let this happen?'

I shrug, trying not to laugh some more. I want her to take this seriously and really hear what I'm saying. 'Why wouldn't you be in love with him? He's wonderful and handsome. And just because it hasn't been some dramatic thing doesn't mean it's not super romantic.'

'But wait, it can't be love,' Clara says impatiently, her eyes getting even wider and more confused. 'He's nice to me, he's my friend. He's thoughtful and kind. What kind of monster does that make him underneath?'

I shake my head. 'No monster. Just a real life, flawed, sometimes-idiotic, sometimes pompous, sometimes-brilliant human man.' I side-smile at her. 'One who is crazy about you. Like crazy-crazy. Like, forces your sister to realize what a cow she's been and flies with her to America to bring you home kind of crazy.'

She nods dumbly, looking suddenly intensely vulnerable. 'Oh my god, Jem, this is really scary stuff.' She regards me fearfully. 'Are you *sure* he's into me, too?'

I nod, smiling. 'I know you've only dated shitheads and it's probably scarier to like someone who could give you a healthy, kind, compassionate sort of love, but you can trust this. Believe me.' She nods with understanding, then leaps up out of her seat, nearly knocking over a passing steward who glares at her suspiciously.

'Ma'am, is this actually your seat?' he asks, and Clara grabs him by the shoulder.

'Nope! But I'm leaving, don't worry. I need to go find my friend Harry and tell him I love him. Isn't that ridiculous?!' The steward gapes at her and she turns on her heel to go before suddenly turning back. Her eyes are wild and excited. 'But hold on, before I go, you said you knew for sure it wasn't Harry writing your notes. Does that mean you have a name? Who is he?'

I reach into my coat pocket and pull out the envelope, waving it. Then I make a face. 'I'm afraid it's a total anti-climax. He told me his name, and it's no one we know.' Her face falls with disappointment as I add, 'He's called Eliot. He's a random stranger.'

Chapter Forty-One

CLARA

I speed-walk through the plane, looking for Harry's familiar messy hair. I'm so pumped up; so ready to tell him how I feel.

Jesus Christ, I'm going to tell a boy I like him. I haven't done anything like this since I was a teenager. I haven't put myself on the line like this, maybe ever.

And oh god, what if he doesn't feel the same?

I know Jemma said he does, but what does she know? She hasn't had a proper boyfriend before.

And I married a cheating, love-bombing narcissist on a whim, so who am I to talk?

My heart is pounding out of my chest as I spot his dark hair on the far side of the plane. There's a whole row of seats between us.

'Harry!' I yell spontaneously. A few heads between us turn, mostly with irritation. Harry's does not. He's asleep, I realize. Bugger.

Ugh, I'm on the wrong side of the plane, I'll have to go all the way to the other end to get to his aisle. Unless I'm willing to climb across the laps of three people. Would they mind? I shift back and forth for a second, unsure what to do, and then I shout again. 'Harry?' I'm louder this time and a few people tut. Some make a show of turning away or putting on their headphones. I'm about to shout again, when I make eye contact with the woman beside him. I gesture for her to wake him up; she looks alarmed. I wave again, more insistent this time, and she gives in, gently nudging the big lug. Harry jerks awake, looking confused and sleepy. It makes my heart squeeze, seeing him like this; all vulnerable and uncertain. Oh god, I love him so much.

I see the woman mouth something to him and he turns in my direction, his eyebrows knotted with confusion and sleep.

'Sorry, mate,' I call out to him across the plane. 'Are you feeling rough?'

He tries to sit up properly, still half asleep, but replies after a moment, 'Not too bad, just tired.' I stare at him, frozen, and he stares back, waiting. His bafflement is clear. Oh god, I'm screwing this whole thing up. Eventually he calls out, 'Um, do you maybe want to get over here somehow and sit down?'

I nod slowly, then shake my head. I don't know what to say and I can't bring myself to move. Someone clambers past me, heading for the loo, and still I stand there, staring helplessly over at Harry.

And suddenly I'm speaking, breathing too hard.

'I've been fighting this for a while now, Haz, but I can't anymore. I can't push down these feelings. I have to tell you right now – right this second – how much I genuinely like and fancy you.' I take a deep, shuddery breath, trying not to be put off by the alarm on his face. 'I know telling you this is ridiculous and everyone we know – all my family and friends – will think I'm mad. I mean, I *also* think I'm mad, for the record.' I shake my head, knowing this isn't going well. 'Like, we're *totally* wrong for each other. No one would put us together as a couple. It's completely irrational and unlikely, but I can't help how I feel. I think I'm realizing now that I've fancied you right from that first day, from the first moment. When I saw you outside my mum's house. You gave the door this adorably rubbish, tentative knock that no one would've heard, and I remember my chest filling with – I don't know – something like *admiration*, despite my better judgement. Oh god, it's all so stupid and ridiculous – and *embarrassing!*' I pause, feeling many eyes on me. An air steward calls across the plane at me to *sit down, miss*. Someone a few rows back starts sarcastically slow-clapping me. I ignore it all. 'Haz, this is all making me feel really shit and weird, so can you just let me off the hook and tell me if you're interested? At least in a shag or something?'

He eyeballs me for a moment, then snorts. 'Clara—' he begins, trying to stand up but trapped by his seatbelt.

'You doofus,' I yell at him, laughing. 'I can't believe I fancy you. I'm so disgusted with myself.'

He releases the belt and runs up the plane. I run along my aisle to meet him at the break in the seats. Finally face to face, we just look at each other for a moment, breathing hard.

And then he takes my face in his hands and he kisses me.

It is the most romantic, sincere, tender moment of my life – until a trolley slams into my ankles. The steward driving it calls out sternly, 'You shouldn't be out here, please return to your seats.'

Harry and I pull apart, laughing some more, and staring at each other. I really do fancy him so much. How could I not have noticed? It's so completely obvious.

'You know your speech was absolutely terrible,' he tells me as we walk hand in hand back towards his seat. 'Like, *really* bad. There was so little effort at civility. You basically told me that you like me against your will, against all reason and against everything you care about.' He laughs and I grimace.

'Sorry. It was my first attempt at professing undying love to someone.'

He pauses at this. 'Love?'

I feel myself pale. I didn't actually use that word, did I? Fuck. 'God no!' I try to regain some ground. 'That is *rank*. I said ... glove. Undying glove. Please try to listen to the words I say and not make nonsense guesses, Haz.'

He laughs again. 'God, you're a pain in the arse, Clara,' he tells me affectionately. 'But I do want you to know that I glove you, too.'

Beside us, a passenger groans. 'Ugh, you two are the absolute worst.' She starts to get up, gathering her things. 'Where are you sitting, young lady? I'll swap with you.'

I gleefully thank her, pointing in Jemma's direction, and then we collapse into the seats, kissing some more. I can't believe I get to just . . . kiss him? Whenever I want? It's so lovely.

After a moment, Harry pauses. 'Not to ruin the moment, but what about . . . him?'

I frown. 'Him who?' I gasp. 'Do you mean Brandon? God, I never want anything to do with that guy, ever again. I didn't leave without a word this time, I messaged to tell him it was a million per cent over – for ever. I hate his guts. When I went to grab my stuff from Enya's, she told me he'd been banging half our friendship group since I've been gone as well! He's a total arsehole, really. I can see straight through him and I feel like such a fool that I believed in him. How I felt about him, even at our best, doesn't compare—'

Harry shakes his head, half laughing. 'No, no, I mean Milo Samuels! The *Book Boyfriend* actor. Have you forgotten about him already? We went through so much to find him and help you make a connection. I saw the way you looked at him. And I can't deny he's awesome! He's, like, the coolest guy I've ever met. I would *totally* fancy him if—'

I laugh, cutting off his obsessive fan-boying. 'Well, sure, he's *hot*.' At Harry's crestfallen face, I add, 'But not as hot as you!' I pause. 'Look, sure, I know I went a little mad over him for a minute. I think I was just looking for an escape. Something to keep me distracted from what had happened over in New York.' I realize as I say this that somewhere inside me, I've known all along that it was just made up. It was easier to focus on the fantasy than face up to my lame, everyday life. I look at Harry properly. 'This is real between us. It feels so real.' I add anxiously, 'Is it real for you, too?'

He nods a lot. 'Really, really real.' We kiss a second time and my stomach flips over again and again. I want to do this with him for ever.

'Also,' I say, pulling away, 'when I actually had a proper chat with Milo, he wasn't exactly . . . I mean . . .' I grimace. 'I dunno, he just wasn't really my bag. I'd built up this dream man – some fictional ideal – in my head. He wasn't what I'd imagined. I don't think we really had anything in common. He had more in common with Jemma than me!'

Harry raises an eyebrow. '*We* have nothing in common.'

I snort. 'Well, yeah, but we have nothing in common in, like, a fun way. We may not have the same interests, but we are the same kind of silly. We can both laugh at ourselves. We love a night out and we love people. Milo seemed kind of . . . low key and shy. Nice, sure! But happier at home on his own with old people telly on.' I make a face. 'I liked him as a person but I think the novelty of his hotness would've worn off pretty quickly.' I brighten. 'He really would be perfect for Jemma – maybe we should try to get them together instead!'

'Fair enough,' Harry says smiling, and I can tell he's re-assured. I hope so. I hope I can always make him feel safe, secure and wanted, like the way he makes me feel.

'Can we kiss some more now?' I ask, raising my eyebrows at his obliging smile.

'I think that would be acceptable,' he says, nodding and moving in closer.

Chapter Forty-Two

JEMMA

'God, Clara' – I roll my eyes affectionately – 'you're on Instagram *again*? Don't you get bored of looking at the same five profiles the algorithm shows you over and over?'

'Never.' She shakes her head vehemently. 'I love it.' She pauses. 'I get so excited when I see a green story on Instagram Stories. Like I'm part of the in-crowd and it's totally going to be something exclusive and exciting, just for the chosen few. I'm like, "Ooh, I can't belieeeeeeeeve I'm in the inner circle – the shortlist of cool people!" – and then it's *always* more pictures of people's boring babies.' She rolls her eyes, and Harry – whose lap she's sitting on – laughs and squeezes her.

These two are already irritating the fuck out of everyone with their non-stop love-in.

Obviously I'm incredibly happy for them, but yeughhhh.

'Anyone for brownies?' Angela calls, entering the living room with a large plate of cakes. She adds reproachfully, 'Since you ate every single one the other night . . .'

'Over here!' Buffy shouts, throwing herself onto the sofa and reaching for a brownie and the TV remote control.

The wedding is tomorrow and we're having a big old sleepover as a sort of hen night stand-in. Because literally nobody was up for a hen do. Especially not me, Clara and Harry who are still jetlagged to buggery from our flying visit to the States.

So no penis straws, no creepy stripper and no booze. Just the core gang of us – Mum, Angela, Buffy, me, Clara, Harry and Salma – eating loads of lovely food and falling asleep in front of the TV, where we've just watched the final episode of *Book Boyfriend* on catch-up. Not that I have any idea what's going on, having watched so little of it. And it's so different from my novel.

I can't tell you what a joyful moment it was, turning up on Mum's doorstep with Clara in tow. Mum cried absolute buckets. And even more so when we revealed she and Harry were dating. Though – after that fake engagement thingy a few months ago – she's taken some convincing that it's legit. Seeing them spend the last three hours with their tongues down each other's throats has probably helped.

'I've just spent £150 to avoid a £2.99 delivery charge,' Salma announces, looking up from her phone. 'Someone take this device away from me.'

'Can someone take mine, too?' Clara begs, holding her phone in the air. 'Amanda won't stop sending weepy voice notes about me being back.'

I collect both, throwing the phones into the pot pourri on the coffee table.

'They're going to smell great when you get them back,' I tell Salma and Clara, who grin at me and then each other.

'Shall we watch a film?' Mum suggests, arriving in the doorway holding bowls of crisps this time.

'How about *Die Hard 2*?' says Harry innocently, as Clara squeals a protest.

'Nothing scary,' I shout over the din. 'I can never sleep after all that adrenaline.'

'I thought you'd love horror movies,' Angela says from the sofa, sounding confused. I blink at her and she continues, 'You're a ghostwriter, aren't you? You write ghost stories.'

Clara snorts and Buffy moans with embarrassment. 'Er,' I begin as nicely as I can, 'that's not actually what a ghostwriter is, Angela.' I sigh. 'And technically I'm not even a ghostwriter – I assist.'

'You could be, though,' Clara says, bouncing slightly on Harry's right leg as he winces. 'Why don't you pitch directly to the publisher or get your own agent? You must've made some contacts by now!'

I blush, feeling self-conscious as the room turns to me. 'Maybe one day.'

Clara raises a finger importantly. 'Now is the time for risk taking and chasing the big dreams, dude!'

I smile shyly. 'I have been thinking about it actually. I've got a proposal I've been quietly working on and I think it's ready to submit to some agents.' I sit up straighter. 'You're right, it's time. I'm going to bite the bullet and send it out.'

'Oh Jemma, that's brilliant!' Clara claps her hands excitedly as Salma regards me proudly.

'You can call me Jim-Jems if you want,' I tell my sister, shrugging like I couldn't care less. But I do actually. I've decided I quite like being Jim-Jems.

Clara smiles at me, a little misty-eyed. 'OK, you got it, Jim-Jems. I can't wait to read your first solo author venture in the near future.'

I grin at her. 'Speaking of reading and jobs—'

'Ugh, don't remind me!' she wails, burying her face into Harry's shoulder.

'What about the library?' I ask innocently, and she looks up, pouting.

'What are you talking about? I didn't turn up on my actual first day. That's kind of frowned upon by employers, I believe.'

I smirk at her. 'I *may* have told them you had a brutal stomach bug and were throwing up all over the place this whole week. Anita was really lovely about it.' I make a face. 'Obviously Mack was an arsehole but Anita told him to shut up. They said you can start next week – as long as you're feeling better.'

Clara leaps up. 'No way!' She hugs me hard and I let her. 'You're the best sister in the universe. Thank you so much!'

Salma leans in impatiently. 'Speaking of the library, where

are we with the note writer, Eliot? You've replied, right? Have you made plans to meet up?'

I squint at a point above her head. 'Ummmmm ...'

She gasps. 'You haven't replied!' she says accusingly. 'Why the hell not? You asked him for his name, like, two weeks ago! Were you hoping it would be someone you knew? Was there someone particular you wanted it to be?'

'I was hoping it would be the sexy mountaineer,' Clara says dreamily. 'He's perfect boyfriend material, with the exception of his missing toes.' Harry grabs at her waist and she giggles, falling into him for another kiss.

'No, it's not that!' I protest. 'It's just ... well, it *has* been a busy week since I collected the note. Give me a break! I barely had a chance to read it properly before we were flying across the Atlantic to fetch a wayward child.'

'Who's happening, what?' Clara looks up from Harry's mouth, her eyes unfocused and hazy. 'What am I?'

'Never mind,' I tell her, smiling warmly. 'You get back to checking Harry's saliva pH levels.'

Salma rolls her eyes. 'So come on then, was the last note not all that exciting? What did it actually say? Please read it to us.'

I go to fetch it from my coat pocket, where it's been sitting on and off since I retrieved it from *Too Good to Be True* well over a week ago.

As I re-enter the living room, Salma and Clara are filling Mum, Angela and Buffy in on the whole saga. They are wide-eyed, enraptured by the story of a pair of strangers swapping notes via a library book. I feel embarrassed as they all look up at me, one by one, universally awed by the romance.

'So you have this man's name?' Mum asks, her voice high and enthralled. 'You know who he is? But you also *don't* know who he is? So he could be a serial killer?'

I shake my head and Salma whips the note from my grasp. 'I'll read it aloud,' she announces excitedly, unfolding the piece of paper.

She clears her throat, and begins reading to a captivated audience.

Well hi, Jemma, what a genuinely lovely name.

I always think names define us, don't you?

Like, Lyndseys – however they spell it – are always no nonsense go-getters, aren't they? And Millys and Mollys always have the biggest hearts. Fatimas are always super cool. Lucys are always hilarious. Aishas are fashionable. And I think Jemmas are kind and funny and – I'm hoping – might want to meet up with me one day soon. My name is Eliot, I'm 32, and yes – obviously my mum named me for George Eliot. If she could've got away with calling me the author's real name, Mary Ann Evans, she would've. I can't remember if I've mentioned, but she was a librarian, so everything had to be book themed for her. And it's why I still make sure I check books out regularly instead of buying them. My brother got the same treatment, by the way. He's called Austen – I'm sure you can guess who that's honouring. We were both into drama as kids, and even the plays we did had to be book themed!

Anyway, it's really nice to meet you, Jemma. If you'd be keen to meet in person, I can't promise a rose in the lapel, but I could wear tiger print in honour of The Tiger Who Came to Tea, *or green for* The Very Hungry Caterpillar. *Maybe we could go for dinner, and eat one shortbread, two chocolate Hobnobs, three digestives, four jaffa cakes, five Viennese whirls (or custard creams) and then a whole box of chocolate fingers. Never forgetting the solitary Garibaldi for afters.*

Hoping to hear from you soon.

Eliot x

God, that's a great note. I've been wandering around with all of that in my pocket for a whole week – even taking it with me on the aeroplane! – and yet I'd barely taken any of it in, beyond his name. I was so focused on that Eliot part – on what it meant – that I hadn't really absorbed the rest of it. There's such a warmth to him, such a loveliness. And I immediately know I want to meet this guy. I have real feelings for him, I realize. I don't care what he looks like and I don't care that he's a complete stranger, I want to see him; to touch him.

'What a sweetheart!' Mum announces. 'But that sounds like an awful lot of biscuits he's proposing you eat between you.' She sounds worried. 'Especially for a first date! Goodness! You'll spend all night high as a kite on E numbers.' She frowns, looking at Salma. 'And why would he wear tiger print? Is that in fashion these days?'

Salma laughs. 'Tiger print is a neutral,' she says, eyeballing me.

'He sounds really delightful,' Angela declares happily. 'Although what's wrong with a nice rich tea or Bourbon biscuit?' She pauses. 'Did you know Brits eat more biscuits than anywhere else on earth? We consume 204 million biscuits a day.'

I shake my head in amazement. 'You know stuff like that, but you don't know what a ghostwriter is?'

Angela raises her eyebrows in confusion and takes another shot. 'So you write about ghosting? I've heard about ghosting! Before I met your mum I got ghosted quite a few times!'

'Never mind,' I mumble, as Buffy whines with frustration.

'Can you stop going off on fucking tangents?' Buffy shouts. 'Look, I didn't understand any of that dumb note, but if a real life living man is willing to meet up with *you*' – she jabs a finger in my direction like I'm the most disgusting creature to walk the earth – 'then you should probably take him up on it.' She gives me a withering look. 'It's not like you've got many choices. Especially at *your* age.' She smirks. 'Although, hello, if you've ignored him and this note for a couple of weeks when he's put his heart on the line like that, he's probably found someone else by now. I bet you'll never hear from him again!'

I stare at her, blinking hard. 'Shit,' I reply quietly, as alarm fills my chest. She's right. We'd been exchanging regular notes for months, and now I've disappeared completely! He must think I'm blowing him off. He must think that the name Eliot was a dealbreaker for me and I'm no longer interested. Oh god, have I really missed my chance? What if he never comes back to the library again? It's not like he's included a number or a surname in this note – I can't just look him up! OH GOD I'VE FUCKED THIS UP!

Salma catches my panicked expression. 'Don't listen to her, Jem!' she says with confidence. 'There's no way he'd give up on you after just a bit of silence.'

I shake my head, knowing *I* would have, if it were me. If I'd written a note like this – so heartfelt and lovely; putting myself on the line like this – and he hadn't replied, I'd have quit my library membership and hidden in my room for the next six months.

'I've messed up,' I say. 'I was so obsessed with my own stuff and worrying about ruining this magic little corner of my life, that I've gone and done exactly that: I've ruined it.'

'Don't say that!' Mum cries, looking agonized. 'Do you really think?'

'You should reply right now!' Angela says with determination. 'We'll get it into your book.'

Salma checks her watch. 'It's seven o' clock at night! It'll have to wait until tomorrow.'

I stand up. 'No, it doesn't have to! The library isn't staffed at this hour, but there's access all evening!' I pull out my purse, brandishing the fob that lets me in, out of hours. 'I'll go right now,' I say breathlessly.

Maybe it's not too late. There's a chance, right? I have to try!

'Let's all go!' Salma says excitedly. 'Right now!'

'Yeah!' Buffy actually looks enthusiastic, as Angela and Mum regard each other with bright eyes.

'Ummmmm.' Clara makes a weird noise as we all grab at coats and bags. 'Um, look, there are loads of you, right?' She glances over at Harry, who nods at her encouragingly.

'Right, exactly!' he says, trying to swallow down obvious excitement. 'You don't really need us, do you, guys? We're just going to . . . I mean, I'm actually not feeling that well, y'know . . . um, yeah, I might just . . . get an early night.' He elaborately fake yawns and Clara joins in.

'Yeah, gosh, boy, am I tired!' She blows out her cheeks really unconvincingly. 'Huge day, *massive* day tomorrow' – she gestures at Mum and Angela who look amused, but nod along – 'and it's my first time as a bridesmaid. I would *not* want to mess that up. So I'll probably, y'know' – she nods at Harry again as they both start backing away and out of the living room – 'just get an early night so I'm – we're – well rested, yeah? So . . . yeah! See you guys later?'

'Good luuuuuuck!' Harry yells as they both take off running towards the stairs, hand in hand.

The rest of us look at each other and start laughing. Horny idiots.

Chapter Forty-Three

CLARA

I am immensely relieved to report that sex with Harry is absolutely brilliant. Bloody fantastic. MAGICAL.

We've done it three times now, and each time has been better than the last. I even had a couple of orgasms! I'm delighted.

'I'm back!' Harry announces from the bedroom doorway, bouncing back onto the duvet, naked and gorgeous. He hands over the tub of ice cream he's been to fetch from the kitchen.

I sigh happily and point at his crotch. 'That is such a lovely penis, is it all for me?'

'You bet,' he says, grinning and offering up a spoon. I take it, still staring at his dangly bits as I remove the plastic from the lid. 'Honestly, though, Haz, it's really, *really* lovely. I must've been a super nice person in a previous life to deserve this. I was probably, like, Tom Hanks or Dolly Parton.'

'Both still alive,' he points out, reaching over to steal a scoop of my Phish Food.

'Oh.' I see the flaw in my logic, but am instantly distracted by the taste of creamy fat and sugar. 'Aaah man,' I breathe out blissfully, 'I am so happy with my life choices.'

Harry glances over affectionately. 'Aw, Clara!' He strokes my leg. 'That's actually genuinely sweet of you.' He beams. 'I glove you.'

I smile back at him. He doesn't need to know I was actually referring to this massive tub of ice cream, not the awesome sex we just had.

He rolls closer, reaching over and gently stroking one of my boobs.

'Wow, this is really nice too,' he murmurs.

'Yeah, you like that?' I say. 'I have another one over here.' I gesture at my other tit and he puts down his spoon to cup both.

'I like this one best,' he says decisively, lightly bouncing the right one in his palm.

'Me too!' I say delightedly. 'It's always been my favourite.' I grin at him. 'You're so lucky to have me and my one nice boob.'

He frowns. 'Hey, I'm not saying I don't like lefty, I really do! I'm just saying there's no point pretending I don't have favourites. The right one just has that je ne sais quoi. It's just got a bit more sass, y'know?'

'I get it,' I say, nodding. I do get it, I get *him*. Then I sigh heavily, checking the time on my phone. It's late. 'They're still not back.'

He shakes his head, helping himself to more ice cream. 'No, but maybe that's a good sign? Like, maybe they found Eliot, the note man, in the library waiting for Jem, and now they're snogging each other's faces off and deciding on a favourite boob.'

'I hope so,' I say, perking up. 'I feel a bit bad about not going along with them all. Do you think we were really out of order?'

'I feel zero guilt,' Harry says happily, squeezing righty again. He pauses and looks up. 'But I think it's really nice that you're worrying about Jemma.' He smiles softly. 'Don't take this the wrong way, but I don't think you'd have given not going along a second thought a few months ago.'

I hit him lightly with a pillow, but feel warm inside. I do feel like I've grown up a bit recently. I feel like I'm surrounded by people who care about me – and I care about them. 'I haven't changed that much,' I point out, laughing. 'I still didn't actually go along to offer any support.'

Harry looks concerned. 'I do really hope it works out. This Eliot dude sounded like a genuinely decent guy in that last note, didn't he? And Jemma deserves someone great.'

I widen my eyes. 'You were listening earlier when they read it out?' I shake my head. 'When Salma started reading, I was too busy licking that sensitive bit behind your ear.'

He snorts. 'Ohh, I remember. You're a very good girlfriend.'

I look over at him. 'Girlfriend?'

He grins. 'If you're up for it?'

I nod silently, feeling a lot of emotions overwhelming me at once. He takes my hand and squeezes it.

Downstairs the front door slams and we both scramble to throw on clothes. I reach the landing first, yelling over the banister, 'How did it go? What happened?'

I throw myself down the stairs, almost winding myself on the chest of drawers, still sitting in the hallway. I really should do something about it.

'Was there a new note? Did you find him? Are you and Eliot in love now?' I'm breathless as I glance anxiously between Jemma, Salma, Angela, Mum and Buffy. They are a collective expression of misery.

Jemma slowly shakes her head, staring down at the ground. She pulls a note out of her pocket and hands it over. I feel Harry behind me and he reads over my shoulder.

Hi Jemma,

It's been just over a week since I left you the last note and I'm guessing that means you've made your decision. For the record, I don't blame you at all. I know it was a lot — asking you to meet up with me. I'm sorry if it made you uncomfortable — I'm really sorry. I want you to know how much I've loved talking to you. It meant a lot, being able to talk about books, and other silly things. I loved being able to share this passion with you. I won't send any more notes after this one, I'd hate for you to feel under pressure to reply. I just wanted to say goodbye, I guess, and no hard feelings. In fact, lots of soft, warm, biscuity feelings. I still think you're really wonderful and I won't ever forget how special this was. You made me feel seen and

more like myself during a weird time in my life. Thanks,
Jemma.
    Yours,
    Eliot x

I gasp. 'No!' I cry, genuinely devastated. 'Have you written back? He might come back just in case?'

Jemma doesn't say anything and Salma sighs, explaining, 'We sat there for ages while Jem tried to come up with something to write back.' She glances at Jemma with sympathetic eyes. 'In the end, we left a short, simple note saying she was really sorry and that she'd been away.'

Jemma pipes up, 'I put my phone number on there just in case.' She looks crestfallen. 'But he won't be back. I know he won't, I can feel it. I'll probably get a text in a few months from some other creep who got the book out and found my number.'

Everyone falls silent and the group's disappointment fills the hallway. I'm heartbroken for Jemma.

'Let's all get to bed,' Jemma says at last, cutting through the awful atmosphere. She glances at Mum and Angela with forced excitement. 'Tomorrow is going to be so lovely, and we can't let this silly let-down taint it. I can't wait to see you two get married.' We all crowd in for a cuddle, holding one another for the next couple of minutes. Even Buffy allows herself to be group-comforted. Eventually, we disengage, each of us heading back to our own rooms to get no sleep; half excited for what's to come, half sad for what's happened.

Chapter Forty-Four

JEMMA

I never cry; I hate crying. Except I seem to be crying a lot right now – like a *lot* lot. But they're nice tears; happy tears. Definitely happy tears.

We've just finished the ceremony, where Mum and Angela exchanged personalized vows and a sweet little kiss. There were beautiful speeches that also managed to squeeze in a cool fact from Angela about a wedding in 1993 with thirty thousand guests. The officiant – (Va)Gina – was great and fun, moving us to tears in one moment, then making us laugh the next. It was all just . . . perfect.

And now we're heading to a nearby pub, where lunch is waiting for us.

We bundle in the door, all speaking at once, full of happiness and emotions.

It's the core family, along with Salma, Harry, plus a handful of Great-Aunts thrown in for good measure. Clara is delighting in torturing them about Harry – after all, the last time they saw these two, they were faking an engagement. But there's definitely nothing fake about all the kissing and hand holding today. Meanwhile Buffy is calling the Great-Aunts *sluts* in a really casual and upsetting way.

And I'm still crying, silent tears rolling down my face as we take our seats.

'This way, sluts!' Buffy calls to the stragglers now, and I catch several Great-Aunt tuts.

I fiddle with my paper napkin, trying not to think about things.

It's been a really lovely day and I've barely even given a second thought to E – to Eliot.

Barely a thought.

Some *small* thoughts, but few and far between.

OK, a handful of possibly larger thoughts, but it definitely hasn't affected how special the day has been. These tears are *all* happy tears and definitely not for him. This is joy. Pure joy for my wonderful, kind, generous mum who has always put everyone else first, and has – at last – focused on her own happiness. I look over at Angela as everyone settles into seats, making small talk about the gorgeousness of the day. Mum has found someone really special and I couldn't be more thrilled for her.

The waiter loudly asks if anyone wants anything and we all ignore him, still too busy talking excitedly. I let out a small sob, and beside me, Clara leans in. 'Are you OK, Jim-Jems?'

'Yep!' I say in a low, strangled voice and Salma joins us, crouching down by my chair. 'These are all happy tears!' I insist to their concerned faces. 'Everything has worked out so perfectly. Mum and Angela are married, you and Harry are in love.' I gesture towards Harry, who is also watching our exchange from across the table, his brow furrowed. 'No, really!' I insist. 'Please stop all looking so concerned, I'm fine! Everything has worked out how it's supposed to. The mountaineering memoir I've been working on is finished now, too. I just had an email from my boss to say he's really pleased and submitted it to the publisher – so no more meetings with sexy Aarav!' I try to laugh, which feels very strange, as tears continue to fall. 'And the whole, silly note thing . . .' I wave my hand dismissively. 'It was mad! I don't know why I got so obsessed. I accused Clara of falling in love with a fantasy when she was chasing that Milo actor around London, but I've been doing the same thing!' I pause, realizing how true this is. 'This guy Eliot, whoever he was, and our conversations, it was all just another fantasy world to hide in. It's time I stopped writing notes to imaginary men and start living in the real world. I'm going to be braver and stronger and experience life outside of fiction and novels.' I take a deep breath, the tears drying up at last. 'I need to stop re-reading the same old tattered book from the library and get out there. It's time to live my life.' I bark a laugh and add, 'Maybe I'll even get on Tinder.'

Clara and Salma are silent for a moment, regarding me. And then Salma takes a deep breath. 'No.'

I glance up at her. 'Huh?'

'No,' she says again, her tone mild. 'Nope, nah, negative.'

She glares at me. 'I'm not letting you give up on this.' She pauses. 'Look, I agree to some extent that you should get out there more and experience life. But we're already going to do that! Haven't we already started talking about travelling to Denmark in the autumn?' She frowns. 'But there's nothing wrong with re-reading books and enjoying a fantasy. *And*,' she exaggerates her words, 'Eliot was not a fantasy! Sure, you don't know what he looks like, but you guys exchanged messages for – what? – months! You got to know each other and shared things. He told you stuff about his life and his values and his family.' She inhales sharply. 'In fact, look, surely we could find him from clues in the notes! He's a big library fan, right? We know that much, maybe we could break into the library computers to find his surname. Or get Clara to sneak a look when she's working there!'

Harry stands up. 'MACK!' he shouts and we all look at him, startled. He lowers his voice, hissing now, 'What if it's that guy Mack? I've heard you guys talking about him a lot in the last few months. What if it's him?'

I gasp. 'He did start working there around the same time E began checking out *Too Good to Be True*.'

Clara, Salma and I regard each other, wide-eyed and silent for a minute, before erupting into the wildest peals of laughter.

Harry looks put out. 'Why are you all laughing? It sounds pretty possible to me.'

'You don't know him,' Clara shrieks through tears. 'You only met him at kickboxing, which was not enough to fully

349

enjoy the Mack experience. He's awful, Haz. Sure, I mean, he has his moments of being fake nice on occasion, but mostly he's an absolute, irredeemable arse.'

'He really is!' I agree wholeheartedly. 'Honestly, mate, I've searched so hard for a secretly decent person under all that broodiness, but Mack's just a dick. There have been moments where I thought maybe he had a sad, damaged past or a complicated present, but nope, I don't think so. I reckon some people are just plain old arseholes – and he's one of them!'

Salma is first to stop howling. 'Guys, I have to confess something.' She looks mortified. 'I shagged him! I was seduced by all those brooding black clothes and sexy sullen glares. We did it one time and it was awful. Lasted three seconds and he asked me to leave immediately afterwards – but not before trying to get me involved in a multi-level marketing scheme.'

'Nooooooo!' I scream, as Clara squeals with delight.

'A multi-level marketing scheme?!' Harry looks horrified as Salma nods.

'Yep,' she says, enjoying the horror she's inflicting. 'He ended up telling me how he's really into bitcoin and recently lost his elderly dad's savings on one of those betting apps.'

'Oh my god,' I breathe out. 'That's why he always seemed so upset at the library, fiddling about on his phone or computer so much. And why he has a second job at a wedding cake shop!' I glance over at Mum and Angela down the end of the table. They're joyfully feeding each other red velvet cake. Bless them.

'Please don't sleep with any more dickheads like him,'

Clara implores Salma. 'Honestly, I can't recommend a nice guy highly enough.' She and Harry beam at each other and Salma laughs warmly.

'Don't worry, I can safely say I'm never going near Mack again.' She glances anxiously at me and I nod encouragingly. 'Actually, Jemma set me up on a date with her sexy mountaineer Aarav last week. We had a great time. We're going out again this weekend.'

There are excitable gasps around the table and I grin with delight, feeling proud of my part in this budding new romance.

Salma waves away happy questions, zeroing back in on me. 'But seriously, we are all smart, inquisitive people who can figure this out. Who is Eliot?' She considers this. 'That penultimate note – the one where he told you his first name – had plenty of info about his life.' She ticks facts off. 'Name, Eliot, a drama club kid, Mum's a librarian, he has a brother called Austen.' She trails off, realizing this isn't that much. 'There must be loads more in the rest of your notes, surely? We must be able to put this together.'

I consider this. Is she right? Should I keep trying to find him? I give myself an internal pat down. The feelings I have for him do *seem* real. I like him, I really do. I loved speaking to him. I feel terrible that I've hurt him. I *miss* him.

On the other side of me, Clara stands up suddenly. 'Wait,' she says loudly, causing some Great-Aunts to start with their tutting again, 'everyone just hold on!' She looks stricken, her face pale.

'Er, holding,' I say mildly, as Harry stands up too, coming over and touching Clara on the arm.

'What's the matter?' he asks so nicely, with such concern. God, they're cute.

'Oh my god,' Clara mutters. 'Oh my *god!*' She scrambles for her phone and we collectively look at one another. What's the matter with her? She jabs at the buttons furiously and looks up at me after a few seconds, wild-eyed. 'OH MY GOD!' she says again, even louder this time, and I swallow hard.

'What's going on?' I ask nervously, glancing fearfully around the table at Mum and Angela, who reflect my expression of confusion.

'Jemma!' Clara splutters, waving her phone in the air. 'JEMMA!'

'What is it?' Salma asks, sounding exasperated.

Clara crosses the room, getting too close to my face. 'Jem,' she says quietly now. 'It's fucking Milo Samuels.'

I shake my head. 'What? What are you *talking* about?'

'Eliot!' she exclaims. 'It's him! It's Milo! It's the *Book Boyfriend* actor! That's probably why he's been so obsessed with reading that novel in the last year or so! Because he got the part of George and was filming the series. He obviously wanted to re-read the source material over and over.'

She's mad. She's completely lost it.

Catching my expression, she groans impatiently. 'I'm serious, Jem! It's him! That mum librarian thing rang a bell. I remembered reading an interview with him once where he mentioned it. And I just double checked Wikipedia – his full name is Eliot Milo Samuels. He goes by Milo for work, and Eliot at home with his family – which *includes a brother called Austen!*'

I gape at her, her words sinking in. It's ... my note writer ... my E is ... Eliot is ...? No, surely this is nonsense. It's got to be nonsense! But if it's true ...? Then – oh god! – I gave him such a hard time at that party when I was drunk! I was awful to him, ranting away about him ruining my favourite book. He thought I was mad! And then I *threw up on him* after the kickboxing. Oh my god. And – even more oh god! – he's so horribly horribly horribly handsome. This is *awful*! There's no way he'll be interested in me when he sees I'm just a plain old beige civilian.

'You can't be right,' I say in a low voice, my brain buzzing and my heart racing. I try to match the sincere, funny, sweet note writer – Eliot – with the actor we've watched on the TV every week. The one we helped Clara chase around London all this time. 'No,' I say again, surer this time, my head shaking involuntarily. 'You're wrong, you have to be.'

'No way!' Salma breathes out beside me. 'But the drama kid thing ... it does make sense!' She turns to look at me, her whole face alight. 'I'm interviewing him this afternoon! I'm supposed to be leaving here in a few minutes. I'm heading straight for a hotel where there are interviews happening with the actors from the show. It's an end of series thing.' She swallows, her eyes bulging. 'You have to come! You have to

353

see him and speak to him. Tell him who you are! You have to tell him, Jem! He thinks you ghosted him!'

'No!' I exclaim, unable to find any other words. 'No, I can't! If it really is him — if! — then it's . . . absurd. It's stupid! He'd never be interested in me in a thousand years. I'm just a nobody and he's . . . oh my god, he's *famous*.'

Harry moves closer. 'Firstly, Jemma, one British TV series does not really a proper famous make.' He smiles before continuing, 'And more importantly, he'd be insanely lucky to be with someone like you. You've always put yourself down and you really shouldn't. You're my best mate—'

'I'm her best mate,' Salma interjects as Clara elbows him.

'I'm her twin sister,' Clara huffs, 'that's, like, auto best mate.'

'I really, really don't like any of you,' I say as sincerely as I can, and we all burst out laughing.

Harry stops first. 'Seriously, though, Jem, you're a major catch and he is going to be so ecstatic to find out it's you who's been writing the notes.'

Mum leans across the table. 'Sweetheart, you absolutely *must* go with Salma!' She glances at Angela affectionately. 'Call it our wedding present?'

'I mean,' I frown, 'I *did* actually get you a wedding present so—'

'Come on!' Salma says impatiently.

'Yeah, come on!' Clara says, standing up.

'Why are you coming?' I ask and she looks baffled.

'Are you fucking kidding me? You think I'd miss you

propositioning my famous friend after all I've done to bring you two together?'

'Er, you seem to have that a bit confused,' I begin, but no one is listening.

'All of you go!' Mum calls happily. 'We'll stay here with the Great-Aunts and have a romantic lunch just, er, us.'

'Much cheaper that way,' Angela says gleefully.

'And more romantic,' Mum laughs, giving the nearest Great-Aunt a small wave.

Beside Angela, Buffy pulls a face. 'Oh what? You're saying I have to go, too? I couldn't give a fuck about any of this.'

'Come on, Buffy!' Clara calls cheerfully. 'It's time to slay.'

She rolls her eyes, standing up. 'Fine!' She turns away from the Great-Aunts. 'Bye, sluts!' she shouts and they regard one another with fury.

I stand up. I'm wearing a hideous greenish, ruffly brides-maid dress, I have makeup stains all over my face and swollen eyes from crying. And I'm going to tell a famous actor I might kind of be into him – that is, if his real name happens to be Eliot and he leaves notes for strangers in romantic fiction.

'What's happening?' A Great-Aunt peers over at us with confusion as we gather bags.

Clara leans across the table. 'We're off to track down this guy,' she explains, flashing the screen of her phone, still in her hand. The Great-Aunt squints at what I can now see is Milo's Wikipedia page. I catch a glimpse of his picture, sitting in the top right corner. He's laughing and gazing off into the distance, looking gorgeous and happy.

Something tickles at the back of my head and then the truth hits me – just like that.

I *do* know him. I recognize him. Every time I've seen him, I've wondered why he was familiar; at the party and again at kickboxing. I wondered what other shows or films I might've seen him in. And suddenly it's so clear. It's not what I've seen him *in*. It's *where* I've seen him. I've seen him at the library. Not for ages, but definitely, definitely, definitely. I've seen this man in passing at my library.

Milo is my note writer. He's my E. My Eliot.

Oh my god.

'Let's go,' I say calmly as everyone cheers and bundles out of the pub.

Chapter Forty-Five

CLARA

Wow, this is a mega fancy hotel. I bet they have really nice loo paper.

I make a mental note to steal a few rolls for the house.

Salma is leading the charge up ahead, since she knows the way and also because she's technically the only one allowed to be here.

'This way!' she yells with authority, leading us past a cavernous room with a bar in one corner and sofas scattered about. I fight an urge to drag Harry to the nearest of them for a lie-down snog. Instead I squeeze his hand in mine and we exchange a grin. God, I like him. It's scary but also so suddenly easy and straightforward. For so long I've felt like love was a battle. I thought it was meant to be! I saw it as a constant stressful rollercoaster of fear and self-loathing and disappointment. Will he text, what does this text mean, should I text back. Never knowing where you stand, never understanding intention, never feeling safe.

With Harry, it's just ... effortless. I know that he likes me because he tells me and he's showing me every day. He has been showing me all along, but love and romance had become such a twisted-up, knotted thing in my head, I couldn't see it. I couldn't recognize goodness and loveliness for what it was until my sister clonked me on the head with it.

'It's through there!' Salma shouts, pointing towards a door at the end of a long corridor. A sign outside reads, 'Press interviews', and underneath the magical words, '*Book Boyfriend*'. She gathers us up in a huddle.

'Look, we probably can't get you all in.' She glances at Buffy, adding, 'Definitely not the teenager.'

'I'll sue you for ageism,' Buffy says mildly, breaking away from the group and wandering off down the corridor, back towards the sofas. And the bar.

Jemma and I exchange a look, wondering what our responsibility level is here. She shrugs and I beam back. *Minimal*. After all, Buffy only became our step-sister literally today, and she is, like, seventeen, right? Shebeaight.

Salma clears her throat. 'My name will be on the list, obviously, so one of you can be my photographer.' She nods. 'Harry.'

'Don't we need, like, official press credentials or something?' He looks worried and Salma scoffs.

'Nah!' She waves her hand dismissively. 'Nobody gives a crap at things like this. I've never ever had to show any form of ID. And quite often, some intern's forgotten to add my name to the list anyway and they don't much care about that either. The team organizing this just want as many faces in that room as possible, so it looks like the show had loads of excitement and interest around it.' She looks at Jemma with determination. 'Which is why this is going to work.'

'What is, exactly?' Jemma asks nervously and Salma takes her by the shoulders.

'Through that door will be a woman with a clipboard. You're going to go up to her and you're going to have *so* much confidence. You're going to say you're Jemma Poyntz, a magazine freelancer, here for the *Book Boyfriend* round tables.'

Jemma is already shaking her head. 'I can't!' But Salma glares her into silence.

'You are! And when they run their pen lid up and down that list and can't find you, you're going to tut and seem harassed. I'll be arriving just after you, and if the woman starts to make noises about it being a problem, I will tell her I know you and confirm you're an industry colleague. You will also have your photographer with you.' She waves in my direction and I gasp excitedly. I *love* this. This is proper stupid, mad drama that has the potential to go so wrong and be so embarrassing. I *live* for this stuff!

But it's clear Jemma does not.

I swing an arm around her shoulders. 'Look, I could do it if you want?' I offer nicely. 'I could be the big time journo, and you can be my pap?'

Salma looks at me with annoyance and I understand. She's

trying to force Jem out of her comfort zone and I've just given her an easy out.

Jemma takes a deep breath. And then another one. 'No,' she says at last. 'I'll do it.' Her face takes on a steely expression. 'I'm ready to do something ridiculous and brave.'

'Amazing!' Salma grins, looking delighted. 'And then, once we're in there, it'll be a bit of a messy melee. We can totally hang back and grab Milo – Eliot – and ask him if he's your library letter man.'

Jemma pales again, but after a second, her determined expression is back. She nods fiercely and takes off, leading the four of us to quiver in her wake over the thrill of this absurd plan.

As Salma predicted, there is a clipboard, but it's a man holding it. He shoots Jemma a distinctly surly, impatient look as she approaches and I almost step on her heels as Jemma suddenly slows down, her confident strut morphing into a Valium-y slouch.

'Stand up straight,' I hiss at her, giving her a little shove, and she does so.

For half a second she stands in front of the clipboard man, and I fear she will bottle it until—

'Er, Louise Theroux here,' she shouts in his face and I look at her in confusion. This was so not the plan. 'Louise Theroux for the round table.' She barks it this time and the man glares back. She swallows, her face utterly unconvincing. When he still doesn't speak after a second, she starts talking. 'I am a journalist, a freelance journalist, called – as

I said – Louise Theroux, and I'm here to interview the cast of *Book Boyfriend*. I know all about *Book Boyfriend* because, again, I am a professional freelance journalist who is here to interview the cast and therefore have seen the whole series for research purposes and am prepared with questions. I work with many different kinds of media outlets, but mostly . . . magazines. I will be selling my wares to . . . a magazine after this – my wares being interviews with the cast of *Book Boyfriend* – which is what I do for a profession. I have a press badge here if you need to see it?' He looks at her blankly and she starts patting herself down with stupidly exaggerated movements. She looks at me and I stare back at her with genuine horror. She is *so so so* bad at this! 'Have you, er, got my press badge?' she asks me and I dumbly shake my head. Jem turns back to the man, who is looking increasingly bewildered and pissed off. 'This is my photographer, by the way,' she says in a tone that I assume she thinks is breezy. 'She is called . . . Andi Leibovitz.'

Oh fuck.

'And she is a very, very good photographer. She has won all the different photography awards like . . . the main ones.' She looks inspired. 'She won the Photos R Us award. And the . . . Nobel photography prize. And she has photographed . . . the Queen actually.' She pauses. 'Before and after she was dead. King Charles asked her personally to come take that . . . final shot.' She licks her lips. 'And she didn't even have to queue! Um, just like Holly and Phil, eh?' She nods now. 'But they've had a rough time of it since, haven't they? That felt like quite a pile on and I felt bad that they both ended up quitting *This Morning*. They'd done it for a long time, hadn't they? It seems a shame they had to resign but I'm sure they are both doing well now and will stage a comeback. So anyway, to recap, I am a freelance journalist called Louise Theroux and this is my photographer, Andi Leibovitz, but I can't remember if we said she's freelance or not.' She stares at me in a panic and I stare back at her.

Eventually the man speaks. 'I'm sorry, my lovely, what did you say your name was? Louise, was it? Soz, I'd totally zoned out there!' He looks at me when Jemma doesn't reply.

'Louise Theroux,' I offer quietly, adding, 'And I'm Andi . . . Leibovitz. We're not sure if I'm freelance or not.'

He cocks his head and breaks into a huge smile. '*So* great to meet you, Louise and Andi! I'm George and you can go right in! We're just about to start. We're so glad you could make it!' He beams and all the terrifying energy from before is gone.

Jem looks at him. 'Um, don't you have to . . .' She waves at the clipboard in his hands and I elbow her. Is she determined to fuck this up?

George giggles. 'Oh my gawd, lovely, this is just my to-do list. It's mostly my grocery shopping actually, if I'm honest with you, babes! Running out of hand soap at home and I *never* remember to get it when I'm in the shop. Do you do that?' He rolls his eyes laughing. 'I'm such a scatterbrain. Anyway, the intern couldn't get the printer to work for the attending list and lord knows where all the iPads are that we're supposed to be using these days!' He waves at the door just as Salma arrives behind us. 'Go on in, my lovelies, have fun!'

Salma passes him breezily, unfazed by the lack of list checking, but Jemma is still standing there, stock still, staring at him.

'Come on, er, Louise Theroux, let's get in there.' I grab her arm and frogmarch her in. If I can just get her past this man and inside the room, she'll *surely* chill out. She won't be under scrutiny, no more one-on-ones with clipboards, where she has to lie. She can just be Jemma again and we can find Milo – or Eliot, whatever we're calling him now – and she can be normal.

I force her through the doorway into a slightly fancier version of a boardroom. The lights are bright and there are a lot of people milling around chatting, large tables dotted about. I spot Salma about ten feet away, but before we can regroup and get searching for our man, a woman approaches. 'TV, radio or print?' she asks impatiently and I jump in quickly with an answer. Don't want Jemma to start making any more speeches about Holly and Phil.

'Print,' I say and she points towards the closest table.

'Sit,' she instructs and stares us out, until we move to take our seats. Several others sit down around us as the woman continues smoothly, 'We're starting in ninety seconds. You've got Milo Samuels coming to your table first. He plays George in *Book Boyfriend*. There are bios in front of you. We'll do intros first—'

Wait, what the fuck is happening? Did she say ninety seconds? And Milo's coming *here*? Oh god oh god oh god. Jemma grabs for my hand under the table and squeezes it until I nearly scream. I can feel the terror pulsing off her. Maybe there's still time to—

The room falls silent as everyone else takes their seats and a door opens at the back. A select few are brought out. I recognize the cast of the show – and Milo among them. I glance around fearfully, spotting Salma being ushered away – presumably to the radio section. She looks over in our direction and her face says everything.

Fuck. This is a disaster. We're screwed.

Chapter Forty-Six

JEMMA

My heart is beating too loudly for me to actually hear any-thing. There's a roaring noise in my ears and I honestly think I'm about to vomit across this table.

I need to calm down. This man has already seen too much of my vomit.

OK, you can do this, Jem. You were absolutely brilliant out there, talking to that guy George with the clipboard about hand soap and the Queen. You can hold your own in here, too. It's just a matter of *believing* in the story. I *am* Louise Theroux. I am the younger sister of legendary TV journalist Louis Theroux, who initially resented her big brother's suc-cess and wanted no part of his career in journalism, but the pull was too strong. Louise is a *born* freelance journalist! She was born for interviewing TV stars about their acting skills and then selling those interviews to magazines. I am Louise Theroux! I can do this – I believe in my character!

My heart rate slows down as Milo-Eliot takes a seat at our

table. He looks tired and waves everyone a generalized hello, taking none of us in. I think of the endless enthusiasm and excitement in those notes he left me. Can this really be the same person? What if we've got all of this wrong? Maybe it isn't Milo at all.

The people around the table introduce themselves one by one, naming the publications they're from. *OK!*, *New*, *Closer*, *Heat*, and then the freelancers. Clara and I are last, and when his eyes arrive on mine, they narrow with shock.

'Wait, hold on.' He recognizes me immediately. 'What are you—' He looks to Clara next. 'And you—' He swallows, glancing back towards the publicist on his right. Thank god Katies must finally be on her maternity leave. I wonder if this new publicist has managed to get Milo lost and trapped in a vomit-covered lift yet?

I hold my breath waiting for Milo to give us away, for us to be ordered out of here. Instead he continues smoothly. 'Erm, yeah, I recognize you guys from that other . . . interview I did a while ago, right? You're from . . .'

He swallows and I say as quickly as possible, 'I'm a free-lance journalist – born to it actually and would've made a success with or without my brother's help – but yes, we've um, totally interviewed you before, El— er, Milo. Great memory! I'm Louise Theroux and this is my colleague—' I stop because I've forgotten the amazing pseudonym I came up with for Clara.

She sighs, looking defeated, then mutters into her own lap, 'Andi Leibovitz.'

I catch the rest of the journalists exchanging looks, but Milo just nods with understanding. 'Of course, I do remember now.' His mouth twitches and I smile at him as professionally as I can.

'So how are you, Milo?' I ask and the stern publicist gives me a look.

'We'll start at this end of the table, if you don't mind, Louise. We'll go one question at a time. We only have fifteen minutes.'

Tiny recorders are thrown into a pile on the table between us, and I retrieve a note book and pen from my bag. Milo watches me do it with curiosity.

The real journalists begin asking about the show and Milo's process, as I panic. It'll be my turn in a minute – what can I ask?

'Louise?' the publicist prompts as the whole group turns to stare.

'Um,' I begin slowly. I can't just ask him outright, can I? 'Um, Milo, have you ever been . . . ghosted?'

He raises his eyebrows and the publicist frowns. We're supposed to stick to questions about the show, but he answers before she can interject.

'I have actually.' He looks at the table. 'Quite recently, as it happens. It's not the nicest feeling, but some people just find it easier to close the book, right?' He offers a short, unhappy laugh and I fight an urge to grab his hand across the table.

I didn't ghost you! I want to shout, desperate to explain.

'OK.' The publicist sounds bored. 'Andi? Next question?'

Clara leans across the table. 'Oh my god, Milo, did you, like, totally get a boner doing all those sex scenes on the show?'

Milo gives a shocked laugh as the publicist angrily tuts. 'Can we keep things appropriate, please?' She waves at the next journalist. 'Let's move on.'

When it comes to me again, I swallow. 'So, Milo, this question was an email from a, er, reader and they were wondering—' I pretend to check something in my notebook. 'How forgiving are you? For example, if someone forgot to let you know they were going to America for a few days when you were waiting to hear from them about something really important, would you, like, hate them for ever, or would you get over it pretty quickly?'

He frowns, then regards me curiously. 'That's a . . . reader question?'

I nod enthusiastically.

'Well, er' – he searches for an answer – 'I guess it would depend on the situation. But I do think open communication and forgiveness are hugely important in any relationship, romantic or platonic.'

I nod quickly, as Clara sits up straight, ready for her turn. 'So, Milo, babe!' She sounds really professional. 'From all the sex scenes you look like you'd be *super* good at IRL sex. Is that something they taught you at drama school, or were you already, like, naturally amazing at shagging?'

The publicist pushes her chair back furiously, scraping the chair legs loudly against the floor. 'Andi! That is not appropriate!'

Clara adds quickly, 'And how many people *have* you had sex with?'

'I'm afraid I'm going to need to ask you to leave,' the publicist snaps, striding around the table to Clara, who looks delighted. She leaps up, then shoots me a look. 'Sorry, I couldn't resist.'

'Out, please!' the woman says loudly and Clara waves a goodbye to our group.

'Laters, everyone! This was fun!' She beams at Milo and reaches out a hand to shake his. 'See you soon, dude!'

He grins at her. 'You bet.'

We all watch Clara being escorted out and the publicist returns quickly. 'Right, can we continue? One more question each now, and we'll have to move on with the next interview.'

This is it, my last chance. My stomach flips over and over as the group powers through more tedious questions that feel straight out of the press release. At least Clara was asking fun things.

'Final question,' the publicist barks at me and I look down at my shaking hands.

'Um, Milo.' I clear my throat, knowing it's now or probably never. I have to be braver than I've ever been in my life. 'Have you ever, um ... have you ever ... left a note – or, um, like twenty notes! – in a library book?'

I feel the tension shift at the table. There is a mix of confusion and intrigue. Milo stares hard at me, his dark eyes searching mine. Then – as if in slow motion – he looks between my face and the notebook I'm holding. I realize in that moment that of course this is the paper I've been using for my messages. Pretty much everything I wrote to him came from this notebook. The pages are fairly distinctive pale blue sheets, with a green border of ivy. His eyes return to mine and we stare at one another for a long few seconds. My heart is racing hard once again and I find myself swallowing away tears.

'You know I have,' he says at last, softly, in a voice meant just for me.

I shake my head. 'I didn't!' I exclaim, then add, 'I only found out today, honestly! I wasn't sure ... I ...' I frown. 'But you knew? You *know*? How?'

He cocks his head. 'I think I knew that first day we met, at that awful party. When you were drunk and falling about, stealing drinks from other tables. When you attacked me with such passion about your favourite book. Something in me said *it's you*.' He laughs sweetly. 'Then I picked up your note the next morning – where you told me your name – and I thought, *it must be her*. I wanted to ask you at the kickboxing class, but' – he pouts playfully, then laughs – 'you pretty much threw up every time I tried to speak to you.'

I burn with shame at the memory. He's known all this time. How is that possible?

We stare at each other, my heart in my mouth. Beside Milo – Eliot – the publicist frowns. 'Er, Milo,' she mutters, 'is everything ... shall I?' Her eyes dart between us but we keep staring at each other, the rest of the room falling away.

At last, I drag my eyes away. 'I'm so sorry for not replying,' I say, 'y'know, I mean, to your last message. I wanted to – and I wanted to say yes to your question – but there were . . . distractions.'

He shakes his head, smiling. 'Don't apologize, I under-stood.' He laughs again and it's such a nice sound. 'To be honest, I thought you'd realized who I was, too, and that you couldn't handle the whole' – he makes a face, waving his hand at the room – 'fame thing.' He sighs, adding hastily, 'I couldn't blame you. It's a lot to ask of anyone and—'

'No!' I cry. 'It wasn't that at all. I just had to go and save Clara! She needed me.'

He glances at the empty seat she recently vacated. 'That makes sense. You're sisters, you've got each other.' His eyes find mine again as he adds shyly, 'And hey, sorry I'm not wearing tiger print. I didn't know you were coming.'

The publicist stands up. 'We need to move on, Milo.' She looks confused by our exchange, as do the rest of the table. 'Um, thanks everyone for your time. I'll be in touch to talk embargoes and run dates.' She looks at me, then at him. 'Come on, Milo.'

'One more minute?' he pleads. She shakes her head.

He stands up at last, looking at me apologetically. 'I have to go.' He shrugs lightly. 'Work, y'know.' He grins. 'But leave your number with the front desk? Or with the team?' He nods at his confused publicist who nods back slowly, still baffled. He smiles one last time, staring at me intently. 'We'll go for that dinner of one shortbread—'

'Two chocolate Hobnobs,' I interject.

'Three digestives,' he says solemnly.

I make a face. 'I can't remember what's next.'

'Four jaffa cakes,' he smiles widely. 'Then five custard creams.'

I snort. 'You mean Viennese whirls!'

'Fine!' he laughs. 'Then a whole box of chocolate fingers—'

'And one Garibaldi,' I finish for him, smiling.

He holds our eye contact as he whispers, 'For all those healthy currants.'

The publicist sighs as we stare at one another. 'Come on, they're all waiting. Say goodbye.' She pulls him away and the journalists around me shout in a chorus, 'Thanks, Milo! Bye!'

'Bye, Milo,' I call out last and he turns around, smiling from ear to ear.

'Eliot,' he reminds me, and I nod.

'Eliot.'

Narrator:

Well, gosh!

And I promise that is my last ever gosh.

For you at least. Clara, Jemma and Salma are going to have to put up with quite a few more from me in the years ahead.

Do you know what I've realized? All this fuss over the note writer's name – over my friend Milo's name – and I forgot to introduce myself!

Hello, my name is Harry. And I'm feeling a bit emotional right now. Maybe you are, too? It's a nice feeling, isn't it? I can't imagine why some men don't cry, it's really lovely and liberating. I'm just so happy for Jemma. I'm happy for her finding her book boyfriend and him being a lovely person, but I'm even happier to see how brave she was about it all. Because – let's face it – that whole thing could've been an absolute disaster.

Although – good god – she should never, ever try to lie again. She's utterly terrible at it. I can tell you now, that nice man George with the clipboard – though he was professional at the time – was left quite shaken by her behaviour. He even forgot to buy hand soap again, when he finally made it to Tesco. They had to use body wash and his partner was in a mood with him all night about it.

It's now been a few weeks since that ridiculous day, where we gatecrashed those hotel media interviews. And guess what? Our Jemma is going to Australia tomorrow! She's flying out with Milo, her IRL boyfriend, who's heading there for six weeks of promo for Book Boyfriend. *Jemma's not going for the whole time. She's earmarked a couple of weeks in Byron Bay to hang out with Milo – though they're both going to be working. Jemma's got her first solo ghostwriting commission and she's planning on using her time over there to write. And probably shag her new man a lot. Then she's going off on her own to travel around Australia a bit for ten days. She's also taking a whole load of books. In fact, she's paid to take an extra suitcase, literally just for her paperbacks. That's despite Milo buying her a Kindle last week to celebrate five months since he wrote that first note to her on a whim.*

They seem really happy. They're good together, y'know? Though Jemma insists that they're taking things slow, and seeing what happens. She's not getting lost in any fantasies this time.

As for me and Clara, we're great. Brilliant, actually. She's obviously still just as obnoxious and hard work as ever. Oh, and we did have our first big fight when I heard about all those sex questions she asked Milo at the round tables. But, god, I totally adore her.

She's having a great time at the library where they're already talking about making her permanent as events manager. I'm sure she's being a bit insufferable, bossing everyone around, but her work's already had a huge impact on the place. They've started a romance book club, which meets there every week – and its membership is growing all the time. Jemma suggested to Clara that she also start a group to discuss unsolved murders every Thursday, but neither of us understood that reference. Clara's booked a few big name authors to visit for Q&As over the next few months, and the tickets sold out in no time. Even Mack is apparently pleased with how she's doing so far.

Oh, and the chest of drawers is gone. Thank god! Apparently Clara's mate Amanda bought it back after seeing it in our hallway that day. She realized she was sick of having all her clothes piled up on a chair. Clara made her pay extra, so I got my investment back after all, with that agreed upon 3.5 per cent interest. I told her to put it towards her debt hole. Speaking of – she has at least managed to pay her mum back for all that rent, thanks to none other than Milo's old publicist Katies! Yes, she's still on maternity leave, but it seems she's planning to launch her own celebrity PR company when she returns to work. And she – for some confusing reason – really liked the name and branding of Celebs R Us. She's bought the website me and Clara made. Apparently the page about all the Chrises was a big selling point.

Jemma and Clara's mum, Sara and Angela are both doing really well, thank you for asking. They went on a lovely honeymoon cruise to Finland after their wedding, where they bumped into Jemma's favourite librarian, Anita. She was – of course – wearing another Christmas jumper and was apparently on the hunt for St Nick himself. She seemed happy, and promised she'd be back at the library one day.

Who else?

Oh, Buffy still hates us all. Jemma insists it's just a pretence and she loves us really, but you should've seen her when we got back from America, having forgotten to get her any Twinkies. I can tell you, it was bad. We barely got out alive.

Right, I promise we're nearly done here – you need to go to sleep, you've got work tomorrow. But I want to return one final time to Jemma on that flight. On the flight we now know was her travelling to fetch her silly sister – my Clara – back home.

Jemma had just found me, down the end of the plane, and given me a hug. I'll be honest with you now, I'd just woken up from quite a long, groggy sleep. I'd had a fair bit to drink at the airport – being so excited at the prospect of seeing Clara again – and passed out before we even took off. Damned Baileys! I was absolutely busting for a wee when I found Jemma wandering the aisles, looking lost. Of course, I didn't know she'd just read her note from Milo – Eliot – but it was clear she was happy to see me. I was happy to see her, too, because, for the record, I'm incredibly fond of my friend Jemma. I absolutely adore her. And it really freaked me out when Clara started going on about us fancying each other. Not least because I happened to fancy Clara at the time. But also because friendship is really important to me – Jemma's friendship is so important to me. I had quite a lonely time of it growing up. I wasn't close to my family and went to a horrible all boys' school where I had no mates at all. I think that might be why all my friends are women? Or maybe women are just better. Either way, when Salma and Jemma came into my life, they became like my family.

Anyway, back to the plane.

'Are you OK?' I ask in a hushed voice, searching her face.

Jemma shakes her head, pauses, then nods. 'I'm fine,' she says at last. 'Just sitting with annoying people. One of them looks like a middle-aged zombie. I needed a break.'

'You're not regretting our secret mission?' I ask, wiggling my eyebrows to emphasize the secretness of said mission.

She smiles. 'No, not at all. It's time to show my nightmare sister how much I goddamned love her. Warts and all.'

'Has Clara got any warts?' I enquire as innocently as I can. Not that it's a dealbreaker, I'm just curious. To be honest – and this is quite pathetic to admit – I don't think I'd be put off if she had an extra seven limbs under those onesies she wears every day. I've properly fallen for Clara's whole high-maintenance, easily distracted, self-involved, obsessive vibe.

Jemma side-smiles, giving me a knowing look. And suddenly it's all too clear that she knows how I feel about her twin sister. I feel my eyes widen with shock as she asks, 'Are you ever going to tell her?' Her voice is soft, kind. 'Will you tell her how you feel?'

I swallow hard, looking away. 'Does it bother you?' I ask by way of answer. Because this has been a huge concern of mine. Jemma may not think of herself as much cop, almost prides herself on it as a matter of fact, but I do. I think she's one of the best people I've ever met. Granted, I did grow up mostly surrounded by rich twats who are all now bankers or Conservative MPs registered as living in the US for tax purposes.

It takes her a moment, but she answers at last. 'It did at first,' she admits, shrugging slightly. 'It really did. I felt like you were choosing her over me, like everyone always seemed to.' She adds quickly, 'But *not in a romantic way.' She laughs lightly. 'We're on the same page about that, right?' I nod, relieved Clara was so completely wrong. Jemma smiles, continuing, 'But I feel fine about it now.' She cocks her head. 'Better than fine – great. I'm thrilled for you both. You're always giggling in corners about dumb stuff I don't think is funny. You bring out the best in her, and I hope she could do the same for you.' She gives me a shy gentle punch on the shoulder. 'Though your best side is all your sides, mate.'*

I feel a warmth spread through me. 'Right backatcha, Jem.' We hug again and she laughs into my shoulder. I can tell it's her way of not crying.

And it's right then – right in that very second – that I know everything is going to be OK. Whatever happens in America, whatever might happen with Clara, whatever and whoever this pen pal of Jemma's ends up being, I just know with absolute certainty that it's going to work out. I'm surrounded by good people, doing their best with whatever life nonsense is thrown at them and it'll be all right. Things will work out how they're supposed to, and it's going to be OK.

And I need you to know it's going to be OK, too.

So that's it, I think. I hope I've done OK for you, as your narrator. I've enjoyed it immensely – all those embarrassing goshes aside.

Now I'm off for a Mia cuppa. You go get some sleep.

Lots of love xx

Acknowledgements

Dear nine-year-old Lucy Vine,

OMG dude, look at what we did. No, I mean it, look! Tear your eyes away from Point Horror's *Freeze Tag* and LOOK. We made a book! Not just one either – this is number SEVEN. Can you believe it?!?!?!

Of course you won't, because I hardly believe it myself. But I'm very grateful to you, Past Lucy, for all that reading you did, and all those stories you're writing. Because look at what it led to! Even though your narrative arcs are absolutely terrible, mate. Maybe you should read some books on how to write a book – it would make my present-Lucy life a lot easier. But then, if you read *Save The Cat!* now, that'll mean I would have and also won't have, and then it starts to get a bit Save the Schrödinger's Cat, doesn't it?

I've lost you back to that Point Horror, haven't I? Oh? It's another Sweet Valley High book now? You read fast.

Well, before I lose you completely, we have so many

people to say thank you to – and the readers are always number one. They make it possible for the present-me to do this job and I sincerely love them so much. Readers are the very best people in this world, and I wish I could go round hugging them all.

We also have to send out the next biggest thank you to one of the loveliest people who ever lived: my editor Molly Crawford. We had so much fun working on *Book Boyfriend* together and I'm so grateful for all her wisdom and know-how. She is incredible – as is the whole team at Simon & Schuster. I'm obsessed with them all – especially beautiful Sabah, who blows my mind with her continued brilliance. Thank you so much for always being just so goddamned good at what you do. Thank you a million, Amy, for your marketing hard work, and to SJV for the many brilliant brainstorms and for always sharing your honesty and your genius. Thank you as well to Clare, to Pip, to Jess, to Harriett, to Kate, to Misha, to Tamsin Shelton and Gillian Hamnett and to the awesome rights team who work so hard – Amy, Ben and Maud.

Oh, Past Lucy, you are going to DIE when you hear about your agent, Diana Beaumont. We're so in love with her, I can't even tell you. Long may our romance continue. Although, be warned that she doesn't understand voice notes (I know you don't either – mobile phones are going to be a massive thing, invest in Apple). Either way, as long as Diana limits her phone calls to fifteen minutes, we will continue to be mad about her for the rest of our lives. She deserves so many thank yous, as does everyone at the DHH agency and Marjacq.

You will also be ridiculously, weepily grateful to all the amazing, generous other authors you're going to meet. If you can imagine, you're actually FRIENDS with authors!!!! I know! It's like being friends with Taylor Swift!! Oh yeah, you don't know who that is. Believe me you will.

Anyway, thank you so much to my Diana's Dames gang: Daisy Buchanan, Caroline Corcoran and Harriet Johnson. Thank you Lindsey Kelk, Cesca Major, Kirsty Greenwood, Lauren Bravo, Milly Johnson (JOHNNYYYYYY), Beth O'Leary, Holly Bourne, Paige Toon, Ayisha Malik, Isabelle Broom, Rosie Walsh, Kate Riordan, Caroline Hulse, Eva Verde, Sukh Ojla, Marian Keyes, Mhairi McFarlane, Salma El-Wardany, Laura Jane Williams, Louise O'Neill, Lia Louis, Justin Myers, Lizzy Dent, Beth Reekles, Hannah Doyle, Oenone Forbat, Poorna Bell, Sophie Cousens, Kate Weston, Mike Gayle, Olivia Beirne, Elena Armas – and so many more I've definitely forgotten, sorry.

I'll let you return to your book now, Past Lucy, and I won't give you anymore life spoilers. Mostly because you'll be SO grossed out if I tell you we got married EWWWWW. But I should probably thank him (thank you, David) and all my wonderful family and friends. Love you all.

Yours sincerely and you sincerely,

Present Lucy xx

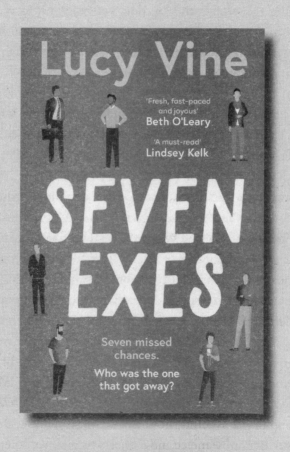
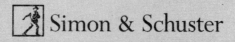

PROLOGUE

Are you my person?

Are you him? Are you the person I will finally, somehow, be fully *me* with?

Imagine if you were that person! Imagine if you were someone I could just *let go* with. Someone I could stop worrying about holding it all together in front of. Imagine if I could be all of the *me* I hate so much; if you were the one person in the world who wouldn't judge me for it. Imagine if I didn't have to say sorry when I let those parts I don't like leak out of me. If you just held me close when I was anxious for no reason. If you stroked my head through hangovers without judgement, if you brought me tea with three sugars in the morning without being asked, if you left the towels in the specific way I like them. Imagine if you were someone I could show my saggy stomach and boobs to, and you only fancied me *more*. Imagine if you pretended you weren't awake when I farted in my sleep, or bought more chocolate without saying anything when I ate all our supplies for breakfast a week before my period. Imagine if you were him.

Are you the person I'll be able to talk to about all the things I feel sad about? Will I be able to cry in front of you about everything that's happened, without feeling embarrassed and ashamed of myself? Can I get too drunk with you and talk nonsense too loudly, and obsess about that girl I hated at school who has her own cake business on Facebook that seems to be doing annoyingly well now – and *not* wake up at 2am, heart thudding with horror that I have alienated and disgusted you with the real me? Are you him?

I look into those beautiful big eyes, examining the long, dark eyelashes – so much nicer than mine – and wonder silently: are you The One?

You take my hand, kissing the throbby, veiny bit on the inside of my wrist and finally – after seconds that feel like a lifetime – move closer to kiss me on the mouth.

Fuck. I think you might be.

CHAPTER ONE

THREE MONTHS EARLIER

'So then we took his dog for a walk, and it turned out he'd forgotten to bring any of those tiny poop bags.' I grimace, remembering the horror. 'So we had to pick up dog shit with' – I pause dramatically to check they're listening – 'a condom.'

'Jesus.' Bibi shifts above me as she covers her face with a hand.

'Wait.' From her position on my lap, Louise turns to see me better. 'What does that mean?' Her lovely face is screwed up in confusion. 'Like, a *used* condom?'

'No, no,' I say and stroke her arm reassuringly. 'New. But yeah, in front of a bunch of old ladies and a postman – all angrily watching from across the road to make sure we picked up the dog's mess – he tore open a brand new condom he happened to have in his back pocket and scooped the whole thing up.'

'Why did he have a condom with him?' Bibi is still hiding behind her hand. 'Did he think you were going to have sex with him on a *dog walk*? Like, is this a thing now? Is this what dating has come to?' She shudders.

The three of us are lying like a human centipede on my bed. Bibi is at the top, our house alpha propped up against the pillows, while I'm sprawled across her with my head on her lap. Louise lies on me, squashing my thighs and stretching her toes over the end of my bed. It is oddly comfortable and oddly comforting to be so entwined with these people I love – particularly when pulsing, as I am, with a truly awful hangover.

'Why are condom packets always so purple and metallic?' Bibi muses, idly picking up the remote control and turning the sound up on the TV. *BBC Breakfast* gets vaguely louder, but still beige and easily ignored. 'Do you think a bunch of condom manufacturers were sitting around in a condom marketing meeting one day, and some junior condom exec – looking for his big condom break – leaned forward with intensity and said, "Has anyone considered just how *sexy* shiny purple foil is?"'

'I'm sure that's exactly what happened,' I nod earnestly. 'Oh, hey, maybe you should get a job in condom marketing, Beeb?' Bibi currently works as a barmaid, but she used to do marketing for a big firm before getting made redundant last year. She's tried for ages to get another job in the same field, but it turns out her many years of training and that MA in psychology were all an expensive and useless waste of time.

All it's apparently good for is a job in a pub. Poor old Bibi and her pointless £25k of degree debt.

Actually, I nearly made the same mistake at eighteen – starting a degree in history before quitting only a term into it. Oh, except I failed to let the finance department know, and managed to spend an entire year's student loan before they stopped depositing funds into my account. It's fine, though, because a term of history studies I'm still paying for is *super* handy for my job as an events planner, I can tell you. Louise – an actress who never works and lives on baked beans with the occasional, decadent slice of bread – is carefully straight-faced whenever we moan about the student loan letters sent only to mock us. We are suckers; the by-product of our parents' generation who got it all for free and pushed us to do what they did but without all their fun consequence-free drugs. Or the £35k houses waiting on the other side.

But sure, scold us some more for not having any direction.

'Nah.' I feel Bibi's body shrug again beneath me. 'I think condoms are probably over. Nobody uses them anymore – even STDs are more fun than using condoms. I might as well get a job promoting CDs or floppy discs.'

'Is floppy discs a euphemism?' I murmur, as Louise sits up straight, taking her body heat with her. My legs feel suddenly cold and lonely.

'Do you think condoms are really bad for the environment?' Louise looks anxious. 'They're very plasticky and I can't imagine they rot away very easily.'

Louise is, like, properly pure. She's always trying to be a

better person, always worrying about the world and society; wanting to learn and teach – although that mostly means reciting things she's memorized from Florence Given's Instagram page.

'If they are, Esther is personally responsible for a lot of climate change,' Bibi sniggers. 'They should bring up her sex life at the next G7 Summit.' I sit up so I can give her a full-faced scowl.

'It's not my fault dating people is so terrible,' I say. 'I only have sex with them because it's the best way to speed up boring dates.' Bibi nods, accepting the truth of it, even though she never really goes on dates. She's been single for a few years now, but she doesn't mind. The fucking bitch actually genuinely *likes* being single.

I used to be like that. I didn't used to mind.

'I got through a hell of a lot of condoms before I met Sven.' Louise still looks concerned. 'Maybe I should go vegan to compensate for my carbon vaginaprint? I need to be more Greta Thunberg.'

'Oh fuck, please *don't*.' Bibi collapses forward on the bed, burying her face in my duvet. 'I know she's doing super important stuff, Lou' – Bibi's voice is muffled in the foul sheets – 'but GOD, imagine how tedious it would be hanging around her. No one wants to be *friends* with Greta Thunberg.'

I nod emphatically. 'Yeah, Lou, by all means try veganism. But do it because Beyoncé was vegan for half a minute, not to be a good person – boring.'

'Oh, OK.' Louise still looks worried. 'I didn't eat beef for a week after I saw *Cowspiracy* – that probably helped the environment, didn't it? And I only eat bacon when I'm *really* hung-over, or when I'm comfort-eating after another failed audition or an argument with Sven.'

I hold back an eye roll because – the truth is – she and Sven never fucking argue. They're both too nice.

Louise has been dating Sven for nearly three years now, and they're, like, the most gorgeous, sweet couple ever – everyone says so.

But they're not exactly perfect, I remind myself. We all know their sex life is dull AF. But they're close enough to make my whole body surge with a jealous fury I hate, whenever I walk in on them giggling together in the living room in that soul-contented, intimate way only long-term couples have. Obviously I'm happy for them and I love to see my friend happy, but also, ugh, fuck them both for finding something that has proved so impossible for me.

DISCOVER MORE FROM LUCY VINE

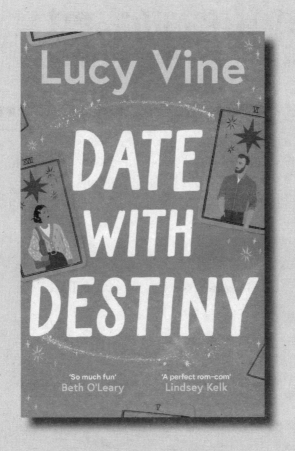

AVAILABLE NOW

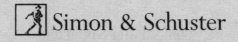 Simon & Schuster

booksandthecity.co.uk
the home of female fiction

NEWS & EVENTS | BOOKS | FEATURES | COMPETITIONS

Follow us online to be the first to hear from
your favourite authors

booksandthecity.co.uk   **@TeamBATC**

Join our mailing list for the latest news, events and
exclusive competitions

Sign up at
booksandthecity.co.uk